THE
Sapphire
Cove

BOOKS BY SOPHIE ANDERSON

The Butterfly Garden

THE
Sapphire
Cove

SOPHIE ANDERSON

bookouture

Published by Bookouture in 2022

An imprint of Storyfire Ltd.
Carmelite House
50 Victoria Embankment
London EC4Y oDZ

www.bookouture.com

ISBN: 978-1-80019-993-4
eBook ISBN: 978-1-80019-992-7

For my parents, Charlie and Fenella

PROLOGUE

She knew something was wrong before she had even opened the door. She had practically skipped home from the doctor's, buoyed by her news and excited to share it. But there was something about the silence as the door creaked open to the flat that made the hairs on her arms prickle. Something about the way it swung open with uncanny ease, unobstructed by a pushchair behind it, that pulled at her insides as if they might be attached to a weight teetering on the edge of a cliff. And there was something about the tidiness and the smell of the lilies that he had brought home two days earlier. They had smelt sweet then, but now the ammonia caught at the back of her throat. There, propped up against the vase, was a letter. She could see her name in his slanted scrawl on the envelope, smeared with the burnt-yellow sap from the stamens. Then the weight tipped over the edge and dropped into the precipice, dragging with it her insides down towards her toes. But she didn't pick the letter up; she averted her eyes like a horse with blinkers and walked straight past it into the kitchen. There was a trail of crumbs on the work surface, a circle of spilled milk. 'Mummy's home!' she called, but there was no reply.

She walked down the corridor towards the bedroom. The bed was made but there was a dip in the eiderdown where something heavy had left its mark. The cupboard doors on his side were open and in the mirror on the dressing table she saw the empty hangers. Down the corridor she walked, on wobbly legs. Past his office, as much of a jumble of boxes, paper and chaos as ever. But the poetry anthologies, his prized collection of leather-bound classics normally lined up on the shelf, were gone. In its place, lines of dust from between the books, some veering off into neighbouring lanes where they had been dragged across the shelf. The weight pulled harder. Into the nursery, where everything looked normal. She let go of the breath she hadn't realised she'd been holding. The cot was as she had left it that morning, sheets and blankets in a muddle, but the top drawer of the chest of drawers was ajar. She curled her fingers over the lip and pulled it open to reveal a drawer, normally full of neatly folded clothes in orderly lines, now empty. Babygros, vests, muslins, flannel nighties... all gone. No, not all; there was one left. A tiny babygro, the only one to survive her recent cull. Not normally sentimental, she had kept it to remind her of that day they left the hospital. It had tiny roses on a frilled collar. She picked it up and held it to her face, breathed in the smell, then she stuffed it in her mouth and screamed.

CHAPTER ONE

ROMY

'Do you have any family who would consider being a donor?' He threw the line away quite carelessly while ruffling through papers on his desk. When Romy didn't answer he looked up and peered at her over the top of his glasses, his pupils widening momentarily as he caught her expression. But he was a professional bearer of bad news and his face quickly softened, a smile tweaking the corners of his lips, a tiny nod willing her to respond.

'I don't think so,' Romy answered slowly, hoping that the wobble in her voice wasn't nearly as obvious as it sounded in her head.

'It doesn't have to be a family member, of course, though the chances of a match with someone biologically related to you would be significantly higher.' She didn't know how to respond to that either, so she looked out of the window to avoid his penetrating gaze. They were on the twenty-fourth floor and the sky was the same blue as the scrubs that hung on the back of the door. Skyscrapers in varying sizes and tones of concrete protruded from the swathe of green forest in the distance. She thought how urban the city felt at ground level, yet up here the green seemed to outweigh the grey.

'Romy?' He brought her attention back into the room.

'Sorry,' she murmured and looked him in the eye.

'I'll give you some time to think about it. But there is also the option of the scheme.'

'The scheme?'

'Yes, if there is someone, a friend, or... well, someone who would be willing to donate their kidney. And if it is not a match for you, then it would go into the scheme for someone else waiting. And you would also be in the scheme.'

'So let me get this straight.' Romy leant forward and placed her hands on the cool tabletop for gravitas. 'If I can convince someone I know to offer up their kidney to some stranger, then I could get some random person's kidney from the, er, scheme?'

He shook and nodded his head at the same time and rolled his answer around in his mouth before letting it out. 'M... m... more or less.'

He continued talking about drugs and dialysis and waiting times, and she could see his lips moving and hear the murmur of his words but she had lost the ability to focus. She was dying; he was telling her that she was going to die unless she could convince some poor sod to have major surgery and give up one of their kidneys.

When she walked out of the hospital the sun scorched her eyes as if she had been in there for weeks, not just the hour that it had taken to deliver her death sentence. Everybody was going about their day as they would on a Wednesday afternoon in downtown Hong Kong. The streets glistened in the wake of a downpour. She hailed a taxi outside the hospital, but as it pulled up, she decided against it. She would walk; she needed the time to collect her thoughts. She had more energy right now than she'd had for months – the irony! It was back in July when the headaches had started coming and the relentless fatigue that dragged her down for weeks on end. She thought it might be dengue fever at first. Most of her friends had caught it in the fourteen years she had been living in the city, and she had always thought she was invincible having never succumbed. And yet here she was, at the mercy of a disease so rare, so unpredictable it had taken them seven months to diagnose it. She tried to recall the doctor's words. Had he told her how long she might have to live without a transplant? She couldn't remember. He had talked about treatment, about having to come into the hospital three times a week for dialysis if they couldn't find a donor quickly. Three times a week? How could she work and go to the hospital three times a week?

Her heart thumped loudly in her chest and up the back of her skull; tick, tick, tick it reverberated around her head. The ticking of a time bomb. She walked towards the harbour. Cars honked and exhaust fumes from the queuing traffic seeped into her nose, her mouth and caught at the back of her throat like a poison making her retch. Was this how it would be from now on? Everyday sights and smells were to become a threat to her already weakened body? The body that was failing her. An image of her father flashed into her mind, the blisters at the corners of his mouth, his grey pallor on a hospital bed. She had experienced more than her fair share of death, but not like this. Now it slapped her round the face and poked her in the ribs and she wanted to scream. 'Arghh!' She shouted up at the sky, and an old man cycling past nearly fell off his bike. This wasn't how it was going to be for her. She was strong, she was in her prime. She had just got her shit together and had a job that she liked, wonderful friends – she was even dating a nice guy who wasn't a waster and wanted to take her hiking. This was not going to be her end.

She passed a small boy on the pavement with stumps for legs; he looked up at her through sticky eyes with a resigned misery. She handed him a coin and he smiled and kissed it before putting it in the tin cup on the street. She wanted to pick him up and shout at him to wake up, that it didn't have to be this bad. That getting a measly coin from a stranger shouldn't be as good as it gets. And then the tears came. They began rolling down her cheeks and tasted salty in her mouth and once she had started, she couldn't stop. She hid behind her sunglasses and crossed the street, away from the boy and his desperate fate. She sat on a bench overlooking the harbour and squeezed her eyes shut to halt the tears. The noises echoed around her head: the chains of the boats, the tinny voice on the loudspeaker announcing the next ferry departure, the splashing of the water against the harbour wall, the shouts of the newspaper vendor, the indignant scream of a berated child, the hustle and bustle of a world that would go on living without her.

Her phone vibrated in her pocket. It was Mali. *How was the doc?* she messaged. And then, seconds later: *S and I are going for noodles after work if you wanna join?*

Her fingers hovered over the keypad. How she longed to be back in that life of only an hour ago when a decision about whether to go for noodles or not wasn't loaded with mind-altering significance. She wanted to call but didn't think she could hear Mali's voice and not cry, and this wasn't the sort of conversation she could have sitting on a bench by the Star Ferry.

Mali was her best friend. They had met when she first arrived in the city fourteen years ago as a wide-eyed eighteen-year-old, hungry for adventure yet overwhelmed by this new and alien world. It was Mali who rescued her when the man she had run away with turned out to be scum. And Mali who found her a job in a hairdressing salon and introduced her to the tribe that became her family. A bunch of disparate souls trying to keep their heads above water in this metropolis of money and fumes and buildings that grew faster and higher than she had ever thought possible. It was Mali who had picked Romy up off the floor after so many nights of overindulgence, who had dried her tears and licked her wounds and helped to mend her repeatedly broken heart. But this wasn't just another hangover or failed relationship, and she wasn't sure she could face her friend's heartache at her news just yet.

Can't do tonight, will call later x

Romy scrolled through her contacts. She could call Jed, the hiking not-boyfriend, but this news would surely see him off forever. Or Ray, her boss at the tattoo parlour, but he didn't *do* emotion. He communicated solely through thrash metal and mono-syllables. They'd had some pretty intense discussions in the eight years she had been working for him, but generally under the influence of something and on a more abstract level. She scrolled down to Joseph's name. She hadn't seen her father for fourteen years. There had been many times in that period when she had nearly called. When she had traced the edges of his smiling face on his picture on the screen, when her finger had hovered over the call button. A memory of grazing her knees as a child popped into her head. How he would clean the wound so gently, calling her 'little bear' in his dulcet tones. And something pulled at her heart, a thread connecting her useless organs to her soul, and before she knew it, she had hit the call button. The ring echoed down the phone. Where would he be? Under an upturned boat fixing an engine, or in the kit room, or teaching a group of young travellers? Did he still teach? It had been so long.

'Romy?' His voice was soft despite the urgency. 'Is that you? Romy, are you there?'

'Hi,' she whispered, barely audible even to herself.

'It's you!' He half laughed in disbelief, or was it panic? 'Oh god, are you OK?'

'Yeah, I... I just wanted to hear your voice... I know it's been a long time, I...'

'Has something happened, Romy? Where are you?'

'Hong Kong, by the Star Ferry, where are you?'

'Where am I? Well, I'm, I'm on the beach, I just took Skipper for a swim...'

'Skipper?' Her heart lurched at the mention of the dog's name. 'He's alive?'

Joseph laughed a little and she could imagine the smile lines at the corners of his eyes. 'Yeah, he's alive, fifteen and still going. He's pretty slow and doesn't walk much now, but every day we go for a swim and he still tries to catch fish. He gets one every once in a while, too.' The tears streamed down Romy's face as she imagined Skipper; he was only a puppy the last time she saw him. Bounding with energy, he would sit at the stern of the dive boat, his ears flapping behind him as they picked up speed. She sniffed and then regretted it. Joseph never missed a thing.

'Romy, has something happened?'

'No... I... just... can I come home?' The words were out of her mouth before she had time to consider them. She heard his sharp intake of breath, and then a longer exhale. Her skin prickled at his silence; his deep, conscious breathing in moments of crisis had always infuriated her.

'Of course,' he said eventually. 'When are you thinking? You can come any time, I... I... would love to see you.'

'Tomorrow.' Her words were choked, but she tried not to sniff, or even breathe, so he wouldn't know that she was crying. 'I'll find a flight and be there tomorrow.'

'OK... I...' She heard him say as she hung up, not trusting herself to speak any longer.

When Romy stepped off the plane at Cebu, the heat and frenetic energy was a shock yet within minutes her heart settled into a more comfortable rhythm. She had become acclimatised to the urban and more tempered pace of life in Hong Kong. But there was something about the dust in the Philippines, the dry heat, the beeping of horns and the bustle of whole families on one bike, the smell of rotting rubbish and barbecued chicken that made her feel at home.

She took a taxi to the port and then a ferry to Siquijor. She wasn't allowed to travel on deck like they used to, and was herded into the air-conditioned cabin where the windows were so steamed up, she could barely see out. She leant her head against the wet glass and shut her eyes. The rising and falling motion of the waves rolled her stomach, churning it up and down. She tried to recall her trips on the dive boat as a child, the smell of petrol and wet rubber, the clanking of the machinery and the spray of the sea. She had taken herself to this happy place so many times in the last seven months. In the tunnel of the MRI scanner she would imagine she was lying on the bow of the boat. As they stabbed her with needles she would remember the sensation of the silky water rippling through her fingertips. And as they hooked her up to relentless machines that beeped and bleeped, and injected her with drugs and radium, she would go to the jungle of coral beneath the glistening turquoise water and follow the brightly coloured fish in and out of the shadows. Romy had barely slept since leaving the hospital the day before, and the whir of the engine helped to numb the anxiety that twisted her stomach into knots and she drifted into a deep sleep. When she woke it was to the sound of shouting and the vibration of the boat in reverse as they arrived at the dock.

The sun was bright and scorched her sleepy eyes as she emerged up the stairs of the ferry and made for the railing at the back of the boat. She wasn't getting off yet; Negros was the bigger island en route to Siquijor.

She turned to lean on the railing and tilted her face to the hot sun. The sea ahead was so blue and stretched for miles, her tiny island in the distance. She remembered taking a trip to Cebu with Ted as a child. They had been shopping for clothes for her and new notebooks for him, and they had stood on deck and looked at Siquijor in the distance just as she did now. Her biological father had held up his forefinger and thumb and shown her how it fit between them. And then he had told her a story about a little girl who had saved the island with a death-defying mission to collect lava from the volcano at its heart. Ted was full of wonderful stories in which she was always the plucky protagonist. For years after his death, it had hurt too much to remember them. But as she breathed in the warmth of the sun on her face at the back of the ferry, she pictured the sparkle in his eyes, his clawed hands and gnarly, villainous voices, his roaring dragons and squeaky little pixies, and she smiled.

The gangplank was being withdrawn and Romy was ushered back inside the ferry for the crossing to Siquijor. Joseph had grown up on Negros, but it was Siquijor that captured Ted's imagination when they arrived together with Romy as a baby nearly thirty-two years ago. The island was famous for its witchery and shamans who concocted potions made from the earth of cemeteries and the melted wax of church candles to cure people of their diseases. Ted was a dreamer and enchanted by these spiritual traditions which had been passed down through the generations. Romy had always shared Joseph's scepticism, but as she sat there with nausea pulsing through her body with every lurching wave, she couldn't help entertaining the idea that her beloved island might save her too.

She emerged up the steps forty minutes later on jellied legs and walked tentatively across the gangplank onto the hard of the shore. As she rummaged for her sunglasses and flung her rucksack on her back, she looked up to see Joseph standing on the other side of the pontoon. She hadn't told him when she was coming; thought she would just take a tuk-tuk. How long had he been waiting there? He smiled and waved. His face was more lined, but still Joseph. She wasn't prepared for their reunion, thought she would have the journey from the ferry to think about how he might have changed, how she would greet him. She was relieved to see that he wasn't grey, still had the thick black head of hair he'd always had. And she swore he was wearing the same clothes that she had left him in all those years ago. A red Sapphire Cove t-shirt so faded now that it was pink and the logo barely visible, a pair of khaki shorts and flip-flops. She looked down, unable to hold his gaze. The flesh on his legs looked older. They had always been smooth and hairless. As a child she would make her two dads sit together and compare their legs, one smooth and brown, the other pale and hairy. Joseph's legs were still brown and hairless but they had age spots and the veins were visible under the skin.

He walked towards her but she remained rooted to the spot. Her legs felt so unsteady that she worried she might topple over if she moved.

'Romy,' he said softly and stopped in front of her.

'Hi, Joseph, I... I didn't think you would be here... how long have you been waiting?'

'I looked up the flight times and figured you'd be on this boat.'

Of course he did! 'Well, thanks.'

He smiled and looked her up and down, his eyes resting on the octopus tattoo on her arm, the piercing in her nose, her cropped hair. She wrapped her arms around her middle and pulled her t-shirt down to cover up the flesh and the orchid tattoo on her tummy. He had always been OK with silence. She hadn't, nor had Ted; they had filled it with an abundance of chat, and those months after he had gone the quiet had driven her mad.

'You look... beautiful.'

She pulled at the short hair around her ears. 'Don't lie, you hate short hair!'

He smiled and shook his head. 'Not on you.' She tilted forward, unsure whether to run into his arms. But he didn't move, and her heavy legs were still anchored hard to the ground.

'It is so good to see you,' he said and held out his hand. He hooked his finger around hers and she held on. And then a rush of nausea fizzed up her body and flushed to her head.

'Are you OK?' Joseph looked at her, concerned.

'Yeah, I'm still bobbing up and down from the boat.' She pulled her hand away from his and ran it across her brow, which was cold and damp.

'You were always sick on this ferry! The truck is just over there.' He picked up her bag and walked across the road. She followed, taking deep breaths to calm her racing heart.

As they pulled out onto the road, she was relieved that the truck windows were down and the hot air moving across her face. She had never got used to the air-conditioned taxis in Hong Kong, with their closed windows and artificial air. She wanted to feel the heat, to smell the sea, the trees, even the fumes and rotting rubbish. As she breathed in the warm, salty air her heart settled to a more normal rate and the nausea subsided. They were on the coast road and the waves lapped at the sand beneath it. Palm trees protruded from the shore at an angle, hovering over the turquoise water. The road was dusty and bumpy and Joseph's truck and everything in it clattered around. Romy could feel his eyes on the back of her head but she didn't dare to look round, and was grateful for his silence for once. They climbed the hill above the cove and she waited for the bay to come into view just as she had as a child every time they drove up this road. They reached the summit through the trees and then the jungle cleared and beneath them was The Sapphire Cove. The surface of the water shimmered and sparkled like the precious jewel, giving way to the varying shades of blue beneath it. The indigo of the deep water fading to lapis as it neared the shore, and the band of turquoise over the reef. The dive boat was moored up at the jetty that stuck out into the sea like an extra limb. She could just make out the thatched roofs of the guest huts and Joseph's house, her home on the beach. There were a couple of bodies snorkelling on the reef and more outstretched on towels on the golden sand.

'Are you busy at the moment?' It was the first thing she had said since they'd got in the truck. She was aware how trivial the question was, given the time that had passed and the nature of their last conversation before she left.

'Yeah, it's high season now, so we are pretty much full all the time.' Romy dared to look at Joseph, who kept his eyes ahead. On closer inspection there were a few grey hairs in among the black. They had turned off the road and were working their way down the bumpy track towards the beach.

'Do you still do all the diving?'

'No, I go out sometimes but I have a young Australian guy who does most of the courses.'

'And the kitchen? Is Angel still running the show?' Angel had been with her dads from the start. They had met her at the port where she was selling Adobe Chicken to the travellers and locals off the boat. Ted said it had been 'love at first taste!' that it was the most delicious thing he had ever eaten, and she had to come and cook for them when they opened their guest house. Angel had been as constant a presence in her life as her two dads.

'Of course! Her daughter helps out now, too.'

'Jasmine?'

'Yes, you remember her?' He turned to look at her then, but she couldn't hold this gaze, had to look away from the lines around his eyes, his puffy jaw.

'Of course,' she said. 'But she was just a kid, maybe ten when I last saw her.'

'Well, she is definitely not a kid any more. She has her own baby on the way.'

'Wow!' They pulled into the clearing halfway down the hill. There were several other cars there, which was not as Romy remembered it.

'Do the travellers all have their own cars now?' she asked as they got out of the truck.

'Quite a few. There are more families coming to stay here now, who rent cars. Not just the young kids who pitch up on the bus.'

'Really? Have you put your prices up?'

He smiled as he pulled Romy's bag out of the back of the truck, now cased in a layer of thick dust. 'Maybe a little!'

'Well, good for you.' She tried to take her bag from him but he held onto it tightly and gestured for her to go down the steps ahead of him.

There were one hundred and twenty-seven steps down to the guest house. She had spent her whole childhood running up and down them, counting as she went. The first thirty-four are in the darkness of the trees, and then you emerge into the sunshine and the view of the sparkling sea over the top of the restaurant. The Kalachuchi plant was in full bloom and tumbling down the sides of the steps. Bright fuchsia flowers had been flattened and squished into the bricks by the feet of the guests. The smell was so strong and so nostalgic that it made Romy lose her footing, and she had to hold onto a vine which snaked its way down the side of the path.

'You OK?' Joseph asked from behind.

'Yeah, just, well, I can't believe I'm here.' She turned to look at him and a smile lit up his whole face, narrowing his eyes and creasing his cheeks. She tried to smile back but her nerves were too fraught, her face held too tight with anxiety. She carried on walking down into the restaurant, which hadn't changed a bit. A couple sat at a table overlooking the beach with banana lassis and a backgammon board. The rest of the tables were empty. Skipper was asleep under the bar at the far end, but his ears pricked up at the sound of them and he got up slowly and hobbled over on creaky limbs.

'Skipper!' Romy crouched down and buried her face in the hair on the back of his neck. The smell was musty and familiar; he had way too thick a coat for a dog living in that heat. Ted had bought their first dog off an eccentric Englishwoman who lived in Manila. He met her on a writing retreat when Romy was four and he travelled the length of the country to collect Stella, a twelve-week-old retriever. She had mated with a local mongrel a couple of years later and the pedigree lineage had weakened. They kept one puppy, Roxy, and then there was Flossie, who was Skipper's mum. And then Skipper, the end of the line. Romy hadn't thought about it until after she had left the island, why they had kept a male puppy for the first time. Ted must have known he wouldn't outlive Skipper when they made that call. The dogs had always been his domain rather than Joseph's. He licked her face and she wondered whether there was any part of him that remembered her.

'Romy, *Romy!*' It was Angel, who came screeching around the back of the bar from the kitchen. She was wearing a uniform of a yellow t-shirt and black shorts and a purple Sapphire Cove apron which was covered in flour. They definitely hadn't worn uniforms in the kitchen when she left. Angel wiped her hands down the front of her apron as she ran towards Romy and enveloped her in a sweaty hug. Her big boobs squished up against Romy's flat chest. She smelt of garlic and freshly baked bread.

Angel pulled away but held onto Romy with her arms, looking her up and down. Tears poured from her eyes and down her sticky cheeks.

'Aaah, Romy, you are so thin! And what has happened to your hair?' She pulled at the tufts of bleached hair on Romy's head.

'Ow! Angel, you're pulling my hair!'

'Ah, I'm sorry, it is just so good to see you.' She pinched the flesh on Romy's cheek just as she used to when she was a child, and then drew her in for another hug and kissed her all over her head.

Romy laughed and wondered how she had stayed away for this long. 'I hear you're going to be a grandmother, Angel.'

'Yes, Jasmine has gone for a rest. She is so fat she cannot work all day. She will be back for supper, though. How long you here?'

Romy glanced back at Joseph who was quietly surveying the scene, trying not to look too interested in her response.

'I don't know.' She shrugged. 'But I'm desperate to get in that sea.' She walked over to the railings at the edge of the restaurant and leant over. She felt the pull of the sparkling water but resisted the urge to run into it there and then.

'I remember when you were little and we had been to the mainland, you would run straight into the sea when we got back without even taking your clothes off!' Joseph said. She was unnerved by his uncanny ability to read her mind. When she didn't answer he picked up her bag. 'Come,' he said. 'Let's get you settled in the house.'

She followed him to the other side of the restaurant and over the rocks towards the house on the headland that her two fathers had built. It was on the furthest part of the bay, only accessible from the beach or the sea. She thought now how indicative this was of her dads. And she wondered why she had never before considered how difficult it must have been to lug all the building materials across the beach. But neither Ted nor Joseph shied away from challenges, and they appreciated aesthetics and nature more than anyone she had ever come across in the bright lights of the city.

It was a glorified bamboo hut on stilts with a thatched roof and balconies on all three floors. As it was on the piece of land that stuck out between the two beaches, it had one-hundred-and-eighty-degree views of the sea, and you could see the sun both rise and set from either end. Romy followed Joseph up the steps where he stopped and took off his shoes and washed his feet in the bucket of tepid water. Romy smiled at the familiarity of this ritual. Twenty times a day he dunked his feet into the bucket and then dried them on the sarong that hung over the balcony next to it.

She washed her feet and followed him into the house. It was as meticulously tidy as ever. A large wooden room lay open to the sea on three sides. There were no windows, but wooden shutters that remained on their hinges for most of the year except when the typhoons struck and the rain drove in at such an angle that it would flood the house if they were left open. There was a table on one side with an arrangement of white candles of varying sizes. Romy wondered whether he still lit them in the evenings when he dined alone. On the other side of the room was a wicker sofa and two chairs around a coffee table. There was a yoga mat in the middle of the floor, with two balding patches halfway up, worn away by years of kneeling. There was the faint aroma of sandalwood incense and the stubs of the sticks and a pile of ash on the floor next to the mat. And there were plants everywhere, both inside and out on the balconies. She pictured Joseph talking to them, pruning them, shining their leaves. Everything had its place in this house. It had infuriated Romy as a child, who just wanted to shed her clothes and leave them where they landed. She liked the ramshackle chaos of the fishermen's houses and the carefree abandon with which the travellers exploded out of their rucksacks in the guest house. And yet more recently, while Romy was beginning to restore some order to the chaos of her own life, she found herself longing for Joseph's calm interiors She wondered what he would make of the flat that she had been so proud to acquire just a year ago.

'Shall I take your bag up to your room?' Joseph asked.

'Thanks, but I can manage it.'

She walked up the wooden stairs. Her room was on the first floor along with Ted's study. Joseph and Ted's bedroom was on the top floor, with the best view. The door was shut to the study and she couldn't bring herself to open it. Inside her room everything was as she had left it. There was a single bed in the middle with a pink mosquito net tied above it. Her collection of shells and sea glass was still on the wooden desk under the open window. There were photos all over a pinboard. Of her as a child, her and Angel, her and Jasmine as a baby. With Flossie and Skipper as puppies. There was one of her holding a fish she had caught, a huge gummy smile on her face with both her front teeth missing. And one of her, not much older, in full diving gear. There were pictures of her with guests whose names she couldn't remember. Lots of her with Ted at various ages; but it was the one just before he died that caught her attention. He was horribly thin and quite grey in the face but his cracked lips were smiling and he had his arm around her. And there was one of her with Scott – she was sitting on his lap. He was whispering something in her ear and she was laughing. There was only one of her with Joseph; he had taken most of these photos. They were on the dive boat, sitting on the edge, their faces reddened by the sun and their hair crispy with salt. They both had wetsuits rolled down to their waists, and were holding their fingers up in that 'OK' diving sign.

Romy threw her bag on the bed and rifled through it for a bikini. Angel had noticed how thin she was, and she wondered whether Joseph had thought it too. Not a lot got past him. She could have dyed her hair blue and had a hundred tattoos without Ted noticing; he lived in a parallel world to the one they actually inhabited, always immersed in a new piece of work. But Joseph was different. It was he who had realised when she had got her period and bought her tampons and talked her through the birds and the bees. And it was Joseph who noticed when she stopped eating in an attempt to lose the puppy fat that had gathered around her middle. She looked down at her concave stomach, the tattoo of an orchid which wound its way from her back and circled the gold hoop with an amethyst in her belly button. Of course Joseph would have noticed her weight loss. She wrapped a sarong around her emaciated body and walked back down the stairs.

Joseph was spraying the plants with water, and a rainbow had formed in the mist where it caught the sun.

'It's just the same,' Romy said, walking out into the middle of the room.

'I don't like change,' Joseph said. 'As you well know.'

'Yeah. I'm beginning to think you might have something there.'

'Really? Are you mellowing at the grand old age of thirty-two?'

She was relieved when he got her age right, hadn't even paused to think about it. 'Maybe a little.' She walked over to the balcony and looked out over the glistening sea. He followed her and leant against the railings next to her.

'I had forgotten quite how amazing it is, the view from here.'

'I know, I don't think I will ever tire of it.'

'Well, I don't imagine you're planning on going anywhere.'

'No, no. I'm not.' They looked down at a family on the beach. A couple with a baby, they were dunking his chubby legs into the sea and he squealed with laughter every time they touched the water. They both smiled at the infectious giggles of the parents.

'Romy. Listen, I... I'm sorry for the things I said back then. I wasn't thinking straight, I wasn't right in the head after Ted, and...'

Romy didn't look at him. She looked up from the family and out at the patch of bleached-out sea beneath the sun. 'We both said things we regret. But let's not go over it, hey?'

'But...'

'Joseph, please...' She turned towards him.

'OK, I won't, but I just want you to know how sorry I am. About everything, and... well, it is really great to see you.'

'Yeah, you too.' She held onto his arm and he put his hand over hers and squeezed it tight. 'But right now, I am really desperate to get in that water.'

He smiled, and looked at the same time relieved and disappointed that the conversation was over. 'I bet.'

'You wanna come?'

'No, you go.'

CHAPTER TWO

FLORA

'So, Flora – can you tell me why you have come to see me today?' Dr Jane Campion's voice was dripping with caramel and sincerity. She wore a white caftan over khaki linen trousers and her feet were bare, her toenails naked and too long. Her hair was grey and hung limply over her shoulders. She had no make-up on and wore wide purple glasses that framed her small eyes.

'My friend Lisa, I think you know her, she's one of your... you know... well, anyway, she suggested I come.' Lisa had been seeing Dr Jane, as she called her, for a couple of years now. Lisa swore that she had saved her from mental ruin, but Flora was sceptical. She could already feel herself getting hot, and she wished she hadn't worn the thermal vest underneath her dress, but it had been so cold at home that morning. There were actually icicles on the inside of her bedroom window. But now here in this airless room she could already feel damp patches under arms and she would have to remember not to lift them up.

'Has something happened? Something that prompted Lisa to suggest it?' The corners of Dr Jane's mouth were pinched into a benevolent smile as she spoke; her head was tilted, her legs crossed, one bare foot nestling into the sheepskin rug on the floor.

'No, not really. Well, kind of, I mean, I guess something happened...'

'You are going to have to be a bit more specific, I'm afraid, Flora.' She smiled as she said this but there was an icy undercurrent to her honeyed tone, and Flora felt berated.

'Of course, sorry.' She looked down and wanted to bury herself under the sheepskin rug. She would not forgive Lisa for making her do this. She took a deep breath and then expelled her words fast.

'I think my husband might be having an affair.'

'You think?'

'I saw him, and Lisa thinks I'm mad because I haven't confronted him about it yet. She says that I have issues with men – my father, stepfather, brothers, ex-boyfriends – and she says I need to sort it out so that I can tell Jake, my husband, where to go.'

Dr Jane nodded with consideration. 'Do you want to tell Jake where to go?'

'Yeah, yeah.' She said it with more authority the second time, nodding and trying to convince herself that it was true. 'I mean, I do. But, well, I just need to be sure first.'

'Sure?'

'Yeah, sure that I don't want to be with him any more, because if I tell him that I know, he'll just leave me, right? For this woman, Jodie, who has known him all his life, his soulmate, they birth lambs together, for god's sake. She understands him in a way I never could, and...' She felt her jaw wobble under the pressure of all that bottled-up emotion and willed it to stay still. 'And, and I don't think he likes me very much, I think he regrets marrying me, so if I tell him I know, he will just leave me for her.' Flora pursed her lips together; she pressed them down tight with her teeth and could taste a hint of iron where they broke the skin. She blinked away the tears that were stinging at the backs of her eyes.

'And how did that make you feel?'

'What?'

'When you saw them. How did it make you feel?'

'Well, pretty upset, really, I mean, I didn't think he would actually do it. Have an affair, I mean. He is so loyal and has such high moral standards. But the way they were holding each other, so tight – her knuckles were white as she gripped the back of his jumper. And she was smiling, a sycophantic, sickly smile with glassy eyes as she clung onto him and then she buried her head in his neck. All I could think of was what he would smell like, of dried hay and pears soap, and I could feel the scratch of his beard on her face, and...'

'And what did you do?'

'I ran away. I had brought him a flask of tea, which I ceremoniously emptied into the mud and then I ran back to the house.' Flora picked up the fabric of the dress in her lap. It was heavy cotton, floral and shapeless in what was meant to be a cool, androgenous kind of way, but which Jake had already told her was unflattering. He didn't understand fashion – he wanted women to either dress like men, like Jodie, or to wear skintight trousers and low-cut tops that left nothing to the imagination. She looked down at the dress now and felt ridiculous; she had dressed up to come to see the therapist, who wasn't even wearing shoes. Had she come here purely to have an excuse to put on a dress? Her eyes flickered towards the door and she wondered if she could leave, just like that, with no explanation.

'And then what did you do?' Dr Jane pressed her.

'Sorry?'

'What did you do when you got back to the house?'

'Well, I sobbed quite a lot and then I pulled myself together and went to pick the kids up from school and cooked him supper as usual and never said anything. We watched *Breaking Bad* after the children had gone to bed, and I pretended that nothing had happened.'

'You are not the one in the wrong here, Flora.'

'I know that, but it is pretty sad that I didn't have it out with him, isn't it?'

'Not necessarily. you were being sensible, not rash, considering all the possible consequences.'

'I am sensible. I have always been sensible, never rash, and look where it's got me.'

'Are you dissatisfied with other elements of your life?'

'You could say that.' She didn't prompt her for more information, just nodded at her with that serene half-smile until Flora could bear the silence no more and felt compelled to fill it. 'I'm thirty, and most of my friends from school and university are still partying hard and forging ahead with their ground-breaking careers, and I'm stuck out here in the countryside with two kids and a husband who has a mistress who looks like a man, so yeah, I'd say I'm pretty dissatisfied right now.'

Flora shifted uncomfortably in the seat, the combination of her woolly tights, the thick cotton of her dress and the felt chair making the backs of her legs itch. She wriggled her hands between her legs and the seat. It was one of those Scandinavian designer chairs, mustard yellow and curvaceous. It wobbled precariously on the single metal pole beneath her as she moved around. She knew there was a clock on the wall behind her head, perfectly positioned in Jane's line of sight but invisible to her patients. She had no idea whether she had been in there for ten minutes or an hour: it felt like days.

'Where would you like to be now?' Jane asked, as if reading her mind.

'What, right now?'

'Not now in this room, in your life. If you could be doing anything with your life right now, what would it be?'

'Gosh, that's pretty hard.'

'Don't think too much about it.'

'Well, I love my kids, don't get me wrong, I wouldn't swap them for anything...'

'I'm not asking you to swap them, Flora...'

'No... right, well... I guess I would like to still be working and maybe not living in a dilapidated farmhouse with ice on the inside of the windows.'

'Did you grow up in the countryside?'

'Yes, I was born in London, but then my mum got together with my stepdad and they moved into his house outside Oxford just after my first birthday.'

'And would you say your childhood was happy?'

Oh, here we go. This is what she had expected from therapy. She could feel a trickle of sweat working its way down between her shoulder blades, and the room was becoming more and more airless. She took in a deep breath but it felt warm on her pursed lips and offered no refreshment. She looked at the door, still firmly shut, and felt a familiar sense of panic fizzing up her legs and making her heart beat fast in her chest. 'Look, Dr Jane, sorry – Dr Campion. I'm fine, really I am. I have two gorgeous, happy, healthy children and a roof over my head – a holey, leaky roof, but I have a roof. And yeah, I think my husband is having an affair but I'm sure there are lots of women out there whose husbands are having affairs and they don't need therapy... no offence, but I don't think this is really me. So, I'll, er, pay you for today and then I'll just get going, if that's all right... because...' Flora stood up and rifled around in her bag for her purse, and she was alarmed to see that her hands were shaking as she retrieved it. Jane stood up and walked around the glass coffee table between them and put her hand gently on Flora's arm. Her face was still painstakingly calm but tinged with sympathy now, a sympathy that made Flora's head pulse.

'It's OK, Flora, there's no charge, this was just a trial session.' Flora put her purse back in her bag and went to put on her coat but realised that in doing so she had lifted her arms up. She caught sight of herself in the mirrored shelves on the other side of the room. Her face was flushed, her hair slightly static and there were big, dark patches under her arms where the floral pattern on her red dress had become maroon.

'I'm sorry, I didn't mean to waste your time. I just, well, I'm fine, really, and this just – it isn't for me...'

'OK. That's OK, you are free to leave at any time.' Flora's eyes darted to the door, and then Dr Jane's hands were on hers. they were surprisingly soft and powdery. 'Flora, if you change your mind, I am here.' Jane nodded slowly with infuriating empathy as she clasped both of Flora's sweaty hands between her own.

'OK, bye, then.' Flora pulled her hands away and waved inappropriately cheerily, as if to a child, and then cringed all the way down the stairs and out into the street. She breathed for what felt like the first time in hours and felt the cool drizzle of rain on her flushed face. She walked down the high street, dodging the shoppers, terrified she might bump into a mum from school and have to talk as her throat tightened and tears rolled down her cheeks.

Her phone rang as she got to her car – it was her mother. She ignored it and started the engine. She was halfway home, winding her way through the narrow lanes, dodging the torrents of muddy water that ran down the sides of the road when her mother rang again. She let it ring this time, listened to the relentless chirping of her ringtone over and over until it finally admitted defeat. It was unusual for her mum to ring in the middle of the day; she liked to call after six, with the safety of a glass in her hand. And so when she called for a third time as Flora swung into the driveway of her house, she answered out of frustration more than anything else.

'Mum?'

'Ah, Flora, you answered. I've tried you a few times.'

'I know, I was driving. What is it? Has something happened?'

'Why do you say that?'

'You don't call in the middle of the day, ever, and certainly not several times.'

'I just wanted to hear your voice, that's all. Is that too much to ask?' She had a slightly manic tone and Flora felt a pull at the bottom of her stomach.

'No, not at all.'

'So where have you been?'

'What?'

'You said you were driving, aren't the children at school?'

'Yes.'

'So where were you?'

'I don't spend the whole day sitting at home, you know. I do go out of the house sometimes.'

'Do you? Where do you go?'

'Mum.'

'Well, I didn't think you got out much, have you been to the supermarket?'

'No, I... if you must know, I've been to talk to someone.'

'Who?'

'A therapist.'

'What?'

'Lisa recommended her, she goes to see her all the time.'

'Lisa with the tarot cards?'

'Yes, that Lisa.'

'Why does she think you need to see a therapist? Has something happened?'

'No... I...' Without warning the tears were back and she heard a tremble in her voice.

'What is it, Flora? Is it the children?'

'No... they're fine.'

'Jake, is it Jake? Is he ill?'

'No, he's not ill, he just. Well, he's, he's having an affair.'

'Oh.'

'Oh? Is that all you have to say?'

'Well, I'm not that surprised, darling.'

'Why not?'

'You do come from very different backgrounds.'

'Oh, come on, Mum, no we don't, and that's got nothing to do with it.'

'I just think you both want different things from life, always have.'

'Maybe.' Flora sighed with resignation. This was not a new conversation.

'There is no maybe about it, Flora. Did you ever think you were going to be a farmer's wife?'

'You don't choose who you fall in love with, Mum.'

'I don't know about that, Flora. And do you really love him? It's not as though you have gone out of your way to keep him.'

'What do you mean?'

'I just, well, sometimes I wonder whether you might try a bit harder, if you really loved him, I mean.'

'Try what, Mum? What exactly are you getting at?'

'Let's be honest, darling, you have let yourself go a bit.'

'Thanks a bunch, Mum.'

'I'm sorry, but, well, you have to work hard to keep your man.'

'What? I can't believe you're actually saying that!'

'There's no point being all feminist, Flora, it's true.'

'I wasn't aware of you going out of your way to keep Jeremy.'

'I'll have you know I have worked very hard indeed to keep your stepfather!' She sounded indignant. 'I have kept his house clean, and food on the table, and I make an effort with my appearance, and...'

'Jesus, Mum, you sound like something out of *the Truman Show*. And you don't exactly keep his house clean, or put food on the table, Mrs Jenkins does—'

'No, Flora, Mrs Jenkins has gone, it's her daughter Tracy now, and anyway, it doesn't matter. I'm just saying that you need to work hard at a marriage, they don't just tick along without you putting in the graft.' Flora watched the rain streaming down the windscreen, the tributaries meeting and forming wider streams. She could see the blurred outline of her house beyond it with its wonky roof and faded red bricks.

'I can't believe I've just told you that my husband is having an affair and you've told me that it's my fault.'

'I didn't say that.'

'Yes, you did, you said I had let myself go. That I hadn't tried hard enough to keep him.'

'Oh, Flora...'

'No, seriously, please tell me what your secret is because I really have watched and admired your behaviour over the years.'

'That's not fair, Flora, you're being oversensitive.'

'Oh for god's sake, I'm not listening to any more of this.' And she hung up the phone. She could imagine the incredulous look on her mother's face. Flora had wanted to hang up on her so many times over the years, but had never dared; couldn't face the inevitable retribution and guilt, too scared of the consequences that might follow. She felt a bizarrely warming sense of pride for a fleeting moment, before it was replaced with a more familiar sense of panic. Her finger hovered over the callback button, but there was a knock on her car window that made her jump. She opened the window to find Larry, Jake's faithful eighty-five-year-old farm-hand with water pouring off the hood of his waxed jacket and breakfast still clinging to his beard.

'Your goats have got out again, Flora, they're eating the laurel hedges. It's poisonous for them, you know...'

'Oh god, I'm sorry, Larry, I'll come and get them.'

So Flora didn't call back. She spent the next two hours in her nice red dress and a pair of wellies and Jake's too-big raincoat that was ripped down the back and let in all the rain, trying to catch the pesky goats that Jake had bought her for her birthday last year, and which had done nothing but cause trouble since the day they arrived. She chased them round the entire perimeter of their garden and eventually captured them by dragging the picnic table to block off one exit and driving the car across the lawn to block off another, leaving deep crevices of tyre-tracked mud across the grass. She was then late for school and was berated by Mrs Humphrey as she collected her snivelling children from the empty playground.

By the time Flora got home that evening and changed out of her dress, which now had a mud-crusted tear down the front. She considered not putting on the grey tracksuit bottoms, in light of her mother's candid advice, for all of ten seconds before climbing into their fleecy lining.

She was on the sofa with a large glass of red wine, a bag of pret-zels and *Grey's Anatomy* when Jake finally arrived home just after eight.

'You're late,' she said as he walked into the room.

'I had to go to the Parish Council meeting about the solar panels, I told you.'

She had forgotten about the meeting and been imagining him in the arms of Jodie in her dingy little cottage on the other side of the village. 'Did you?'

'Flora, we had a whole conversation about it this morning. I told you to eat without me, that I didn't know what time I would be back.'

'I don't remember,' she said, and it was true, and that was a worry in itself. Were her brain cells so devoid of stimulation that they were melting away?

'How was your day?' he asked, while going to the fridge and opening a bottle of lager.

'Pretty awful – the goats got out again. And I churned up the lawn trying to recapture them.' She wondered whether he would be cross about the lawn and part of her wanted him to reprimand her, to open the door to a confrontation.

'Poor you,' he said and sat down next to her on the sofa. He rubbed her leg underneath the tartan blanket and she felt her whole body flinch under his touch. 'Flora? Has something happened?'

'Why do you ask?'

'You're a bit touchy.'

'I'm just tired, Jake, and I had a run-in with Mum this morning.'

'Oh god, you and your mother. What was it this time? Was she pissed again?'

'It was eleven o'clock in the morning.'

He looked at her, but refrained from mentioning the time when they had left their son Toby in her care while they went to a wedding. It was the first time they had left him overnight, and they came back at a little after eleven to find her mother slurring her words and Toby screaming in a dirty nappy in his cot. Flora thought back to the conversation that morning; her mother had seemed quite coherent, punchy even, stiffening for a fight. But then she was a master at hiding her drinking.

'What was it about?' Jake asked.

'What?'

'The run-in.'

'Oh, er, you, actually.'

'What?'

'Yes, she told me I should be a better wife to you, keep the house tidier and make myself look more beautiful.'

'What? She actually said that?'

'She wasn't mincing her words.' Flora took another sip of her wine and kept her eyes focused on the operating theatre on the TV.

'That's ridiculous.'

'Is it?'

'Of course it is.'

'So you don't think I have let myself go?'

'Well, you've just had two kids in quick succession.'

'Olive is four, and that wasn't a no.'

'I didn't mean...' He rubbed her leg under the blanket again and she pulled it away, hugged her knees tight into her chest. 'Oh, come on, Flora, it's not like you to be so self-pitying. You're a mum now, a beautiful mum bringing up our two gorgeous children. You don't need to be dolling yourself up.'

'What if I want to?'

'Then be my guest! What else did your nutty mother say to put you in such a funk?'

'Not a lot.' Flora shrugged.

'Then why don't you take your wine up to the bath and have good long soak?' He squeezed her shoulder then and she forced out a smile. It was one thing picturing him as an evil adulterer when she wasn't with him, but when he was here, and looking at her with those big blue eyes, his cheeks flushed and his dark hair matted, the thought of him with another woman literally tore her heart in two.

· · ·

Flora was woken by the phone in the middle of the night. It was the hardly used landline that rang maybe twenty times in her wine-induced dreams before she realised it was real. She climbed out of bed so fast that her head swam and threatened to topple her over until she steadied herself on the bedpost. She made her way down the stairs in the dark, willing the children to stay asleep. Her feet icy on the brick floor in the hallway.

'Flora?'

'What is it, Jeremy? What's happened?'

'It's your mother, she's, er... she's fallen.'

'Is she OK?'

'We're in hospital in Oxford, she hit her head and broke her leg.'

'Oh, god...'

'They say she's going to be OK, so I didn't want to bother you in the middle of the night, but...'

'But?'

'Well, she's quite distressed, keeps asking for you and, er...'

'I'm on my way, Jeremy, which hospital are you in?'

'The Radcliffe... I'm sure you can wait until tomorrow, I just... well, I...'

'I'm coming now. It's OK, tell her I'll be there soon.'

It was still raining on the M4. It had rained relentlessly for about four months. The headlights shimmered on the road ahead, and Flora worried that she might be over the limit after the two thirds of a bottle of Malbec she had proceeded to drink in the bath the night before. It was five o'clock; surely the sun would be coming up and relieving the strain on her eyes soon. She nursed her regret for the entire journey, tortured herself with guilt and shame. She should have called her mother back; the goats could have waited; Larry could have waited; even Mrs Humphrey could have waited. There was a reason why Flora had never hung up on her mother before. Why she never dared to challenge her or touch upon those unspoken truths. Because she was scared. Scared of triggering a binge, scared of what her mother might do when tipped over the edge of the precipice that she lived so dangerously close to every single day.

It was seven o'clock by the time she arrived at the hospital. She let go of the steering wheel that she had been holding so tight for nearly three hours and rolled her creaking shoulders down from her ears.

'Hi, I'm Flora Harris. My mother was brought in here last night. Lizzie Harris?' she said to the surly receptionist, and was told she was in the Lindley Wing. Flora followed signs down lengthy corridors and through heavy doors until she found the Lindley Wing, where the floors were carpeted and there was a trolley of freshly pressed bed linen like you might find in a five-star hotel. Of course she was in the private wing! Jeremy was asleep in the chair and her mother looked impossibly pale and small in the big bed. She had a big gash at her hairline and a trail of blood was crusted onto the side of her face. She was wearing a blue-and-white-striped shirt, the collar of which was stained red. Her eyes were closed but sprang open as soon as she heard the door.

'Flora?' she said.

'Hi, Mum,' Flora said, walking towards the bed. She took her hand and Lizzie's chin quivered as she looked up at Flora. She pressed her lips together so hard they formed white ridges and she nodded her head vigorously, tears spilling out of her watery eyes.

'I'm sorry, Mum, for what I said on the phone.' Flora squeezed her hand. Lizzie shook her head then, as forcefully as she had nodded it, and lifted her finger. It wobbled as she placed it on Flora's lips.

'Shhh, shhh,' she said, and Flora took the shaking hand and placed it back on the bed beneath her own.

'OK, let's not talk about that. Are you in a lot of pain? That looks like a nasty gash.'

Flora watched as her mother braced herself to speak. 'It's...' She coughed and cleared her throat and Flora could hear the phlegm rattling around. 'It's my leg that hurts, there are shooting pains all the way down it. My head, bah.' She tapped the scab on her head with her finger as if to prove that it didn't hurt. It turned Flora's stomach to see her touching the wound and she grabbed her hand and pulled it back down onto the blanket.

'Have they given you anything? For the pain, I mean.' They both knew this was a loaded question, and her mother considered her response for a while before answering.

'Yes, they gave me some painkillers, and some...' Flora lifted her eyebrow and then realised what she was doing and so consciously relaxed it. 'Oh, for god's sake, Flora, they gave me some valium as well. I was quite distressed last night.' She had raised her voice and woke Jeremy in the chair.

'Flora, *brrr*, hi.' He blew air out of his puffed cheeks like a horse and blinked a few times to rid his eyes of sleep.

'Hi.' She let go of Lizzie's hand and walked over to the other side of the bed to kiss him. He tried to hold on for a little longer than she'd expected and they were left in an awkward tangle of limbs.

'So good of you to come.' He picked up his glasses from the table next to the bed and after putting them on he looked at his wife. 'How are you doing, old girl?'

'How do you think I'm doing? Bloody awful. I need some more painkillers. Would you go and fetch the nurse, Jeremy?' Flora exchanged a look with her stepfather.

'I think they write it all down on a chart, Lizzie. I'm sure they'll come round with some more drugs when you need them.'

'I think I know whether I need them or not, Jeremy, there are sharp pains shooting up my leg. If you're not going to go and find the nurse, I will just ring this bell here.' She fumbled around with all the various leads and wires and pressed one that made the bed whir and tilt her forward.

'Arrgh!' she shouted in pain, but couldn't take her finger off the button. Flora leapt up and released her mother's finger and then pressed the other button to lower her back down.

'Everything all right in here?' A male nurse in blue scrubs popped his head round the door.

'Yes, we just pressed the wrong button,' Flora explained.

'I need more painkillers,' Lizzie called to him, not remotely hiding the desperation in her voice.

'Right, well, let's have a look, shall we?' The nurse came into the room and picked up the chart at the end of the bed. 'Well, Mrs Harris, it says that you only had painkillers and sedatives two hours ago, which means really you're not due any more for a while, but if you are in real pain...'

'I am.'

'Let me just go and get the doctor and I'll see what we can do...'

Jeremy and Flora looked at each other and then back at Lizzie in the bed. 'I might go and grab a cup of coffee. Would you like one, Flora?'

'Yes please, that would be lovely.'

'I...' Lizzie started to say.

'Not for you, Lizzie, nil by mouth, remember? They've got to operate on that leg this morning.'

'Oh really?' Flora flushed with shame; she hadn't even asked what the diagnosis with the leg was.

'Yes, she's broken it in two places. They have to reset the bones, stick some pins in, I think.'

Flora looked at her mother, whose eyes were starting to fill with tears again.

'What if I can't walk again, what if I'm crippled?'

'It's just a broken bone, Mum.'

'Two, two broken bones that need pinning!'

'You'll be fine.' Flora sat down in the chair next to her mother and pulled it closer to the bed. 'So, are you going to tell me what happened?' Lizzie stared ahead and scrunched her nose up like a petulant child refusing to speak. 'Come on, Mum, were you drinking?' Still nothing. She hunched her shoulders like a hedgehog puffing out its bristles in defence. 'Look, I know I upset you, and

I'm sorry. I was going to call back and then the goats got out and... were you very upset?'

'Of course I was fucking upset, Flora! You basically told me I was a useless mother, and...'

Flora took in a deep breath, 'I didn't say that... look, I'm sorry. Where did you fall?'

'Down the stairs.'

'All the way?'

'I... I... don't remember.' She looked pitiful then; her hackles had dropped and so had her shoulders.

'Jeremy said you were asking for me... that you were quite distressed...'

'I just, well, I wanted to see you, to tell you that I know I haven't been the best, the most stable mother, and I just... well, I just needed you to know that I'm s... s... I'm sssorry.'

'Shh, Mum, it's OK.' She drew her mother into her chest and patted her bony shoulders as she sobbed. She hadn't seen her like this for a few years. It used to be more of a regular thing when Flora was growing up. She would drink herself into self-loathing and then beg Flora's forgiveness. It was usually followed by weeks of disdain. To make up for the weakness she would then go the other way, spitting vitriol at Flora. It was during one of these post-breakdown periods that she packed Flora off to boarding school at age nine: she physically dragged Flora out of the bathroom that she had locked herself in, and without a tear and barely a hug sent her off with Jeremy to a Convent school three hours from home.

'Ah.' Jeremy was coming back into the room with two coffees. Flora untangled herself from Lizzie and took the cup sheepishly. She was feeling light-headed with exhaustion and tipped two whole sachets of sugar into her coffee. Her mother hissed and blew her nose loudly and Flora walked over to the window to inhale the sweet, hot coffee without reproach.

'Hello, Mrs Harris, I'm Dr O'Brien.' The voice was vaguely familiar. Flora turned round to see a blond man in a suit, no scrubs.

He was clean-cut and baby-faced, he had bright blue eyes and a dimple on the side of his cheek.

'Douggie O'Brien!' Flora said, without pretending to hide her surprise.

His cheeks flushed red and he smiled, revealing a mouth of bright white teeth. 'It's Doug now, Flora. Hi.'

'You two know each other?' Jeremy asked while slurping his coffee loudly.

'Er, yeah. Douggie – sorry, Doug and I were at school together.'

'I thought there were only girls at your school?' Her mother found her voice, though still wobbly with emotion.

'The sixth form, remember, when you finally let me leave that awful place and go somewhere without nuns and with boys.' She turned back to Doug. 'Wow, I can't believe it, you've obviously done well for yourself.'

'Yes, I'm an orthopaedic surgeon now, which is why I am going to operate on your leg, Mrs Harris.' He had recovered himself and his cheeks had faded to a gentle glow as he turned to her mother in the bed. 'I gather you've had a fall?'

'Don't say that. Old people have falls, I just fell, past tense. I fell down the stairs and now I'm in crippling agony and no one will give me any more drugs.'

'Mum.'

'I'm sorry, Mrs Harris, I didn't mean to patronise you. Could I have a look at your leg?' He walked around the bed and lifted the covers to reveal Lizzie's naked thigh. Someone had removed her trousers and her fraying, not-quite-white underwear was there in all its shameless glory, along with horrific purple and red marbled bruising down the side of her leg. Jeremy removed himself from the room and Flora followed.

'Was she really pissed?' Flora whispered to him with one eye on the open door.

'I think she must have been. I was out at a dinner and came home and found her at the bottom of the stairs. She was barely conscious. It was quite, well, quite alarming, actually.'

'Has she been drinking a lot recently? I thought she seemed quite good at Christmas.'

'Yes, she was. And she has been better. I don't know what tipped her over the edge yesterday...'

The coffee gurgled inside Flora's stomach and she wrapped her arms around it in shame. 'Yeah, well, that might have something to do with me. We had a bit of a row on the phone, and...'

'Oh for god's sake, Flora, you know how fragile she is...'

'Yes, I know, but she said some really harsh things to me, and...'

'She doesn't mean it,' he said, not hiding the irritation in his voice. 'You should know by now to tread carefully around her. It's not as though you have to see her very often. Is it really too much to ask you to suck it up on the phone?'

Flora hung her head. 'I'm sorry, I'll make it up to her, to you, I promise...'

'There is something. I was going to ask whether you can come and look after her when she gets out of here.'

'Oh, right, um, well, the kids – they have school, and...'

'I've got my AGM next week in Holland, and I have to be there. So if you can't look after her then I will have to find a nurse.' Jeremy ran a shipbroking firm which seemed to involve a lot more dinners in private clubs in London than actual work. The AGM took place on a different European golf course every year.

'She would hate that,' Flora said through gritted teeth.

'Yes, she would, but if you can't do it... your brothers are all working and there isn't anyone else.'

'I'll see what I can do.'

'Great, that's sorted then.'

'I said I'd see...'

'Yes, well, it will be good for you two to spend some time together, and you did say you wanted to make it up to her.'

'Right, so...' Doug O'Brien was coming out of the door, his head down as he scribbled some notes on a chart while he spoke. 'The scans show that she has broken her leg in two places, which I think you already know. We are going to have to put some metal pins in there to hold it all together. Someone will be along to prep her for theatre in the next hour or so.'

'Right-oh,' said Jeremy, and walked back into the room.

'It's good to know she's in safe hands,' Flora said cheerfully.

'She's going to be in quite a lot of pain afterwards, won't be able to walk for a few weeks. Is there someone who can look after her?'

'Yeah, we're just trying think that through as I don't live around here, you see, and my kids are at school in Dorset, but they're only little, so maybe I could take them out for a bit and... we'll figure it out.'

'OK, great. I'll come and find you after the surgery to let you know how it went.' He touched her arm as he left and it was this sudden gesture of unexpected kindness that brought tears to the backs of Flora's eyes.

'OK,' she whispered, swallowing down the emotion and hoping he didn't notice. He smiled and walked down the corridor. He wasn't that tall but he had a very upright posture that gave him gravitas, and the baby-faced skin that had made him look immature at school now clung to his cheekbones with age-defying definition.

'Flora!' her mother shouted from the room, and Flora jumped to her call as she always had.

CHAPTER THREE

LIZZIE

Nerves jangled in the pit of Lizzie's stomach as she made her way to school that first morning. Her father dropped her at the gate and she wondered whether he might offer to escort her in, but he just gave her a quick peck on the cheek before driving off to catch his train to London. A gang of girls with skirts rolled up to reveal varying shapes and sizes of thigh approached Lizzie. She braced herself but they didn't even seem to notice her as she backed off the pavement to let them pass and landed in a slimy pool of water that had gathered at the side of the road. It seeped through the seams of her loafers and for the second time that day she wished she had won the battle with her mother over the Doc Martens.

She followed the girls through the gate and straight into a flow of teenage traffic that was fast and loud. Wafts of cheap aftershave and cigarettes, talcum powder and body odour. Up the steps they moved as one and into a concrete courtyard where they all dispersed. It was a very different place from that sunny day in the holidays when she had come to meet the head teacher. Ghostly quiet, the concrete had glistened and the plants around the courtyard seemed positively tropical against the deep blue sky. But today it was grey and the tarmac was littered with pools of murky water; the leaves on the trees were already starting to fall and the air was heavy and damp. She realised that she had absolutely no idea where she was meant to go as she stood in the courtyard being battered repeatedly by passing backpacks and shoulders.

'You look lost.' It was a lady with grey hair that surrounded her head like a bowl and too-big tortoiseshell glasses.

'Yeah, it's my first day.'

'I can tell. What is your form?'

'Um, Mr, Br, Brad...'

'Mrs Bradley?'

'No, it's a man.'

'Mr Brewster.'

'Yeah, that's it.'

'Over there.' She pointed to the other side of the courtyard where pupils were funnelling in through a green door. 'Through that door and turn right. Mr Brewster's class is the first on the left. His name is on the door.'

'Great, thanks.'

'Er, wait, Miss...'

Lizzie turned round to look at her. 'Claybourne, Lizzie Claybourne,' she said, and she could have sworn she saw the lady's eyes widen with recognition behind those thick lenses.

'Of course, well, Lizzie Claybourne, enjoy your day.'

'Thanks.'

There were only desks left at the front of the classroom when she walked in. She anticipated a ghostly hush and turning of heads, but yet again no one seemed to even notice her arrival. As she settled down at the window end of the front row a squat bald man with thin glasses and a wide gait marched into the room. He threw a pile of exercise books and files onto the desk and removed his glasses, wiping them on the tail of his tweed jacket.

'OK, everybody,' he shouted. 'Quieten down now, can everyone please take a seat. Thank yooouuu.' He extended the end of every word, dragging it out for dramatic effect, sliding down a scale of notes. 'Right, and we have a couple of newcomers in the class todaaay.' Lizzie braced herself.

'Edward Thatcher.' He scanned the room for Edward, but no one confessed to the name. 'Uh, well, maybe he got lost somewhere, sure he'll turn up. And...' he looked down the register and she kept her head down, her heart in her stomach. 'Lizzie, where are you, Lizzie? Lizzie Claybourne?' She didn't speak but lifted her hand and imagined every eye in the room burning into the back of her head. 'Right, well, I hope everyone makes Lizzie and Edward, wherever he is, feel welcome. Lizzie, you need to go and register and pick up a welcome pack from the office at break. That is the oh-so-desirable Portakabin by the front gate.' She nodded and swore she could hear whispers from the back of the room, not specific words but indecipherable utterings that caused the hairs on the back of her neck to stand on end. Mr Brewster continued to talk about timetables and lunch vouchers and rules, and halfway through his diatribe about chewing gum underneath desks, Edward Thatcher made a fraught and sweaty appearance in the classroom.

'How nice of you to join us, Edward.' There was not an iota of warmth in his sarcastic tone, and Lizzie winced for the awkward-looking boy with glasses and floppy hair and limbs that seemed too long for his skinny body. He collapsed into the desk next to hers. She stole furtive glances at him throughout the rest of Mr Brewster's speech. He had moved on to Sixth form responsibilities: how they were to lead by example now that they were at the top of the school. And then to tutors and A level mocks in January. Edward Thatcher was wiping the sweat from his brow. He looked even more flustered than her, and she wondered how many classrooms he had been into before eventually finding theirs. He kept his head lowered, his face obscured by a thatch of brown hair that came down to beneath his round glasses. His hands were long like everything else; his fingers looked soft and girlish. They shook slightly as he rustled around in his pencil case to find a pen, to make notes she presumed, and wondered whether she should be doing the same. But once he was safely with pen in hand the shaking seemed to stop and he doodled around the edges of the piece of paper.

'Right, so I know that was a lot to take in. Are there any questions?' Mr Brewster looked exhausted by the session and Lizzie wondered how he was going to get through a day's teaching after this. How was she going to get through the day? She looked at the clock; it was not even nine. Six more hours until she could go home, and to what? Her parents with their furrowed brows and pained expressions and the web of lies that she had wrapped herself in. The panic tightened around her neck a little more every day.

She muddled her way through Maths and Biology. They were behind her last school in the syllabus, and so she could let her shoulders drop a little. She hadn't seen Edward again and imagined he was taking Art and English Literature; maybe Theatre Studies or History? He had that whimsical look about him that she had always found intriguing in others, so far from her own mind. She had a scientific brain, a neurotic one that couldn't cope with hypothesising. She needed raw facts, they made her feel safe. She grounded her overactive mind in science, in how and why things worked. That was how she stopped her head from exploding on a trajectory of infinite impossibility.

In the echoey and brightly lit lunch hall she queued for a plate of meatballs that were swimming in a sauce with such a thick layer of fat on the top that it had hardened into craters. It came with that dry yellow rice which she had only ever seen in school canteens, and sweetcorn and peas mixed together. She found an empty table at the edge of the room and sat down with her tray. She recognised a girl from her form on the next-door table, one of the crowd from the back of the room. She had a high ponytail and big brown eyes, and she was pretty until she opened her thin lips to reveal a mouthful of yellow, stained teeth. She caught Lizzie's eye and then started whispering to the other girls on her table who turned round to look at her, and Lizzie felt her face flush with heat. She picked at the meatballs, put a piece in her mouth, but it congealed like cement and she couldn't swallow it down.

'Hey, Lizzie, isn't it?' the girl with the yellow teeth called across the table.

'Yeah,' Lizzie squeaked, her mouth full.

'Where were you at school before?' Should she lie? Add another thread to the web? But she was so very tired of lying.

'Highfield.' The girl's eyes widened and the whispering continued.

'Isn't that a boarding school?'

'Yeah.'

'Why did you leave?' The meatball was stuck halfway down her throat now and she coughed, spluttered, in fact. She picked up her glass and hoped the girls couldn't see her hands shaking as she swallowed several gulps of icy-cold water and the meatball thankfully disappeared.

Lizzie shrugged her shoulders and tried with all her might to look nonchalant. 'Parents couldn't afford it,' she said with a shrug. The girl's eyes widened in surprise and Lizzie felt a flash of hope that this might stall them. They went back to their whispers.

'Go on,' Lizzie heard one of them say. 'Ask her.' Lizzie braced herself; she held onto the cold metal chair with her thighs, ground the soles of her feet through the loafers and into the sticky floor beneath. She picked up a pea and squashed it between her fingers; the husk separated from the flesh inside. 'Go on,' the girl whispered again with more urgency. But the girl with yellow teeth, for whatever reason, decided to let it go.

'Come on, let's get out of here,' she said as she scraped her chair back across the floor. The screech of metal on wood echoed around the rafters of the dining hall. She carried her plate away and they all followed, one larger girl shovelling in the last mouthfuls of meatball before she rushed to catch them up. They would be back. She had been on the wrong end of girls like that all her life. They had let her off this time, but only because they wanted to leave her hanging.

'Do you mind if I sit here?' She was so consumed with her own thoughts that she hadn't noticed him standing there, Edward

Thatcher. He was eyeing the girls that were still moving across the dining room like a pack of wild dogs, and Lizzie felt the colour flush to her cheeks as she imagined him witnessing that exchange.

'Sure,' she said, without properly looking at him.

'You new too?' he asked as he tucked into a bread roll.

'Yeah.'

The flour stuck to his lips and hands, which he wiped on his blazer. Powdery white smears now streaked his top pocket but he didn't seem to notice.

'Is this as disgusting as it looks?' he asked, sniffing his plate of food.

'Worse,' she said, moving the meatballs around her plate with her fork.

'Can't be as bad as my last school. Here goes.' He took a mouthful and chewed hard, his face contorting into a series of expressions while he chewed, from not so bad, to not sure, to grimacing in distaste.

Lizzie smiled. 'Where was your last school?'

'Slough.'

'Why did you move now? In the final year, I mean?'

'My dad got a new job, had to move last minute.'

'What does he do?'

'What is this, the Spanish Inquisition?'

'Sorry.' She looked down, embarrassed.

'Hey, I'm kidding, he runs the telesales department for a travel insurance company. Their office in Slough was requisitioned for a block of flats and they relocated the whole thing to some industrial estate here in Crawley. Most of the staff were laid off, think they'd been waiting for an excuse to do that for years. But Dad was one of the lucky few they asked to move with them. So here we are.'

'So you had to leave all your friends and everything?'

'Yeah.'

'Have you got brothers and sisters?'

'No, it's just me and my dad.'

'Oh.' Her mind rattled with reasons why, and she realised too late that her face had given her away.

'My mum died when I was four,' he said and shovelled in another meatball.

'I'm sorry.'

'Thanks. It was a long time ago, I don't really remember her. What about you? Why did you move schools at this impractical time?' he asked.

Maybe he hadn't heard after all. 'I was at a boarding school just outside Oxford, but my parents can't afford it any more so now I'm here.' It sounded more credible second time around, and she wondered whether she might even convince herself if she said it enough.

'Must be hard too,' he said and pulled something out of his mouth. He inspected it before putting it on the side of his plate. 'I bet you didn't get gristle in your meatballs at a posh boarding school.'

She laughed. 'No, we had a baguette bar.'

'Baguette bar? Wow, how the mighty have fallen!'

'Yeah, well, it wasn't that great. There were ferocious nuns that made sure we ate every morsel of food on our plates.'

'Seriously?! Well, give me meatballs with gristle over ferocious nuns any day, they sound like something out of a horror movie. Are your parents really religious then?'

'Not really, they go to church on Sundays, we all do. But they don't preach it much at home. It is not like we say grace or anything.'

'What subjects are you taking? Religious studies?'

'No! Maths, Biology and Chemistry. You?'

'English, Art and History.' She smiled, delighted with herself for getting it right.

'Quite opposite ends of the spectrum, then – we must be friends.' She felt a warm, honeyed glow creeping up her body. She had never been friends with a boy before. Not much scope for that in a girls' boarding school in the middle of nowhere. They had organised dances with the local boys' school where Lizzie had skulked at the edges of the dimly lit school hall caught between her own conflicting desires to be both invisible and under bright lights. She never made out with a boy, though; the only ones that approached her were covered in spots or an extra layer of fat, and she wasn't that desperate. So she got her kicks elsewhere; stole bottles of wine from behind the bar, which she drank in the woods, and smoked cigarettes, one after another. Sometimes Mary joined her – only if she hadn't managed to pull, though. Mary had a less discerning taste in men and would happily pick up the strays from the edges if approached.

Lizzie watched Edward plough his way through his lunch. For a skinny guy he had quite an appetite. He finished every morsel on the plate and moved on to the chocolate mousse that Lizzie hadn't dared touch. It had formed a leathery layer that he had to puncture with his spoon a couple of times before reaching what looked more like custard than mousse below. His eyes were big and blue, in contrast to his dark hair. His skin was incredibly smooth, with only a smattering of fair hairs on his chin. He reminded her of a character in a historical novel, pale and interesting; he would be the one under a tree reading a book with a blanket over his knees while others played games in the sunshine.

'What are your teachers like so far?' she asked.

'Well, I've had Mrs Carruthers for art, who is like every art teacher I have ever met. She wears long floaty clothes and has different coloured nails and thinning hair, which she hides under a flamboyant scarf. She speaks incredibly softly and slowly about perspective and detail and integrity, but she seems OK. And I've got Mr Brewster, our dreaded form tutor, for History and he is about as dry as the Sahara.'

'Yes, he didn't seem especially inspiring.'

'Smelt funny too, did you notice?'

'I thought that was just the general aroma of school.'

'Nah, it was definitely him. Eggy, I'd say. I guess that's why everyone bagged the desks at the back.'

'Leaving the loser new ones to sit at the front.'

'To endure the horrific stench of the Brewster.' He put on a dramatic voice, slowly labouring every word as he looked over the top of his glasses at Lizzie, his eyes sparkling with mischief. 'What about you?' he asked, scraping the corners of the mousse pot out with his spoon.

'My teachers?' she asked.

'Nah, that's boring. Tell me about you, your home, your family.'

'Well, my dad works in the city in London. He spends the whole week in a flat there and comes home on Friday evening. My mum doesn't do much apart from the odd church lunch or flower arranging for a wedding but she always seems to be in a rush. We live in a house in the middle of nowhere about twenty minutes away, and I have two brothers and a sister, all older.'

'Wow, youngest of four. Must be fun in your house.'

'It's loud and sometimes fun, but on the whole we just fight and Mum shouts at us not to. My sister and older brother are away at university, and my other brother is on a gap year. He's meant to be earning money to go travelling later this year, but he just sits in his bedroom and gets stoned most of the time.'

'Doesn't your Mum notice – that he's not at work, I mean?'

'Yeah, of course. She pretends to care – he's meant to be working with a friend of my dad who runs a photocopier business, but he comes up with a whole myriad of excuses not to go and Mum goes along with it. He's her favourite. He's handsome and funny and popular and can basically get away with anything. They will pay for him to go travelling in the end, just like they did for my brother and my sister, so what's the point?' He looked at her like she was from a foreign land then, and she wished she hadn't revealed so much. That bit about the money had really contradicted her story about her parents being too poor to let her finish her last year at school. 'I mean, maybe they won't, actually give him the money for travelling, not now, with their finances and my school and everything...' He looked at her quizzically for a moment but then changed his expression quickly, a habit she was becoming familiar with, and didn't ask any more questions.

'Well, I'd better get going to my English class. *Macbeth*, apparently. "Fair is foul and foul is fair".' Lizzie smiled to hide the fact that she had no idea what he was talking about.

'Yeah, I've got Chemistry now. See you around.'

'OK, bye, Lizzie.'

The following day Edward found Lizzie in the lunch hall, and then every day that week until it became a thing. Apart from their weekly form sessions with Mr Brewster, they didn't see each other around the school at other times, their classes occurring at opposite ends of the concrete sprawl. But Lizzie found herself looking forward to lunchtime, despite the horrors that appeared on her tray every day. Edward didn't seem to notice or care and he encouraged Lizzie to eat up, told her she was too thin and would waste away. Her parents had been saying that all her life, but coming from him it didn't make her skin crawl in the same way. She was flattered by his interest, and so she did. She chewed down the rubbery macaroni cheese, totally devoid of sauce, and the fish and chips which oozed so much oil they caused slick-like rainbows on the edge of the plate. She even stomached the semolina for him because he was so excited by the hundreds and thousands that melted into the crust on its surface and created a multicoloured paint effect when you stirred them in.

She hadn't made any other friends; most of the girls ignored her. Even the ones who had been interested that first lunchtime hadn't spoken to her since. She was both relieved and disappointed. She had lived in fear, those first few days, of more invasive questions and had come up with some better responses which now lay useless, like the paintings her parents never put up on the fridge. The only people who talked to her were the nerdy brainboxes in her maths class who wanted to compare formulas. She was falling behind in maths; working hard was evidently not enough at this level. She didn't have the natural geek brain that fuelled those at the top. She had always been near the top, if not actually at the summit, but it wasn't without effort – she worked hard. It was what she did, had always done. She didn't have anything else to make her shine. She was skinny and had thin lips and mousy hair, not ugly exactly but no defining features to get excited about. And no accompanying skills that could brand her. She played the violin, but without 'va-va-voom', as her teacher repeatedly reminded her. She was useless at sport, could barely draw a stick man and had very little charm, according to her siblings. So, she worked hard and got good results. She'd had one consistent friend at Highfield – Mary – who was an even less bright, and plumper, version of her. Mary followed her around like a puppy and Lizzie tolerated her because it was better than being on her own and because sometimes Mary deflected the bullies' attention from herself. And then there were the other fleeting friendships – girls who Lizzie flattered or bribed with homework or presents. Girls who humoured her for as long as it took for them to get what they wanted, before flinging her to the bottom of the pile again.

But Edward was nothing like those girls. He was funny, clever and handsome and didn't ask anything of her in return for his friendship. It was week three, and he still hadn't dumped her for a more interesting lunch buddy. She was eating more, and taking more care over her appearance. She had stolen one of Bella's Alice bands and found that if she pushed her hair forward with it then it didn't stick so limply to the top of her head. It was bouncier, and so was she. She didn't even care that much about only getting sixty-three per cent in the recent maths test. Lizzie had never got below seventy-five per cent in anything, and if someone had told her six months earlier that she would only be two thirds of the way down the class at a new school she would have been horrified. But she was still doing well in Biology and Chemistry, and maybe she didn't want to be up there with the super-nerds in maths anyway. This carefree recklessness was a novelty for Lizzie, and she liked the light-headed feeling it gave her when she really focused hard on it. She even went so far as to try to explain it to Edward over lunch one day.

'So let me get this right, you are elated about the fact that you got a less than mediocre result in your maths test?' He had picked up a chicken leg and was eating it with his hands, licking his lips at regular intervals. It made Lizzie feel a bit sick to watch but she kept her head down and tried not to let it get to her.

'It's not that I'm happy that I didn't get a good result. Just happy that I'm not a dribbling wreck. You must understand, Edward, this is very unchartered turf for me. I really don't care that much!'

'If you say it enough times it might actually become true.'

'I'm serious, it's the new me.'

'I'm not sure I get why you not caring about your results is a good thing, as we're starting the most important year of our education so far?' He looked at her more confused than ever, and she worried that she might be weirding him out. Her siblings told her she did that every day.

'Do you think I'm nuts?'

'Not exactly.' He spoke slowly, considering his response. Then smiled. 'No, I'm delighted that you've found this sudden sense of abandon, Lizzie. I think we should celebrate!'

'How?' She laughed, and actually picked up her own chicken leg and gnawed at the flesh. It was surprisingly good, even if the jelly was now all over her fingers.

'How about you invite me to your place this weekend? I want to meet this crazy family of yours.' She put down the chicken leg and felt her muscles tighten as the smile fell from her face.

'What?'

He looked at her, surprised. 'Anyone would think I'd just suggested you jump into a pool of shark-infested water.'

'They're a bit like that, my family. I mean, they'll eat you alive.'

'I can't wait!'

'No, Edward, I'm sorry. I can't, everyone is home this weekend, it's a family get-together – another time, maybe.'

'Well, I wouldn't want to intrude on your family get-together.' He shrugged, pretending to be nonchalant, but she could tell he was disappointed. She knew her parents would welcome him with open arms; the only friend she had ever invited home was Mary, and they hadn't even pretended to find her anything other than drab. Imagine the look on their faces if she told them she was inviting a boy home – it might be worth it just for that moment. But then she considered the inevitable conversation that would follow, the lies that she had told him about why she had moved schools shamefully revealed. And her family were a bunch of live wires. They would grill Edward about every tiny detail of his life, and they were bound to reveal all sorts of details about Lizzie that she would rather keep under wraps. No, she wasn't brave enough, not yet. But she picked up the chicken leg again and took a big bite of flesh. Baby steps, she told herself.

That night at dinner she told her mother and brother Jamie about her less than satisfactory maths result.

'I don't believe it, little miss brainbox got sixty per cent! What is the world coming to?'

'I'm sorry, darling, were you dreadfully upset?' Her mother looked at her with that familiar pained expression.

'Actually, I'm OK.' They exchanged a look across the table, something else she had grown accustomed to over the last few months. The exchanging of expressions, angst, sympathy, terror, despair – did they really think that she couldn't see these supposedly furtive glances? It made her want to scream. She gripped her skirt under the table and waited for the rage to pass.

'Don't get complacent, Lizzie, you won't get that place at Oxford with sixty per cent, you know,' Jamie said, the mocking tone ever-present behind his words.

'Actually, I might have changed my mind about Oxford.' More exchanged glances.

'Really?' Her mother tried to hide the alarm in her voice.

'Yeah, a friend of mine, Edward, he's going to Manchester. Apparently the faculty of medicine there is even better than Oxford.' At the mention of Edward, Jamie spat his potato across the table. 'I'm sorry, Jamie, did I say something funny?'

He had his hand over his mouth and was trying to shovel the food back in. He coughed to regain his composure.

'And who is Edward?' her mum asked, painfully calmly.

'A friend at school.'

'A boyfriend?' Jamie asked.

'Well, yes, Jamie, Edward is a boy's name and he is a friend.'

'Ooohhh,' Jamie mocked, and Lizzie rolled her eyes.

'That's great, darling.' Her mother's voice was sickly-sweet. 'I'm so pleased you're making friends at your new school. You see, I knew it wouldn't be so bad.' She reached over and squeezed Lizzie's hand. It was small, like her own, the only feature she had inherited from her beautiful mother. Her nails were painted bright red and a large sapphire shone from her ring finger. Lizzie pulled her hand away.

'And boyfriends, no less! Lizzie, you dark horse, is he devilishly handsome, or does he have horns and two heads?' Jamie sneered.

'Oh, do shut up, Jamie, I'm sure he's very nice-looking. Where does he live, darling? What do his parents do?'

'His mum is dead and his dad works for an insurance company.'

'Oh, poor boy – you must invite him over, Lizzie.'

'Oh yes, ask him, Lizzie, it's time we had a laugh – it's been a while since Mary came and blocked the downstairs loo.'

'Oh Jamie, poor Mary, that is very unfair.'

'Come on, Mum, you must admit it was pretty hilarious when Dad had to stick his arm down there to pull out the wads of paper napkins and beetroot roulade.'

'Shut up, Jamie.' Lizzie scowled at him but couldn't stop the smile that was creeping over her face. She wanted to feel indignant for poor Mary, who had snaffled her beetroot roulade into a napkin in her lap, to dispose of later down the loo. She wasn't to know that the dodgy Georgian plumbing wouldn't stand for it and that it had been drummed into them all for as long as they could remember not to put so much as a tampon down the downstairs loo. They had all feigned ignorance, and no one had cast any blame while their dad cursed and swore in his rubber gloves. But they had all had a really good laugh about it when Mary left later that afternoon.

'Oh, Lizzie, even you have to admit it was hilarious. She went the colour of the beetroot when Dad stormed in with the plunger and swore at everyone.'

'Oh, poor Mary,' her mother said again.

Lizzie rolled her eyes. 'In fact, I was wondering whether Edward might be able to come over this weekend.' The words were out of her mouth before she had given them any thought, the memory of Mary and her ridicule still rattling around her subconscious.

'Of course, darling.' Her mother shot Jamie a glance, willing him to shut up and he did, with a smirk.

'Great, I'll get him to come for lunch on Saturday, shall I?'

'Yes, of course. Bella and Damian will be home too, but I'm sure they would love to meet Edward – we all would, wouldn't we, Jamie?'

'You bet,' said Jamie. 'Can't wait to meet Eddie.'

'Edward.'

'Whatever.'

'And, er, you won't mention anything about why I left High-field, I mean...' She looked at her mother and then at Jamie, the smiles on their faces dropping to infuriating sincerity.

'Of course not, darling, wouldn't dream of it. Would we, Jamie?'

'Nope, not a word, scout's honour.'

CHAPTER FOUR

ROMY

Romy walked to the end of the pontoon. It was missing various planks along the way, and the dark gaps reminded her of the missing teeth of the beggars that lined the streets in Hong Kong. When she reached the end, she sat down and dipped her feet in the water. A shoal of silvery fish was feeding on the weeds underneath the wood. They scattered at the intrusion and then reformed and inspected her toes. She lay back on the warm wood and closed her eyes. She could hear the sound of the waves lapping gently against the shore, the creaking of the pontoon and the tinkling of the bird scarers on the dive boat tied up on the other side of it. She had dreamed about this moment so many times since she had left, and she resisted the urge to pinch herself.

When she felt her flesh tingle under the intensity of the sun, she pulled herself up to sitting and then standing, the blood rushing from her head to her feet. Then the familiar anticipation of the jump. It wasn't high. In fact, now she looked down it can't have been more than a couple of feet between the wood and the surface of the water. But it had felt so much higher as a child, when she had run and jumped and flipped and dived over and over again. Kids from school would stop on their way home to jump with her, their dark skin glistening with dripping water as they bombed their way in.

She did a shallow dive into the sea. In the years since she had left, the world had zoomed in on the dying reefs and she had anticipated a graveyard of grey, but the coral there was as abundant and bright as she remembered. She swam down into the forest of magenta, fuschia, turmeric, through the purple tendrils and the golden fronds. She followed shoals of silver angelfish and then a lone parrotfish, its pink scales glowing like fluorescent skeletons down the side of its body and its turquoise belly kissing the tops of the sea fans. How had she stayed away for so long? She came up for air and looked around at the vast expanse of blue sparkling sea with no hint of the world that was hidden beneath it. The laughter of the children on the beach was echoey and distant. She was alone. So wonderfully and horribly alone. She lay back on the surface of the water and her ears filled and her mind numbed momentarily until it was flooded again with the same dark thoughts, the same bleak reality of her prognosis. She dived down again, into that magical world of silence and colour and dreams. She swam deeper, her ears popping with the descent, further down, further away from the horrors that plagued her mind on the surface. She held onto a weed that swayed in the water and relaxed her limbs, willing her body to stillness. It floated up but she grabbed the weed tighter and forced herself back down. A clownfish swam past, a real live Nemo looking for his dad. The irony wasn't lost on her. The last of the bubbles came out of her nose and still she held on, desperate to stay down there where she felt safest. But her legs started to float up and she lost her grip on the weed. She grabbed onto a piece of nearby coral that was sharp, and punctured her palm. She tried to swim back down but there was no air now and nothing to fuel her limbs. Water seeped in through a crack between her lips and she coughed and panicked. She looked up at the light beaming its way down through the shadows, but it was so far away. She kicked her legs and swam towards it. It was difficult, and the muscles in her chest clamped down hard around her heart, squeezing the last pockets of air out of her lungs. When she finally emerged out of the water, she was gasping, her throat raw, her body exhausted.

She swam back to the pontoon with defeated limbs, climbed up the ladder and lay on the end. Her nerves were shattered and her body shivering despite the blistering heat of the sun. What just happened? Was she really that desperate that she would have been willing to end it all? Without a fight? Obviously not, but she had come close and it scared her. That glimpse of the end and what it really meant, leaving everything and everyone behind. Her heart thumped in her chest and her mind raced. She felt the pontoon shake under the weight of some feet and looked up to see a couple approaching. She pulled herself up to standing.

'Lovely spot!' the guy said, and she forced a smile but couldn't respond. She bowed her head after seeing their exchange of glances and stumbled back along the length of the pontoon, up the beach, into the house and her room, where she lay on the bed and watched the fan blow the mosquito net above her.

She fell into a deep sleep, and when she woke it was dusk and her room glowed as if it was on fire. She scrambled out of her bed and over to the window. She had seen sunsets in the fourteen years that she had been away, in fact she and Mali would often climb to the top of a peak on Lamma Island with cold beers and crisps to watch the sun falling into the sea. But there was a power station in their line of sight, and the sea was densely populated with boats. She had taken the magic of the sunsets at The Sapphire Cove for granted and pined for them after she had left. Romy looked out at the sky streaked with fuchsia and orange, the colours reflected in the sea so that it was impossible to tell where sky stopped and the water began. The dark silhouettes of the boats seemed to hang in the air, suspended in the infinite blaze. In the restaurant, candles flickered on the tables and she could hear the murmur of the guests and the clinking of ice in their sundowner cocktails. Her own

stomach growled and she rummaged through her bag for something to wear.

Ted and Joseph always had dinner with their guests in the
restaurant. At one long table, they sat with people from all over the
world; said it kept them young and in touch. They made an excep-
tion on Sunday nights, family night, when they would have dinner
just the three of them on their balcony in the house. They would
play cards and tell stories, listen to music and quiz Romy about
school. She spent the whole week looking forward to Sunday
nights. She resented having to share her dads with these strangers
who came and went. She was initially relegated to the kitchen,
where she ate with Angel and Jasmine, and then on her tenth
birthday her fathers asked her to join them the restaurant. She
could remember that first night, the candles dancing in the breeze;
she wore a yellow dress, and was given a fruit cocktail with a pink
umbrella. But the novelty soon wore off. Some people were
intrigued by their set-up and would grill her about her unconven-
tional life, but mostly she was ignored. And so she sat quietly and
listened. She learned more about life from that dinner table than in
the whole of her school career. As she got older and more attractive
some of the young travellers paid her more attention, but her dads
were always quick to intervene. That is, until Ted became too sick
and Joseph too preoccupied, and at seventeen Romy often found
herself entertaining the guests alone. She kidded herself and
everyone else that she was doing it for the business, but they all
knew that she just needed to get away from the sickness in the
house. The smell of vomit, faeces and disinfectant which Joseph's
relentless burning of incense couldn't help to mask. And then after
he died and Joseph went to pieces, Romy still continued to have
dinner with the guests. 'To hold the fort and keep the business
afloat,' she said, but by then it was the silence that she was
desperate to avoid, and Joseph's all-consuming grief.

That was when Scott arrived. He was from Australia, twenty-
three and taking some time out to travel the world after uni and
before settling down in Hong Kong with a job at a bank that his

dad had already lined up. He was handsome in that shaggy blond hair and piercing blue-eyed surfer way. He was working his way around Asia with his best friend Alex, and they arrived at Sapphire Cove to do their advanced diving course. After completing it, Alex was keen to move on to Palawan, but Scott and Romy had fallen into a relationship that was deep and intense. Still raw with grief, she was desperate for distraction and attention and Scott gave it all in abundance. He showered her with so much love that she found herself riding an emotional wave of euphoric highs and lows so potent she couldn't breathe. When Joseph was drowning in his own grief, Scott was always there to pick her up and take her on the next ride. Alex left, and Scott stayed and helped to run the dive shop. For the next four months while he should have been travelling around Borneo, Indonesia and Malaysia, he stayed at The Sapphire Cove. Joseph didn't approve, but he didn't have the strength or mental capability to do anything about it. And the more he withdrew, the more Romy grew, fuelled by her grief and a compulsive desire to live life to the max. So, when Scott asked her to go with him to Hong Kong, she didn't hesitate. She was eighteen and bursting at the seams with vitality and frustration with this tiny island and its strangling limitations and memories. And she was terrified about Joseph dying too, having to go through it all again only to be left on her own.

Romy came out of her room in a bright red sundress that revealed the tattoos on her arms and back. She had wondered whether Joseph would forgo dinner with the guests to welcome her home after all this time, but wasn't surprised to find the house empty. There was a momentary flash of childish resentment followed by a cooling sense of relief. Her feet were bare and the now cool sand was soft between her toes as she walked across the beach. The smell of citronella candles and freshly baked bread was as familiar as an old blanket. That was Ted; he had been horrified at the lack of bread when he arrived here and so baked his own. In time he had taught Angel how to make sourdough just the way he liked it, and The Sapphire Cove quickly became renowned for its freshly baked bread and pastries, quiches and cakes.

She spotted Joseph talking to a couple on the other side of the restaurant.

'Romy.' He smiled at her. 'This is my daughter. Meet John and Suzanne, they're from Singapore.' It was the couple with the baby that they had watched from the balcony earlier.

'Hi.' Romy forced a smile.

'Did you grow up here?' John asked, while fanning away a mosquito from the baby asleep in his arms.

'Yeah, I did, until I was eighteen, and then I moved to Hong Kong.'

'Lucky you,' Suzanne said. 'I don't think I'd ever leave.'

'Well, the bright lights of the city called,' Joseph said. 'We knew we couldn't keep her here forever.' They smiled.

'How long have you been here?' she asked.

'Just a week, unfortunately. Tonight is our last night, but we'll be back. We come every year.'

'Oh really?' She was surprised; there hadn't been much in the way of returning trade in her day.

'Well, for the last three years,' John said. 'We moved to Singapore six years ago from London and spent the first few years travelling around when we could, and then we discovered this place and figured it's as good as it gets, so now we just come here.'

'This is the first time little Jack has been here.' Suzanne stroked the fuzz on the top of her sleeping baby's head.

'And has he liked it?'

'Yeah, I think so.'

'He likes the water,' Joseph said, and put his finger underneath the hand of the baby who latched onto it in his sleep. She couldn't help feeling put out by their familiarity. 'I'm just going to get a drink,' she said, and excused herself. Joseph said something that Romy couldn't hear as she walked towards the bar, and she saw Suzanne laugh and touch his arm.

'Hey, what can I get you?' There was an American guy behind

the bar. He had long brown hair, still wet, that he pushed behind his ears. He wore a grey vest over tanned shoulders.

'Uh, a beer, thanks.'

'You must be Romy.'

'Yeah, and you are?'

'I'm Bob, I help Joseph out with the diving.'

'And the bar too, I see.'

'I'm a man of many talents.' He passed her a bottle of beer. It was cold and beads of water dripped down the side. 'You want a glass?'

'Nah.' She put the bottle to her lips.

'You look like you needed that.'

'Do I?' She was aware of the defensive tone in her voice.

He laughed. 'Yeah, long day?'

'I guess, I hate travelling.'

'Hong Kong, right?'

'That's right.'

'I don't know how anyone lives in a city like that where you can't breathe for all the pollution. I went there last year and felt strangely light-headed the whole time. Apparently it's a thing, pollution sickness.'

'Yeah, well, you get used to it.'

'Each to their own. Personally, I'd much rather breathe this in and see that sunset over the water every night.'

'You don't find it a bit quiet here?'

'Nah, I like it.'

'OK, everybody sit down, dinner is served.' It was Angel, coming out of the kitchen with baskets of bread, which she put out on the long table.

'I'd better go help serve up,' Bob said and retreated to the kitchen.

'I'll come with you.' Romy followed him into the kitchen and scanned the unfamiliar faces for Jasmine. There were three ladies in there, a bigger operation than when she had left and it was just Angel. They were all wearing the same yellow t-shirt and black shorts. She spotted a hugely pregnant girl at the back spooning rice into serving dishes.

'Jasmine.' Romy approached her and she smiled. 'You don't remember me?'

'Romy – yeah, er, kind of.'

'Wow, you were just a little girl when I left. Look at you now! When is it due?'

'A month.' She rubbed her belly in a circular motion.

'Congratulations.'

'Thanks.'

'Romy, you here to help, or what?' It was Angel coming back into the kitchen.

'Sure, what can I do?'

'Take this out to the table.' She handed her a big plate of salad with orange flowers on the top and carrots and cucumbers carved into flowers around the edges.

She was wondering whether she could get away with helping Angel all night and not sit down when Joseph called her over.

'Romy, come and sit here.' He beckoned to a seat next to his at the head of the table.

'Julian, isn't it? This is my daughter, Romy.' He talked to the guy on her other side, who was wearing an ethnic striped shirt with a waistcoat and was pale with a bead of sweat trickling down the side of his face into his ginger beard.

'Hi.' Julian smiled a meek smile.

'Hi there.' She sat down with regret.

'And this is Saira.' Joseph gestured to the lady opposite Romy on his other side. She was beautiful with long dark hair and a white sundress with thin straps revealing smooth, tanned arms.

'Hi.' She took Romy's hand across the table and flashed her pearly-white teeth at her.

'Mummy, can we have some bread?' A boy with huge brown eyes ran at the table and helped himself to the bread, tipping the basket over in the process.

'Indy, hey, look what you've done. That bread is for the grown-ups. You've already had your supper.'

'But I'm still hungry, and it's warm.'

Joseph laughed, and put the bread back in the basket and offered it to the child. 'Here you go, Indy, it's delicious, isn't it? Angel has perfected the art of baking bread over the years.' Indy grabbed three pieces and ran off to find his brother on the beach.

'Where do you live, Romy?' Saira asked her across the table.

'In Hong Kong – and you?'

'We did a stint in Hong Kong a few years ago. My husband, Tim, works for an airline and we move around a lot. Right now, we are in Kuala Lumpur.'

'Oh right, how is that?'

'It's OK. I preferred Hong Kong, there's a bit more of a scene.' Romy could imagine exactly which scene she was referring to; in fact, she probably knew Scott and all his cronies.

'I spend most of my time trying to escape the scene.'

'I guess it can get a bit much sometimes. Where do you live?'

'On Lamma Island, I moved there a few years ago.' Romy watched as Joseph spread some butter on his bread and put it in his mouth. She thought she detected a smile and couldn't tell whether he was enjoying this bizarre process of fact-finding through others. He obviously wasn't going to ask her anything about her life, wouldn't want to expose himself as the father who had no idea where his daughter had been living for the past decade and a half.

'I know Lamma. I used to go there on the company junk. What do you do there?'

'I work in a tattoo parlour.' She looked at Joseph for a response, wanted him to choke on his bread or guffaw or laugh, but there was nothing. He just carried on chewing.

'Cool, is that your own work?' She gestured to Romy's arms.

'No, the guy I work with did it. It's pretty hard to work on yourself.'

'How did you learn how to do it?'

'I met my boss at a party, got chatting about how I had always wanted a tattoo, that I had designed my own as a teenager. I was working at a hairdresser's at the time, but he agreed to train me if I helped out at the parlour in the evenings and on my days off. Eventually he gave me a job.'

'Wow, that's pretty cool. I have always wanted a tattoo but never quite had the balls, and now I'm getting old and think I may have left it too late.'

'Nah, never too late. You could just do something subtle where no one can see it.'

'Maybe I will!'

At that moment someone came down the steps and into the restaurant. Romy was still looking at Joseph and waiting for his reaction to her career in tattoos, and she saw his eyes narrow slightly before breaking into a smile.

'Sorry I'm late,' a male voice came from behind her. 'Glad you didn't wait!'

Romy looked over her shoulder to see a blond man, probably in his fifties. He wore a pale linen shirt that was creaseless and darker linen trousers with navy espadrilles. He was tanned with blond stubble. He smiled and scanned the table. Then he spotted her and his smile widened.

'Stefan!' Joseph said. 'Come and meet Romy.'

'Romy! Hi, I've heard so much about you.' He leant down and kissed her, his stubble grazing her cheek.

'Hi,' Romy said warily. His familiarity was unnerving. And then Stefan put his hands on Joseph's shoulders and gave them a squeeze and left them there for a while.

'Is there a space for me?' he said, standing at the head of the table, his hands still on her father's shoulders.

'Yeah, over here,' John called from the other end of the table.

'Or do you want to sit here?' Saira was standing up and offering her seat.

'No, no, no, I'm gonna let Romy catch up with Joseph. I'll be fine down there. Thanks, Saira.' He moved to the other end of the table. Smiling, he clapped John on the back and engaged them all in animated conversation. Romy couldn't take her eyes off him. Then she did, and she looked at Joseph, who was also watching him at the other end of the table but looking more uneasy than she had seen him all day. His eyebrow twitched when he was nervous; she had forgotten about that until now.

'So, is there something you want to tell me?' She turned to Joseph, and Saira turned to her husband on the other side and pretended not to listen to their conversation.

'I- I'm sorry, I was going to tell you but it was all such a rush, and I wasn't sure how, and...'

'How long has it been?'

'Two years.' It felt like a long time, but then Romy remembered that she hadn't been home for nearly fourteen years. That Ted had been dead all that time.

'And does he live here?'

'Yes, he moved in about a year ago. But he travels a lot. He's a journalist.'

She nearly spat out her water. 'Another writer?'

'Yes, but it's different. He writes about war and economics and climate change...'

'So did Ted.'

'I guess, but in a very different way. He was making art, and Stefan is reporting news.'

She picked at the salad on her plate. 'Well, I'm happy for you. That you've found someone. You've been alone for a long time.'

He didn't answer, and suddenly Romy wondered whether Stefan was just the latest in a long line of suitors that had replaced her father. But she didn't ask, didn't want to know. Angel came out of the kitchen at that moment with steaming bowls of Adobe chicken.

'I'm going to see if Angel needs help.' Romy stood up.

'I'm sure she's fine, Romy, she does this every night,' Joseph said, placing his hand on top of hers.

'I know, but I'd like to.' She took her hand away and followed Angel back into the kitchen.

'I cooked Adobe chicken just for you, Romy,' Angel said, and came and pinched her cheek.

Romy was still reeling from the arrival of Stefan. 'Thanks, Angel, my favourite,' she said unconvincingly.

'You didn't know about Stefan?' Angel asked.

'Er, no. Is he... nice?'

'Very nice man, made Joseph smile again. He good thing, Romy.'

'Yeah,' she whispered.

'Here, you wanna take this out?' Angel handed her a big bowl of white rice which she carried out to the table, and then sat down again. She was relieved to see that Joseph and Saira were engrossed in a conversation about feeding the whale sharks – Joseph's favourite topic even after all these years. So she chatted to Julian, who was a marine biologist and here to investigate the reef and its decline. Her eyes kept finding Stefan over Julian's shoulder. She was relieved to see that he wasn't sitting in Ted's seat at the other end, but maybe that was just because he had arrived late. He seemed to be the life and soul of the party, and really focused on whoever he was talking to as if they were the only person in the world. Once he looked up and caught Romy watching him, and he smiled at her. It was a kind, knowing smile, and she figured that in any other circumstance she might like him, but then she thought of his hands on Joseph's shoulders and her toes curled into the sand beneath the table.

After dinner, Joseph and Stefan retreated to the house and asked Romy to join them, but she couldn't face them yet, and so she sat on the beach with Bob and Saira and Saira's husband Tim. He was drunk and ranted about American politics, and Romy was happy to feign interest while drinking rum and coke and soaking up the sounds of the sea and the sight of the stars in the night sky that she had longed for in the polluted city. She hoped Stefan and Joseph might have gone to bed by the time she returned to the house an hour later, but they were sitting on the balcony, talking quietly in the light of several candles.

They both stood up when they saw her. 'Romy, come and join us,' Stefan said, gesturing to a third chair in the circle.

'I'm kind of tired. it's been a long day,' she said, hovering in the doorway.

'Please, Romy, just for a bit.' It was Joseph who spoke then, and she couldn't refuse. 'What can I get you? We are having Jasmine tea.'

'That sounds nice.' Joseph disappeared into the kitchen and left her with Stefan, who lit a cigarette and offered her one.

'No thanks. I've given up,' she said, and then changed her mind. 'OK, yeah, why not?' She took one and he lit it for her. She breathed the smoke down into her lungs and then couldn't help picturing it circulating around her organs, already struggling to breathe. The taste was stale in her mouth; she exhaled and stubbed it out in the ashtray.

'Not as nice as you remember, yeah?'

'No, it was quite gross, actually.'

He threw his head back and laughed, but it felt forced. 'Well, good for you. I wish it tasted like that to me.'

'Joseph said you're a journalist.'

'That's right.'

'For a specific paper?'

'Not any more. I'm freelance, so I go wherever the work is. I'm just back from the US, covering the election.'

'Oh right. Where are you from? Originally, I mean.'

'Denmark.'

'Cool.'

'Yeah, it's a beautiful country, very far away from here.' He took another drag and Romy looked around for Joseph, but he was tactically absent. 'Joseph is very pleased to see you.'

'Yeah, well, it's been a while.'

'What brings you back here after all these years?' He blew the smoke out into the air and looked out to sea as if it were not the most significant thing he had said so far. She prickled at his audacity. Her own father had been treading so lightly, and here was this strange man, larger than life in his uncrumpled shirt and slacks going straight for the jugular.

'Dunno.' She shrugged. 'Like I said, it's been a while.'

Joseph arrived at that moment with the tea, and she wondered whether he had been cowering at the kitchen door, if he might have put Stefan up to it, too frightened to ask himself.

'Here we go. What have you two been chatting about?'

'Romy was asking about my job,' Stefan replied a little too quickly, and they sipped their tea in silence.

'I would like to go to Apo Island.' Romy was the one to break it.

'I hoped you would.' Joseph turned to her, unable to contain a huge smile. 'Although you might be disappointed. I'm afraid it is no longer our hidden treasure. It was named as one of the best diving spots in the world a few years ago, and since then it's been seething with tourists. But if we go early, we should get some time there before the hordes descend. I can't do tomorrow – I've got to finish Saira and Tim's Open Water with them. But we could do the day after?'

'OK, cool.'

'Have you done any diving since you've been in Hong Kong?'

'Nah, the water is too dirty there. I did go out once quite soon after I arrived. I was missing the sea. But the visibility was so bad, and not a lot of fish to look at, so I never did it again.'

'That's a shame. The day I don't get in the sea it will be all over for me,' he said, and then obviously regretted it.

'Do you dive, Stefan?' Romy asked.

'No, it's not for me. I have bad ears. I swim, but Joseph says I don't know what I'm missing under the water.' He placed his hand on Joseph's bare knee where his shorts ended. There were age spots on his leg and the skin looked old against Stefan's smooth pale hand. 'Joseph told me you're working in a tattoo parlour. He said you're a great artist, that you were always drawing as a child.'

'Did he?' She looked at Joseph.

'Well, you did. You drew these amazing doodles of fish and coral and birds all over everything. And not just on paper. I would find them on the back of cigarette packets and beer mats, menus and even furniture sometimes.'

'Furniture?'

'Yes, in the restaurant, not up here, you wouldn't dare! But on the tables and chairs down there. If they weren't so good I would have been livid.'

'You should do some drawing while you're here,' Stefan suggested.

'Maybe I will,' she said.

'Do you know how long you're staying?' It was Joseph who asked this time, and she was tempted to tell him why she was here. To unload the burden of her news that weighed so heavily on her heart, but she was so tired, and she just couldn't find the words.

'I don't know.' She shrugged. 'Maybe a week or so, is that OK?'

'Of course.'

'Did you have to take time off work?' Stefan asked.

'Yeah, but I'm owed some holiday so they were fine.'

'And is there anyone you've left behind?' Again, it was Stefan who asked the probing question, and Joseph seemed to wince a little at his shamelessness.

'No, I live alone. I am dating someone, but it's not serious.'

'Is that a guy or a girl?'

'Stefan! Leave the poor girl alone.'

She didn't want to answer that; didn't want to give him the low-down on all the intimate details of her life without his having to work a little harder for it. She felt boosted by Joseph's outrage, and yet part of her wanted him to ask these questions, to show some interest in her and the life that she had led for more than a decade without him. Why did he seem not to care?

'You know, I'm really tired. I left home in the dark this morning. I think I'm just gonna crash.'

'Of course.' Joseph jumped to his feet. 'Have you got everything you need? I put a towel on your bed. And there's water in the cooler in the kitchen.'

'OK, I'll grab some.' They stood facing each other, only inches between them and yet a whole life's worth of things unsaid and feelings so suppressed that they charged the air like a negative magnet holding them apart.

'Night, then,' she said and turned away.

CHAPTER FIVE
FLORA

Flora waited until her mother had come round safely from the operation before setting off on her three-hour journey home. It was dark again, but the rain had finally ceased, leaving the streets wet and shimmering. She called Lisa from the car, who had picked her children up from school.

'How are they both?'

'Fine, Toby and Elsie are watching *Spider-Man* and the little ones are in the bath.'

'Thanks, Lis, I don't know how long it's going to take me to get home, but Jake should be back any minute.'

'It's fine, Flora, just focus on the driving. You must be exhausted. Have you got caffeine to keep you awake?'

'I've drunk my body weight in hospital coffee today and I've stocked up on chocolate from the vending machine.'

'Good for you.' She knew Lisa didn't really mean that; she was a staunch vegan and wouldn't dream of eating a Mars bar. It was a sign of how pitiful Flora must have sounded that she didn't reprimand her.

'Lisa, you're not going to say anything to Jake, are you?'

'What? You mean, I can't ask him about his illicit assignations in the cow barn with not-so-lesbian Jodie?'

'She's not a lesbian, Lisa.'

'Are you really sure about that, Flor?'

'I know what I saw.'

'But do you really?'

'Yes! And anyway, she told me once about her relationship with this Shaman guy.'

'That's not a sexual relationship, Flora.'

'No, I mean, yes, it was, they had tantric sex in some sand dune in Wales.'

'Sounds... gritty.'

'Very funny, but I mean it, Lis. Promise me you won't say anything? I don't think I could cope with that tonight. I will talk to him, just not yet...'

'Yeah, I get it.'

'No, you don't.'

'No, maybe I don't. I just don't understand why you don't want to string him up by the balls, why you don't kick him out of the house and tell him you don't want anything to do with him ever again.'

'Lisa, can the kids hear you?'

'No, well, only the little ones and they don't know what balls are. Not that sort.'

'Lis, please, I know you think I'm pathetic, but I just need to sort it all out in my head first.'

'Don't worry, my lips are sealed. I can't promise to shower him with love and affection, but I won't say a word. Did you talk to your mum about what she said to you?'

'Only to apologise.'

'What! She's the one who should be apologising, Flora.'

'Yeah, but she's the one with a smashed-up leg and in hospital. Anyway, she doesn't do apologies.'

'Jesus, no wonder you can't confront your husband.'

'I know! Dr Jane would have a field day.'

'She would if you hadn't run out. Hey, Tommy, stop hitting Olive with the sponge.' Flora could hear the splashing and indignant screams of her daughter and it pulled her insides tight, like a drawstring. 'I've got to go, world war three breaking out here.'

'OK, tell her I love—' But the line had gone dead, and the unrelenting beep pulled the string on her insides tighter and tighter and her eyes blurred, and she had to open the car window and breathe in the damp night air and blink away the tears.

Flora had met Lisa at a mother and toddler group when Toby was eighteen months old and she was heavily pregnant with Olive. It was an excruciating affair in a draughty church hall. The children played with filthy toys while the mums sat on plastic chairs around the edges of the hall and pretended to be interested. Halfway through the painful hour, the coordinator brought out her guitar and the children and parents sat in a circle on the floor and sang along to her tuneless nursery rhymes, while the children mashed pieces of regurgitated toast into the plastic matting. Flora was making a hasty escape and swearing never to return when she literally bumped into Lisa, who had a baby strapped to her chest and was dragging a screaming and snotty child behind her.

'Oh no, have I missed it?' She swore as she careered into Flora.

'Yeah, it's finished. Well, pretty much, unless you want to help with the clearing up.'

'I was trying to leave the house but had a yellow peril emergency.' Flora looked at her, bemused. 'You know, one of those explosive shits that spurt up the back and down the sides and require a whole change of clothes and then another feed to calm the trauma, and then...'

Flora laughed. 'Oh, one of those! Well, you didn't miss much.'

'Was it Gertrude on guitar?'

'I don't know.'

'Red hair, boobs hanging out, probably a large child hanging off them?'

'Yeah, that was her!'

'Right, sorry Elsie, looks like Mummy screwed up today, no playgroup. Shall we go to the library instead?' Elsie, still snivelling, erupted into full-blown sobs. 'I know it probably doesn't sound that appealing right now...' She gestured to her child. 'But would you like to join us?'

So they did. Dr Jane may have saved Lisa from mental ruin but Flora was pretty certain that it was Lisa who had saved her. They had spent at least three days a week together since that morning. When Olive was born just six weeks later, it was Lisa who had Toby for the night and was the first person to visit them in hospital the next morning. She had taken Flora under wing and introduced her to music classes and swimming classes and farm school and forest school and surf school. None of which Flora would have had either the inclination or stomach to face alone, but with Lisa and her acerbic wit and gung-ho spirit at her side, she discovered joy in them all.

Lisa's other half was a gentle soul. Caspar was an anthropologist and lecturer at Exeter University. He was quiet and softly-spoken, in direct contrast to his mouthy partner. He was a talented musician, and when the four of them spent the evening together he would often retreat with a guitar and strum away on the periphery. Jake would join him; they had also developed a friendship that, unlike the women, wasn't based on sharing stories and secrets, and could happily spend hours in each other's company barely exchanging more than a few words.

As Flora strained to keep her drooping eyes focused on the road ahead, she thought about her husband's quiet apathy. Why didn't he crave success or recognition? Why wasn't he driven by social interaction or creative stimulation like her? And were their contrasting characteristics a perfect union or a perfect storm? Would he be better off with Jodie, an equally reclusive soul who was more at home with sheep than humans? Or was she? Had Jodie and Jake found solace in each other on a level that Flora could never understand?

The rain came down on the road and the trail of crimson headlights blurred in the distance. She blinked hard and shook her head to wake up her mind. She thought back to that day in the library, the first time she had met Jake. Flora had been looking for her reading list in among a pile of papers when she dropped her ring binder on the floor. It sprang open and all of her notes flew across the carpet, down the aisle and fluttered up against the shelves of books.

'For fuck's sake,' she cursed and bent down to retrieve the far-flung pages.

'Here, let me help.' A tall guy with a mop of dark curly hair was picking up some of the pieces that had flown to the end of the aisle.

'Thanks, sorry, I'm so clumsy.'

'Happens to us all.'

'Yeah, some more than others.' Together they collected all of the notes and he tried to hook them through the clasps in the binder.

'Oh, don't worry about that, I'll sort it out later.' She stuffed the notes in a dishevelled pile inside the folder and snapped it shut. He picked up her copy of *Tess of the D'Urbervilles* from the floor and handed it to her. 'Thanks,' she said.

'*Tess* is my favourite.'

'Are you studying English? I haven't seen you.'

'No, unfortunately not.'

'Oh right, how come?'

'It's a long story,' he said, and then seemed to regret it as she turned to walk away. 'Hey.' He followed her. 'Do you fancy a coffee in the canteen?' She turned back to look at him: his hair had fallen in front of his face, hiding one of his eyes, but the other was a dark indigo and was focused on her with an intensity that made her look away.

'Oh, I'd love that, but I've really got to write this essay. Left it to the last minute, as usual.' He pushed his hair back from his face to reveal the other eye; it was framed with a dark eyebrow. There was a shadow of stubble on his face. He was wearing a shirt, an old-fashioned checked Viyella shirt, like something Jeremy might wear. And cords – he was actually wearing cords! They were a faded sand colour and balding at the knees.

'OK, well, I'll see you around then.' He turned to leave and she wanted to call him back. The essay could wait – why couldn't she be impulsive? But she didn't, she just watched as he walked to the end of the aisle and turned to smile at her before disappearing.

'Yeah, see you around,' she called after him.

But she didn't see him around, though she found herself looking. Not for three whole weeks. And then she spotted him on a bench outside the student union. He was totally absorbed in the book on his lap.

'Is it Hardy?' Flora asked as she approached.

He looked up, disorientated, and then smiled. 'Er, yes, actually.' He flashed the front cover of the book at her.

'*Return of the Native*. I haven't read it, is it good?'

'It's pretty much what you'd expect from Hardy, full of sexual politics and thwarted desire.'

'I can't believe you're reading it for fun.'

'It's a good antidote to crop production systems and soil science.'

'Oh wow, are you an agric?'

'For my sins. You can leave now, I won't be offended.'

But Flora sat down on the bench next to him. 'You don't seem like a typical agric.'

'I don't know what you mean,' he said, feigning offence.

'Well, they, sorry, *you*, have got quite a reputation.'

'There are always exceptions to the rule.'

'So they're true, then?'

'What?'

'The stories, about agrics having to go through these initiation ceremonies where they have to down vodka out of pigs' heads and drink their own piss.'

He smiled and shook his head. 'There may be some truth in them.'

'Did you do that?'

'I did not.'

'But I thought it was compulsory, that you wouldn't be accepted into the gang if you didn't do it.'

'Maybe I didn't want to be in that gang.'

'Fucking philistines. Wasn't there an agric guy who died here a few years ago?'

'I don't know about that.'

'There was. He was found with his head shaved, lying in a dark alley in town in a puddle of his own vomit.'

'Look... er?'

'Flora.'

'Right, Flora, well, if you've just come to sit down here to tell me how awful all agric students are, then I really don't need to hear it.'

'I'm so sorry! You're right. I just, well, you don't seem anything like them. Not that I have actually met one before.'

'We're not an alien race, you know.'

'Sorry, I should probably just stop talking, right?'

'Maybe we could change the subject.'

'Yeah, OK. Let's do that.' But Flora couldn't think of anything else to say. She swung her legs back and forth under the bench like a child. When she turned to look at him, he was watching her, a smile peeking from the corners of his lips.

'What? What are you smiling about?'

'It seems we don't have anything else to talk about.'

'Sure we do. Where do you live?'

'I live in Jesmond.'

'Of course you do.'

'What's that supposed to mean?'

'Isn't that where all the... posh people live?'

'I thought we were trying to move away from stereotypes.'

'Yeah, sorry. So, why aren't you studying English then?'

'Because my father wants me to take over the family farm. In Dorset.'

'Oh right, and he hasn't given you a choice?'

'Has anyone ever told you your line of questioning is quite, um, invasive?'

'Uh, yeah, sorry. They have, actually.'

'How about I ask you some questions?'

'Sure, fire away.' She peeled the cling film off her tuna and sweetcorn sandwich and bit into it.

'So where do you live?'

'Fenham.'

'Thought so, with all the hippies.'

'We're meant to be avoiding stereotypes, remember.'

She looked at him; he was smiling, but not in a triumphant way. He was totally right, of course. In just two minutes of talking to her on a bench he had seen right through her in a way that so many of her friends of nearly three years had not. She had tried desperately hard to recreate herself here at university. To be someone more interesting than the spoilt, middle-class, privately educated girl from the home counties that she was. And it was exhausting. She was exhausted by the constant pressure to challenge. Challenge views, challenge labels, challenge her own upbringing and in doing so, deny who she really was.

'Do you want to go and get a pint?' she asked him.

'Sure. I'm Jake, by the way.'

'Nice to meet you, Jake.'

And so she took him to a pub on the quayside which she knew none of her friends would dare to frequent on account of it being a chain. It served beer in tall iced glasses and little bowls of Japanese rice crackers. He was easy to talk to. He was funny in a dry way, and obviously fiercely clever, and very well read, and yet he knew next to nothing about music or popular culture.

'You seriously haven't heard of The Super Furry Animals?'

'Well, we have plenty of sheep on the farm.'

'Jesus, Jake, they've been around for a decade! You really need to get out more.'

'So, take me somewhere where we can listen to some hip music. Educate me.'

'I, er...'

'Or would you be too embarrassed to be seen with me?'

'No, it's not that.' But he had done it again, seen straight through her. 'Look, I'll play you something.' She took out her phone and scrolled through to find something radical and obscure.

'OK.' He smiled and took a sip of his beer and she thanked him for not pushing her further.

When they left the bar, they walked along the quayside. It was dark by then and the reflection of the lights glowed in the inky water. It was cold and she was still in the hoodie that she had left for classes in that morning, when the sun was shining and bringing a promise of Spring.

'Here, you're freezing.' He took off his coat and she welcomed its warmth as she pushed her arms into the fleecy lining.

'Don't worry, if you see anyone you know you can just tell them it's my coat.' She laughed and elbowed him in the ribs and then let him take her hand as they continued to walk in silence. The streets were beginning to fill with Friday-night revellers. Scantily clad women and men in buttoned-up shirts and gelled hair. Friday night was Geordie night on the town – it was an unwritten rule. The students had the weekdays but the weekends belonged to the locals. And anyone who disabused that rule did so at their own peril.

'I think I'd better be getting back,' Flora said as they reached the bus stop.

'Well, it's been fun.'

'Yeah, it has.'

'Maybe we could do it again sometime,' he said and leant in to kiss her on the cheek. His lips were soft and surprisingly warm, and as they grazed her skin she turned and caught them on her mouth. He pulled her close and she wrapped her arms around his neck, ran her fingers through the matted curls on his head. Then he pulled away and left her at the bus stop with a fire burning inside of her.

It was a whole week before she heard from him again. He

called the following Friday, asked if she fancied a trip to the beach at the weekend. He had a battered old Land Rover and picked her up from the pub at the end of her road.

'Did anyone see you leave?' he asked as she finally wrenched the door open and climbed into the passenger seat. The leather was fraying and bits of orange foam peeked through the worn stitching.

'Very funny,' she said, but didn't offer any further explanation as to why they were meeting there rather than at her house just thirty metres up the road.

It was cold and an icy rain whipped at their faces as they walked along the beach. The waves thundered into the shore with a ferocity that was both exhilarating and terrifying. And the wind was so strong that when they leant into it with their arms spread wide, it held them suspended in its power. Flora screamed and then laughed; she felt like she was flying. Jake smiled at her, but he didn't shout or scream. He closed his eyes and held his face up to the elements. She watched as the rain streamed down the dark stubble on his cheeks. His eyelashes were surprisingly long and beads of water were suspended off the ends.

They walked along the sand but it wasn't long before Flora's ears throbbed in the cold and her trousers became drenched and clung to her legs. So, they retreated to a tiny tea room on the promenade. It had doilies on the tables and yellowing net curtains on the fugged-up windows. They hung their dripping coats on the radiator next to their table, and Flora snuggled up to it in an attempt dry her trousers too.

'You know, if you wore trousers made from material that is actually equipped for the outdoors they wouldn't absorb so much water.' He had a twinkle in his eyes as he spoke which simultaneously infuriated Flora and made her belly flutter.

'Yes, but then I'd look like such a dag.'

'No offence taken.'

'None intended.'

They ate scones loaded with thick cream and strawberry jam

and drank hot sweet tea that slowly thawed the ice from her bones. Then they walked a few doors down to the games arcade and put their pennies in the slot machines, and Flora thrashed him at air hockey and he lapped her three times at the Grand Prix when she kept crashing her car into the barriers.

'I think I need to get outside for some air,' she said as she climbed down from her seat.

'Are you all right?'

'Yeah, I just feel a bit carsick. That's quite lame, isn't it, getting sick from a simulated game?'

'You are obviously a very delicate little flower,' he said, holding open the heavy door for her.

The rain had stopped and the sun was trying really hard to break through the blanket of thick grey cloud that hung above the still-raging ocean. Shafts of light lit up the grey water like spotlights on a darkened stage. Flora breathed in a few deep breaths of the cold salty air.

'Better?'

'Yeah.'

'We could get fish and chips?' She turned to look at him with a scowl.

'Not that much better, and we only just had scones.'

'True. So, do you want to come back to mine?'

'Will your flatmate be there?'

'No, he's gone to his girlfriend's in Edinburgh for the weekend.'

'OK.' He grabbed her hand as they walked back to the car and she curled her fingers around his and held on tight.

His flat was typically male. A Victorian maisonette on one of Jesmond's gentrified residential streets. He had the ground floor with a small sitting room at the front, two bedrooms behind and then a tiny kitchen and bathroom at the back. It was sparsely furnished and totally devoid of any aesthetic adornments. He showed her into the sitting room and she sat on a chocolate leather sofa, willing the sickness that had come back in the car ride home to disappear while he fetched her a glass of water. She had suffered from carsickness all her life. There were times that she was left behind on long car journeys as a child so that they wouldn't have to stop for her to vomit. When she was twelve she missed a family holiday to Cornwall and spent an entire week living with Mrs Jenkins and her daughter Tracy who was two years older than Flora and called her a 'stuck-up bitch' behind her mother's back.

Jake came back into the room with two pint-glasses of cloudy water.

'Have you spiked my water with some date drug?'

'If I have, then I've spiked my own too. It's just sediment – it settles down after a while. Don't you have sediment in your water in Fenham?'

'Probably, but my flatmate has an alkaline filter so we drink our water out of that.'

'Of course you do.' He smiled and handed her the glass of water which she sipped tentatively and then glugged the rest.

'See, nothing wrong with a bit of acidic tap water, is there?'

'You think I'm a fraud, don't you?'

'What?'

'You're laughing at me, and I'm not sure I like it.'

'Hey.' He took her hand. 'I'm sorry, I didn't mean to upset you. To be fair, you've done your fair share of ribbing too.'

'Fair enough,' she said, and didn't take her hand away. 'It wasn't a criticism, by the way. I like it. Some of my friends are too bloody sincere for mockery, they would think it was a violation of their civil liberties.'

'Wow, you need to tell them to lighten up a bit. Life's too short for all that.'

'Yeah, probably.' He put his other hand over hers and drew small circles on the top of it with his thumb. The skin was a bit rough when it made contact with hers and it set her nerve endings on fire.

'Still feeling sick?' He looked up at her through the curls that had fallen in front of his face. She could see her own bedraggled reflection in his dark blue eyes. Her long brown hair, now curled by the rain, hanging limply around her pale face.

'Much better, thanks,' she said, and he removed his hand from hers and wiped a smudge of mascara from beneath her eyes. His touch was surprisingly delicate.

'I must look a mess,' she said.

'A beautiful mess,' he said, pulling her hair out from behind her ear so that it fell down the side of her cheeks which flushed with heat. And then his hand found its way under her hair to the back of her neck and he pulled her towards him and kissed her gently on the lips.

She spent the whole weekend at his house, and then every weekend for the next six weeks until the end of term. She pined for him over the Easter holidays and they spoke only a couple of times. His father was ill, and so there was no question of their meeting up. Jake was pretty useless on the phone and Flora worried that he was having second thoughts, but when they found each other again at the beginning of the summer term their relationship was renewed with an increased intensity.

Flora eventually introduced Jake to her group of friends, and as predicted, they pretended to like him but thought he was unsophisticated and square. He tried hard to ingratiate himself and went along to art house films and raves in warehouses where he bobbed up and down in the corner, sipping on a beer while everyone else was getting high. But afterwards he would moan to Flora about her pretentious and unwelcoming friends and she felt conflicted. She loved spending time with him alone in his flat or out on the moors, at the coast or in the secret woodland they had discovered just outside the city. And yet she felt embarrassed by his parochial ways, and found herself ignoring him and belittling their relationship when they were out with her friends. And she hated herself for it.

One day towards the end of the summer term, they were

having a picnic on the grass in the park. It was just the two them, and everything glistened in the sunshine. Having gorged themselves on mini pork pies and cherries, Flora was lying on Jake's stomach while he twisted her hair around his fingers.

'We need to talk about what happens when we leave here,' she said, and his fingers stopped twisting momentarily before carrying on.

'No we don't,' he said sleepily.

She turned over, onto her elbows. 'Yes, Jake, we do. You have to go to Dorset and I am going to London, and so I don't think we can carry on seeing each other.' He didn't even open his eyes, just smiled a little.

'Of course we can,' he said and fumbled for her hair again with his eyes shut.

'Jake, you're not taking this seriously,' she said and sat up.

'OK, sorry.' He opened his eyes and propped himself up on his elbows. 'What do you think we should do then?'

'I think we should split up.'

Again he smiled. 'Don't be silly. I can come to London at weekends, and you can come down to Dorset. Well, after Dad, you know...'

'I just don't think that's going to work, Jake. I know you have to go to the farm and be with your dad before he dies, and I know you've made him a promise to take it over after he's gone. And that's truly admirable and amazing, but I don't see how we can carry on if we're going to be so very far away. it just wouldn't work.'

He picked her hand up and kissed it. 'Look, Flora, I know it isn't ideal but we can make it work if we want it to. If we... love each other.' It was the first time the word *love* had been mentioned, and it sent a lightning bolt of fear, or delight, or overwhelming panic through Flora that she didn't know what to do with. She didn't answer and could feel her silence crackling with meaning. 'Do... we... love each other?' he asked tentatively.

'I... I...' She fiddled with the bangles on her wrist and looked up at the dazzling blue sky for inspiration. 'I... don't know...'

'Oh.' He dropped her hand and rubbed his along his stubbled jawline.

'I mean, I'm not saying no, I'm just saying that right now, I don't know. I don't know what I want. Well, that's not totally true, I know that I want to go to London and try to get a job in a publishing house, and have some fun, and go to bars and gigs and markets and live with friends in East London... and I know that's not what you want to do.'

'OK.'

'And I know we could try to see each other at weekends and stuff, but it's pretty far, and you need to be with your dad, and...'

They left Newcastle the following week, promising to keep in touch while both knowing that they wouldn't. Flora went to London, and after three months of trying she got an internship at a publishing company. She moved into a flat in Bethnal Green with two of her flatmates from uni and they partied hard, and went to gigs of new underground bands and exhibitions of alternative artists and occasionally got cheap seats in the gods at the theatre, and it was all she ever dreamed it would be. Except that it wasn't. She had no money, and she was lonely. She went on a few dates and even slept with Otto, her flatmate's brother. But their limbs clashed awkwardly and she got dreadful cystitis afterwards and spent the following few weeks putting him off with various excuses.

Then one day in May Jake texted her to say that he was in town for a cousin's wedding and did she fancy meeting for a drink. They met at a wine bar in Marylebone. He had lost weight and his trousers hung loosely from his hips, his face was more chiselled, his deeply sunk eyes somehow even more blue.

'Did your dad...?' Flora asked once they were both safely settled with drinks in hand.

'Yeah, back in February.'

'I'm so sorry, I should have...'

'It's OK, I'm sure you've been busy. Like the hair, by the way.' She ruffled her short hair and new fringe self-consciously.

'Thanks.'

'So you got your dream job?'

'Not yet, it's just an internship. They're taking on an editorial assistant at the end of the summer, though, so I'm trying to be as efficient and inspiring as I possibly can.'

'I'm sure you're doing brilliantly.'

'I don't know, the lady who runs the show is this terrifyingly clever woman, and every time she talks to me, I just get all sweaty and say ridiculous things.' He smiled at her across the table and his eyes sparkled. She had forgotten how totally at ease she felt in his company. 'How's life as a farmer?'

'Well, it's busy. I've got lots of ideas about how to modernise and generate more income. Dad had let it all go while he was ill.'

'That sounds exciting.'

'Don't go overboard, Flora.'

'I'm sure you'll do a great job.'

This more formal interaction was new territory for them both, and it made Flora feel sad for what they had lost. 'I miss you.' The words came out of her mouth before she really had time to consider them. He leant forward and grabbed her hands across the table.

'I miss you so much,' he said, and her stomach did a flip up into the back of her throat.

They went back to hers and barely made it through the door before they were pulling each other's clothes off. And afterwards he slept in her bed and she scanned the familiar lines of his body. His stubbled jaw, the dip between his shoulder blades, the birthmark behind his ear. She wanted to savour them, to remember them after he was gone. But he didn't go; he spent the whole weekend with her in the flat. Her flatmates came home and they hid in her bedroom, giggling behind the closed door until they heard them leave again and it was safe to come out. She needed little convincing to agree to a trip to the farm the following weekend. As the train made its way out of London and the concrete gave way to green fields and endless blue sky, she felt her shoulders drop and her heart lift. Maybe the countryside wasn't so bad after all. Jake picked her up from the station in a slightly less battered Land Rover in which the leather on the seats was still intact. A bouncy yellow Labrador puppy jumped up to lick her face as soon as she was inside the car.

'Tess, down,' Jake said, laughing.

'Tess?'

'Of course!'

Once out of the town, they turned off the main road and up a winding lane to the top of the hill where there was a view of the sea. A huge expanse of shimmering blue against the white chalky cliffs of the coastline and the green of the rolling hills beyond. There wasn't another soul, another car, even another house in sight for miles. And then the road headed back down the other side of the hill. It narrowed even more, and the overgrown hedges that curled over at the top like a Hoxton hairdo brushed against the side of the car. They turned down a track that was so bumpy the Land Rover rattled and their bums left their seats as they bounced over the holes. At the end of the long track was a red-brick building with a wonky tiled roof. The windows were small and crossed with lead. There was a porch at the front with a white front door and a black horseshoe for a knocker and the house was covered with creepers; the purple fronds of wisteria climbed all over one side and a pale pink rose clung to the bricks on the other.

'Oh, Jake, you never told me it was so beautiful,' Flora said while getting out of the car.

'Come,' he said and took her hand.

It was cool and dark inside. There was an uneven brick floor in the entrance hall, which led into a dining room with a huge polished wooden table and two tatty armchairs either side of an inglenook fireplace. It smelt of old ash from a recently lit fire. She followed Jake into the kitchen. It was warmer in there, with an Aga and a cork floor. There was a pine table and four chairs in the middle of the room and chipped, mint-coloured formica cupboards all around the walls. She walked over to the sink, which looked out on to the garden, a ramshackle arrangement of lawns that needed mowing and flower beds bursting with colour and weeds. And beyond you could just make out the blue shimmer of water bleeding into sky.

'You can see the sea from here!'

'On a day like today you can. You might struggle when the fog rolls in in the winter.'

'It's wonderful.'

'Really?' He put his arms around her and kissed the back of her neck. 'You really like it?'

And she really did. She was so surprised. She had spent all these months imagining a bleak, exposed headland and a dilapidated farmhouse. But this was charming, this was, well – it was like something out of a Hardy novel!

After some lunch at the rickety picnic table in the garden they walked down an overgrown path at the end of the lawn towards the sea. They crossed three fields and clambered down the cliff with the assistance of a rope onto a tiny shingle cove almost entirely covered in a blanket of seaweed. They left their clothes on a rock at the back of the beach and stumbled across the stones to the water. It was icy-cold and thrashed at their knees. Flora squealed but Jake took her hand and led her deeper into the waves. When it reached her chest, the cold made her organs contract to the point that she felt she couldn't take in any air.

'Just breathe, don't talk, just breathe and swim, you get used to it quickly.' And so she followed him out into the water, her heart still pounding with every stroke. But her breathing soon slowed and a tingling sensation fizzed up and down her body, filling it with light and warmth.

Jake had brought a flask of hot tea and a bar of chocolate, which they devoured on the rocks at the back of the beach. The stone was hot and her back tingled as she lay each vertebra down one by one, soaking up the warmth.

'I think I'm beginning to see what you love about this place,' she said, her eyes shut to the mellow glow of the sun.

'Yeah, it's pretty special, hey? Sometimes I forget, so it's good to see it through fresh eyes.'

Flora visited the farm every weekend that summer. Jake drove her on a quad bike around the fields of sheep and wild flowers that he had planted in an attempt to bring back bees. Tess balanced precariously on the handlebars, her ears flapping in the wind. They went further afield, to beaches and clifftop trails and village pubs, and Flora began to think differently about what happiness meant to her.

One Sunday evening at the end of June when Jake was dropping her at the station, he caught her hand as she was climbing out of the Land Rover.

'Why don't you just stay?' he said.

'What do you mean?'

'Why don't you not go back to London? Stay here with me, and Tess.'

'But my job.'

'You love it here, Flora, and we, Tess and me, we love having you, and...' She laughed and turned to leave but he kept hold of her hand. 'Just think about it.'

'Jake, I can't...'

But she did think about it, in fact it was all she thought about for the following week, And then the week after, and the week after that. Jake didn't ask her again, and she was thankful for that. At the end of July her internship was coming to an end and she applied for the editorial assistant job. Everyone said that she had a good chance. So she was beyond devastated when they gave the job to the other intern. It had been a very tough call, said the terrifying editor-in-chief, but the other intern just had the edge on Flora. For twenty-four hours Flora cried and racked her brain about which edges she should have sharpened. And then she made the call; it was fate. She would leave London and move to Dorset with Jake.

. . .

The children were already in bed when Flora finally arrived home that night, and Jake was nursing a large whisky with a book by the unlit fire. The lights were mostly off, the curtains open and there wasn't the smell of supper cooking that she had pined for on the motorway. Tess was at his feet, but unlike her master she immediately got up and came to greet Flora with a wagging tail and drooling mouth.

'Have you eaten?' she asked Jake pointedly as she crossed the kitchen. She couldn't bring herself to look at him and he remained firmly planted in his chair. There was a time when he couldn't keep his hands off her, when he would kiss her all over when they were separated for just a couple of hours. When he would race home at various intervals throughout the day to make love to her, in their bed, on the sofa, in the orchard at the bottom of the garden. Yet now, he hadn't even got up to give her a kiss hello when she had just had a very long, gruelling day.

'Yeah, sorry, I made myself a sandwich. I figured you would have got something on the road.'

'I couldn't quite face a Ginsters.' She opened the fridge and eyed up the congealed remains of the kids' supper. Lisa had made one of her vegetable risottos with undercooked rice and pulses that her children had evidently rejected. Flora didn't blame them, she couldn't face it either, and took out the pot of hummus and some breadsticks. She sat down at the table and dipped the sticks. The hummus was out of date and fizzed on the roof of her mouth.

'So, I'm going to take the kids to stay with Mum at the weekend. Jeremy is going away and someone needs to look after her.'

'Oh right, how long for?' he asked, and she tried to gauge his reaction from the other side of the room. He flicked the top corner of the pages of his novel between his fingers but held the features on his face perfectly still.

'Not sure really, probably a week or so. The doctor...' She considered telling Jake about Doug but decided against it. 'He said that she would be in a lot of pain after the surgery, that she wouldn't be able to walk. God, she's going to be a nightmare patient.'

'Maybe it'll be good for you two to spend some time together.'

'Unless we kill each other.'

'Yeah.' He smiled, and she longed for him to offer some words of encouragement, to tell her that it would be OK. But Jake didn't talk about emotions. He looked back down at his book but she could tell he wasn't reading.

'Will you be all right here on your own?' Flora asked.

'I guess.' He shrugged, and there was a look of self-pity in his eyes that she knew to be false, and she crunched down on a breadstick and bit the end of her tongue.

'Ow,' she muttered into her hand, which she'd lifted to her mouth.

'You all right?' he asked without looking up.

'Yeah, I'm shattered,' she said. 'I'm going to bed.'

'I'll be up in a bit,' he called after her but she knew he wouldn't; she knew that he would wait until she was safely asleep before he dared to join her.

CHAPTER SIX

LIZZIE

Lizzie's emotions fluctuated between dread, excitement and abject terror in the few days that led up to Edward's visit. He had been delighted when Lizzie told him he could come after all.

'But what about the family gathering?' he asked. 'Won't I be intruding?'

'Nah, it wasn't, well, isn't really a thing...'

'You just panicked at the prospect of your family meeting me and then thought better of it?'

'It was more *you* meeting *my* family that I was worried about, but yeah. They do love to have new flesh in the house, though. So be prepared, they will grill you.'

'I have nothing to hide!' he said. Such a throwaway line, and Lizzie reflected on a time only six months ago when the same could have been said of her.

It was one of those glorious September days when the sun is low in the sky and casting a mellow glow on the still-green leaves just clinging onto the brittle branches of the trees. The table was laid on the terrace with brightly coloured linen napkins and jam jars of flowers from the garden. The barbecue was lit and the smell of charcoal and grilled meat was intoxicating. Edward arrived on his bike. He had taken a bus and a train and then biked from the station and was rosy-cheeked and slightly clammy when he pulled up at the house with a bunch of wilted chrysanthemums. Lizzie had been waiting in the window; she knew what train he was getting and had calculated the time it would take him to bike from the station. She watched as he dismounted in the circular gravel driveway, as he looked up and down at the Georgian Manor House and took in the topiary trees either side of the front door and her father's vintage sports car with the roof down. The door was open – it had been since April despite her father shutting it ten times a day. 'It gives off the right message,' her mother said with her broad, lipsticked smile as she opened it every time he shut it, 'that anyone is welcome.' What she didn't appreciate was how unnerving it was to anyone who lived on a populated street in the middle of a town. For anyone who didn't have the privilege of a sweeping driveway and dogs that announced arrivals. Lizzie watched as Edward hesitated on the front doorstep, as he winced at the licking that Banjo, the bouncy Springer Spaniel, greeted him with.

'Hello…?' he called, and tentatively stepped inside. Only then did Lizzie reveal herself from behind a heavily draped window.

'Hi,' she said. 'You found us.'

'Yeah, it wasn't hard. The road is named after your house.'

'I think you'll find the house was named after the road.'

'It's yellow, your house,' he said craning his neck back to take in the whole height.

'Yes.'

'I don't think I have ever seen a yellow house before. I like it.'

'Well, that's a good start. Come in.'

He walked past her through the door and onto the black and white chequered tiles in the hallway. He looked up at the glass-domed ceiling and down at the circular ray of light it cast across the floor. He stepped into it and his skin glowed red.

'Edward, welcome.' It was her mother, coming out of the kitchen, wiping her hands on her floral dress.

'Mrs Claybourne, hello, it's nice to meet you.' He held out his hand to her and she took it and then linked her arm through his.

'Lizzie has told us all about you. Come and have a drink. We are eating outside – got to make the most of the sunshine at this time of year, haven't you?' She led him off through the kitchen and out onto the terrace on the other side. Lizzie followed.

'Everyone, this is Edward,' her mother said, still holding onto his arm.

'Hi, everyone,' Edward said modestly, pushing his glasses back up his nose with this finger. 'Thank you for having me.'

'Edward!' Her father emerged from behind the barbecue. He wore an apron with a naked woman on the front and carried tongs that dripped fat as he walked. He wiped his free hand on the pink breasts and then shook Edward's. 'Lovely to meet you, I'm Lizzie's father.'

'I think that's pretty obvious, Dad,' Lizzie said. 'Do you have to wear that apron? It's really quite offensive.'

'What? Oh, come on, Lizzie, nothing wrong with a pair of breasts, you've all got them.'

'Er, no, Lizzie doesn't.' Her eldest brother sat up from the table where he was reading the sports pages of the paper. 'Hi, I'm Damian.'

'Hi,' Edward said, blinking furiously.

'Thanks, Damian,' Lizzie said, and swiped him round the back of his head. 'I'll get you a beer.' She disappeared into the kitchen and by the time she came back with two beers, Edward was sitting at the table between Bella and her mother. She handed him one and sat down opposite them.

'Lizzie, what are you doing? You don't like beer,' Bella said with scorn.

'Maybe I do now.' She took a sip and tried not to wince as the cold, sour bubbles hit the back of her throat.

'So, Eddie, can I call you Eddie?' Bella asked, and Edward half shook, half nodded his head. 'Edward is a bit formal, isn't it?'

'It's his name, Bella,' Lizzie said, and Bella shot her a look.

'Where do you live, Eddie?'

'Broadfield. It's, er, the other side of town.'

'Oh right, yeah.'

'Don't pretend you know where that is, Bella.' It was Jamie coming out of the kitchen. 'Hi, mate, you must be Edward.'

'This is Jamie,' Lizzie said. 'And now you've met the whole tribe.'

'Yeah,' Edward said, and Lizzie wondered if this was a horrible mistake. He had barely said anything other than 'hi' or 'yeah' since he had arrived. Where was the sharp-tongued boy she had fallen for?

'Have you got brothers and sisters, Eddie?' Bella leant over him to take a crisp from the bowl on the table. She dipped it in the pink dip and sucked it off the crisp, curling her tongue.

'No, it's just my dad and me. Quite quiet, really,' he said, and took his own crisp. He hovered over the dip and then thought better of it.

'And what does your dad do, Edward?' Damian asked, looking up from his newspaper.

'He works for an insurance company.'

'I'm sorry,' Lizzie said. 'I did warn you.'

He smiled his sparkling smile. 'No, really, it's fine. You did warn me about your shark-like family, and I came prepared. I thought about bringing a slide show but couldn't really fit the projector on my bike.' Lizzie beamed at him – this was more like it. 'Come on, then, I can take it, fire away.' He looked around at her family who seemed momentarily stunned, and she wanted to punch the air in triumph.

'OK, Eddie, I've got one for you. How on earth did you end up meeting my square little sister?' Her moment of glory was quickly and predictably slashed by her sister.

'Thanks, Bella,' Lizzie sniped.

'Well, she was the other newbie in Mr Brewster's class on that first day. I got horribly lost and arrived sweaty and flustered, in fact, not dissimilar to how I look right now.' They all laughed. 'And then I spotted her again in the dining hall at lunchtime, and contrary to what you may think of your sister, Bella, I thought she looked quirky and interesting.' A warm, melting feeling began in the depths of her core and then worked its way up her spine.

'She certainly is quirky,' Jamie said from behind Lizzie, squeezing down on her shoulders with affection and a little too much force.

'Do you study the same subjects, Edward?' her mother piped in. She had been serenely surveying the scene until that moment, smiling all the while as she sipped her gin and tonic at the head of the table.

'No, god no! I don't have a scientific bone in my body. It's arts all the way for me. I'm doing English, Art and History.'

'Thank god for that,' Bella said. 'We don't know where Lizzie came from, she's a total anathema to the rest of this family.'

'Yes, we are more arts and humanities-focused,' Jamie said.

'Not sure I'd class Home Ec as an art.' Lizzie directed her words at her sister and watched as she squirmed ever so slightly in her seat.

'At least I'll know how to cook a meal, which is more than I can say for the rest of you. Speaking of which...' Bella got up from the table and walked over to her father, who was looking hot and flustered behind the barbecue. 'How are we doing, Dad? Shall I bring out the salads?'

The rest of the day passed in a haze of beer, wine, charred sausages and sunshine. After lunch they played croquet. Edward's only point of reference for the game was *Alice in Wonderland*, and he was amazed yet enchanted that people actually played it in real life. He was pretty useless, but he laughed his way through. And then, just as it looked like he was going to lose, he hit Damian's ball onto the central post meaning that he had to start all over again. Damian tried to laugh it off but Lizzie could tell he was seething under the surface as Jamie wheeled Edward around the garden in the wheelbarrow for a lap of honour.

Everyone dispersed after that and Lizzie and Edward found

themselves on their own. He asked if she would show him around the garden.

'Sure,' she said, and they headed off across the lawn at the front of the house.

'We'll have to jump across the ha-ha,' she said as they reached the bottom of the lawn.

'The what?'

'The ha-ha!'

'And that is what, something hilarious?'

'This ditch here. It's to stop the animals coming into the garden without having to have a fence so it doesn't upset the view from the house. We don't actually have any animals, just fruit trees, but there would have been sheep here once upon a time.'

'And it's called a ha-ha because…?'

'I have no idea.' She jumped across the ditch which was full of nettles and brambles, quite incongruous to the uniform stripes on the lawn next to it.

'Don't fall in. Jamie pushed me in there when I was younger and I got tangled up in all the brambles, covered in nettle stings as well. He left me there for half an hour and every time I tried to climb out, I became more and more ensnared.'

'Charming.'

'Yeah, I told you he was the charming one.'

They walked through the orchard; the grass was long and scratched at Lizzie's bare legs. The branches on the trees were weighed down with plums, apples and pears. The sun was low in the sky and cast long shadows across the ground. Wasps hovered over the fallen fruit, crawling dozily out of the holes inside.

'Don't you get fed up with them taking the piss out of you all the time?' Edward asked.

'I've never known anything different.' She shrugged. 'I did used to dream of being an only child when I was younger, not having to share, not getting everything fourth-hand, being the sole focus of my parents' attention.'

'It's not that great, believe me.'

She climbed up and over the gate that led into a field where two Shetland ponies were grazing. Edward followed, but his glasses fell off when he was swinging his leg over the top bar. 'Here,' Lizzie retrieved them from the ground and went to hand them to him but they were smeared with sap from the grass. 'Hang on,' she said, and wiped the lens with the edge of her tartan shirt and handed them back to him.

'Thanks,' he said and lowered himself down the other side of the gate gingerly, his eyes following the horses as they came towards them.

'Are you scared of horses?' Lizzie laughed.

'No,' he said a little too quickly. 'They just, well, I have never been this close to one before.'

'You're kidding.'

'No, I grew up in a town. My dad is pretty urban, and we never did much in the way of country pursuits.' The ponies approached them and Lizzie picked a handful of grass and held it out to them while Edward stepped into her shadow.

'Edward, these guys are smaller than you. What do you think they're gonna do?' She grabbed his hand and pulled it towards the mane of the pony and he smiled nervously and patted its neck.

'You see, perfectly harmless. They're called Laurel and Hardy. We've had them since I was tiny. Bella was horse mad, and my parents have bought her several ponies over the years. Although they sold her horse last summer when she discovered boys and neglected her duties. These guys were bought to keep her horses company. They're not really for riding, but when I was little, I used to jump on their bare backs and plod around the field. I used to spend hours talking to them. They've got far more grit and character than any of Bella's prissy ponies.'

'The underdogs?'

'I guess!'

'Have you always gone for the underdog?' he asked.

'I haven't really thought about it. Are you an underdog?'

'Definitely. I've never been part of the cool gang.'

'Me neither.'

'What about your friends at your last school?'

'What about them?' she said, and then realised how defensive she sounded.

'What were they like?'

'Well, there was Mary, I've been friends with her since we were five. She is sweet and loyal, but never going to set the world on fire. And there were a few other girls along the way who picked me up like a plaything and then dropped me when they'd had enough. Then there was Isabelle...' Even saying her name out loud made her heart miss a beat. 'She was pretty, and daring, and really good at art. She lived abroad, her dad worked for the Foreign Office. She actually *was* part of the cool gang and I couldn't quite believe she wanted to be friends with me, and...' Suddenly she could see the flashing lights of the ambulance, the stretcher, the hushed voices of the girls, the housemistress forcing them back inside... 'And...'

'Are you all right, Lizzie?' She felt light-headed, and she looked at the concern on his face but struggled to bring him into focus.

'I... yeah... I...' She backed away, towards the gate. 'Sorry, I just...' But she couldn't find the words. She knew she was freaking him out but she couldn't help it. She climbed over the gate and ran through the orchard and back towards the house.

'Lizzie, wait... I'm sorry, I didn't mean to upset you...' She could hear him behind her, knew she should turn round and say something, convince him that she wasn't a freak. But the hysterical screams of Vanessa Simpson who had found Isabelle in the woods now echoed around her head. The siren of the ambulance, the thumping of her heart as the police arrived. She ran up the lawn towards the house and past Jamie smoking a cigarette on the terrace.

'You all right, Liz?' he said as she pushed past him and through the back door. 'What's going on?' she heard him say to Edward as she ran up the stairs and into her bedroom. Then she watched them out of the window; she could hear their muffled tones but not what they were saying. She could see the concerned crinkling of Edward's brow above his glasses as he listened to Jamie tell him the secret that she had been so desperate to hide.

Edward left before she came back downstairs. The panic had ceased and in its place was a numbing shame. She didn't imagine Jamie would have minced his words about her breakdown. About how she had been sent home from school a few weeks after Isabelle's death because she had locked herself in her bedroom for two days and refused to come out. They had to knock the door down eventually. There was a bucket of piss and shit in the corner of her room. She had survived on individually wrapped biscuits that she had stolen from the kitchen and the wrappers were strewn all over the floor. Had Jamie told Edward about the state of the room? About the state of her? Her insides lurched and twisted themselves into knots about the freak that he would now know her to be. Her siblings were all in the sitting room when she finally came down. Her head hung low, she didn't dare look at their raising of eyebrows and exchanging of glances.

'Edward had to catch his train,' Jamie piped up eventually. 'Said he was sorry he didn't say goodbye.'

'Did you...?' She couldn't quite get the words out to ask him.

'He was worried about you, sis, so I told him, yeah. But don't worry, I left out the really psycho bits.' Damian sniggered and Lizzie shot him a hateful glance.

'Eddie is really cool, Lizzie, we approve,' Bella said from the sofa.

'His name is Edward.'

'Whatever.'

'And now he thinks I'm a total freak.'

'No, he doesn't. I just told him you were really upset when your friend died, that's all. And he felt bad about bringing it up, and...'

'Did you tell him why I left school?'

'I just said that you freaked out a bit.'

'You didn't go into details?' Jamie's face flushed red and she could tell that he had. 'Jamie, you promised.'

'What? I didn't!' But he had always been a useless liar, and Lizzie stormed back upstairs and spent the rest of the weekend almost paralysed with fear about what she was going to say to Edward on Monday.

She didn't see him until lunch, when he found her at their usual table in the corner of the dining room.

'Hi,' he said with casual good cheer and sat down opposite her.

'Hi.' She kept her head down and pushed the chicken and rice around her plate with her fork.

'I'm sorry I rushed off...' he said.

And she said, 'I'm sorry I didn't say goodbye...' at the same time. The both laughed awkwardly.

'You go...' he said.

'No, you...'

'OK, Jamie told what happened to your friend and why you left school, and I'm really sorry, Lizzie, it must have been so awful to lose a friend like that, and I am so sorry I brought it up, and...'

'It's OK, Eddie, sorry, Edward...'

'I think I quite like Eddie after all, the way your family said it, I mean. It felt like, I don't know...'

'What?' She smiled and willed him to continue.

'Well, like they accepted me or something.'

'They did, they were all raving about you after you left!'

'Really?'

'Yeah, it was nauseating.' He rolled his eyes but smiled a coy smile and she was pleased that it meant so much to him. 'So, you don't think I'm a total freak?'

'Of course not, Lizzie. You went through something horrible and upsetting and it's fine to be freaked out by it.' He looked at her, his brown eyes focused on her with what seemed to be genuine sincerity and she had to look away before the tears that were stinging at the backs of her eyes escaped.

CHAPTER SEVEN

ROMY

Romy spent the following day lying on the beach and then jumping in the sea when it became too hot to bear. In the middle of the day when the heat was so stifling that she felt giddy, she found an old sketchbook of Ted's in his study and sat on the balcony and doodled as she had as a child. She started with the reef under the sea, the fish weaving their way among the forest of coral and weeds. Then up to the birds in the sky, the children on the beach, the jungle behind. It was here that Joseph found her as the sun was falling into the sea.

'Hi, Romy. I'm sorry I haven't seen you all day, I've been out on the boat.' He looked tired, his eyes puffy and his movements slower than she had noticed before.

'Yeah, you were gone by the time I got up. But I've had a great day on the beach, swimming and lying in the hammock.'

'And drawing, I see.'

'It's been a while.'

'Can I see?' She gave him the drawing pad.

'You haven't lost your touch. Do you do similar designs with your tattoos?'

She was still wearing her bikini with a pair of shorts and realised that this was the first time he would have seen the orchid tattoo. He looked from it to the octopus on her arm, and the Chinese symbols on her other arm, the bird on her chest above her bikini.

'Well, I kind of have to do whatever the client wants. But yeah, I have come up with some designs of my own, and I guess they're based on these kinds of things. Flowers, the coral. I like doing birds.'

'They're beautiful. I am so glad you've found an outlet for your talent.'

'Really? You hate tattoos! I remember there was that guy who came to dive once who had them on his face and you couldn't even look at him.'

'That was pretty extreme. You won't do that, will you? Not on your beautiful face?' He touched her cheek so gently with the tip of his finger and she flinched, so he withdrew it immediately and she wished he hadn't. She had spent the last two days longing for him to reach out and touch her, and yet when it happened it had been a shock and her body reacted before her brain. He looked down at her drawing and seemed to be mustering the courage to speak again. Romy held her breath, not knowing what was to come.

'That day, when you called. I felt so happy to hear your voice after all this time. I wasn't sure if I ever...' He stopped then and swallowed hard. Took in one of his long signature breaths. She knew better than to interrupt him. 'But you sounded so... scared... and... Will you tell me what's going on with you, Romy?' He dared to look up at her then and she tried to hold his gaze but couldn't. She wanted to tell him, she wanted him to hold her and stroke her hair, to tell her it was all going to be OK in that soft whispery voice. But he would want to know everything that the doctor said and she couldn't remember; he would research her condition and make copious notes, just as he had done with Ted. He would want to find a donor. Maybe he would delve into her family history, try to find her mother, the surrogate who carried her or a long-lost cousin of her father. Part of her wanted him to take control and yet she wanted, needed, just a few more days like today, days when she could almost forget about the death sentence that weighed her down.

'Joseph, I'm so sorry if I scared you, I just... well, I guess I just missed you, and this.' She gestured around the bay with her arm. 'I missed this like you wouldn't believe.' He looked sceptical and she nearly faltered in her resolve, but then relief flooded his face and he grabbed both of her hands in his.

'Really? Is that all it is?' She nodded and smiled and he closed his eyes and seemed to offer up a little prayer of thanks to someone somewhere.

'Yeah, and I really want to go to Apo Island tomorrow. I've been dreaming about the turtles.'

'OK, let's do it. We'll leave first thing. I'll go get the boat ready.' He started to walk away and then stopped at the top the stairs. 'Will you dive, Romy?'

'Of course.' He beamed at her and her conflicted heart sang and cried all at once.

'Will Stefan be joining us?'

'No, he had to go to Manila this morning, he won't be back for two days.'

'OK.' She felt Joseph's eyes on her, scouring her response, and she looked down at the sketch pad in her lap to avoid his gaze and swallow her relief.

The sun was just peeking over the brow of the hill when they left for Apo Island the following morning. The air smelt different at this time of day. It was warm and sweet, like tropical fruit. The screeching and buzzing of the jungle echoed across the glassy water. The engine chugged into action and they pulled away from the pontoon. Romy sat at the front of the boat and dipped her toes into the silky water. She turned to look at the fanlike ripples that the boat created behind them and the beach just beginning to glow in the light of the morning sun.

As a child it was her favourite time of day. School started early and finished at lunchtime so as to avoid the heat of the afternoon. Joseph would take her on the boat around the headland. The water was always at its stillest first thing in the morning and the light was soft and sometimes hazy. On the nights when the air temperature dipped below that of the sea there would be a blanket of mist shrouding the surface of the water; it felt other-worldly, and Romy would imagine she was on one of Ted's missions to save the island from certain doom as they motored through the fog. Joseph would drop her on the beach and she would make her way along a dust track through the jungle to the school. The monkeys howled above her head, the cicadas buzzed and the macaws screeched. Sometimes Romy would run the entire length of the path and on other days she would wander slowly, kicking her heels in the dust and imagining she was Mowgli and this was her domain.

Siquijor Elementary School was a collection of red buildings with corrugated roofs around a dusty patch of land with raised flower beds made from rocks and old tyres that the children painted in brightly coloured stripes. She had been happy there. The teachers and students never grew tired of playing with her long blonde hair and pinching her freckled cheeks. They were taught in English and learned basic arithmetic, reading and writing. But she was always ahead, her dads supplementing her schooling with additional lessons at home. Joseph would take her out on the reef and for walks in the jungle explaining biodiversity and weather systems, while Ted taught her to read and write, about onomatopoeia and alliteration and how to dissect works of literature and appreciate fine art. She never thought she was different, not to the other children at the island school, not to the travellers' children who stayed at the guest house, not even to the children in the American movies she was allowed to watch on Sundays. She just accepted her small yet utterly safe existence. Until she hit her teens, that is; and then a whole life's worth of questions tormented her. It was like a light was shone on this infinite realm of other lives, other possibilities, other selves. The questions came and they wouldn't stop. And today as she looked back at the island glistening in the dawn, and spotted the red roof of the school in the jungle, she longed for those days of blissful ignorance.

'The school has been shut down,' Joseph shouted over the engine from behind the wheel of the boat.

'What?' She moved back to sit next to him so she could hear him better.

'Yeah, lack of funding, apparently. The kids have all been moved to Solangon on the other side of the island, but there are loads who can't get there, so they have just stopped going altogether.'

'That's awful. How can they just close the school?' He shrugged and she was reminded of his infuriating apathy. It was one of the rare things that Ted and Joseph had in common: they were both so happy to just roll over and accept their lot. They considered themselves to be fortunate. More than that, lucky! So lucky with their idyllic life in paradise that they had lost the power to complain, to fight back. Even when Ted became sick and the horrendous disease that obliterated so many started to rot his body from the inside out. Even then they didn't complain, just accepted their fate as was their due. 'But Joseph, we must do something, all those kids not going to school.'

'There is nothing we can do, Romy. It's all about money, as usual, and in the hands of the local government.'

'There's always something to be done, Joseph. You could fight for those kids. You're a respected member of the community here, they would listen to you.'

'I don't know about that.' He looked back at the school and she wondered, hoped that she might have ignited something in him. 'Do you think you suffered from not having a good education?' His question startled her – he had never asked anything like that in all the years she had known him.

'Why do you say that?'

'Well, we brought you here to this tiny island and forced you to live this quiet life, and we worried that you wouldn't be prepared for the world.'

'You did?'

'Of course! Well, I did anyway. Ted always told me to stop worrying. He said you were strong, that you would cope with whatever life threw at you.'

'I don't know about that.'

'But were you?'

'Was I what?'

'Prepared for the big bad world? What was it like when you first arrived in Hong Kong?'

'It was different.' She hesitated, not sure how much of her life she wanted to reveal. But he looked at her with big, wide eyes, desperately wanting her to let him in, and so she did. 'Yeah, the pace of life was definitely faster than here. The crowds, the buildings, the traffic – but I loved it. Had you prepared me? Probably not. I could talk about Seamus Heaney and rainforest ecosystems, and I could bake bread and make a mojito, but I didn't know how to buy a metro ticket, had never even been on a train. I barely knew how to cross a road, in fact I had several near misses with trams in my first few months there.'

Joseph winced and shut his eyes. 'I'm sorry, we just didn't know. I... There was no we, it should have been down to me, and... well, I guess I lost myself for a while.'

'Yeah, you did. But it's OK. I learned the hard way. Scott wasn't much help in the end.'

'So what happened with him?'

She sighed; that period of her life still hung heavy in her heart. 'He had fallen in love with me here, or so I thought. But when he took me back into his real world, I didn't fit. I tagged along and tried to keep up with his pretentious friends. But he started working more and more, and then he would go out with his colleagues and party hard and I barely saw him. Then one day I found him with another woman in our bed! I couldn't believe it, he obviously had so little respect for me to actually bring someone home to our apartment. But it wasn't ours, was it? Everything in it was his. His eyes had been opened to another life, a more glamorous and sexy life than I would ever give him. He didn't even try to apologise or explain. I honestly think he brought the girl home that day so he wouldn't have to dump me.'

'Oh Romy, I'm so sorry.'

'Yeah, well, you never liked him. And you did try to warn me.'

'I didn't do it very well, did I?'

'Hey, don't beat yourself up, OK?' She touched his arm, which was gripping the steering wheel. 'He was an arse, but he bought me an airfare out of here, and I had to get out. I couldn't have stayed here forever, you must see that.'

'Yes, Ted and I both knew you wouldn't want to stay. But I am so ashamed of how you left, the things I said to you that day.'

'Yeah, well, me too. Let's just forget about it, shall we?' He looked like he was about to object and thought better of it.

'So what happened when you found Scott with that girl? Where did you go?'

'I went to Mali's. She was, still is my best friend. I slept in her bed for a few months and then we got a place together for a few years.'

'Did you move with her to Lamma Island?'

'Eventually, yeah. We lived on Hong Kong island for a few years but we grew tired of the manic pace of life and so we moved to Lamma. There's a cool scene there. A more alternative tribe of artists and musicians, and the rent was cheaper. We would get the ferry over to Central every day to work in the salon and sometimes we would go out partying after and stay with friends. But then we would come home to the peace and quiet of the island.'

'How long did you work in the salon for?'

'Quite a while, about four years. I got promoted to junior stylist and then senior stylist. I was colouring as well as cutting. It was fun, but I knew I didn't want to do it forever.'

'And then you went to the tattoo parlour?'

'Yeah, then I met Ray and went to work for him. I've been there for eight years now.'

'And you like it?'

'I love it! I meet some great people. I get to design stuff and be creative all day long. Definitely beats working in an office.'

'I never thought you would work in an office.' He focused on the sea ahead. It was easier to ask questions that way. 'And is there anyone special in your life?'

'There have been a few along the way.'

'Boys or girls?'

'Both.'

'Really?'

'I was pretty confused for a while.' Neither of them spoke, just listened to the chug of the engine, their hair blowing in the breeze. She didn't mean to have a dig, but he would feel responsible. And it had been hard, figuring out who she was. She still wasn't sure, but she was becoming more comfortable with not being sure.

'And now?' Joseph asked eventually.

'Well, there is still no one serious. I have started seeing a guy, but I don't know.'

'Romy, I'm so sorry if the way that your father and I brought you up was confusing.'

'It was hard when I got to Hong Kong. I guess everything was new and different and I just had no idea who I really was.'

'And do you know who you are now?'

The question struck a nerve. She had, she had found herself, and in doing so had become happy, and that was why it all just seemed so incredibly unfair. She could feel his gaze penetrating the back of her head and she didn't know how to answer without giving herself away. But she wasn't ready, she hadn't been to the island, hadn't had her day. She shut her eyes, felt the cool spray of the water on her face and braced herself. But she didn't have to, because when she opened her eyes again, there in front of the boat was a school of dolphins, their fins surfing the foam-crested waves.

'Joseph, look!' But he had already seen them, seven or eight dolphins just ahead of the boat, one at the tip and the rest fanning out behind, like stunt planes flying in formation. Their fins appeared first, all at the same time, and then their bodies, arcing and soaring out of the waves until their noses hit the water and they dived back in. Romy made her way to the front of the boat and lay on the end like she had as a child. She imagined she was at the tip of the pod as the sea sprayed her face and the salty water mixed with the tears that poured down her cheeks.

CHAPTER EIGHT

FLORA

Flora called the school and explained to Mrs Herbert that she would have to take her children out the following week. She found herself saying that her mother had broken her hip rather than her leg, thought it sounded more dramatic somehow and more in need of care. But then she spent the next two days panicking that Toby would talk about his grandmother's broken leg, not hip, and she would be called up on her pointless lie. She had decided to leave them in school until the end of the week while Lizzie was being looked after in hospital and Jeremy was still around. But she had promised him that they would stay with Lizzie for the whole time he was away. The prospect of ten unadulterated days with her mother made her feel quite sick.

'Will Granny Lizzie be able to walk at all?' Toby asked from the back of the car as they headed up the M4.

'I'm not sure, Tobes, maybe she'll have crutches. But she won't be able to do much, so we're going to have to do all the cooking and running around after her.'

'Don't worry, Mummy, I'm an excellent cook. I can make Granny chocolate rice crispies and ice cream sundaes.'

'She would love that, Toby. Shall we listen to *The Gruffalo* or *Paddington?*'

'*The Gruffalo!*' Olive chanted from her car seat and kicked the back of Flora's seat.

They arrived at the house before Jeremy and Lizzie had got back from the hospital. Flora ran around turning lights on. She had presumed that Lizzie would sleep in the guest room downstairs, but Jeremy hadn't so much as cleared the piles of laundry off the bed. So Flora set about making the room look more appealing while cursing her useless stepfather. The closest he came to helping in the house was lighting a fire and sorting out his wine cellar. He thought all other acts of domesticity would signify a depreciation of his manhood. Not that her mother did much either. She considered herself too clever for most household chores, and spent her days doing crosswords and reading biographies of surgeons and politicians while letting her band of cleaners, gardeners and handymen carry out the grunt work.

It was one of the reasons she had warmed to Jake; he wasn't afraid of cleaning, and he actually enjoyed cooking. Sure, his repertoire was somewhat old-fashioned with a heavy emphasis on meat and two veg, but at least he tried. In fact, he had tried so hard to please her at the beginning. Flora thought back to that first day when she arrived from London for good, her bags at her feet, her heart in her mouth and Jake had picked sweet peas from the garden and put them all over the house. Knowing how apprehensive she would be about giving up her job and having too much time on her hands, he gave her some of his father's inheritance and told her she could do up the old farmhouse any way she liked. And while she was slightly put out by his gender stereotyping, she embraced the challenge and surprised herself by how much pleasure she got from painting the chintzy bedrooms in bright, modern colours and wallpapering the bathrooms in contemporary prints. She bought new bedding and kitchen equipment and converted the dining room into a cosy snug. But that was during the summer months when the fields around them were lush and green, and blue sea sparkled at her through the windows. It was when the days shortened in October and the leaves fell from the trees and all around the green faded to brown, that the doubt crept back in and gnawed away at her insides. Then it rained for three whole months, unrelenting downpours that swept in from the ocean on bitter winds that whipped your cheeks and soaked your bones so that you never properly dried out. For twelve whole weeks she felt constantly damp and the water seeped through the bricks of the four-hundred-year-old walls, staining the fresh paint and dulling the vibrant colours. It was freezing; none of the windows fitted their frames and the arctic winds rattled through them, leaving icicles on the inside of the glass in their bedroom. Jake was used to it, hardened to the cold through a lifetime of exposure. But she had grown up in a centrally heated Victorian house outside Oxford with thick carpets and heavy damask curtains and was totally unprepared.

Flora pulled the heavy curtains shut in her childhood home and lit the fire while the kids raced around the house at top speed. Flora let them run in the hope that they might wear themselves out by the time her parents arrived. The car pulled up and she could see the sour look on her mother's face as she closed the curtains on the other side of the glass. It didn't bode well. The children rushed out to greet them and she followed hot on their tails, but not quickly enough to stop Toby throwing himself at his grandmother and nearly toppling her over. He was told off by Jeremy and retreated back into the house, sobbing.

'Sorry, Mum, he was just excited to see you.' Flora took her mother's arm; she had a cast on her leg, all the way up to her thigh.

'Yes. Well, he is going to have to be more careful, Flora, or I'll break the other one.'

'Don't worry, they'll calm down. So how do we do this?' Lizzie was leaning on Flora and hovering the bad leg above the floor. Her mother was pretty skinny, but Flora's arms were beginning to shake under her weight.

'I- I don't know, they put me in a wheelchair to get to the car, but...' Lizzie's eyes filled with tears and she leant more heavily on her daughter.

'It's OK, Mum. Did they give you crutches?' Flora looked around for Jeremy, who had followed the children into the house with the bags and not returned.

'Er, yes, yes – they're in the boot.'

'Right...' Flora looked at the boot and tried to figure out how to get there without letting go of her mother, whose nails were now digging into her forearm and actually breaking the skin. 'Jeremy!' she shouted, and then louder: 'Jeremy!'

He came out through the front door, his normally combed-over hair fallen in front of his flustered face, revealing the shiny bald patch beneath. 'What?'

'Where are the crutches?' Flora said with a hint of irritation.

'Oh yes, they're in the boot.' He retrieved them and between them they balanced Lizzie on the metal poles.

'Didn't they teach you how to use these at the hospital?' Flora asked as her mother wobbled between the sticks and looked at the front door doubtfully.

'Well...' Lizzie began.

'Your mother refused to wait for the nurse who was coming to show her how to use them. She said she wasn't an imbecile and it couldn't be that hard,' Jeremy said, rolling his eyes.

'Oh, right,' Flora said. 'If you remember, Mum, I twisted my ankle at school once and had crutches for a few days.'

'Did you?' Lizzie looked at her, bemused.

'Yes, I did, and you just need to step with the good leg and then put the crutches down ahead of you and put your weight into your arms and pull yourself forward.' Lizzie tentatively stepped onto her good leg but then couldn't bring the crutches off the floor to follow. She tried to drag them across the gravel and gathered a pile of stones in front of the poles, and her body was left behind. Her hands were shaking and her bottom lip quivered.

'I... can't... I can't do it,' she said, her voice trembling.

'Yes, you can.' Flora tried to sound reassuring. 'You just need a little practice. You'll be hopping around the house in no time.'

'Come on, Lizzie, you can do it. Just try what Flora said, put the weight into your arms and hop forward.' Jeremy tried to sound encouraging but the impatience lingered behind his words like a bad smell. Lizzie moved the crutches further forward but failed to get her body to follow. She was bent over with her arms outstretched in front of her and her bottom protruding towards the car. Flora hooked her arm underneath her mother's and Jeremy did the same on the other side and between them they picked Lizzie up and carried her into the house, the redundant crutches banging against their knees as they walked.

'I'm assuming Mum is going to sleep in the guest room downstairs,' Flora said as they entered the hall. Lizzie and Jeremy both looked at each other perplexed, as if they really hadn't given this any thought. Not for the first time Flora wondered how on earth the two of them had reached their fifties relatively unscathed with barely a practical bone between them.

'Er, yes, that's a good idea, Flora. Isn't it, Liz? Then you don't have to deal with the stairs.'

Lizzie looked horrified at this suggestion. 'Couldn't you just carry me up the stairs to my own room?' she asked.

'We could, but Mum, you're not going to stay in bed forever, and Jeremy is going away tomorrow and I can't carry you up there on my own.'

'She's right, Lizzie, much more practical for you to be down here. And you'll be up and about in no time.'

'It sounds like you've both made up your minds,' Lizzie said with a huff and they carried her into the guest bedroom and lowered her onto the bed.

'There we go. It's nice in here, Mum. I'll leave you to get settled and go and make us all a cup of tea, shall I?'

Flora retreated out of the room before her mother had time to say another word. This was going to be harder than she thought. It wasn't unfamiliar territory, looking after her mother, but Lizzie was normally smacked out on valium or so pissed she didn't know what was going on when Flora had been forced to intervene over the years. This was different; Lizzie was *compos mentis* and humiliated and full of self-loathing and rage. It wasn't a good combination. And trust Jeremy to do a runner. Lizzie had always been so pathetically grateful to him for rescuing them both when Flora's father died in a car accident when she was only two months old. Lizzie had met Jeremy just four months later at a birthday party at her sister's. He was drawn to the wide-eyed waif her mother had become; liked to think of himself as her protector. He rescued Lizzie when she was down and never really let her get back up. Auntie Bella once told Flora that Jeremy had been jilted by the love of his life just before he met Lizzie. Neither he nor her mother ever spoke of it. Nevertheless, they were two lost souls who found each other at a time when both of their lives were in ruins. Yet it wasn't as romantic as that made it sound. He was controlling and pompous, but he had money and offered stability to Flora and her mother at a time when Lizzie was desperate. Jeremy had inherited the family business five years earlier and he had this big house in Oxfordshire which he placed them in, like figures in a doll's house. It didn't really matter that they weren't the figures he had bought it for. Or did it?

They went on to have a family of their own. When Flora was just two Tommy was born, and then eighteen months later came Arthur and then Billy two years after that. Flora recalled her mother during those early years of her brothers' lives. She wafted around the house, often in her nightie, her hair unwashed and greasy, her skin pale and her eyes wide. There were nannies, of course – Lizzie couldn't have coped with four young children on her own. In fact, Lizzie barely contributed to the rearing of her children at all. Mrs Jenkins, the housekeeper-cum-cleaner-cum-cook-cum-general dogsbody, who had looked after Jeremy when he was growing up, did everything. And there were various young nannies and au pairs, who changed nappies and played games with them, taught them French songs or German swear words, but they rarely lasted more than a few months. The combination of Lizzie's unhinged behaviour and Mrs Jenkins' bossy firm hand was enough to send anyone running for the hills.

It wasn't as though Flora's early years were unhappy, exactly – she had no other points of comparison. When they weren't pulling her hair or farting on her pillow, she loved her brothers. Well, maybe not at the time, but she loved them now. She was jealous of them back then, of their uncomplicated relationship with their mother who adored them and asked nothing from them in return. Lizzie smothered 'her boys', as she called them, in kisses and love that she never bestowed upon her daughter. While she berated Flora constantly, she laughed and delighted in the boys' bad behaviour. And where were they now? Not unlike their father, they were nowhere to be seen. They had all tired of Lizzie's histrionics years ago and only came home at Christmas or the odd birthday celebration to drink their wine and eat their food. Tommy had at least called Flora after the fall. He lived in Scotland, and was clearly safe in the knowledge that he wouldn't be called back to help. Arthur and Billy, however, were in London and perilously close and hadn't made contact at all. Not that they would be of any use, but Flora would have liked to have their company.

The kettle hissed and Flora was snapped out of her reverie. She made three cups of tea and juice and biscuits for the kids, who were now safely ensconced in front of *Winnie-the-Pooh*. At home Toby would claim he was too old for *Winnie-the-Pooh*, but it was something of a tradition to watch it here at Granny Lizzie's house, and they were both smiling at the TV when she walked in. She was tempted to snuggle down with them on the sofa but dragged herself back to the guest room.

'It's freezing in here, Flora, and the bed is too soft. I really do wish I could be in my own bed if I am going to be stuck here day after day.'

'Well, Mum, it will be an incentive to get you out of bed and up those stairs then.'

'Don't talk to me about incentives, Flora, I'm not one of your children.'

Flora took a deep breath and went over to the chest of drawers in the corner of the room. She opened the top drawer; it was full of photographs.

'Shall I clear out this drawer for you? Then we can bring some of your things down here.'

'What? No, don't bother, it's just full of old photos. There's too much to clear out. You can just get me whatever I need from upstairs every day.'

'No, really, I don't mind. It might be fun looking through some of these pics.' She picked up a photograph: it was of Jeremy and all three boys sitting on the tractor mower. Jeremy was laughing and so were the boys. Tommy was sitting on the hood, Arthur standing on the back and Billy was just a baby sitting on his father's lap.

'Look at this,' Flora showed the picture to her mother.

'I really don't want to go through old photos now, Flora, I'm tired, I just…'

'Oh, come on, Mum, it might cheer you up. Look how little Billy is here.' Lizzie took the photo and the corners of her mouth peaked in a reluctant smile.

'He was the most beautiful baby! You know you entered him into a…'

'I know, a beautiful baby competition.' Flora finished her sentence. She had heard this story so many times before. 'And I was incensed when he didn't win.'

'I'm sorry if I'm boring you, Flora, but you really were—'

'Look at this one. Why do I look so miserable?' It was a picture of Flora at about nine. She was holding a book; it looked like it might be *Anne of Green Gables*, and she was scowling at the camera. She handed it to her mother.

'I'm afraid, darling, you looked like that most of the time.'

'What? No, I didn't.'

'You were quite a serious child, and you had obviously been interrupted while reading one of your precious books and were shooting daggers at whoever had disturbed you. It's an expression I remember well.'

'Really? I don't believe it, there must be some pictures here of me smiling.' She rummaged around in the drawer and found loads more of the boys: in their school uniforms on the front doorstep; on the local steam train; at the zoo; blowing out candles on their birthday cakes. There was one of her on a pony, also scowling; she had always hated riding. And one of her in a ballet tutu, not scowling exactly but not smiling either – she wasn't a huge fan of ballet either. And then she found one, of her holding Billy as a baby. She was smiling and so was he.

'Here, you see. I did smile.' She handed it to her mother.

'Yes, you did love Billy, he managed to make you smile. Made us all smile, laugh in fact. I wish he was here now. Does he know about my accident?'

Flora took the photo back from her mother and continued to rifle through the photos in the drawer. 'Yes, he said he has a big job on and he can't come down. Maybe at the end of the month when it's done.'

'Oh.' Flora could hear the disappointment in Lizzie's voice and she felt a twinge of sympathy for her.

'Flora, please stop rummaging around in that drawer, you're not going to find any more photos of you smiling, I can assure you.' The sympathy rapidly diminished. 'Could you go and get me my reading glasses from by my bed? Jeremy brought me the wrong ones to the hospital. And there is a pile of books on the bedside table, things I have been meaning to read for ages. Could you grab them? I may as well make the most of this static time.'

But Flora was determined to find another photo of herself smiling and so she dug deeper into the drawer. There was an envelope at the bottom. She pulled it out and opened it up. There was a photo inside of a baby in the arms of a man. He had glasses on and smiling eyes beneath a mop of floppy hair. He was gazing adoringly at the child.

'Who is this, Mum?' Flora watched as the colour drained out of her mother's already pale complexion.

'Er, I don't know, Flora. I told you to stop rummaging. Now please could you go and get me my books.'

'Is it me? Is this me and my father?' She handed Lizzie the photo and she took it with trembling hands.

'Um, I, yes, I suppose it is.' She tried not to look at the photo but something drew her in and locked her eyes there on that man and baby. Flora took it back.

'But Mum, I asked you so many times whether you had any photos of him and you said you got rid of them all. That you burned them after he died!'

'Yes, well, this one must have got away.' Her words were quiet, barely more than a whisper.

'So, is this really him? And me? I look older than two months here. You said I was only two months when he died, I look at least six here.'

'You were a big baby.'

'Really? I never knew that.' Flora found herself smiling down at the photograph and a sensation of pride, of belonging, of love, warmed her body. Here she was. Evidence of her as a baby, of her father. 'I'm going to keep this, get it framed. A photo of him, and me! I can't believe it. I look so like Olive! I'm going to show the kids.' She practically skipped out of the room, and then faltered in the hallway, looked back at Lizzie through the crack in the open door. She was sitting up in the bed, staring ahead of her, her eyes glassy, pulling at the bedspread with restless fingers. And quickly that warming sense of pride chilled to a cool foreboding. Flora had never been able to talk to her mother about her father. Lizzie had always said it was too upsetting, and they had tiptoed around her mental fragility with such trepidation that Flora had never pushed her. Well, apart from once when she was sixteen and Jeremy had grounded her when he caught her stealing booze for the Mistletoe Ball. She had screamed at Jeremy, and Lizzie too, said that he wasn't her real father, that she was sure her real father wouldn't be so uptight. That he might have actually given her a drink so she didn't have to steal it. That they had never loved her like they loved the boys. That she hated them both. And later that night her mother had taken an overdose. It was Flora who found her, caked in her own vomit. Flora who had to call an ambulance and watch as they pumped her stomach and the little pills flooded out on a river of bile and gin.

Flora had never dared to mention her father again.

She walked back through the doorway.

'Mum?' Flora said quietly. 'Are you OK?' She didn't answer, just picked at the threads on the eiderdown with her fingers. 'Look, I'm sorry if I upset you. I just, well, I'd never seen a photo of him, of us before, and you said there weren't any and—'

'It's fine, Flora,' Lizzie said, her words hard and full of contempt, and without turning to look at her daughter she said, 'Just go and get me those bloody glasses and books, would you.'

'Yeah, sure.' Flora stuffed the photo into her back pocket. She would show it to the children another time.

CHAPTER NINE

LIZZIE

As the winter drew in Lizzie and Edward's friendship deepened. Her family was quite enamoured with him and he was flattered and intrigued by them. He came out to the house again the following Saturday and then the one after that until it became a regular event. He stayed for two nights over the Christmas holidays. Came for the Claybournes' infamous 'Carols and Canapés' party. Her mother went totally over the top at Christmas. She put up a huge tree in the hallway that was as tall as the double-height stairwell. The fairy on top hit the glass of the domed ceiling. There was even an electric train that wound its way through the branches of the tree. The banisters of the stairs were wrapped in green foliage and fairy lights, and there were Father Christmases everywhere. A hundred of her parents' closest friends and their children arrived for mulled wine and canapés and sang carols with gusto and little finesse, accompanied by Lizzie's eccentric piano teacher. Edward's eyes bulged in amazement. 'It's like a scene out of Dickens!' he said, half disparaging, half enchanted. Lizzie had come to recognise the effect that her family had on him. She could see him wanting to hate them, their sense of privilege. Yet he was a romantic at heart and couldn't help being charmed by the smells of pine and wine and freshly baked pastry, the candles and open fires, the laughter and the singing. He was there in full voice at the front of the crowd around the piano, Jamie with his arm around his shoulders as they bellowed 'O come let us adore him'. Lizzie was never at the forefront of the Christmas party, or anything if she could help it. She usually hung out in the kitchen with Magda, their Hungarian cleaner who had been helping at this party since before Lizzie was born. Lizzie had no interest in cooking or even food, but it gave her a purpose. She carried round the plates of canapés and never had to talk to any of her parents' friends for longer than it took them to dip their melba toast in the melted Camembert. That year, however, she was torn between the kitchen and Edward at the piano. So she hung out in the doorway to the drawing room, halfway between them both, and watched his face flushed with wine and festive cheer.

He and Jamie had formed quite a close bond, and Lizzie was trying not to be jealous. Bella and Damian had only been back from university once since that first lunch, but Jamie was there every Saturday. He had taken it upon himself to teach Edward the ways of country living, clay pigeon shooting or quad biking around the field, followed by tennis and pints in the local pub. Lizzie went with them to the pub but found their conversations about rifles and targets increasingly dull. She was pretty sure Edward didn't care about such things either, but he was surprisingly eager to please her brother. On reflection, it wasn't that surprising; Jamie had that effect on everyone. But he was going travelling around Thailand and Malaysia after Christmas and she would have Edward to herself for five whole months.

There was never any question of her friendship with Edward being more than just that. She had deluded herself in those early, balmy days that he might try to hold her hand or even kiss her. But she had given him every imaginable opportunity and he hadn't taken the bait. So she had reconciled herself to being just friends. *Just*, she almost had to laugh at herself. There was no *just* about it. Her track record with friends wasn't great, and now she had a best friend who was a boy and one that wanted to spend time with her and her family. One that her family actually thought was worth spending time with.

'There's something beautifully romantic about him, darling,' her mother had said after that first visit. 'Like a wounded soldier, the unsung hero.' She was a sucker for a period drama and was evidently charmed by Edward's eccentricities. Even her father seemed impressed. 'A very charming chap,' he said. 'Clever, too, has something to say for himself, which is unusual in your generation.' And Jamie, well, he was just delighted to have a plaything, someone who would laugh at his jokes and follow him around the fields like a loyal puppy. Bella and Damian were hardly there, but when they were Edward gave Bella a reason to put on her tightest top and brightest lipstick, and Damian enjoyed thrashing him at tennis.

His visits continued throughout the spring term and over the Easter holidays. They either met at the library in town to revise together or Edward would come to the house and they would lay their books out on the dining room table. And then as the weather grew warmer, Lizzie followed Edward around the garden with his easel. He had to complete a substantial portfolio for his art A level and had left it all rather late. So he was churning out paintings daily of the orchard or the front of the house or the vegetable garden, and Lizzie would lay a rug down next to whatever spot he had chosen and work on her quadratic equations or anatomy diagrams. Lizzie's carefree attitude towards her results had rapidly diminished as their A levels loomed closer and the novelty of Edward faded. She found herself haunted by the same anxieties that had rattled her at this time of year since the first time she had taken summer exams aged twelve. Edward of course was remarkably calm: he was top of his class in English. In fact, his teacher had recently submitted some of his poems to a national competition which he had won, and one of them had even been published in a broadsheet. He was too lazy to be top of history but he would cruise it on the day. And his art teacher said that if only he would just focus on the matter in hand, he could be something really special. But Edward never focused on the matter in hand. He was like an overexcited puppy, constantly distracted by a passing butterfly or scuttling rabbit. It was as if his brilliant mind was on high alert at all times, determined never to miss a thing.

And yet for all his shiny brilliance, he was still an enigma. Lizzie had long since tired of asking him questions about his life, his father, friends at his last school. He always batted her away with some quip about how horribly dull it all was. But there were times when his eyes glazed over and his mind wandered into the darkness. When she had to call his name several times to bring him back to the here and now. She recognised that look; she still went there herself, less regularly since he had come into her life. But there were days when the black cloud wouldn't lift and the past weighed down on the present like a pillow over her head.

Then there was one day when she caught a glimpse of his demon. It was a Saturday at the beginning of the summer term. He was late and arrived in the middle of lunch, which was unusual for a start. He made up some excuse about the train being delayed but he blinked a lot as he spoke, and she had come to recognise that as a rare sign of his anxiety. Then after lunch when Jamie suggested tennis, he feigned tiredness, said he had some reading to do for English. And as he walked away from the table Lizzie noticed that he was holding himself differently, slightly cocked to one side. She followed him into the kitchen with a pile of plates and dropped a fork. His chivalrous manner prompted him to bend instantly to pick it up, but he got stuck halfway down and couldn't quite reach it. A piece of potato clung to its prong on the tiled floor beneath them. Lizzie dived down to grab it and looked up at the pained expression on his face.

'You all right?' she asked as he pulled himself up gingerly, holding onto the base of his back to support it.

'Yeah,' he sighed through gritted teeth. 'Must have slept funny.'

'Can I see?' She went to pull up his shirt, but he pushed her hand away violently.

'No,' he said with a sterner tone than she had ever heard before. 'Sorry, I just... I'm fine, really.'

Later that afternoon, they were sitting outside in two wicker armchairs. He was reading and annotating *Who's Afraid of Virginia Woolf*, while she pretended to study the *Let's Revise Biology* book in her lap.

'Can I come and meet your dad next weekend?' she asked.

'We've been through this before, Lizzie. You really wouldn't like it, there is nothing to do at my house.'

'There are chairs, aren't there? We could sit and read like we're doing here.'

'There isn't room. Dad likes to watch snooker on Saturday afternoons. He wouldn't like us to be there.'

'Then how about Sunday? Is snooker on Sundays too?'

'No, but he goes to the pub on Sundays. And anyway, you go to church on Sundays.'

'Only in the morning, I could come after. What do you do when he is at the pub?'

'Enjoy having the house to myself.'

'So why can't I come and be with you then?'

'Lizzie, please.' He looked at her with pitiful eyes and she nearly relented, but then she remembered the fork and the pain in his side.

'Look, I don't have to meet him if you don't want me to. I'll come when he's at the pub, just for an hour. You can't stop me. And it'll be fun.'

But he did try to stop her, over and over again that week at school. Then on the Wednesday she caught a glimpse of the bruises on his side when he took off his jumper and his shirt rode up with it. Angry swirls of purple and red with the rib bones prominent under the skin. He didn't know she had seen, and given his reaction to the fork, she didn't say anything. But she was more determined than ever to visit the house, and so she held her ground.

Wilton Street was long and straight with a hill in the middle.

The terraced houses on either side were all the same, apart from the odd brightly coloured front door or window box. Number 54 was halfway up the hill and there were no window boxes and the grey paint on the front door was peeling. But the path was swept, unlike next door where a bin bag was propped up beneath the front window. It had been ravaged by animals and there was curdled milk and baked beans dripping from the holes, beer cans and soggy pizza boxes piled up next to it. Lizzie rang the bell.

Edward answered. He looked different, somehow; sheepish. He was wearing the same clothes that he wore to her house every weekend, the same glasses, the same hair that hung over one side of his face. But he wasn't smiling and his shoulders were hunched, his feet dragging across the floor as he ushered her into the hallway.

'So, this is it,' he said with a shrug.

'Is he here? Your dad?' she asked.

'No, he just left.' She wished she'd had the courage to come earlier than she said she would. She had considered it, of course, just so she could meet him. But given the battle she'd had in the first place, she had decided it wasn't worth it. Maybe she had passed him on the street? She should have been paying more attention.

'OK, so are you going to show me around then?' she said, peering over his shoulder and down the dark corridor to the stairs.

'Sure.' He walked into the room on the right of the front door. It was small; there was a brown leather armchair beneath the window and a matching sofa facing the TV. It smelt a bit musty but it was impeccably tidy. There was a photo of Edward with his front teeth missing in a frame on a small table next to the TV. 'There's really not much to see, Lizzie.'

'I just want to see where you live, so I can picture you here. Is that weird? You know everything about me.'

'Not *everything*.' He didn't look at her when he said that, just picked at the stitched seam on the corner of the sofa.

'What do you mean?'

'I mean, Lizzie, that you pretend to be this open book, but we both know you have secrets too.'

She couldn't answer; didn't dare look him in the eye. She walked over to the window and looked out at the street through the net curtains. There were a couple of boys playing football in the middle of the road. One of them hit a parked car and the alarm sounded. They laughed and ran out of sight. 'It's OK that you have secrets, we don't need to know everything about each other, you know,' Edward said.

'Yeah, I know.' Her voice was high and she hoped he couldn't hear the tremor behind her words. She walked back towards the door. 'Come on then, show me the rest.'

The rest took less than a couple of minutes. There was a small kitchen behind the sitting room. The vinyl floor was sticky under her feet. It had mock-wood shiny cupboards with a cream tiled work surface that was criss-crossed with thick brown grouting. It smelt of bacon and lemon washing-up liquid.

'Where do you eat?' she asked.

'On our laps in front of the telly.'

'Always?'

'Yeah.' His voice rose at the end in indignation. She had never seen him like this before.

Upstairs there were two bedrooms. His dad's at the front – the door was shut and there was no question of looking inside. Then there was a small mint-green bathroom, still wet and fugged up from the morning's ablutions. And Edward's room at the back. There was a single bed under the window and a bookshelf bursting at the seams with tatty-looking books, classics mostly and poetry anthologies.

'Where do you get all your books from?'

'Charity shops, and there's a second-hand bookshop on the way back from my dad's office. He sometimes brings them home.'

'That's nice,' she said, running her finger along the spines of the books. 'You've got a good collection.'

'Yeah.'

There was a desk under a small window which looked out over the roofs of the houses behind. You could see straight into the bedroom of the nearest house, its pink curtains and collection of My Little Pony figures on the windowsill.

'Is this where you work?' she asked, pointing at the desk.

'Yes, Lizzie, this is where I work.' He sighed wearily. 'Are we done now?'

'Done with what?'

'The tour.'

'I guess.' She shrugged. 'So, what shall we do?'

'I told you, there's nothing to do here.'

'Oh, come on.' She sat down on the bed. The blue-and-grey-striped duvet cover was soft and faded. 'What do you do all day?'

He shook his head and rolled his eyes. 'I don't know. I read, watch telly, same as anyone else.'

'Shall we watch something then?'

'I don't have any films. I guess we could go and rent one?'

'Great.'

And so they walked to the Blockbuster three streets away. Edward didn't lighten up on the walk; he was twitchy and quiet. She chose *Heathers* in the shop. It had only just come out and she had heard girls talking about it at school. Edward had no input at all. He pretended to pick up the tapes and read their covers, but she could tell he wasn't actually taking anything in. He was merely enduring the whole experience, willing it to be over. But Lizzie had taken a train, a bus and two quite substantial walks to get here and she wasn't ready to leave. She bought popcorn and sweets in the shop and they sat side by side on the sticky leather sofa.

Heathers was macabre. The bitchy girls and Winona Ryder's dark retaliation were unnervingly close to home for Lizzie. She wished she had actually read the synopsis before choosing it to impress Edward. It unsettled her, along with his twitching leg that squeaked with friction against the sofa seat and his flinching at every passing shout or noise that came from outside the window. The minute the credits rolled he jumped up from the sofa and switched off the TV. It was dusk and shadows had crept into the room.

'I'll walk you to the bus stop,' he said.

'Can I just do a quick pee?' He started to roll his eyes at this and then corrected himself. She looked up at the mildewed shower curtain as she sat on the loo, brown stains streaked down the side of it. She thought about the brooding and twitched Edward here, and how different he was to the bright and carefree boy that came to visit. She wanted to tell him that she didn't care about the size of his house, the differences between their families, but she knew that just by saying it, it would imply that she did. She worried that they would never be able to recapture what they had before today. He was right; she never should have come.

He had his coat on and was holding hers as she came down the stairs. The door was open and he was already halfway out of it. As they stepped out into the cool evening, his eyes darted up and down the street.

'Come on,' he said, 'or you'll miss the bus.' He walked fast, his long legs taking big strides so she had to run to keep up.

'Edward, wait. Chill out.'

He kept looking over his shoulder and she was pretty sure she saw his eyes widen momentarily, before he put his arm through hers and hurried her even faster. She tried to look back at what he had seen but he was pulling her along too fast. When they arrived at the bus stop minutes later, there was no sign of the bus. They were both out of breath and her heart was thumping in her chest.

'Was that him? Your dad?' she asked, her words still punctuated by wheezy breaths.

'What do you mean?'

'He was arriving home from the pub, wasn't he? Why were you so determined I didn't meet him?'

'You've got an overactive imagination, Lizzie. I just didn't want to miss the bus.' They waited in silence then for what felt like an interminably long time.

'I'll see you at school tomorrow?' she said as the bus eventually pulled up.

'Yeah.'

'Thanks for having me.'

He didn't answer, just smiled. But as the bus pulled away, she saw him kick a bottle that had been abandoned on the pavement. He kicked it hard with the front of his foot and it obviously hurt because he winced and then hopped a few steps, shaking out the pain. And as she watched his figure grow smaller and smaller in the distance, a familiar emptiness began to grumble inside her belly. She had blown it again.

CHAPTER TEN

ROMY

It was two hours on the boat out to Apo Island, and after the dolphins Romy didn't return to Joseph at the back of the boat but put her headphones in and lay down on the bench at the front. While it was nice talking to him, and he did seem genuinely interested in her life, she really didn't have the energy to dissect the last twelve years. There was so much she couldn't tell him. About the nights when she had taken so much ketamine that she didn't know where she was or how she got home. Or the mornings when she woke up in the bed of strange men or women or both, and crept back to her and Mali's apartment with shame weighing down her heart and limbs. Mali was always there at the beginning of the evening, but she had an off button that Romy didn't possess. She would know to go home before it became impossible. She tried to take Romy with her, but she was defiant when she was high on drugs and booze and the potential lure of a lover, and there was no way she was going to cut her night short. And faithful Mali was always there to pick up the broken pieces of her friend the following morning. She nursed Romy's hangovers without sympathy or reprimand and listened without judgement as she beat herself up with loathing and regret about the previous night's antics.

But then Mali got a girlfriend, a Cantonese girl called Symphony. Mali had brought girls home before and some of them had even stuck around for a few weeks. But Symphony was different. She was tiny, barely even five foot, but she had the sharpest mind and quickest wit of anyone Romy had ever met. She was an investment banker and so far from their world of hairstyles and tattoos that it was laughable. But she was nothing like Scott and his awful friends. She had a scepticism that grounded her, and a hairdresser girlfriend with dreadlocks and nose ring that kept her even more real. Romy had known that Mali was bright; she read Kafka in her spare time and did sudoku for fun. But Symphony brought her brain out into the light. They sparked off each other with an electrifying magnetism, and Romy was left feeling inept and stupid. She tried to join in their conversations, dredging up the literary and artistic references that Ted had taught her, but she didn't have it in her like they did. And so she partied harder than ever before. She stayed out for nights on end, going straight to work in the morning fuelled by coke and speed. One day she rocked up at the parlour having not been to bed and her hands were shaking so much she couldn't hold the needle. Ray sent her home and told her not to come back until she got her shit together. But she didn't go home. She went on a bender and ended up in a squat in Sham Shui Po with a guy who gagged her while they were having sex. They did heroin and she shat herself in her sleep. The following morning after she had washed herself in a bucket because there was no running water, she ran five blocks from the squat, her pants sticking to the backs of her legs. She could still smell her faeces when she collapsed in a doorway and rang Mali. She came with Symphony who had a car and who couldn't hide her disgust at the sight and stench of Romy. They took her home and Mali put her in a bath and washed her body, her face, her hair while Romy cried. She had hit rock bottom and it frightened her. There had been other girls in that squat, filthy girls with greasy hair and scabs on their faces. And their wide, frightened eyes had been the wake-up call that Romy so desperately needed. Mali was there to help her – she wrapped her in blankets in the middle of the night when she was shivering so much from withdrawal that the bed squeaked and she was powerless to stop it. Symphony was there, too, not holding her or mopping her fevered brow like Mali, but in the kitchen making her broths and smoothies with wheatgrass and ginger, and watching black-and-white movies with her on Saturdays when Mali had to go to the salon. As Romy's strength grew and her addled mind recovered, she found she was less intimidated by Symphony, who cried at the movies and didn't like taking the bins out in the dark. And so when Mali and Symphony asked her to move to Lamma with them, she did. They lived together in a little cottage on the outskirts of the village, surrounded by trees and away from the temptations of the city. And Romy came back stronger. She begged Ray's forgiveness and he took her back to work where she started creating her own portfolio of designs and built up a list of clients. They were mostly women who were intimidated by Ray and the bar through his nose, the Wolverine tattoo across his face. He didn't resent it; he welcomed and supported the new, shinier version of his sidekick and they took on new premises to cope with the increasing demand. After a year Romy got her own place. Mali and Symphony said she didn't have to move out, but they all knew that she did. She found a flat in a place just back from the harbour in Lamma. It was on the third floor, as high as it gets on the island, and out of her bedroom window she could see the sea through a crack between the buildings. If she shut her eyes at night she could just hear the crashing of the waves against the shore and it felt like home.

Romy had fallen asleep on the boat and woke as the engine cut. She jumped up, conscious that Joseph might have noticed how prone to sleep she was right now, but her head swam with blood and she had to sit back down again.

'You OK, Romy?' he asked as he dropped the anchor.

'Yeah,' she said, leaning over the boat and splashing her face with water. 'Is this the chapel dive?'

'It is. I thought we could do it first before the tourists arrive. Is that OK?'

'Of course! You know it's my favourite.'

He smiled as he hauled up their tanks from beneath the deck. Romy had grown up diving; she used to accompany Joseph on the boat whenever she wasn't in school. Ted didn't love it; he tried in those early years, but he was horribly sick on the boat and didn't like being under the water. In other aspects of life Ted was the free spirit and Joseph so much more in control. The house, the business, the day-to-day maintenance of their lives. And yet under the water something happened to Joseph, all that pent-up responsibility seeming to dissipate, and he was free. In contrast to Ted, the dreamer. Ted, who lived his life in a fictional world of myths and legends, couldn't cope with the underwater world to which there was no end. He wanted walls and ceilings, and he panicked at the prospect of running out of air.

'How long has it been since your last dive?' Joseph asked as he pulled his wetsuit up over his shoulders. There were a few grey hairs on his barrel-shaped chest but not an inch of fat; you could still see the definition of his ribs as he lifted his arms.

'About five years. There was the one just off Hong Kong that I told you about. And then I went to Thailand with some friends five years ago, and we went diving.'

'OK, well, as it has been a while, I just need to refresh a few things with you. OK?' He had his teacher head on and she didn't like it. He had taught her to dive all those years ago, but then she was a child and everyone patronised you. Today it made her hackles stand on end and she had to consciously stop her eyes from rolling when he asked her the basic safety questions. Then they got in the water and he told her to remove her mask and put it back on under the water, the regulator too. She did so without complaint but inside she was squirming.

Once all the technicalities were done, they swam down the edge of the reef wall, stopping to equalise by a pink and yellow sea fan. It looked like the underside of a giant mushroom and its tendrils swayed in the current, which was strong. They had to swim hard against it to stay close to the wall where fish of all shapes and sizes and colours swam in and out of the coral. She could hear the sound of her breathing reverberating around her head. Scott had once told her that the noise of air conditioning made him feel safe and at home. She had balked at this, and when he asked her what noise gave her the same feeling, she told him it was the sound of her own breathing under water. She listened to the hypnotic in-and-out, each breath becoming longer and fuller as the knots of panic in the depths of her stomach started to untangle for the first time since leaving the hospital.

They swam along the edge of the reef wall, stopping at an over-hang to see a Lionfish. And then at another ledge where there was a moray eel weaving its way in among the finger sponges. So aptly named, they looked like the hand of a giant and his fat fingers. All along the wall were leather corals which glowed golden in the light of the sun. They swam down to a cavern where there was a school of silversides hiding from their predators. Their scales were metallic yet iridescent, revealing the stripes of their bones which glowed an electric blue. They startled the fish which dispersed, only to regroup in perfect unity as they swam away as one. Joseph had his camera and took a picture of Romy and then showed it to her. Her eyes were smiling inside her mask and there was a halo of light around her head. An orange coral hung from the opening of the cave, so bright against the deep intensity of the blue beyond.

They swam out of the cave and up onto the reef flat. Yellow furry sponges and pink fungi and green grasses and purple lettuces all swayed in the current as far as her eye could see. It was a world so alien and yet so utterly familiar. Romy heard her own breath falter, and her mask steamed up as she realised she was crying, again! She kicked her legs hard and fast, swimming out over the clouds of fish that weaved their way in and out of the enchanted garden. The abundance of life was overwhelming. Striped fish, spotty fish, clownfish, leaf fish, frogfish, ribbon eels, a sea snake, silver dories with electric-blue underbellies and turmeric tails, sea caterpillars with Mohicans of spiked hair down their backs. And the sea cucumbers that lay in wait on the patches of sand between the coral, the barbs on their backs menacing but still extraordinary. Romy swallowed down the tears with every kick and her breath slowed and deepened. Joseph was just behind her. Every once in a while she caught a flash of him in the corner of her eye. Not too close, but near enough to know she was not alone.

After the dive they motored into the bay. Tourist boats from all the neighbouring islands and dive schools were starting to arrive, and Romy's heart sank at the thought that she would have to share her beloved turtles with the hordes.

'Why don't you go for a swim before they all get in the water?' Joseph suggested as he dropped the anchor.

'But the kit, shouldn't we sort it out? I know how you like to do it straight away.'

'It's OK.' He smiled. 'I'll sort yours out, just this once. Go on, before they all get in with their selfie sticks.'

She dived off the boat and into the turquoise sea. The reef was shallow in the bay and the coral was visible from the surface. And there was a turtle, a magnificent creature with his speckled shell and wrinkled neck just waiting for her by the boat. It headed out to sea and she swam after it. So graceful the way it glided through the water, just one flick of its fin powering it for seconds. The dinosaurs of the ocean, Joseph had always said. He was right: there was something prehistoric about these regal creatures. Their wrinkled necks and hooded eyes, the striking definition of the white webbed pattern across their feet, their fins, their faces. And the shell, so weathered, like the old leather coat of an army general that had seen a life's worth of battles. She followed him around the headland until they were in a little cove all on their own. She had always thought of the turtles as being male, although she knew that not to be true. But there was something so masculine, so solid and unflappable about the way that they moved. The grand-father of the sea.

Romy thought of her own grandfather, the only one she had

ever known, Joseph's father. He was a fisherman and she would accompany him on the boat when she went to stay with them on the larger island of Negros as a child. He was a small, gentle man with kind eyes who hummed his way through life. Her grandmother Lola said he came home humming after a typhoon when he was stuck at sea for three days, and after that he never stopped other than to sleep! Lola was soft and smelt of talcum powder and she kissed Romy all the time. Smothered her in hundreds of little kisses on her head, her neck, her cheeks, in her ears. Romy squirmed and Lola laughed and they made lumpia together – crispy spring rolls which they dipped in a sweet and sour sauce. Her grandfather had died eight years ago, Joseph had emailed to tell her. But it was when Romy was utterly bound by her own self-ishness and she declined to return for the funeral. In fact, she didn't even reply. And then Lola had died only two years later, of a broken heart she presumed; her grandparents hadn't spent a day apart for more than fifty years. By then Romy had already burned her bridges and didn't dare return for her grandmother's funeral either.

She rolled over onto her back and lay suspended in the salty sea. She closed her eyes and let her ears fill with water. The mystery of her own lineage had suddenly become a thing of prac-tical significance. There might be someone out there who could donate their kidney and keep her alive. The doctor had said that there was a far greater chance of someone she was biologically related to being a match, and yet she knew so little about where she had come from. Her fathers had told her when she was old enough to understand that her mother had been a surrogate in England. 'A very kind lady had offered to help them have a baby.' She had accepted that for years, not really bothered to question the finer details. But when she hit her teens and learned about reproduction at school, the questions came thick and fast. They were prepared, of course they were. They'd had fourteen years to anticipate her questions and come up with their answers. 'No, we didn't use an official agency, that wasn't really allowed back then.' 'She was a friend of Ted's, she didn't want children of her own.' 'Yes, they paid her to house their foetus.' It was Ted who made the baby with her. Why Ted? 'It meant more to him that the child was his own flesh and blood.' She had never asked how the deed was done, whether Ted had actually slept with this woman. Or had they inseminated her in some other way? After she had been born, her mother had just handed her over and never wanted to see her again.

Angel, their faithful cook, was the only constant female presence in Romy's life as a child. She was eight when Angel had Jasmine, and was fascinated by the baby that came out of her bulging belly and suckled at her breast just like the litter of puppies earlier that year. Angel had let her help change Jasmine's nappy and even hold her sometimes. When she was a little older Romy would dress her up and stick hair clips in Jasmine's hair like a real live doll. Romy had been too young to question the motives of her own mother at that point. But fifteen years later when some of her friends coupled off in Hong Kong and started having babies of their own, she watched from the sidelines as their bellies grew and with it their love for their unborn child. Romy wondered whether her own mother had been sick in pregnancy, or eaten strange food. Whether she had held her hand under her bump subconsciously, and how she had felt the first time she felt her baby kick. And then she had watched her friends with their babies, been blown away by the love that they so visibly felt. The love that was so primal, so instinctive, so all-consuming. Had her own mother felt none of that? What kind of a person just handed over the baby she had been carrying all that time? She asked each of her dads privately how much they had paid her mother to carry and then give up her child. Joseph told her not be vulgar, while Ted pretended not to remember. She didn't explain to them that she needed to know how much her life was worth. That she needed that figure in order to make sense of it all.

Romy flipped onto her front and dived down. She followed the turtle into a crevice under a ledge on the headland. But no matter how deep she dived, she couldn't swim away from her thoughts. What of her father's family? Ted didn't speak of his parents. Apparently, his mother had died when he was young and he was raised by his father, who was not a well person and died not long after they arrived in the Philippines. Romy had no idea whether Ted's father had brothers or sisters, whether he had any cousins. Why hadn't she asked more questions when he was alive? The turtle came up to breathe and so did Romy. Her lungs were bursting and she gasped for air when she reached the surface. Tomorrow, she told herself. Tomorrow she would tell Joseph and he would know what to do, maybe have answers to some of these questions.

Joseph was tinkering with the tanks on the boat when she swam back. Their wetsuits were lying out on the bow, drying in the sunshine. She tried to climb back into the boat but got stuck halfway – she just didn't have the strength in her upper body to heave herself up. Joseph pulled her into the boat.

'Thanks,' she said, trying to catch her breath. 'I'm obviously out of practice.' He smiled but looked at her warily.

'Did you see some?'

'Just the one, I followed it round the headland.'

'You were lucky. Look how many more people there are here now.' He gestured to the dozen or so other boats that were pulling into the bay. They were lined up like regimented soldiers. Tourists with selfie sicks were jumping into the water. Both children and adults were screaming with excitement and terror at the turtles.

'It really has got busy.'

'Yes. And they fleece you every step of the way. You aren't allowed into the marine park now without a guide. And the restaurant has put its prices up. The whole place is a rip-off.'

'What a shame.'

'I was thinking we could walk over to Cogon, dodge the crowds. They only come for the turtles.'

'Sure.'

Cogon was on the other side of the island. It was about an

hour's walk over two hills to get there, but the views from the top made it worth it. It was nearing the middle of the day when they started the climb, and Romy was already feeling light-headed as the sun beat down on her head. She was still bobbing up and down from the motion of the boat and her dive. It was more exercise than she had taken in months, and her legs felt like jelly beneath her before they had even started.

She was totally breathless and exhausted by the time they reached the top of the first peak. They sat under a tree and drank water and ate some chocolate-chip muffins that she had taken from the kitchen that morning. Below them the boats looked like toys in the bay, the tourists like little specks of dust. There was a band of turquoise shallow water with the reef beneath it that gave way to the deeper blue of the sea sparkling in the light of the sun. The island was a lush green of palms only interrupted by the red roofs of the two restaurants that vied for the tourists' custom. It was wonderfully peaceful, with just the buzz of the cicadas and the odd muffled cry from below. Romy's breath eventually deepened and the hammering of her heart slowed in her chest, but she was worried she wasn't going to make it up the next peak.

'We could go back to the beach after this. No need to go all the way to Cogon.'

Unnerved by his mind-reading again, she responded quickly. 'No, I want to. Just a bit unfit, I guess. I used to walk a lot in Lamma, but haven't done much recently.'

'Why is that?' She could feel his eyes on her, but she couldn't turn to look at him.

'Just busy, I guess. Shall we get going?'

She stood up and a wave of nausea unsettled her and she wobbled. Joseph caught her by the arm. 'Come on, Romy, let's go down. I'll shout you a Coke in the bar.'

'No, I'm fine. Really I am.' She moved away from his arm and strode out along the path. The second hill was even steeper than the first and the sun was gaining in intensity. They didn't talk. She needed to focus all her energy into putting one foot in front of the other and staying upright.

'Romy, let's stop here for some water,' Joseph shouted from behind her halfway up the hill but she pretended she hadn't heard. She trudged on, afraid that if she stopped she wouldn't start again and he would see how broken she really was. She had to make it to the top. Had to prove that this fucking disease was not going to get her. She could see the brow of the hill but her vision was wavy. Spots of light littered the path ahead. She was barely lifting her feet off the ground, just shuffling forward. The dust of the track was collecting in heaps at the fronts of her sliders. She could hear Joseph panting behind her; he was out of breath too, and that was strangely comforting. Sweat trailed down between her shoulder blades. The suntan lotion on her face had melted and seeped into her eyes, making them sting and even more blurry. She took off her sunglasses and rubbed her face with the t-shirt she had taken off halfway up the hill, but she didn't stop. All the while her feet kept moving forward and the muscles in her thighs screamed in agony.

And then they reached the top and the sea on the other side of the island glistened. They could see Siquijor, a tiny shadow of rock in the distance. She shut her eyes and a cool breeze kissed her clammy brow.

'We made it.' Joseph was at her side. He put his arm around her shoulders and she flinched, embarrassed at the sweat, the smell that now oozed from her. But he didn't let go. He squeezed her arm and leant in closer and then she relaxed into him. She laid her head on his shoulder and for the third time that day she fought back tears.

They sat down in silence, catching their breath. Both lost in their separate worlds of thought. It was Joseph who eventually broke it.

'I can't pretend it didn't happen, Romy.'

'Shh, don't, Joseph.'

'I cannot un-hear what you said to me that day.'

She closed her eyes in exhaustion and willed him to stop. 'I was young, grieving. I didn't mean it,' she whispered, her voice weary.

'But you did.'

'I don't know, maybe I did.'

'It should have been me.'

'Says who?' She turned to him suddenly and could feel the fire burning in her stinging eyes. 'No one gets to say who dies and who stays alive, Joseph. We are all at the mercy of something out there that's bigger than us.'

'But it was me, I gave it to him.'

'Sure, you got it first, but you were young and fucking around. And I really cannot judge you for that.' She laughed and sighed at the irony. 'You would have thought I might have learned a lesson, but I went and did exactly what you did. I just knew to use a condom!'

Neither of them spoke for a while, just sat there with their arms resting on their knees, looking out at the sea. It struck Romy that there was a whole world beneath it, a world that they had just visited, and yet still from up here it was hard to fathom.

'I was always the strong one,' Joseph said quietly next to her. 'I guess we should have known that it would get him first.'

'Look, Joseph.' She turned to him and placed her hand on his arm. It was salty from the sea. She squeezed it. 'You can't blame yourself for being strong. And you can't blame yourself for still being alive. Sure it got him first, and it is so unfair that it got him just before the drugs came in. But none of us could have predicted any of this. And I am sorry, I shouldn't have said that it was your fault, I was just so angry. I was angry with the world, for everything. And I thought I would lose both of you. I was so scared of that, I pushed you away. I couldn't go through that again, and it was easier to leave than watch you die too.'

'Oh Romy, I thought I would never see you again. All this time, I know I should have been the one to reach out. I was the adult, you were the child. But every time I tried to pick up the phone I thought of that day, of the fire raging in your eyes. Of you telling me that you wished I had been the one to die, and... and... I just couldn't do it.'

She turned to him and threw herself into his arms. They both cried, and their bodies shook and they clung to each other and absorbed each other's grief and relief on the top of the hill – their beloved island in the distance.

CHAPTER ELEVEN

FLORA

It was no surprise to Flora that her mother was not the easiest patient. On the first morning after she got home from the hospital Lizzie asked Flora to fetch the brass bell which hung next to the fire in the dining room. It had been used by Mrs Jenkins back in the day to call them all in for meals. Even as a child the shrill tones of the bell had made Flora's skin crawl, but she had spent the morning running to her mother's holler and stupidly thought that the bell might be preferable.

She was wrong: the bell made her insides jolt and then curdle with its inflection. Barely ten minutes would pass without its chime. Lizzie wanted tea, or toast, or a scented candle, or a maga-zine, or her face cream. Flora managed to delegate to Olive for a while who was a big fan of Cinderella and enjoyed playing the part of the beleaguered stepdaughter. However, she quickly tired of the fetching and carrying and the ungrateful demands of her grand-mother, and Flora couldn't blame her. Lizzie felt unduly wronged, and rather than thank those around her for their help she snapped at them. It took all of Flora's self-restraint and long deep calming breaths outside the bedroom door not to snap back.

The kids were bored and going stir-crazy cooped up in the house where they weren't allowed to touch anything, or jump on the sofa, or eat anywhere other than in the kitchen. After lunch on the first day Flora had told her mother that she was taking them out for a walk, and that she'd be gone an hour at most, and Lizzie spiralled into an irrational state of panic.

'But what if I need you? Or someone comes to the door? Or I need to go for a pee?'

'Mum, it's just an hour, all of those things can wait. You don't need to answer the door and I'll take you to the bathroom now before I leave.' This in itself was an ordeal; Lizzie had refused to try the crutches again after the first day and so Flora practically carried her into the bathroom across the hall. Thankfully her mother had too much pride and self-respect to let her daughter pull down her pants or, god forbid, wipe her bum. Flora hovered outside the door and listened to her panting and exasperating efforts to do it herself and then carried her back again. They were both exhausted by the experience and so when the bell jangled repeatedly asking for tea or water, coffee or gin Flora didn't always comply. She did worry about dehydration for a fleeting moment until the bell rang again and she decided it was worth it. Dr O'Brien had said she wasn't to drink alcohol on the painkillers, and Flora chose not to mention the fact that Lizzie had spent the best part of her life mixing alcohol with sedatives. And so she agreed with her mother on that first night to two gins a day, and not before six, by which time they were both in dire need.

Flora tried to get the children to engage with Lizzie. She took Boggle into her room and they all clambered onto her bed to play. But Lizzie, whose brain had always been too big for her head, got frustrated with Toby and Olive's two-letter words and feigned exhaustion after only two rounds. Flora then suggested that Lizzie read to the children and found some of her old beloved books in the attic. But Olive wanted to 'snuggle up' and get into the bed with Lizzie, and in so doing she kicked the bad leg and was promptly banished. Flora had to read the story instead, with Olive on her lap in the chair by the window and Toby perching, terrified, on the edge of his grandmother's bed. Within minutes Lizzie was snoring and Flora couldn't help resenting her for not making more of an effort to engage with her grandchildren.

Flora had no one to discuss any of these frustrations with. She would ordinarily have ranted at Jake, and he wouldn't offer much in the way of advice or even sympathy but he would at least grunt and raise his eyebrows in the right places. But she had barely spoken to him since she'd arrived. He called once but it was during that witching hour of seven till eight while she was trying to bath the kids and prepare supper for Lizzie, who was demanding peanuts with her gin and tonic. She had been short with him, exasperated by his monosyllabic tone. She tried to call him back later that evening after the kids were in bed but he hadn't answered, and so she had spent the night imagining him in the arms of Jodie and hadn't called again.

Exasperated by all the running around, on the third day she convinced Lizzie to have another go at the crutches. Toby was on hand to help and between them they carried Lizzie into the hallway where Olive was waiting with the poles. She tentatively placed them under her grandmother's arms and it made Flora's heart squeeze with love watching her daughter take so much care not to hit the bad leg.

'You've got to lean onto them, Mum, with more confidence. They will take your weight.' But her whole body was stiff and as she leant forward to take a step Flora could feel the muscles in her mother's arms quivering.

'That's it, now take a step with the good leg and pull yourself forward with your arms.'

'I can't bloody do it,' she said, and threw one of the crutches across the floor and promptly collapsed onto Toby, who couldn't carry her weight and started to topple himself. Flora rushed in to help and saved them both before they careered into the sideboard and some ornamental vase worth thousands. 'It's OK, Mum, that was an improvement on last time. You'll get it eventually.'

'Don't patronise me, Flora,' Lizzie replied and Flora took a deep breath and closed her eyes for a minute, calling on those calming gods. With as much conciliatory cheer as she could muster, she said, 'OK, well, that's enough for today. Shall we get you back to bed now?'

Dr O'Brien, Doug, called shortly after the crutches incident. He had called every day. Flora was pretty sure that this was above and beyond the call of duty for an orthopaedic surgeon after his patient had been discharged, but she welcomed their conversations and the momentary relief from the monotony of her daily tasks.

'How are you doing?' he asked.

'Aren't you meant to ask how the patient is doing?' Flora replied.

'Yes, but the sigh that you answered the phone with sounded pretty weary.'

'Yeah, well, she's not exactly the easiest patient, as I'm sure you gathered in hospital.'

He laughed. 'Has she managed to get onto the crutches yet?'

'Not really, well, two steps just now. It nearly killed us all.'

'I need to come and do a check-up on her.'

'Oh really? I thought a nurse was coming to do that tomorrow.'

'I told her I would come. That I'd like to see her for myself.' His words tumbled out in an awkward hurry.

'OK, what time are you coming?'

'About elevenish.'

'Great, we'll see you then.'

Flora felt as though a whole day had passed by eleven o'clock the following morning. She had been up with Olive since five. And Lizzie had summoned her with the bell at eight, which was at least an hour and a half earlier than any other morning. She had decided to actually get dressed when she heard that Doug was coming. She was propped up in bed in a pink cashmere jumper and some bright red lipstick. Her lily of the valley perfume caught at the back of Flora's throat as she showed Doug into the bedroom. She left them to it, but could hear her mother's flirtatious chuckling from the kitchen and it made her cringe with shame. He came out half an hour later looking somewhat flushed.

'Your mother has agreed to give the crutches another go while I am here to help.'

'I bet she has.' Flora smirked, and Doug's cheeks glowed an even darker red.

'She asked if you could go and help her get out of bed, she won't let me...'

'Of course.' Flora laughed and left him fiddling with the notepad on the work surface.

'He really is very handsome, Flora,' Lizzie said as Flora levered the leg in a cast over the side of the bed.

'What on earth did you say to him? He looks as if he's been eaten alive.'

'Oh, don't be ridiculous. I just asked him whether he was married, and you will be pleased to hear he is recently divorced.'

'Why would I be pleased to hear that?' she asked as she pulled her mother's arm up over her shoulder.

'Well, after what you told me about Jake the other day.'

'I have a husband, thank you, and I am not on the prowl for another.'

'I'm not talking about marrying him, Flora, just a little dalliance. It would lighten you up a bit.'

'Oh Mum, for god's sake!'

'Has Jake even called you since you've been here? Aren't you worried that he's with that other woman?'

'Yes, I have spoken to him. And no, I'm not worried, well, maybe a little bit. Come on, up you get.' She pulled her up to standing.

'I'm just saying that it might do you good.'

'And I'm just saying don't, I'm fine and I definitely don't need you trying to set me up.'

'Everything OK?' she heard Doug call from the hallway.

'Fine,' Flora called back. 'We're just coming.' Lizzie leant on Flora and hopped over towards the door where the crutches were propped up against the wall.

'Great, Mrs Harris, nice to see you up and about. So, are you ready to give these crutches another go?' He placed them underneath each arm. 'Right, so, take a step with the other leg, that's right, and then lean into the crutches, yes, and then pull yourself forward.' And Lizzie did as she was told: she leant into the crutches with a determination and confidence that Flora had not seen before, and she did it! She took a step and then another, and another. And then Flora let go and Lizzie did a lap of the hallway. She smiled, for the first time in so long that Flora could actually see her mother's teeth. Her cloudy eyes sparkled and her still-beautiful face lit up.

'I did it!' she exclaimed. And she whooped! The children rushed out of the sitting room where they were watching TV to see what all the fuss was about and they danced around Lizzie and she took another turn of the hall and then into the kitchen, and she didn't even comment on the breakfast things still being on the table.

'Maybe I'll have lunch in here today!' she said.

'That's a great idea, Mum, I've got salmon.'

The children groaned and Flora shot them a look and they shut up promptly. 'My favourite!' Lizzie exclaimed.

'I know,' said Flora.

'You must stay, Doctor.'

'Oh no, I, er...'

'I'm sure he's got to get back to work, Mum, this isn't a social visit.'

'No, actually, it's my day off,' he said a little meekly.

'Perfect, then you must stay. Have you got enough salmon, Flora?'

'Er, yes, of course. I'll just rustle up a salad or something.'

'Well, if you're sure you've got enough.'

'Of course we have,' said Lizzie. 'Now Toby, pull that chair away from the table, would you, I think I need to sit down.' They all rushed to her assistance, and Doug pulled up another chair for her to rest the bad leg on. Olive brought her cushions and Toby took her a glass of water.

Lizzie grilled poor Doug over lunch. 'And what made you choose orthopaedics rather than, I don't know, neuro or paediatrics or...'

'Mum watches a lot of *ER*,' Flora said while passing him the salad.

'I'll have you know I had a place at Manchester to study medicine,' Lizzie said tartly to her daughter.

'Did you?' Flora was surprised. She had never heard this before, and struggled to keep the disbelief out of her voice.

'I did, one of my biggest regrets is that I didn't take it up.'

'Why didn't you? If you don't mind me asking,' Doug said.

'Life got in the way,' she said, and no one dared question her further.

'You were always a big brain at school, Flora. What did you study?'

'English literature at Newcastle.'

'Yes, I remember you always had your head in a book. Do you work now?'

'She's a full-time housewife,' Lizzie answered for her.

'No, I, er, worked in publishing for a while but then I left London and had the kids and, well you know, life happened.'

'She lives on a farm in the middle of nowhere. There's ice on the inside of their windows,' Lizzie said, and Flora found herself gripping onto the seam of her jeans under the table.

'We have sheep and goats and pigs and a dog called Tess,' Olive piped up, her face smeared with tomato ketchup.

'That sounds great, I love animals. Sometimes I wish I'd become a vet. Animals are probably easier patients. No offence,' he said to Lizzie.

'None taken,' she said, popping a bit of salmon into her mouth. But Flora could tell she was wounded and couldn't help enjoying a little moment of triumph. Maybe she was overthinking it, but she could have sworn he said that in retaliation to Lizzie's icy windows barb.

'And do you have any children?' Lizzie pressed on with her enquiries.

'I do, a little boy called Harry. He lives with his mum most of the time but I have him every other weekend.'

'Why don't you live with Harry's mum?' Olive asked.

'Olive,' Flora scolded, and then to Doug, 'Sorry.'

He laughed. 'Don't worry. Well, Olive, Harry's mummy and I don't live with each other any more, because Harry's mummy lives with a new daddy. So, Harry is very lucky, he has two daddies now.'

'What?' Olive exclaimed. 'I would not like that – a new daddy or mummy, I mean. I like the ones I've got.' Flora could sense Lizzie shooting her a knowing glance and was determined not to look at her. She felt heat prickling up the back of her neck and fizzing around her head.

'I'm sure you do,' Doug said with a little too much sincerity.

'Right, Olive, Toby, do you want to go and get an ice cream for pudding?' Flora said, standing up to clear the plates.

'Yes! Ice cream!' Olive punched the air.

'But she hasn't eaten her salmon, Flora,' Lizzie reprimanded.

'I hate salmon.' Olive stamped her foot.

'And that is very rude, young lady, when your mother has cooked you lunch. She can't just be given ice cream if she hasn't eaten her main course, Flora, she'll never learn.'

Flora felt her cheeks flush as though she was the child being told off. 'It's just this once, Mum.'

'It's not giving her the right messages, Flora. You'll regret it later, you'll see.'

Olive picked up her plate and with triumph tipped the untouched salmon into the bin.

'I think I need to go and have a rest,' Lizzie said with a sour look on her face, and both Flora and Doug jumped to her assistance. She let Doug accompany her back to her room on her crutches and when he returned, she couldn't quite look him in the eye.

'Sorry about the grilling. You might not have agreed to stay for lunch if you knew what you were letting yourself in for.'

'Don't be silly, it was nice.' He picked up the dirty plates from the table and carried them over to the dishwasher. 'I miss the dynamics of family meals. It's pretty quiet in my house. Even when I have Harry, it's just the two of us.'

'I'm sorry about your wife. Has it been long?'

'Just last year, actually.'

'I take it that it wasn't your idea to split?'

'Not exactly, no. She left me for another guy, an ex-boyfriend, in fact. Think she'd always been in love with him, to be honest. Only settled for me because he shacked up with some Brazilian babe he met while travelling.'

Flora shivered at the uncanny symmetry to her own situation. 'I'm sorry, it must be hard.'

He shrugged. 'Yeah, well, I was pretty broken up for a while, but feeling a lot better now. What about you?'

'What about me?' She deflected his question unconvincingly and took a sip of tea.

'Where did you meet your farmer husband?'

'At university.'

'Really? And you knew that he was going to be the father of your children when you were what, nineteen, twenty?'

'I wouldn't say that. We split up for a while after uni when I went to London and he went to become a farmer in Dorset.'

'But love prevailed?' She didn't answer, just shrugged and put the final plate in the dishwasher. 'I've got Harry this weekend. We were thinking of doing a day trip to the zoo. Would you like to join us?'

'I don't think I could leave Mum for that long.'

'She'll be fine, Flora, she's up and about now. You can leave her some lunch. I insist, doctor's orders. It will be good for both patient and carer to have some space.'

'Carer! God, is that what I am? I always hated that word.'

He smiled. 'That's settled, then. I can pick you and the kids up at ten on Sunday.'

For the next couple of days Lizzie was up and about and making more of an effort with the children. She still snapped at Flora but had the humility to apologise once in a while. And at the end of the week the sun peeked through the blanket of cloud that had been smothering them for months. And whilst the air was still bitterly cold, this glimpse of sunshine brought a hint of spring and hope with it. And so, Flora decided they could have the hamburgers she had bought as a treat, outside for lunch. The children were beside themselves with excitement when Lizzie hobbled out to join them and whilst she pretended to disapprove of the burgers, Flora saw her close her eyes in a brief moment of sheer pleasure as she bit into her brioche bun and the mayonnaise dribbled down her chin. Flora was just clearing the plates off the table when a male voice called from inside the house.

'Hello!' Her stomach lurched as she imagined Doug making his way along the corridor. She looked down at the tracksuit bottoms she had thrown on first thing that morning and ran her fingers through her dirty hair and grimaced. But it wasn't Doug that stepped out onto the terrace, it was Billy!

'Well, this doesn't look too shabby,' he said. His freckled face was ruddy and beaming with a wide smile.

'Billy!' her mother shrieked with glee, and he walked over to her and planted a kiss on the top of her head.

'Hi, Mum.'

'What a wonderful surprise, darling, I thought you were flat out at work?'

'I was.' He walked back round the table towards Flora, who was so pathetically pleased to see him she thought she might cry. 'Hey, sis.' He put his strong arms around her and she hugged him tight. He smelt of slightly rotting cut grass and body odour, but she buried her head into his hoodie and whispered into his neck, 'I am so glad to see you.'

'Uncle Billy!' Olive was pulling on his trousers and Billy untangled himself from Flora and grabbed her, throwing her upside down and tickling her under the arms. Olive shrieked and giggled while begging him to stop. Toby watched, a shy smile across his face. Flora could tell that he longed to join in but didn't dare.

'Hey, buddy,' Billy said to Toby and ruffled his hair. Olive was wrapped around his legs, making it difficult for him to walk.

Billy collapsed into the chair next to Lizzie around the table. 'I've missed lunch, then?'

'Yeah, sorry, Billy, if you'd told us you were coming...'

'We had burgers,' Olive brayed.

'What? And you didn't leave any for me?'

'Yeah, I did,' she said and went to retrieve her half-eaten burger from the stack of plates that Flora was picking up again.

'I don't think Billy wants to eat your half-chewed burger, Olive,' Lizzie said with scorn.

'Oh yeah he does,' Billy said, accepting it from Olive and putting the whole thing in his mouth at once.

'Oh honestly, how disgusting.' Lizzie looked away in revulsion as the ketchup oozed out of the corners of his mouth. Billy had always enjoyed winding his mother up, and while she pretended to be horrified, she loved him more than any of her other children and never made the slightest attempt to hide or deny it.

'So, Mum, it's great to see you up and about. How is the old leg?'

'Yes, well, it has been very painful, and now the cast is terribly itchy.'

'But she's much better than she was, aren't you, Mum?' Flora said.

'I guess so, yes.'

'That's great to hear. I'll go back to London then.'

'No!' Flora and Lizzie both shouted at once and Billy laughed and picked at the cold chips on top of the pile of plates.

'Shall I make you a sandwich, Billy?' Flora asked.

'That would be great, sis, I'm starving.'

'You're always starving, Uncle Billy,' said Olive, climbing onto this lap and giggling as he tickled her ribs.

'That's true, Olive,' he said.

Flora retreated into the kitchen with the plates. She could hear Lizzie asking Billy how he had managed to get away. 'Have you come to your senses after all and decided to get a proper job?'

'Afraid not, Mum, still gardening. I just worked really hard this week and got the job done early so that I could come and see my invalid mother.'

'I am not an invalid, Billy.'

'Course not. You'll be back on your feet in no time.'

After their second lunch when the kids insisted on having sandwiches with Uncle Billy, they left Lizzie at home in front of *ER* and went for a long walk across the fields. Olive didn't whine nearly as much as she had on previous walks that week with Billy there to distract her. It was bitterly cold as they walked along the river that meandered through the fields and into the next village. The sun was losing the battle to shine through the hazy mist that gathered on the surface of the frozen water. Billy and the children threw stones and sticks at it trying to crack the ice. As the dusk crept in, the sky burned a bitter orange and its reflection glowed on the steaming surface of the river. There was something magical and other-worldly about it.

Olive was holding onto a tree on the bank and kicking at the ice at the edge of the river with her boots. 'Olive, please don't do that, it will be so cold if you fall in there and we are really far away from home and any dry clothes,' Flora said.

'She'll be fine, Flora,' Billy said, also stamping on the ice, sending cracks cross the width of the river.

'You can be the one to jump in and rescue her then.'

'OK.' Billy jumped back onto the bank and picked up a stone

and skimmed it across the ice. 'So, how's life on the farm?' he asked.

'Cold and wet, and there is no sushi for a hundred miles and I don't have a job, and...'

'It can't be that bad.'

'It is, actually. Worse, in fact. I think Jake is having an affair.'

'What?' Billy stopped throwing stones and looked up at her in horror. 'Surely not, Jake wouldn't do that. He adores you.'

'Apparently not.' She kicked at the ice at the edge of the river and found it strangely satisfying, the way it creaked under her foot and the crack splintered off into tiny branches. 'Apparently he adores Jodie more.'

'Jodie? The one with the hairy armpits?'

'That's the one.' She dug her heel into the ice again.

'No way, I don't believe it.'

'I saw them, Billy.'

'What, shagging?'

'No, hugging, and she was holding onto him really tight and I could see this look of longing in her eyes. I couldn't see his eyes, but I'm sure they were the same.'

'Have you asked him about it?'

'No.' She looked up at him and he crinkled his brow in perplexity, much like Lisa had. 'I know, I know, I just... well, I was going to and then this happened with Mum and I couldn't face it and I came here. And now I keep imagining them together. She's a vet, you know. They grew up together and they're like two peas in a bloody pod. They're probably discussing a prolapsed uterus while lying in each other's arms right now.'

'Shit, sis, I'm sorry. You've got to ask him about it, though. I mean, you might have got the wrong end of the stick.'

'I don't think so. Mum says I deserve it, of course.'

'Seriously?' He laughed and threw another stone. 'That's Mum for you! How has she been?'

'Demanding. She rang her bell at me for the first four days, it was unbearable.'

'Not the one Mrs Jenkins used to ring?'

'Yes!'

'Oh god, that bloody bell. We never used to come when she rang it. More often than not we would just run further away.'

Flora laughed. 'Poor Mrs Jenkins!'

'There was nothing poor about Mrs Jenkins. She was a battleaxe.'

'She was nice to me.'

'That's 'cos you would spend hours baking with her in the kitchen.'

'Yeah, maybe. Actually, I've made a Victoria sponge for tea, shall we head back?'

'Sure. Come on, kids, Mum's made cake. I'll race you back to the house.' He ran towards Toby, who started sprinting, but Olive stamped her foot and remained rooted to the spot in defiance. Billy scooped her up onto his shoulders and ran after Toby with Olive squealing as she bounced up and down. The hazy sun was setting now, and the pink glow of the sky lit up the children's flushed faces. And for the first time that week, Flora thought that maybe life wasn't so bad after all.

CHAPTER TWELVE
LIZZIE

Neither Lizzie nor Edward spoke of the uncomfortable visit to his house in the week following it. But he didn't come out to hers that Saturday, or the one after that. Said he needed to focus on revision, and the travelling took too much time. She tried to hide her disappointment and went along with his feeble excuses, but she knew something rotten had grown between them. The structure of the school day fell to pieces when the A level exams started, and so Lizzie and Edward stopped even meeting for lunch. She felt the big black hole inside of her that had been slowly closing since the start of their friendship open up again like a raw wound. She had been dumped, and those all too familiar feelings of injustice and self-loathing returned to taunt her. She retreated back inside herself and her parents watched with mindful eyes and tiptoed around her like a porcelain doll that might break at any given moment. Edward had joined the same realm as Isabelle, names that no one dared mention in the Claybourne household. To them he was just another passing phase, a toy they played with for a while and were happy to forget in the bottom of the box when a newer, shinier version came along. But Lizzie couldn't just forget him and move on.

One day she bumped into Edward in the corridor. He was

coming out of an English exam as she was heading to the library. She saw him before he saw her and he looked flushed in the face, his eyes sparkling behind his glasses. He was talking to another boy as they walked towards her. His gestures were animated, and he talked hard and fast. This was the Edward she remembered.

'Oh, hi, Lizzie.' He practically bumped into her he was so focused on his conversation with a guy with dark hair and a wide mouth. She had seen him around school before and thought he looked interesting in his tatty velvet jacket and flared jeans.

'Edward, hi,' she said. 'Have you just had an exam?'

'Yeah, English.' He tapped his feet on the floor, energy buzzing out of every pore.

'It obviously went well,' she said, smiling up at him.

'It did.' He smiled at the boy, who beamed back at him. 'Really well.'

'Great.'

'I'll see you around,' he said and walked on, just like that. He hadn't even been able to talk to her for more than a few seconds. She watched him over her shoulder as he continued with his animated conversation about an exam question on Keats. He hadn't given her a second thought, let alone another glance.

She threw herself into studying, barely sleeping. She pored over her textbooks and old exam papers into the early hours. She was wired on anticipation and loneliness, but it focused the mind. One evening she was reciting the periodic table to her imaginary class of pupils – Edward and Isabelle both featured, and of course she was directing her focus on Edward when she heard her mother knocking tentatively on the door.

'Are you OK, Lizzie?' she asked as she came in with a bowl of spaghetti bolognese.

'I'm fine, Mum.' She grabbed the bowl and shut the door in her face, ashamed to have been caught in the middle of her role play.

Her exams went well. She had a near miss with a panic attack in her first biology paper when she turned over the page to find a question on molecular structure that was in an unfamiliar format.

The fizzing travelled up her body and into her head and then came the sirens and the screams and she had to press down really hard on her temples to make them go away. But they did, and she recovered and after that she was invincible.

She didn't see Edward again. His exams finished earlier than hers and he left the school without a trace. And then hers finished and the loneliness came back and smothered her like a dark blanket under which she struggled to breathe or see the light of day.

Her dad got her a job fruit-picking at a local farm. It was backbreaking, but she welcomed the distraction. Most of the other workers were Eastern European and barely spoke a word of English. They all slept at a nearby hostel and enjoyed the kinship that comes from sharing a bunk bed and bathroom. So yet again Lizzie found herself on the periphery. She listened to the lilting drone of their conversation and closed her eyes and pretended she was in Hungary working the fields, the sun heavy on her shoulders, rather than on Mr Thompson's farm just two fields over from her own house. Mr Thompson was a sour old man who kicked his farm dogs and probably his wife and daughters who scuttled meekly back and forth from the fields to the barns where they sorted the good fruit from the rotten. Mr Thompson owed her father a few favours after he backed him when the local council called into question the arrival of his huge barns and polytunnels a few years back. And so here was Lizzie, the payment for her dad's kindness. Which she knew wasn't kind; there had obviously been something in it for him, other that his youngest daughter's summer job, that is. But it occupied her mind and she found the stiffness in her shoulders and blisters on her fingers at the end of the day bizarrely satisfying.

It was a ferociously hot day in July and she had been there for three weeks and was walking down the lane towards her driveway when she saw Edward cycling towards her. The sun was so high and so bright that the road between them shimmered and she did a double take. Was he just a hopeful mirage like the ripples of light above the glistening tarmac? She rubbed and blinked the blanks out of her eyes but his face still looked disfigured by the shadows. He came closer, his bike wobbling under his weight and then she saw that the shadow across his face was in fact something darker. His eye was half shut, swollen and purpling. There was a trickle of dark red blood making its way down his cheek from an open wound at his hairline. The bike wavered and started to fall beneath him. She ran towards him and tried to catch it but she was too late and it was too heavy and they both crumpled to the floor in a tangle of limbs and blood and bike chains.

'What happened?' she asked, stumbling to her feet and pulling the bike off them. He didn't answer, just looked up at her, his swollen eye filling with tears, his chin gathering into white folds of distress. 'Hey, it's OK,' she said, and held onto him tight. 'It's OK.' His body shook and he held onto her, his fingers pinching the mud-crusted skin on her arms. He opened his mouth to say something but nothing came out. His lips wobbled under the pressure of the unspoken words. And then he pulled himself together, took off his glasses and wiped his face with his sleeve. He was the only person she knew who would still wear a long-sleeved shirt in this insuffer-able heat. He disentangled himself from her and tried to pick his bike up.

'Here, let me get the bike,' she said, pulling it up from the grass verge.

'Thanks,' he said, dusting down his shirt and trousers. 'Can I stay here for a while?'

'Of course.' They started to walk in the direction of the house, Lizzie pushing the bike and Edward limping awkwardly next to her. They rounded the corner and the shade from the trees at the side of the road were a welcome relief from the sun on their heads, the light in their eyes. 'You could come and pick strawberries with me for the creepy Mr Thompson,' she said quietly.

The corners of his mouth lifted almost into a smile. 'That sounds fun.'

'It's not fun, it's hot and hard work. But you do get to eat a few when no one is looking, and they are the most delicious strawberries I have ever eaten. Probably just 'cos I know how much hard graft went into picking them, but...' She turned to him and noticed the pool of blood that was gathering at his neck and turning his collar a deeper and darker red.

'They give me a rash.'

'What?'

'Strawberries.'

'Oh, right. Well, there are raspberries too, and gooseberries.'

He shrugged, the effort of keeping his body upright and moving forward seeming to be all that he could deal with. She shut up and they walked the rest of the journey in silence, and she tried to keep the smile that was filling her with a warm light, from creeping onto her face.

No one was at home when they arrived, and so Lizzie managed to clean him up and put some Steri-Strips on the gash on his head, which looked less alarming once she had wiped the crusted blood away.

'You'll make a great doctor, you know,' he said quietly.

'If I get the grades.'

'You will.'

She smiled and then looked down at him, catching his eyes briefly before he looked away. 'Edward,' she started.

'Don't, Lizzie.'

'But these are quite bad wounds, you should be reporting—'

'No,' he interrupted her sternly.

'But Edward, who did this to you?'

'It doesn't matter, Lizzie.'

'Of course it matters, Edward.'

'I mean it, Lizzie. I am not reporting anything. If you don't feel comfortable with that, I'll go somewhere else. I'm sure John will have me.'

'John?'

'A friend.'

'The guy in the velvet jacket?'

'Yeah.'

'No.' The word came out fast and abrupt. 'You can stay here. I won't ask any more questions. But promise me you won't go back there.'

He didn't answer, but he also didn't question what she meant by 'there' and she had to make do with that. Lizzie showed him into the spare room and went to get him some of Jamie's clothes to wear. But by the time she came back he was sprawled out like a deflated star on the bed, his mouth open, his swollen eyes tight shut. She closed the curtains and left the clean clothes for him on the chair.

Her parents came home before he woke up and she told them not to ask any questions, not to make a fuss, just to make him feel welcome and safe. They exchanged glances of concern which she chose to ignore, but did as she asked. Her mother fussed about Edward when he woke up, making him cups of tea and then giving him a stiff brandy. But she didn't comment on the darkening bruise surrounding his eye, and her father just told him how delighted they were to see him. It had been way too long. He must stay as long as he wanted.

And he did, for the whole glorious summer. He went to work with her at Mr Thompson's farm and together they picked raspberries and gooseberries. It was less back-breaking than the strawberries, and Lizzie was so delighted to have someone to talk to that the days flew by in a hazy blur. Her shoulders turned nut brown and so did Edward's forearms – Jamie's wardrobe didn't include long-sleeved shirts. And after work, they swam in the river and played tennis and took picnics down to the orchard.

Jamie returned from his travels, with long, sun-bleached hair and a tattoo on his tanned bicep. He told them of his adventures, of trekking and leeches and white-water rafting and riding on elephants and smoking opium with hill tribes. And Lizzie watched Edward soaking up these stories with watery-eyed admiration. And Damian returned for a few weeks, and they would all traipse down to the village pub after supper, drink pints and smoke cigarettes in the warm nights, and Lizzie thought she might burst with the happiness of it all.

Bella didn't come home much. She had a boyfriend in London, Tarka, he was called, and Bella was besotted. She did bring him home one weekend but he was like a fish out of water. He talked about the Claybourne's life in the countryside as if they were rugged beasts from a far-off land. Lizzie's mother was quite put out by him; she had been excited by the prospect of her daughter with a titled rogue. But he wasn't interested in her rose garden, and didn't even pretend to like her avocado mousse. And then when he refused to play charades, well, that really made her mind up. He didn't come again, couldn't face the journey, Bella said. They all heaved a sigh of relief.

Tarka's failings only served to highlight Edward's attributes still further in the eyes of her family. Her brothers ridiculed him like he was one of their own. Her mother fussed over him and encouraged him to eat more; she made more puddings and took to serving up chilli con carne at least once a week because he had said it was his favourite food. Even her father welcomed Edward's company; they played chess together most evenings. Apparently her dad had fancied himself as a bit of a chess wizard back in the day but hadn't played for years, till one evening when he heard Edward challenge Jamie to a game. Jamie hadn't a clue how to play chess but her dad stepped in. Edward beat him that first time, but after a week or so he remembered his game and they were more evenly matched.

Two weeks into his stay, Edward left the fruit farm early one afternoon and went back to his house to collect some of his things. Lizzie tried to persuade him not to – he still hadn't told her what had happened that day and she hadn't pressed him, for fear of him leaving. As he disappeared down the drive on his newly mended bike, she worried that he wouldn't come back. But she needn't have. He'd returned within a few hours, laden with books and clothes, which soon littered the floor and walls in the spare room at the end of the corridor. It took on his smell – the musty leather of antique books and Lynx deodorant. Sometimes when he was in the garden with Jamie she would go in there and lie on the bed. She would breathe in his smell and pray that he would never leave.

One weekend Edward convinced them all to put on a play. Bella and Damian were both home for their mother's birthday and the heatwave had given way to relentless rain. All the water that the sky had been holding onto for months was released in torrents. A lake had formed on the front lawn and a couple of ducks were swimming in it. But trapped inside, the Claybournes were at a loss as to how to amuse themselves.

'No way, Edward,' said Damian when he first suggested it.

'We're not five, Eddie, we haven't put on a play at home since nursery school,' said Jamie.

'Oh, come on, it will be fun. And what else are we going to do all weekend? More *Blackadder*? Another game of Monopoly?'

'Yup,' Jamie said while flicking the channels with the remote.

Edward looked at Lizzie hopefully. 'Don't look at me.' She laughed. 'I can't think of anything worse.'

'Bella, come on. It will take your mind off Tarka the Otter and his holiday in the south of France that you weren't invited on.'

She picked up a cushion and threw it at him. 'You really think that's going to get me onside?'

'You could be the leading lady, your name in bright lights. You could wear that sparkly dress you bought for the summer ball.' He had her there. Her eyes flashed with fancy.

'Why? What is the play?'

'Um, not sure, give me a minute.' Edward's eyes darted around the room for inspiration. 'I know – *Pygmalion*!'

'Oh, god,' Damian scoffed.

'What's that?' asked Bella.

'*My Fair Lady*?' Edward said, but she still looked blank.

'For god's sake, Bella, did you ever actually go to school?' Lizzie scorned.

'I'll write a modern-day half-hour version of *My Fair Lady*,' Edward said, standing up on the arm of the sofa. Lizzie recognised that expression. It was the same look of vitality and excitement she'd seen after that exam. They all rolled their eyes at him, but the positivity fizzing from his every pore was infectious and before they knew what was happening, they had all agreed to his hare-brained idea. Their mother was delighted, of course. She wanted to make a birthday celebration of it, and they had to physically restrain her from picking up the phone and inviting all the neighbours. In the end they convinced her to be content with a supper afterwards, outside in the orchard if it had stopped raining. She set to work making pavlovas and coronation chicken.

It did stop raining on the Sunday afternoon, and by the time of the performance in the evening the sun had dried out the lawn and the ducks had flown away. The whole garden dripped and sparkled with renewed vitality. Edward's version of the classic play was brilliantly funny, and Bella was a beautiful if somewhat stiff Eliza Doolittle. Jamie was an overenthusiastic Henry Higgins, and Damian and Lizzie divided up the rest of the cast between them. Edward made a cameo appearance as Eliza's dad, the smooth-talking dustman, and reduced both audience and cast to a giggling hysteria in the middle of the second act. They drank champagne throughout the play and were high on the bubbles and post-performance glow by the time they sat down for supper at a table under the rose arch, where lanterns hung and the scent of citronella mingled with the sweet smell of the roses. They drank more champagne, then wine, then schnapps that Bella had brought from London, and the night melted into a muddle of laughter and joy.

Lizzie looked at Edward on the other side of the table, his face flickering in the mellow light of the candle. Only the faintest hint of a bruise was left now, a darkish circle around his eyes that enhanced the blue of his cornea. He was still wearing the dustman's scarf tied around his neck, sooty smudges on his cheeks. He looked like a pirate from a bygone age. Jamie was telling a story about the night he was caught drinking by his housemaster. How he swore it wasn't booze in the bottle of body wash and how the teacher made him walk in a straight line all the way round the tennis court to prove it. Everyone was laughing, Edward was laughing. Jamie was laughing. Edward was watching Jamie laughing, and then Jamie put his hand on Edward's knee and Edward flinched and Lizzie watched as Edward's laughter became forced as he looked at the hand that remained on his knee. Then it was gone, and Lizzie watched Edward looking at the place where Jamie's hand had been and placing his own hand there and holding onto his trousers as if he might fall off the chair.

Her parents went to bed, and they smoked a spliff and giggled some more. Then Bella and Damian went to bed and they had another spliff and stared into the starry sky. Jamie went inside and Lizzie watched as Edward's eyes followed him stumbling all the way down the path and into the house.

'Think I'll head to bed too,' he said, his hands heavy on the table as he pushed himself up.

'Wait, Eddie.'

'What?' He was standing now, wobbling slightly on his feet.

'Stay for another schnapps.' Without waiting for an answer, she filled both of their glasses. The syrupy liquid spilled over the top and she laughed.

'No, Lizzie, I don't think I want any more of that.'

'Oh, come on, I don't want this night to end. Nor do you, I can tell.' He hovered, swaying back and forth on his feet, towards the house then back to her, forward and back, forward and back.

'I think I've had enough.' He looked up at the window in the attic which had just filled with light. 'I'm going to head in, sorry.'

'OK, night then,' she said with a smile, trying to hide the disappointment that pulled at her heart.

'Yeah, night,' he said, already halfway down the path, his strides fast and purposeful. 'Don't do all the clearing up, will you? We'll do it together in the morning.' And without waiting for her to reply he entered the house.

Lizzie slumped back into the chair and ran her finger round the top of the glass of schnapps and licked it. The light was still on in Jamie's bedroom, and she thought she could see shadows moving behind the closed curtain. She stood up and busied herself with clearing the table loudly and cursing her family for leaving it all to her. She had done three trips into the kitchen and back and was just stacking the last of the glasses at the table outside, when Eddie walked back down the path. Gone was the purposeful stride. He kicked at the loose stones with his hands in his pockets.

'Thought you'd gone to bed,' she said as he approached the table.

'I did, and then I could hear you clearing up all this on your own and...' He ran his fingers through his hair over and over again and his eyes darted back to the house, back up at the window in the roof that was now dark. He lunged for one of the glasses of schnapps still there on the table. 'Maybe another schnapps is not such a bad idea after all,' he said, and held the other one out to her.

'You said you'd had enough.'

'Yeah, well, you're right, it is such a beautiful night, and... Let's go and sit on the swing bench over there.' She took the other glass of schnapps and he picked up the bottle. She sat down on the bench carefully so as not to spill the schnapps but he landed with a thud next to her and spilled both glasses.

'Oops, sorry,' he said, and she laughed.

'It's OK. Cheers!' She clinked his glass and watched as he knocked it back. He closed his eyes and scrunched up his face and then she drank hers and the warm sticky liquid burned its way down her throat. He picked up the bottle and poured another shot into his own glass and then went to pour one into hers.

'No, I don't think I want another... oh, OK!' she said as he ignored her and the schnapps spilled over the top of the glass. He downed his and winced again, then leant back and shut his eyes.

The silence lingered in the air like a bad smell until she felt compelled to fill it. 'I still can't believe you convinced Damian to dress up in those breeches!'

'Yeah.' He shrugged, his eyes still closed.

'And that toe-curlingly awful cockney accent.'

'At least he tried.'

'At least *I* didn't humiliate myself with my efforts. Or did I?'

'How could you when there was so little effort made?' His words were quiet and slightly slurred, his face tilted up towards the stars.

'What?' She turned to look at him with feigned indignation. He opened his eyes and forced a conciliatory smile.

'I guess you made an effort in your own way,' he said.

'Well, you know me, not big on performance.' She sipped at her glass and he picked up the bottle.

'Not really,' he said and took a swig.

'What's that supposed to mean?'

'It means there is still so much I don't know about you.'

'It's not like you're an open book either.'

'Fair enough,' he said, and had another swig. 'I've got an idea.' He turned to face her, suddenly animated. 'How about we both get to ask one thing about each other that we don't already know?' Lizzie felt the weight inside, pulling down. And a sharpness, bringing her thoughts back into focus.

'I don't know, Eddie.'

'Come on, there must be things you want to know about me.' His eyes were wide and he touched her arm with his fingers, sticky from the schnapps.

'Yeah.'

'So, ask away.'

'I don't know, I—'

'Oh, come on, Liz...' She didn't answer. 'OK, if you don't want to ask me, I've got one for you. What happened with Isabelle?' And there it was. The knot inside of her pulled tight and she edged away from him on the bench.

'You already know, I saw Jamie telling you out of the window that day.'

'He didn't tell me very much, just that she had died and you were so upset you had to leave.'

'And that's all there is to it.'

'I don't believe you.'

'What?'

'Did something happen, were you involved in some way?'

'What is this, a police interview?' She tried to laugh it off, but it wasn't funny.

'It's just, well...' His tone changed then, became softer, and he took her hand and clasped it between his sticky fingers. And he looked at her with an intensity that was both unnerving and endearing at the same time. 'Sometimes you just get this look in your eye, and you go somewhere and I can't reach you, and I just... I want to help, Lizzie. You have helped me so much...' It was the nicest thing he had ever said to her and she smiled a tight smile, her lips curling over the top of her teeth. She kicked the ground and the seat began to sway. It made her stomach lurch, but it helped to move.

'She was one of the cool girls,' she began quietly. 'Part of the gang that had always ignored me. The ones who sneaked out for fags in the middle of the night and met up with boys and generally looked like they were having a really fun time. Except Isabelle wasn't. I found her throwing up in the loo one afternoon. She didn't know I was there, and she left the door open and stuck her fingers down her throat and made herself sick. When she had finished she saw me. She got really upset and begged me not to tell anyone. And... well, it felt nice, to be taken into someone's confidence. Especially a cool girl like Isabelle, and to realise she wasn't as perfect as she seemed. The next day I wrote her a note, told her I understood how she felt. Not that I ever threw up or anything, but I told her I knew what it felt like to be scared, and if she ever needed someone to talk to. And she came to my room that evening, and told me about the dark places that she went to in her mind, and I told her that I had been there too. It felt good to talk, to know that there was someone else in the world who felt the same. For two whole terms we did everything together. I was never really accepted by the rest of the gang, but they tolerated me on Isabelle's insistence and she grew away from them. They didn't understand her like I did. We even became blood sisters – how sad is that? We went down to the woods one night with a packet of cigarettes and a knife and we cut our arms and shared our blood. She told me that night that she wanted to die, and... and...' Lizzie faltered; she was so torn between the truth and the lies at this point of her story that she no longer remembered which was which. 'And... well, I didn't take her seriously, and then a week later they found her in the woods with a bottle of vodka and some pills. They took her to hospital but it was too late...' She couldn't continue; her throat swelled and she couldn't quite breathe... the screams, the sirens, the panic started to fizz up her legs.

'Hey, Lizzie, it's OK, it's OK...' He put his arms around her and he held her tight until her heart slowed to a more regular beat. And still she held on. Over his shoulder she could see the nearly full moon and the shadows that crept across its face. He kissed the top of her head and then went to pull away but she held on tight, pulling him closer.

'I guess it's my turn,' he whispered with a chuckle.

'What?' she asked, not daring to move, her head still on his chest. She could hear his heart beating hard and fast against her ear.

'You can ask me a question now.'

And there was one, a question that had flashed into her head like a lightning bolt at supper. The hand on his knee, the dent that it had left in her heart. But she didn't want to know the answer. Didn't want to know if he was even now looking at the house over the top of her head. At the room in the attic with the tiny windows peeking out of the roof like eyes.

'It's OK,' she whispered.

'No, it's only fair, I asked you.'

But she didn't ask; she breathed in his smell and then kissed his neck. And then kissed the flecks of stubble on his jawline. Then she moved her hand down to the top of his trousers and she felt him flinch.

'Lizzie, what are you doing?'

'Maybe you're not who you think you are,' she said and pressed down.

'What?' His voice was incredulous but he didn't move her hand away. He let her slide it over the top of his belt and into his trousers. He squirmed under her touch but still he didn't pull away, didn't remove her hand. She kissed his neck and felt him harden in her hand. She watched as his eyes glazed over and he held onto the side of the seat, gripped it with both hands until his knuckles whitened. And then he was on top of her, pulling her off the bench, scraping and splintering her back as he dragged her onto the ground. He covered her mouth, her nose, her eyes with angry kisses. He was pulling up her dress and pinching her nipples, his body hard and angular. His glasses, hips, ribs, belt buckle and elbows all jutting into her, bruising her with their urgency. Then he was inside her. He was thrusting and his glasses were crooked and steamy. She dug her nails into his back as he tore her apart with every plunge. Desperate, hard thrusts. Further and higher and harder and faster. And then he shuddered and collapsed on top of her, his breathing heavy in her ear. She held onto his back. She held him as he shook and cried and told her he was sorry. And his tears fell into her hair and onto her cheeks, finding and mixing with the tears that spilled from her own eyes.

CHAPTER THIRTEEN

ROMY

The walk back down the hill from Cogon was easier on the heart and lungs but hard on the knees. Romy and Joseph collapsed at a table at the restaurant on the beach and waited an interminably long time for a plate of dried-up rice and chicken and a deliciously cold bottle of Coke with a straw. After lunch Joseph asked Romy if she wanted to dive again, but she said she was a little tired. She lay on the bench at the front of the boat and slept the entire duration of the journey home.

It was dusk when they arrived back at Sapphire Cove and the guests were gathering for sundowners in the bar, their hair wet and their faces shiny.

'You look like you could do with a cold beer,' Bob called to her as she walked through the restaurant on wobbly legs.

'Just going for a shower,' she called over her shoulder and kept walking, her head down, praying no one else would engage her in conversation.

The walk up the stairs to the house and then the next flight to her bedroom made every muscle in her body scream. Her lungs hurt just trying to draw the air down. She didn't change but collapsed onto the bed. She could see the mosquitoes hovering around the light which hung from the ceiling and could feel the familiar pinch as they sucked at her skin, but she couldn't move. She shut her eyes and willed the pounding in her head, the aching of her body, the relentless bobbing up and down to stop, stop, stop, stop.

It was pitch-black when she woke; her light had been turned off. The mosquito net now covered her bed and the sheet had been pulled over her body, still crispy with sand in her bikini and shorts. Her mouth was sticky and dry and she longed for water, but there was none within reach and no way she could get up to find some. Her head still pounded, squeezing her temples like her brain was swelling and bursting at the seams of her skull. She tried to sit up but an overwhelming rush of nausea pushed her back down. She closed her eyes and tried to fight the fear that was circulating around her body and forcing the air out of her lungs. She moaned, a noise she didn't recognise that seemed to come from somewhere deep inside. Then Joseph was there in the doorway, and then kneeling by her bed, his hand on her clammy brow.

'What is it, Romy?' His eyes were wide with fear. 'Are you sick?'

She couldn't bring herself to say the words but she nodded, a slow, painful nod that made her brain rattle.

'Is it bad?'

'Mm...' she whimpered. Another wave of nausea, crashing over her head, tumbling her over and over in its wash. She couldn't breathe.

'I'm going to get the doctor.' She didn't resist, just pulled her knees up towards her chest and hugged them tight. Joseph disappeared from the room but was back soon – or was he? Time was not time as she knew it. She could hear the waves outside, the tinkling of the boats. The moon had cast a silvery glow over her mosquito net.

'He's coming, Romy,' Joseph said and he climbed under the net and into her bed. He gathered her up in his lap and he stroked her hair and spoke in his calm, soft voice. 'It's going to be OK,' he said and kissed her hair. 'I've got you now. You're OK. I'm here and I'm never leaving you again.'

The rest of the night was a hazy blur of comings and goings. She could remember the doctor, a small man with a moustache and a black bag. She thought she recognised him from before but couldn't be sure. She told him between groans about her condition. Kidney disease, transplant – the words she had been hiding clawed at her throat. All the time she could feel Joseph there beside her, stroking her hair, her back, telling her it was going to be OK. And then he was carrying her out of the house and onto his boat, and she was wrapped in a blanket and they were bouncing over the waves and Joseph was holding her head in his lap as Stefan drove. All the time the moon shone. It was three-quarters full and looked wrong, like someone had sliced off the top corner. There was an ambulance at the dock, and she was carried into it and there were sirens and she had a mask over her face and the bed bumped on the uneven road and shook around the corners. And all the while Joseph was there, holding her hand, and the moon, it was still there in the window, still shining its awkward glare. And then the doors opened and there were bright lights, and corridors and people in scrubs and more people and she was on a trolley and she was moving and still Joseph was there, still he was holding her hand, until he wasn't. She was in a hospital theatre, and a light was shining in her face and there were machines beeping and needles in her hand, electrodes on her chest. She still wore her bikini, could still feel the sand crunching on her limbs. Doctors and nurses in surgical masks were asking her questions but she couldn't answer, she was too tired. She just wanted to sleep.

CHAPTER FOURTEEN

FLORA

With Billy in the house Lizzie was tempted from her bed more and more. He brought with him a sparkle that was infectious. On his second evening they all played charades. Even Lizzie took part, acting out *The Hunchback of Notre Dame* from her position of state on the sofa, her leg suspended on a pile of cushions. She had definitely had more than two gins but was all the more charming for it, so Flora didn't challenge her. Besides, Billy was there to carry her to bed.

The bonhomie of the evening took a downturn, however, when Olive, high on Ribena and wired with exhaustion and excitement, had one of her meltdowns when Flora told her it was time for bed. Olive was prone to melodrama, and Flora braced herself for a battle that she knew could take some time. The evening's frivolities fizzled. Toby retreated to the TV in the snug and Billy disappeared to mix more drinks. But Lizzie couldn't escape, and she actually put her hands over her ears while Flora dragged her screaming child out from behind the sofa. She carried her upstairs and left her on the loo while she went to fetch her pyjamas, but when she returned to the bathroom it was empty and she could hear the screams resonating from the sitting room once more. Flora was halfway down the stairs when the holler ceased, abruptly, with a yelp. Flora ran into the room to find Lizzie holding onto the tops of Olive's arms and shaking her violently.

'What is going on?' Flora demanded from the doorway.

'Granny h... hh... it... mm... me,' Olive stammered between sobs and wrestled her way out of her grandmother's grasp and into the arms of her mother.

'What?'

'She was out of control.' Lizzie's lips were pursed together in defiance, her nose in the air.

'You hit her?' A rage bubbled up from somewhere deep inside Flora and made her blood pulse in her ears.

'What's going on?' Billy asked, coming into the room with two gin and tonics.

'Oh, thank god, Billy, I need a drink.' Lizzie held out her arms to take a glass.

'She... she hit Olive,' Flora said, incredulous. Lizzie gulped down half the gin, the ice clinking in the glass.

Flora crouched down to look at Olive, whose whole body was now shaking with sobs. There was a bright red handprint across her cheek. 'Look! There's a mark. You slapped her on the face!'

'She was hysterical.'

'She is not yours to hit.'

'Oh, for god's sake, Flora, stop being so melodramatic.'

'Melodramatic! You slapped my daughter!'

'Look, I think we all need to calm down a bit,' Billy said, hopping from one leg to the other in the chasm between his mother and his sister. 'Flora, why don't you take Olive up to bed?'

'We are not done here,' Flora said while scooping her daughter into her arms and carrying her up the stairs. She lay down with Olive on the bed and held her while she cried herself to sleep. Her little body continued to flinch with leftover sobs after she had succumbed to her dreams. When Flora finally returned downstairs, Lizzie had a full glass again and she and Billy were speaking in hushed tones.

'I will never forgive you for this,' Flora said, striding into the room. 'It's one thing to bully me, but you will never lay a finger on one of my children ever again.'

Lizzie didn't answer. She rolled her eyes in disdain and took another sip of her drink. Her hands weren't shaking any more and Flora had to stop herself from marching over and shaking her herself.

'I know you don't do apologies, Mum, but I really think this is one time you could break the habit of a lifetime.' Lizzie continued to stare ahead.

'Come on, sis, I'm sure she didn't mean it. Olive will be OK. Christ, Mrs Jenkins used to hit me all the time and I'm fine.' Lizzie's head turned in surprise at this.

'*What*?'

'Oh, so it's all right for you to slap my baby, but not Mrs Jenkins and your precious Billy, huh?'

'Oh, Flora, you have always been so emotional.'

'Emotional! Maybe that's because you've always been so fucking *un*emotional, so unloving, so bloody mean to me.'

'Hey, Flora, come on now.' Billy was at her side, putting his arm around her.

'What do you know, Bill?' She turned to him. 'You were always there at the centre of her world while I was stuck out here in the cold.'

'Flora, I know you're upset, and maybe I shouldn't have slapped Olive, but—'

'Maybe! *Maybe*? There is no fucking *maybe* about it, Mum. There is no circumstance in which that would have been an OK thing to do. And you know what, I'm fed up with it. Fed up with being such a mug. All my life I have tiptoed around you, too frightened to challenge you, too afraid of the consequences. Well, I'm done with it. And I don't care what you do.'

She stormed out of the room and up the stairs to her bedroom, her heart thumping in her chest.

'Flora.' Billy came running after her. 'Flora, what the fuck? Flora, wait, what are you doing?' She was grabbing the bag from under her bed, and then she pulled the clothes from the drawers and stuffed them in, took her dressing gown and coat from the back of the door. Billy followed her into the bathroom as she swept the bottles from around the sink into her washbag. 'Flora, calm down. What are you doing?'

'What does it look like, Billy?'

'You can't go anywhere tonight. It's miles back to Dorset, and you've had at least two gin and tonics and two glasses of red wine.'

'I can't stay here, Billy, not after what she's done.'

He grabbed her by the shoulders and looked her in the eye. 'Flora, Flora, please. I know it was bad, and she shouldn't have done it. But just think what this is going to do to her.'

She pulled free from him and pushed past him back into the bedroom. 'That's what I've been doing my whole life, Billy, and I am fed up with it.'

'OK, OK, fine. So don't stay for her, but for your children. Sis, please, you have drunk too much. Just sleep it off and then leave in the morning.' She knew he was right, but she wanted to leave. The rage was still throbbing in her veins and it gave her courage.

'If I don't go now, I don't know if I'll be able to go in the morning.'

'Hey, it's OK.' He put his arms around her and she buried her head in his chest.

'Mummy.' It was Toby at the door in his robot glow-in-the-dark pyjamas. He was holding onto his teddy, McFly, and biting his bottom lip.

'Hey, Tobes, it's OK, darling. Mummy's OK. Come here.' She pulled him onto her lap on the bed and her mind whirred trying to place him in all the drama of the last half hour. He had retreated to the snug when Olive's hysterics had erupted. Maybe he had missed it all.

'Did Granny really smack Olive?' he asked with big worried eyes.

'No, no, it was just a little misunderstanding. You know how Olive gets when she doesn't want to go to bed.'

'But you and Granny were fighting, you said—'

'It's OK, shhh.' She kissed his cheek and pulled him to her chest, kissed the top of his damp curls. 'Don't you worry what Mummy and Granny said. People always say silly things when they get upset, don't they? We're all fine, now let's get you into bed.'

Flora didn't go back downstairs. She finished packing her bags and then she packed the children's. She wanted to call Jake, her finger hovering over the button. But what if he was with Jodie? She sent him a message instead.

We're coming home early. Tomorrow. Had a row with Mum.

His reply was instant.

Are you OK?

Not really.

I love you.

But she didn't reply. Did he love her still? Or was he just conditioned into saying that? And did she love him? She was so confused by the torrent of emotions coursing through her body that she didn't know anything. She looked at her bags piled up against the door. She used to do that as a child, pile chairs and books up against her door when she was upset and then lie in bed longing for someone to push them through and comfort her. But they never did.

She climbed into bed in her clothes and buried her head under the covers. An hour or so later she heard Billy struggling to carry Lizzie to bed. They crashed into the table in the hall and she could hear the expensive vase rattling in its stand. She willed it to crash to the floor. But it didn't and they giggled, like a couple of drunken teenagers.

She left the following morning before her mother had even stirred. She woke Billy to say goodbye and he stumbled out of bed and followed her in his pants out to the car where the kids were already strapped in.

'But Flora, who is going to look after her if you've gone?'

'Don't know, Billy, maybe you can. Or your father, when he gets back from his business trip. Or one of your useless brothers. I've done my bit.'

'But Mummy, Granny can't walk,' Toby said from the back of the car as Flora climbed into the driving seat.

'Yes she can, darling, she's got really good on those crutches now, hasn't she? And Billy will look after her, won't you?'

'I can't, Flora, I've got to be back at work tomorrow.'

'So call Jeremy.' She put the car into reverse.

'Wait, Flora...' He ran after her.

'Sorry, Billy,' she shouted out of the open window. 'Gotta go...' She watched in her rear-view mirror as he kicked the gravel on the driveway. The tops of his skinny thighs were so white. She felt a twinge of regret, but then she looked at Olive in the mirror and the faint redness to her cheek and she put her foot on the accelerator and headed home.

Jake was waiting for them when they finally arrived. He wasn't out at the farm as he would be normally at that time of day. And he had cooked lunch. Roast pork with crackling and apple sauce; he had even made Yorkshire puddings.

'I know they don't go with pork but the kids love them, so I...' She collapsed into his arms and held onto the back of his woolly jumper. She breathed in his familiar musty smell and tried not to think of Jodie. She wiped her eyes on his shoulder and he pulled away at the sound of her sniffs.

'Hey, Flora, was it that bad? What was the argument about?' He wiped a tear away from beneath her eye with his finger which smelt of pork fat. She looked at him, his face bleary through the tears.

'Granny hit me.' Olive was dipping her finger in the bowl of apple sauce on the table as she said it, matter-of-fact, without a hint of emotion.

'What?'

Flora nodded and watched Jake swallow down the rage like a bad dose of heartburn.

'What was she doing?'

'She was refusing to go to bed,' Toby said, still in his coat. He had climbed into Tess's dog bed with her and was cradling her head in his lap.

'Really?' Jake turned to Flora and she nodded, afraid of what would come out if she opened her mouth to speak.

'Jesus, I can't believe this. And you had it out with her? You told her that it was absolutely not acceptable to hit our d- daughter?' His voice cracked.

'I... yeah... I had it out with her. And we left...'

'You just left her on her own?'

'No, Billy is there.'

'Billy? Jeez, poor Billy.'

'Can we eat now? I'm starving. Mummy made us eat salmon at Granny's,' Toby said, still in the dog bed.

'Sure, it's ready now.' Flora watched as Jake gathered up his emotions and placed them tidily somewhere else while he got the pork out of the oven. It sizzled and spat fat at him as he peeled off the layer of golden crackling.

They didn't discuss it again. Over lunch the children told Jake about Billy and their walk along the icy river, and playing Boggle and charades. Flora envied their ability to forget. She looked at their flushed faces and listened to their animated stories and she wondered whether she had ever been that carefree as a child.

After lunch she called Doug while Jake was playing football with the kids in the garden. She had realised halfway down the M4 that he would be arriving to pick them up for the zoo in an hour. Too embarrassed to call and not wanting to hear the disappointment in his voice, she pulled off at the service station and sent him a brief message. She had been really looking forward to their trip to the zoo. Doug was surprisingly good company and so completely different from Jake in so many ways. Despite his learned status of surgeon there was something quite fresh-faced and vulnerable about him, like an excited puppy. And he wore his emotions so close to the surface. With every nervous laugh or embarrassed glance he revealed himself a little more, while after ten years her husband was still an enigma.

'Doug, hi, it's Flora.'

'Flora, what happened? Is everyone OK? I have been so worried about you.'

'Yeah, sorry, we are OK.'

'Did something happen?'

'Just a row with Mum. I had to get out of there.'

'Was it bad? The row?'

'It was pretty bad, yeah. We both said some things that had been brewing for a while.'

'Are you OK?' Flora watched Jake throw Olive onto his shoulders and then chase Toby around the tree, their laughter muffled through the window.

'Yeah, I will be. I'm really sorry about the zoo.'

'Yeah, it's a shame. We were looking forward to it, Harry and me. But maybe another time...'

'I'm not sure I'm going to be coming back any time soon.'

'Oh, right.' She could hear the disappointment in his voice and her shame was tinged with pleasure. 'Well, I guess that's that then...'

'Yeah...'

'Wait, Flora – if you ever need someone to talk to about, well, anything, I'm here...'

'Thanks, Doug,' she said, and a smile pulled at the corners of her mouth as she hung up the phone.

That evening Flora sat in front of the fire with a glass of red wine listening to Jake acting out *The Bear Hunt* upstairs. The children were squealing as he pretended to be the bear and chased them around the room. The ceiling rattled under the weight of his stamping and roaring. He was flushed and still smiling as he came downstairs.

'They missed you,' she said.

'I missed them, and you.' He took a wine glass out of the cupboard and joined her in the other armchair next to the fire. Flora looked into the crackling flames and felt the heat on her face.

'Did you?' she asked.

'Of course I did. What sort of question is that?'

She shut her eyes and took a deep, fortifying breath. 'I know about you and Jodie.'

'What?'

'I saw you, in the barn.'

'Saw what?'

'You and her, holding each other. Jesus, do I have to spell it out? I saw you, Jake.'

He didn't say anything, and something dropped deep inside of her. She realised she had been hoping he might tell her she had imagined it, that she had got the wrong idea all along. 'Say something, Jake, for god's sake.'

'I'm sorry.' And that was it, all semblance of hope smashed into a thousand pieces. She didn't think he had actually done it until now.

'How long?'

'What?'

'How long has it been going on for?'

'It hasn't been going on, exactly, it only actually happened the once.'

'So it did happen? You did sleep together?'

He nodded, unable to say the words, and she felt a weight of darkness pulling her down, down to the bottom of the ocean. Where the light from the sun became dimmer and dimmer until it was just a flicker of something so very far away. He buried his head in his hands and when he looked up at her his eyes were red and pleading.

'Fuck,' he said, shaking his head violently. And then he stood up and paced the room. 'You, you were so miserable. So distant, and cold.'

'Cold? *I* am cold!'

'Yes, Flora, you can be cold too, you know. You just shut down when you're unhappy. I've watched you do it with your mother for years, and then you started doing it to me, too. Blocking me out. And I knew you regretted being here. I knew that you wished you had stayed in London and got a sparkling career in publishing. That you weren't trapped here on the farm.'

'I'm not the one at fault here, Jake.'

'No, no, you're not. But you pushed me away. And Jodie was there. One day after you stormed out of the house and told me how useless I was, she was there. She had come to ask my advice about a patient, a ewe in labour...' Flora laughed at this; she couldn't help herself. It was exactly as she had predicted. She put her hands over her mouth to stifle it but it was too late.

'What? What's so funny?'

'I'm sorry,' she said. 'A fucking ewe, I knew it!'

'What? What did you know?'

'That it would have been sheep, a bloody sheep that brought you together.'

'It wasn't the sheep, Flora.' There was a harsh tone to his voice, to the way he spat the words at her, and it hurt. Her smarting disbelief turned to sadness and the tears came and they poured down her cheeks and rolled off the bottom of her chin. Her nose ran at the same time and all of a sudden she was like a leaking, weeping mess of snot and heartache. Jake picked up the kitchen roll from the work surface and knelt down in front of her and tore off pieces of paper to blot the tears on her face.

'I'm so sorry, Flora.'

She closed her eyes and turned to face the fire, to feel the heat of the flames on her sticky cheeks. 'Do you love her?'

He grabbed her hands between his and turned her face towards him with a finger on her chin. 'I love you.'

'But do you love her?'

'Yes, as a friend, she is my oldest friend. But no, not like that. It was a stupid mistake, and that time you saw us in the barn. That was after it had happened and I had told her that it couldn't happen again, that I didn't love her like that, that I love you.' He pulled her onto his lap on the floor and he wrapped his arms around her and held her tight. She felt safe and she wanted to stay like that forever, but she knew she couldn't. She climbed out of his lap and went towards the stairs, stopping at the bottom to tell him to sleep in the spare room.

CHAPTER FIFTEEN

LIZZIE

A whole week passed before Edward found his way into Lizzie's bed again. A whole week of excruciating normal behaviour. A week of pretending that her internal organs didn't lurch when their fingers met by chance in the raspberry bucket between them at the farm. A week of trying to catch his eye over the table but then not being able to hold onto it. A week of watching him think, watching him read and watch TV and watch Jamie. She was constantly trying to gauge his expressions, read his complex mind, and her nerves were fraught. Neither of them mentioned the night by the bench. If it wasn't for the graze down her back and the spots of blood in her knickers, she might have thought she had imagined it.

And then a whole week later he came to her again. She was asleep when he crawled in behind her and without saying anything, he buried his head into her neck and curled his body around hers, still heavy with sleep. She woke the following morning, her pyjama bottoms gone and her legs sticky, but otherwise there was no sign of her night-time visitor. And again a few nights later, they fucked without kissing. She tried to hold onto him, to make him stay, but he always left. And still not a word of it was uttered during the day.

Halfway through the following week was A level results day.

Lizzie and Edward had planned to take the day off from the fruit farm to catch the train into town to read their results from the board at school. He had come to her in the night and left without speaking again and she had tortured herself with self-loathing and a lust for more until the birds had begun to sing and the light crept into her room with a honeyed glow. She tiptoed down the corridor to Edward's room and watched him as he slept, his face so peaceful, so young-looking without the glasses. She went to touch his hair but something stopped her before she made contact. Her hand hovered over his head, shaking in the air that surrounded him. He woke, suddenly aware of her presence and she jumped back, ashamed.

'It's results day,' she said, backing out of the door. 'Get up quick or we'll miss the train.'

There was already a crowd gathered around the board when they arrived at the school, and a whole spectrum of emotions. Air punching, tears, brave bottled-up faces with quivering lips and glassy eyes, ecstatic smiles and the kicking of pavements. Lizzie and Edward watched from the periphery; it was what they did. And when the groups finally dispersed and scattered into smaller factions, they moved in to scan the board. Lizzie saw Edward's before her own – two As and a B in history. She looked up at his face, at the fleeting flash of disappointment and then the sporting smile.

'Wow, Liz, you nailed it,' he said and she found her own name. Three As. 'Looks like we'll be calling you Dr Claybourne after all.'

She smiled. 'You did pretty well yourself,' she said, nudging him in the ribs, knowing he would be disappointed but that he wouldn't show it. It was not a result you could publicly be disappointed with.

'Yeah, we both did.'

'Hey, Ed.' It was John coming up from behind him. He put his arm around Edward and squeezed his shoulder. Edward turned to look at him and smiled; it was a smile of genuine pleasure and it made her skin crawl with jealousy.

'Hey John, how did you do?'

'An A and two Bs, not too shabby. You?'

'Two As and a B.'

'Great, well done! We're going to the park with some booze to celebrate if you fancy it?' He looked over at a group of boys and girls, Melanie with her yellow teeth and her gang of faithful followers among them.

'Er, I...' Edward looked at Lizzie and then back at the group who were now starting to move as one down the road.

'Come on, John!' one guy shouted over his shoulder.

'Coming! You guys coming?' He looked at Edward and then at Lizzie.

'You go,' she said to Edward, and then to John. 'I've gotta get home, my family is planning a bit of a thing...'

'OK, great,' John said, pulling Edward away by the arm. 'Come on, or we'll lose them.'

'Hang on,' Edward said, laughing and only half resisting John's dragging. 'Won't they mind if I'm not there?' Edward asked Lizzie, his expression torn between guilt and want so shamelessly.

'Don't worry.' She shrugged. 'I'll save you some beetroot roulade.'

And then he was gone, running across the road, his arm still wrapped around John, laughing, his glasses crooked and slightly steamy.

Lizzie fought back the tears on the train home but was suitably buoyant by the time she got to the house. Her family were obviously disappointed and exchanged questioning glances about Edward not being there to witness the balloons and the 'Congratulations' banner. But they didn't labour the point, for Lizzie's sake. There was much talk throughout lunch about how she would be a brain surgeon one day and was she sure she shouldn't be taking a year off and applying to Oxbridge after all? But Lizzie was insistent that she stick to her plan of doing medicine at Manchester, which she heard was one of the best. Nothing to do with the fact that Edward was planning on reading English literature there, of course. He didn't come home after lunch. Damian and Bella left for London and Jamie had a party to go to, so Lizzie was left with her parents for the evening. They opened a bottle of vintage champagne and toasted her over and over again, but as the evening wore on, they all grew tired of forcing the celebration.

'Do you think Edward is OK?' Her mother finally confronted the elephant in the room after supper.

'Why wouldn't he be?' Lizzie shrugged.

'I mean, I'm sure he's just celebrating with his friends, but do you think he will come back tonight? There aren't many trains at this time. Does he have money for a taxi? Or would he go back... to... his house?'

'He's a big boy, Mum, I'm sure he'll figure it out.'

He did come back that night. Lizzie was in bed, unable to sleep, insomnia fast becoming a reliable visitor. She heard a car crunching on the gravel, saw the headlights cast a silvery glow around her room as it turned in the drive. She heard his footsteps, heavy and stumbling on the stairs, and she held her breath waiting to see if he would turn right or left at the top. Hoping for the creak of his footsteps in the corridor, the shaft of light as he opened her door. But no, he turned left, his door slamming behind him.

He didn't get up for work the following day and Lizzie picked raspberries on her own in the rain, the fallen fruit leaking its juice into the ditches that filled with water around her feet and seeping into her white trainers. She came home that day sodden to the core and found Edward on the sofa watching *Ferris Bueller's Day Off*.

'How appropriate,' she said, peeling off the wet layers of her clothes.

'Wow, you are drenched.'

'Yeah, you picked a good day to skive.' She took off her jumper and then realised her t-shirt clung to her body, her nipples poking through unashamedly. She pulled the wet material away from her and it puffed out before clinging back on.

'I'd better go and get changed.' She hugged her jumper in front of her and turned to walk out of the room.

'Lizzie,' he called after her and she stopped in the doorway. 'I'm really sorry about yesterday.'

'Yeah, whatever.' She carried on up the stairs.

It was the end of August and their last week at the farm before it closed up for another year. The leaves on the trees were already starting to brown, the fruit becoming sour and rotten. Jamie had gone to Cornwall with some friends for the bank holiday weekend and Lizzie's parents went to Scotland. So Lizzie and Edward found themselves alone in the house for four days. They had been looking forward to this weekend all summer. Had talked about how they would eat ice cream for breakfast and watch movies through the night. They would make cocktails from all the bizarrely coloured liqueurs in the drinks cabinet and live off pizza and cereal. And yet somehow it wasn't as good as they had imagined. The weather had turned and the house felt damp and gloomy. They neglected to put the lamps on or light the fires, to clear away the pizza boxes or bowls crusted with dried-on cereal and yellowing ice cream. And still they didn't speak of the nights. They sat at opposite ends of the huge sofa and watched film after film, barely engaging with each other except to argue over what to watch next.

They were halfway through *Top Gun* on the Sunday evening, it was dusk and the room was grey with shadows. They had made a lurid concoction of blue curaçao and vermouth. It was bitter and gave Lizzie heartburn with every sip. It was during the steamy sex scene with Tom Cruise and Kelly McGillis that she got up, stormed over to the TV and turned it off.

'Hey, what are you doing?' Edward asked from his end of the sofa.

'I can't do this anymore.'

'All right, we can watch *Pretty in Pink* if it means that much to you.'

'It's not the film.'

'What, then?'

She threw her head back in exasperation, closing her eyes to summon the strength to face the truth. 'Are we just never going to talk about the fact that we have been fucking for weeks now?'

'Oh, that.' He pulled the rug off his legs and swung them to the floor, his hands resting on his knees to prove his engagement. 'What do you want to say?'

'I don't know, I just think it's pretty weird that it's happening and that we're pretending it isn't.'

'Yeah, I guess. I didn't really know what to say.'

'You don't have to say anything, Eddie, but maybe you could acknowledge it sometime. Or touch me during the day, or even kiss me! Anything that doesn't make me feel like a slag.'

'Woah, Lizzie. I'm sorry, I didn't know you felt like that. You could have said something too, you know, it's not just me.'

She shrugged. 'I guess.'

'So...'

'So what?'

'So what do we do now?'

'Do you want to do it now?' She looked at him, at his furrowed brow, his eyes darting from side to side as he considered his response.

'I... er... yeah, I guess, if you do.'

'That didn't sound very enthusiastic.'

'I'm sorry, Lizzie, I'm just not very good at talking about this stuff. And you, well, you're my best friend. I never thought we would be anything else, and it's kind of weird.'

'Do you just want to be best friends?'

'Do you?'

'No, I want more.' She didn't even hesitate.

'OK, I... Yeah, OK, let's do it then.'

'Jesus, Eddie, you really know how to make a girl feel wanted.' She rolled her eyes but smiled as she moved towards him.

'What, like now, here?' His eyes widened in fear.

'Why not? There's no one here.' She took his glasses off and kissed his forehead, his eyelids, his nose, his neck, his mouth. She wrapped her legs around him and took off her sweatshirt. She was naked underneath, her nipples cold and hard.

'Lizzie, I don't know if I can do this.' He protested but she kissed him and unbuttoned his trousers. 'No.' He pushed her off and stumbled to his feet, scrabbling around for his glasses. 'Not here, not now, I can't...' He pulled up his trousers, held them together with one hand as he ran out of the room. 'I'm sorry, I just... I'm sorry.'

She was left sitting on the floor, a draught circling her bare shoulders. She pulled her legs into her chest, curled herself into a ball as tight as she could go. 'No,' she muttered, 'no, no, no, no.' She rocked back and forth as she uttered the words. 'Not again.'

She didn't see him later that night. She waited for him to come back down but he never did. For hours she stayed there, curled up into a ball on the floor. She wrapped the blanket that had been draped over his knees around her. It smelt of him; she breathed it in and waited. She waited as night crept into the room. Eventually when she was cold and stiff and tired of waiting, she climbed the stairs. She hovered outside his door on the way up and whispered his name. She made tiny taps on the door with her fingers but there was no reply.

The following morning he came to her room. He woke her with a smile and a cup of tea. She turned her back on him and pulled the duvet over her head.

'Lizzie.' He held onto her shoulder. 'Look, I'm sorry, this is all new territory for me. I screwed up, I'm really sorry. The last thing I wanted to do was upset you. I'm just, well, I'm a mess right now. I don't know what the hell is going on in my head but it's a mess, and I think I just need some time to sort it out.' His voice was muffled and she could smell her own fetid breath under the duvet. She didn't answer. 'Lizzie, please come out.' He tried to pull the duvet off her but she held onto it tight, pulled it further over her head.

'OK, fair enough, I just wanted to tell you that I'm going to go back home.'

She threw the duvet cover off and sat up. 'What?' She squinted; the light burned her eyes. He was dressed in a crumpled linen shirt, his hair wet and slicked back against his head. 'But you can't. Your dad.'

'Look, Liz, there's something I need to tell you.'

'Don't.'

'What do you mean?'

'I mean, you don't have to tell me...'

'But I want to, I want to be honest with you, Liz. I feel bad about what has happened between us and I owe it to you...'

'You don't owe me anything, Eddie...'

'But...'

'Shhh.' She put her finger to his mouth.

'OK,' he said and pulled her hand away from his mouth. 'I'm going to get a job for a month or so to earn some cash before university.'

'But what about me?'

'You'll be OK, you've got your parents, and siblings, and you don't need the cash like I do. And I just, well, I need some time to sort my shit out, OK?' She nodded her head and held her lips shut tight, not sure what words would come out if she opened them. 'Come here,' he said, and shuffled towards her on the edge of the bed. She leant into his chest and he put his arms around her and stroked her hair. 'I'm so sorry,' he whispered into the top of her head. She could feel his lips brushing her scalp and she clung onto him.

'Please don't go.'

'I've got to.' He kissed the top of her head and then untangled himself from her and walked out of the room.

Lizzie didn't hear from him for a month. She didn't have a number for him and he didn't call her. It was familiar territory; she was back in that lonely place with only her dark thoughts for company. She focused on preparations for university. She bought books and bags of pasta and fairy lights and new clothes and thought about how she might like to reinvent herself when she got there. She didn't have to be the nerdy hard worker any more; she could be whoever she wanted to be. But she missed Edward, with her whole body she longed for him. What was it that he wanted to tell her the day he left? She pushed it to the back of her mind, buried it alongside her memories of Isabelle. She packed and repacked her bags for Manchester. She and Jamie were both starting university at the same time and the anticipation of an empty nest seemed to have prompted a sudden surge in concerned parenting from her mum and dad, who fussed over her relentlessly. They talked to her about how to eat healthily and take enough exercise and not to drink too much and not take drugs and always have protected sex and...

She hadn't had protected sex. And it was as her mother was giving her this particular spiel while chopping onions with a silver spoon in her mouth to stop her eyes weeping that a flush of panic swept through Lizzie's body. A hot, sweaty panic that bubbled up the front of her legs and then surrounded her head with a halo of effervescent fear. She was sick, sick with nerves, sick with anticipation, or sick with... She rushed out of the room to find her calendar to count the days since her last period. Not days, weeks – six to be precise. It was in those heady summer days, just before the play. Just before... She looked at her bags packed on her bed, the folders, the exercise books, books on anatomy, books on... Oh god, she couldn't be pregnant. She ran out of the house, told her mother she had to go to town to get some books. She ran, all the way to the station. Why did they live in the sticks? It was in moments like these that she wished they were in the city, with a corner shop, like Edward. Oh, Edward, what would he do? And then she vomited at the back of the station and it seemed to confound the reality of her situation. The pile of diced carrot and spaghetti hanging from a bed of nettles, her eyes streaming and her throat raw.

She bought a test from the chemist's in town and went into the Gardener's Arms opposite to pee on the stick. She had seen it done in so many movies yet couldn't believe she was doing it herself. She peed on her hand; it was warm and she nearly dropped the stick down the loo. And then she waited, tried not to look until the two minutes was up. Instead she read the graffiti scrawled on the back of the door. 'Lily 4 Jason'. 'Things I hate. Graffiti, Lists, Irony'. 'Is life worth all the bullshit?' 'Your future is in your hands'. Is it? She looked down and there it was, the faint cross that would ruin her future. It darkened as the moisture bled into it, darker and darker, along with her thoughts. She stayed for a long time in that loo, so long that she had ridges on the backs of her legs when she stood up. Her life was no longer in her hands.

The daylight hurt her eyes when she finally emerged. She dithered on the street corner and then headed not for the station but for 54 Wilton Street. It hadn't occurred to her that Edward wouldn't be in as she knocked on the door. In fact, she had been so absorbed in how she would break the news to him that she figured she must have got the wrong house when a sandy-haired man opened it. She backed off the doorstep to reread the number written on the wall.

'Can I help you?' the man said. His voice quivered and his head shook slightly as he held onto the door. He was small and frail, and a tweed suit hung off his skinny frame like a hanger and there was a red spotted hanky in the pocket. He wore thin round glasses which perched precariously on the end of his nose.

'Oh, h- hi,' she stammered. 'Is Edward in?'

'No, he's not. And you are?'

'Sorry, I'm Lizzie.'

'Ah.' He smiled and raised his eyebrows above the frame of his glasses. 'The infamous Lizzie. I'm afraid he's at work.'

'Oh, right, where's he working?'

'At a bookshop on the other side of town. He was really chuffed to get the job, they know he's leaving for Oxford next month, but...'

'Oxford?'

'Yes! Didn't he tell you? He called one of the colleges and sent them some of his poems and they accepted him, even with a B in history. He's over the moon.'

A spark of something hot and fiery ignited in the pit of her stomach from the same place that the baby, his baby, was growing. 'I bet,' she said. 'Maybe I'll go and find him there then. What's the name of the shop?'

'Much Ado About Books. It's on Victoria Street, the north side.'

'OK. Well, it was nice to meet you, Mr Thatcher.' She forced a smile and stepped away from the door.

'You too, Lizzie, I've heard a lot about you. And it was so kind of you to take Edward in and look after him while I was in hospital.'

'Hospital?' She turned back round to face him.

'Yes, after my fall.'

'Your fall, yes, of course. How are you feeling now?'

'Still a bit shaky, as you can see. That's the Parkinson's, unfortunately, but it's good to be home, and with Edward again.'

'Yes, yes, of course, it must be.'

'Please come back, with Edward I mean. You could come for a cup of tea. I've heard so much about your family. Edward doesn't really bring friends home, never has, I think he's a bit embarrassed by his old man.' He turned the corners of his mouth down as he said this, not in disdain but for dramatic effect. And Lizzie could see Edward with the same expression, the same theatrical demeanour.

'That would be lovely, Mr Thatcher,' she said and turned back to the road, her mind whirring with questions and indignation. This man didn't look like he could hit anybody; he could barely hold onto to the door frame for shaking. So who had given Edward that swollen eye, and why had he lied? And Oxford, he had persuaded her not to go there and now he was going himself? She held onto her stomach, swallowed down the bile that was trying to creep up the back of her throat again.

The bookshop was tucked away down an alley off Victoria

Street. There was a cobbled path that led up to it, totally incongruous against the concrete and traffic on the main road. There was a courtyard in front of the shop with geraniums in pots and an old wheelbarrow with plants tumbling out of it. She could see Edward through the window. He was talking to a customer and they were both leaning over a book. He looked serious and absorbed. And then he caught her eye through the window and there was a flicker of shock, then alarm. He would be wondering how she knew he was there, that she must have been to the house, met his frail father. She waved and he held his hands up in query and then beckoned her in. The door chimed as she entered.

'I'll just be a minute, Lizzie,' he said to her over the shoulder of the customer. 'So, do you want just this one, or any others from the series?'

'I think I'll just take this one for now, and come back for more if I like it,' the lady said while rummaging in her bag for her purse.

'Good idea.' He tapped the keys on the till and the drawer opened with a ping. He was trying not to look at Lizzie, who was pretending to browse books on the shelf. But she sneaked glances back at the anxious flush on his cheeks, the darting back and forth of his magnified eyes behind the lenses. Eventually the woman left and they were alone.

'What are you doing here?' he asked nervously.

'I went to your house, met your dad.'

'Oh.'

'He's quite different from what I expected. He thanked me for looking after you while he was in hospital.'

'Lizzie, I tried to tell you.'

'What?'

'That day I left, you were hiding under the duvet, remember, you wouldn't let me speak...'

'But I thought...'

'What, what did you think I was going to say?'

'I... er... I don't know. But Eddie, you had already been living with us for weeks by then. For weeks, months, in fact. I thought you were being abused by your father.'

'I'm sorry.'

'But why did you lie?'

'I didn't exactly lie, Lizzie, you just jumped to the wrong conclusion and I didn't correct you.'

'Come on, Edward, that's basically the same thing as lying.'

'I just, well, I guess I was ashamed.'

'Of what? What actually happened that day?'

'I, er, well, I got beaten up.' He stumbled on his words and couldn't look her in the eye. He fiddled with the roll of receipt paper, turning it round and round in his hands. 'By this bunch of kids. I was leaving the hospital after Dad had been admitted. And this gang jumped me.'

'But... but that's awful. You should have reported it to the police. Why were you ashamed of that?'

'I don't know. I guess I—'

'What?'

'Well, it's just not exactly something that would happen to anyone in your family.'

'That is ridiculous.'

'Look, Lizzie,' he whispered. 'I don't expect you to understand and I know I shouldn't have lied but there are things that I just couldn't tell you. And my dad, well, it's not as simple as it seems.'

'But he seemed so nice, so gentle. So completely different from everything I imagined! That day I came to your house, you were so nervous about him coming home, I thought, well, you led me to believe that he'd been at the pub all day drinking and would be violent.'

'I never said that, Lizzie, that was just your overactive imagination again.'

'My imagination? You had bruises all the way down the side of your body.'

'What?'

'That week, before I came to your house. I saw it, a massive purple bruise on your ribs.'

'I... I don't think so, I can't remember. Maybe I did it doing sports or something.'

'You don't do sports, Eddie!'

'I don't know what that was, Lizzie, but life is not always the soap opera you imagine it to be.'

'It feels pretty dramatic right now.'

'What do you mean? Why are you here, Lizzie? Why did you go to my house today?'

'I...' She tried to find the words, and then the door chimed and a lady walked in with her son.

'I don't want a book, Mum. Can't I just spend Grandad's money in the toyshop?' the boy said, scuffing his feet across the floor.

'No, Grandad said it was to buy a book. Where do we find the children's books?' she asked Lizzie.

'Oh, I don't work here.'

'Over here.' Edward came out from behind the desk and showed them into the children's section through an arch at the other end of the shop. She could hear him recommending some books and the mother trying to sound excited and encouraging with her high-pitched tone while the boy grumbled and groaned. Then Edward left them to it and came back to Lizzie. He held onto her arm and ushered her into another arched section of the shop. Cookery and travel books were laid out on a table in the middle.

'What's going on, Lizzie?' he whispered.

She pulled her arm away from his. 'So your dad told me you're going to Oxford.'

He looked sheepish and straightened some of the books on the table so that their spines were aligned. 'Oh, right, so that's what this is all about. I was going to call.'

'Were you really? Or were you just going to let me rock up at Manchester and try to find you?'

'I'm really sorry, Lizzie, I know how this must look, and—'

'I was only going to Manchester because of you,' she said and realised how pathetic it sounded.

'I know, but I think you'll love it there. And I've heard really good things about the medical faculty.'

'Hello,' the lady called from the other end of the shop.

'Coming,' Edward said, and smiled apologetically at Lizzie before leaving. She picked up a book on birds and flicked through the pages. She could hear Edward telling the boy what a good choice he had made and how *Tom's Midnight Garden* was sure to convert any reluctant reader. And then the bell on the door chimed and he came back to her.

'There's something else,' Lizzie said quietly, and put the bird book back on the shelf.

'What?' He walked towards her and for a minute she faltered. Maybe she shouldn't tell him, shouldn't ruin his life as well as hers. He could go to Oxford as planned, become a famous poet or a lecturer or... But no, she was the one who was meant to be going to Oxford, not him.

'I'm pregnant,' she said, and watched the colour drain from his flushed cheeks, his eyes widen in disbelief.

'What?'

'I'm pregnant, just did a test. That's why I came to find you today.'

He wobbled on his feet, held onto the nearest bookshelf for support. 'But...'

'But what, Edward? We had unprotected sex, remember? Quite a few times. You came to my room.'

'Oh, shit, Lizzie.' He ran his hands through his hair and held onto the top of his head, pressing his fingertips down into his scalp. 'Fuck, fuck.' He kicked the table leg and a large coffee table book on mammals fell to the floor. It lay open at a picture of an orang-utan with a baby on its back. He went to pick it up and place it back on the table. Then he looked at his watch.

'I can shut up here in half an hour. Why don't you go and wait for me in the pub opposite?'

'But—' She started to object, but he interrupted her sternly.

'Just give me half an hour, Lizzie, OK?'

And so she left and sat at a gloomy table at the back of the King's Head and sipped at half a pint of lager. It churned in her stomach and left a taste of metal in her mouth. After the roller-coaster ride of emotions she had experienced that afternoon, she now felt numb. Like she was wearing a fur hat and it had been pulled down over her eyes, her nose, her mouth, muffling the chatter of the guys at the bar, the darts on the TV in the corner, the scraping of chairs and clinking of glasses. She held her head in her hands and gazed into her glass. She lost her mind to the bubbles in the brown liquid which rose to the top and then popped and fizzed on the surface. She had no idea how long she had been sitting there when Edward arrived looking flustered and scared. It could have been the half an hour he had promised or half a day.

'Do you want another one?' he asked.

She shook her head, not sure she could even speak. He went to the bar and got himself a pint and a shot of something brown which he downed before coming back to the table.

'I'm sorry for the way I reacted. For everything.' His voice wobbled and she thought he might cry and she didn't think she could take it. She reached for his hand across the table and held onto it. He wrapped his fingers around hers and blinked away the tears.

'So what are we going to do?' he asked.

'My parents won't let me get rid of it.'

'Are you sure?'

'They're Catholic, Edward, they don't believe in abortion.'

'They're not really religious, though, are they? I mean, they go to church on a Sunday but that's about it. You said it yourself – it's not as if they say grace or anything.'

'I think they might find their divinity when it comes to this one.'

'But Lizzie, we're about to go to university.'

'I'm well aware of that, Eddie.' She had a sip of her beer, forced the cold bitter bubbles down and felt them curdle as they hit her stomach. She hadn't eaten since before the vomiting episode at the station.

'But you're going to be a doctor, Lizzie, a really good one.'

'I know, I *was* going to be a really fucking good doctor.'

'Maybe you don't have to tell them, maybe we could just go and do it ourselves.'

'What?'

'You know, get rid of it.' She felt her stomach heave and for an awful moment thought she might be sick again. She wrapped her arms around her middle and leant over onto the table. 'You all right?'

'I think I need to get some fresh air.' She stumbled out of the pub and into the dusky evening. She held onto the sticky wall of the King's Head and took in a few long, deep breaths, exhaust fumes filling her lungs.

'Are you all right?' Edward was at her side. She hadn't noticed him following her. He rubbed her back and she felt the tears stinging behind her eyes. He put his arms around her and hugged her into his chest. 'It'll be OK, Lizzie.' He squeezed her tight and she held onto the back of his jacket with both fists. 'I'll stick by you,' he whispered into her head. 'We're going to be OK.'

CHAPTER SIXTEEN

ROMY

Romy peeled her eyes open and the light of the day through the window stung her pupils. She shut them again but could hear Joseph's voice, the squeeze of his hand.

'Romy,' he whispered, and she tried to open them again.

'Where am...' She tried to speak, but her throat felt as though she had swallowed fire. Joseph silenced her with his palm on her head.

'Shh... it's OK. Don't talk.' He smiled a brave smile at her but she could see the tears streaming down his face. He took his hand away from hers to wipe his eyes. 'You're in a hospital in Cebu. Gave me quite a fright, but you're stable now. You were horribly dehydrated and your kidneys are inflamed because of your condition, but they have given you some medication and it's bringing the swelling down.'

'I'm sorry...'

'It's OK, I know why you didn't tell me. But we're here now, and we are going to make you better, OK?' He squeezed her hand and smiled his wonderful benevolent smile. And then his eyes half closed and she watched as he drew a long breath down to his core, dealing with this in the only way he knew how. But it didn't annoy her today, didn't make the hairs stand up on her arms. It made her feel safe. And she closed her eyes again and lost herself to her dreams once more.

When she woke again it was dark and Joseph was asleep in the chair beside her bed. She looked around; she was in a private room that looked very much like the one in which her father had died. She turned her head to look at the window, and sure enough, there was the apartment block with the horribly familiar mustard-yellow balconies. She had spent so much time staring at that block, watching the glimpses of life through the windows and imagining the stories behind them. She had also spent way too much of her time counting the windows, figuring out the irregularity in their number. Some floors had twelve, others thirteen. She became so preoccupied with this anomaly that one night while her father slept fitfully in the bed, she had left the hospital and crossed the road to the block. She waited outside for someone to come or go and when they did, she nipped in behind them. And then she climbed the stairs to the seventh floor and she counted the apartments. There were six. And then to the floor above, where there were five. The end one had the large balcony that wrapped around the corner, but one less window. She was still none the wiser as to why they didn't just put the extra window in the bigger flat when the door opened and a man in a sharp suit and briefcase, possibly a doctor, came out of the flat at the end. Before the door shut, she saw a staircase where there should be a window. It suddenly all made sense: the flat was on two floors. Problem solved. She was weirdly delighted and walked back to the lift with a skip in her step. But then she caught a glimpse of the hospital through the narrow window in the lift lobby. The huge concrete slab that towered over the apartment block with its hundreds of windows, some closed with blue curtains and others revealing the strip lights and reflective surfaces beyond. She counted the floors and windows to locate Ted's room. The curtains were partially open, as she'd left them. She had been feeling strangely far away, as though she was watching someone else's life, someone else's demise, but it was this alternative perspective that suddenly brought the horror of her situation into brutal clarity. She had slid down the wall and sat on the floor in the stairwell that stank of piss and rotting rubbish and considered how her life could have panned out differently in another world. A world in which both of her fathers had not contracted this horrific disease and had not been taken away from her. Or a world in which her mother hadn't given her away as a baby but brought her up somewhere else, far away. Or a world where she grew up in this apartment block and looked at the hospital every day and wondered about the lives of the people inside rather than the other way round. Here she was again, back in that hospital in a room so horribly similar to the one she had tried to forget all these years. Wondering again, what if.

She looked over at Joseph asleep in the chair. It was the same royal-blue fake leather chair with plastic arms that her legs had stuck to fourteen years ago. She had spent a lot of time in one of those chairs, sleeping, sitting, reading to Ted. Graham Greene was his favourite, or Tolkien, or Kipling, depending on his mood. He would drift in and out of consciousness but she wouldn't stop reading, she couldn't bear the silence. By the end she and Joseph were no longer taking turns to visit. And so the three of them had that moment together, Romy and Joseph on either side of Ted, each holding onto one of his delicate hands. The hands of a poet, who had barely done a day's manual labour in his life. His long, fine fingers that curled around theirs until they didn't. There was no death rattle, no dramatic grappling for air. He just stopped breathing in his sleep, drifting into the next world in the same graceful and dreamy way that he had drifted through the whole of his life.

'Romy, you're awake.' Joseph blinked away the sleep from his eyes.

'Yes.'

'Hi, how are you feeling?' He leant forward and smiled, taking hold of her hand.

'It's the same hospital.'

'Yes, I know, one floor down.'

'I never thought I would come here again,' she said.

'Hey.' Joseph leant forward and grabbed her hand. 'It's OK. This is different. You're going to be OK. This is definitely not the end for you.' She nodded and curled her lips over her teeth, biting down on them hard. She shut her eyes. 'Look at me, Romy,' he said and she forced them open again and looked at him through the blur of salty tears. 'We are going to fight this. I know you are scared, and believe me, I didn't want to ever come here again either. But you know what? Ted has got your back. He is here, in this room. This is why we're here, not in some hospital in Hong Kong. You came back to him, to me. And he is fighting for you too. Can't you feel him?' He looked up and let go of her hand to wave his around the room. She nodded. She couldn't feel him but she wanted to so much, and Joseph smiled. 'We've got you, Romy,' he said, taking her hand between his, 'and we are never letting go of you again.'

'OK,' she said.

The following morning Joseph wasn't in the room when she woke but he strode back in twenty minutes later with a purposeful look.

'Ah, you're awake. How do you feel?'

'Like I've been asleep for a hundred years.'

'Well, that is good.' He looked twitchy as he paced up and down the room and then fiddled with the cord on the roller blind.

'What's going on, Joseph?' Romy asked.

'What?' He turned to her, lost in a world of thought.

'You seem quite on edge this morning.'

'Me? No, I'm fine. I just, well, I've spoken to your doctor in Hong Kong.'

'Dr Chung?'

'Yes.'

'He's quite dry, isn't he?'

'Yes, not oozing with bedside manner, but he has filled me in. Obviously I can't be a donor because of the HIV.'

'Yeah, I figured.'

'Even if I was a match, which is unlikely as we're not blood-related, but not impossible.'

'And I don't have any other living relatives to call on. But I can go into the scheme, did he tell you about the scheme?'

'Yes, he told me about the scheme.'

'I thought it was pretty insane when he told me, that some poor sod would consider giving up their kidney to a stranger. But I've been thinking a lot about it since the diagnosis, and there is one person who would do it for me. Mali – I told you about her. I know that if I told her what was going on she would offer, and she is young and healthy and—'

'Romy...' Joseph came to sit back down next to the bed.

'I know it's not ideal, Joseph, but I don't really have any other options. And I know you will love her – she's the kindest person I've ever known.'

'Romy, please...'

'What? What is it?'

'There is something I should have told you a long time ago.' He had her attention now. She tried to sit up a bit but hadn't the energy or the strength in her stomach muscles, and so lay back down. 'Here, let me help.' He hooked his arms underneath hers and hauled her up, puffed up the pillow behind her back.

'Well?' she asked as he was still fussing around her.

'I know that we, Ted and I, should have told you this before. And I wanted to tell you when you were younger but Ted didn't think we should – not that I'm blaming him, of course. I could have persuaded him I'm sure, but I was scared. And with every year we didn't tell you, it became harder and...'

'What is it, Joseph?'

'Your mother... she wasn't a surrogate like we told you.' A weird, warm sensation crept up her legs. She felt as though she had been here before, not just in this hospital but in this scene. It had been played out again and again in her dreams, but she had no idea what was coming next. 'She and Ted were married.' He stopped and looked at her, his eyes searching, terrified of her reaction.

'Go on.'

'And then Ted and I met, and we, well, we fell in love.'

'And...'

'And your mother, she was a little...' he searched for the right words '...unstable. Ted was worried about you, and so... so...'

'What did you do, Joseph?' Her skin tingled with anticipation and dread. What did they do to her mother?

'We took you, we brought you here.'

'You stole me?'

'Well, not exactly stole, you were Ted's daughter. But yes, we took you, her daughter, to the other side of the world and lied to you about her for the whole of your life.'

'Wow!'

'I'm so sorry.'

'And is she...' She hesitated, too scared to ask. 'Is she alive now?'

'Yes, yes, she is.' Romy exhaled through puffed-out cheeks and puckered lips.

'Shit.' Her mother didn't give her up as she had always thought. She had been stolen, by her beloved fathers. The fathers who always seemed so kind, so safe, so gentle; they had stolen her as a baby from her mother and taken her to the other side of the world.

'There's more.'

'What?' She turned to face Joseph, could feel the fire burning in her eyes.

'You have a sister.' And then that fire turned to water and her eyes filled, a reaction so immediate, so visceral, and she was powerless to stop it. The tears spilled out and poured down her cheeks.

'What do you mean?'

'Your mother was pregnant when we left. Ted didn't know... he never would have...' And then came the rage. The anger bubbling up inside of her like a shaken-up bottle of fizz. It had its own momentum. Every pore of her body seethed with rage, frothing and foaming.

'And is she...?' The words were stuck in her throat.

'She lives in the South-West of England with her family, and she has two children.' Fire burned up her nose and behind her eyes and the tears came harder and faster.

'I'm an aunt.'

Joseph smiled then and tried to take hold of her hand but she snatched it away. 'I'm sorry, Romy, I am so very sorry that we never told you. There wasn't a day that went by when we didn't think about telling you. But we, well, we were so scared of losing you. And then Ted got sick and we nearly told you then. We tried to one day, I don't know if you remember?' She racked her brains for the moment when this epic conversation might have taken place but couldn't find it. She rolled her eyes and shook her head, no longer able to look at him. 'We took the boat to the Secret Beach. It was one of the rare occasions that Ted joined us. He had just started having symptoms and we knew it was only a matter of time but we hadn't told you yet. Ted didn't want to spoil what little time we had left. We had argued about it that morning, and I told him we had to tell you, that you had a right to know. To know everything, because one day you might need your mother, your sister, when I went too. He begged me not to tell you about them. Said that we could tell you about his prognosis but not about that too. He cried and hung onto me and said it was too much, too much for you to take on. And he was right. When I saw your face, your quivering lip, the fear in those big, wide eyes, I couldn't do it.'

Romy remembered the day then. They had taken all their favourite foods for a picnic. Fried lumpia, freshly baked quiches, chocolate-chip muffins and iced tea. Ted had sat at the back of the beach in the shade. He wrote a limerick about them that had her and Joseph crying with laughter. Skipper was a puppy and Romy threw a ball for him in the shallows. It was as perfect a day as she could remember. Until they told her, as the sun was dipping into the ocean and the sky was glowing orange. She remembered watching the sandcastle that they had built earlier in the day being slowly destroyed by the incoming tide as they told her that her father was going to die. Probably her other father, too; and her world began to fall apart.

'I remember,' she whispered. The tears had dried on her cheeks and she was left with an emptiness, like she had been hollowed out inside.

'We should have told you that day, but it was too much. And then Ted got more and more sick and you were being so strong, so brave the way you insisted on coming to the hospital every day. You had barely left the island on your own before that, and yet every day you took that ferry here and you sat with him, read to him, played your funny games. You seemed so in control, but I was afraid that at any moment you might crumble to pieces.'

Romy shut her eyes and lay back on the pillow. Her head was spinning, round and round and up and down like a roller-coaster ride that she couldn't get off. Joseph was still talking, his voice echoey and distant. 'Turns out I was the one who fell to pieces,' he continued. 'And I should have told you afterwards, I promised Ted that I would. But I couldn't. I thought I would lose you forever. And then I did anyway. Romy? Are you OK? Romy?' But she couldn't answer. She willed the spinning sensation to stop but it just kept turning her round and round. Her heart raced and the blood pounded in her ears. She gripped onto the bed sheets with both hands and squeezed her eyes tightly shut.

'Romy, shall I get the doctor? Romy, what is it?' But still it pounded, still she held on tight. 'It's OK, Romy, I'll be back, just hang on in there. Help,' he called and ran towards the door. 'Help, Doctor, Nurse, someone, please, my daughter...' And then two people in scrubs rushed into the room and they were checking her pulse and taking her temperature and still the blood pulsed around her body and she couldn't speak.

'What is it? What's going on?' She could hear the panic in Joseph's voice.

'It's OK, Mr Cruz, her heart is racing and we need to figure out why. I'm just going to check her blood pressure. Has she been OK this morning?'

'Yes, I, er, just told her something. It was a shock. Oh god, I, did I do this? Romy, I'm so sorry, it's all my fault.'

'Can someone get him out of here, please.'

'Come on, Mr Cruz, come with me, she will be OK. Just let the doctors do their job...'

'Romy, Romy, can you hear me? Romy, can you open your eyes?' She peeled them open and a male doctor she didn't recognise was inches away from her face, glaring into her eyes. She could smell garlic on his breath as he pumped up her arm to take her blood pressure.

'I'm OK,' she said. 'I just, I couldn't breathe and my heart was...' Her words were punctuated with breaths as she struggled to get the air back down into her lungs.

'It's OK,' he said. 'You had a panic attack. Just breathe, deep and slow in, deep and slow out, that's it.' They breathed together for a few minutes and then he released the blood pressure band and placed his hand on her wrist and she felt her heart settling into a more comfortable pace.

'OK, that's good. You're OK. Just keep breathing long and slow, I'll go tell your dad you're OK.' He turned towards the door.

'Wait...' she called after him. 'Could you just give me a few minutes, before you tell him?'

'Sure, I'll tell him you're asleep and to give you some space, OK?' he said, and she nodded and closed her eyes.

Joseph wasn't there when she opened her eyes again, and she wasn't sure how long she had been asleep. She felt disorientated and confused and then she remembered. She had a mother and a sister, a nephew and a niece. Her mother hadn't given her away; she had been stolen by the two people she loved and trusted most in the whole world. The anger crept back into her heart. They had lied to her: her whole life was based on a lie. And all this time there was a sister, a mother, on the other side of the world. How could they do that? How could they take a child away from her mother?

'Romy?' Joseph knocked tentatively at the open door. 'Can I come in?' She shrugged, and he walked in slowly, giving her bed a wide berth as if he was afraid that his proximity might set off another attack. 'I'm so sorry,' he whispered, and walked over to the window.

'Why didn't she come after me?' Romy asked, her voice croaky and faltering.

'We were so far away. I don't know, maybe she did, maybe she didn't know where to look.'

'How do you know about my sister?'

'What?'

'My sister, you said you didn't know she was pregnant when you took me. How did you find out?'

'Your mother's brother, Jamie. He and Ted, they were close, they stayed in touch.'

'So my mother's brother knew where I was and didn't think to tell his sister?'

'I guess not. Please, try not to worry about it all now.'

'It's a bit late for that, Joseph!' She raised her voice for the first time and he winced and backed further away.

'I know, Romy, but please. You're sick, you just need to be calm. To look after yourself.'

'How can I be calm after what you've just told me?'

'I'm sorry, maybe I shouldn't have told you. But you need a donor, and don't you see, there is hope for you now. Your sister might be a match.'

'Does she even know about me?'

'I don't think so.'

'So, what? I have to pick up the phone and say hi, I'm your long-lost sister that you never knew existed, and guess what? I'm dying and need your kidney!' She laughed; it sounded even more insane when she said it out loud.

'I'm going to go and talk to her.'

'What?'

'I just booked a flight.'

'You did *what?*'

'You said it yourself, it is not the sort of conversation you can have on the phone, and you can't go, so I will.'

'No way.'

'Come on, Romy, you know it makes sense. We need her, and if I meet her, face to face, and explain everything...'

'That didn't go so well with me, remember.'

'But she doesn't know me, it's different.'

'I reckon she could be as angry as I am about the lies that she has been fed all her life. What has she been told? About her father?'

'I think they told her that he died in a car crash when she was a baby. Her mother remarried and she has three half-brothers.'

'So I have three half-brothers too?'

'Yes, yes I guess you do.'

'When is the flight?'

'Tomorrow morning.'

'But...' She felt her voice wobble and those bloody tears filling up at the backs of her eyes again.

'Hey.' He dared to come nearer. 'I'll be back in no time, and you're in safe hands here. You know that I have to do this, Romy.'

'But she doesn't know me, Joseph, and she has kids of her own. I can't ask her to give me her kidney. What if something goes wrong, what if—'

'Shh,' he said, holding his finger towards her lips but not quite touching. 'You won't be asking. I will.' And the anger that coursed around her body gave way to a little spark of hope.

CHAPTER SEVENTEEN
FLORA

Flora called her mother's house the day after she got home and Jeremy answered the phone.

'You came back?'

'Somebody had to.' Her stepfather's tone was curt.

'I'm sorry, Jeremy, but I couldn't stay. She slapped my child. I just—'

'It's OK, Flora, Billy told me what happened.' This took Flora by surprise; it was unusual for Jeremy to be conciliatory, and he was rarely understanding.

'How is she?'

'Quiet.'

'Right. And Billy?'

'He had to go back to London so he left as soon as I got back.'

'And your AGM?'

'Well, I'm missing the final dinner and was meant to be playing golf today, but...'

'I'm sorry.'

'Yes, well... Do you want to speak to her – your mother, I mean?'

'No,' she answered a little too quickly. 'No, I'm afraid I'm not ready to talk to her yet. I, er, just wanted to make sure that someone was there.'

'Right, yes, here I am.'

'OK great, goodbye then.'

Three days had passed since that conversation, and she had wandered around the house in a bit of a trance ever since. After she had banished Jake to the spare room, she had told him that she needed some space to think and he had complied. So much so that he had barely come near her. They had skirted around each other for the past three days, exchanging only pleasantries, or discussing plans for the children, or supper, or which car they were going to use that day. She felt hollow inside and could barely eat.

When she told Lisa about their conversation, she was surprisingly optimistic.

'So that *is* good!'

'Why is it good?'

'Well, he doesn't love her. He loves you. He only went to her because he was feeling neglected by you.'

'Now you sound like my mother.'

'Sorry, wrong word. He was feeling shut out by you, and he was so devastated that he fell into the arms of another.'

'I'm still not sure how this is a good thing, Lis.'

'Well, because it's his love for you that was the driving force.'

'The driving force?'

'He was so upset by the thought of you feeling sad and having regrets about your life that he sought solace elsewhere.'

'In the arms of the woman who has been in love with him for his whole life.'

'Yes, but he doesn't love her.'

'He didn't say that exactly, he said he loved her as a friend.'

'As a friend, Flora! Not a lover or life partner, a friend!'

'Oh god, Lisa, I just don't know what to think. I'm such a mess, and then there was the fight with Mum. I feel as though all of the elements in my life are coming to a great big fucking peak, and I just want to run away from them all.'

'Why don't you go for a walk?'

'What?'

'I'll look after the kids for a couple of hours. Take Tess and go and sort your head out. You need some time on your own to think this all through.'

'Are you sure?'

'Totally. Go now before anyone comes to stop you.'

And so she headed through the garden and onto the path that led towards the sea. It was early March, and while the trees were still mostly bare there were glimpses of spring and things to come. Tiny buds were appearing on the brittle branches, and daffodil shoots lined the pathways. By the time she had walked through the fields and down to the cliff edge she was warm and had taken off her coat and then even her jumper. She lowered herself down the rope onto the beach and thought about that first time Jake had brought her here, when the stones were covered in a blanket of stinky seaweed. Today they were mostly clear and glistened in the light of the sun. She walked to the water's edge; it was calm and the waves lapped against the shore with a gentle touch. She took her boots and socks off and rolled up the legs of her jeans and felt her toes go numb and then tingle in the freezing water. She closed her eyes and tilted her head up towards the sun and felt its warmth thaw her bones. She picked up a piece of driftwood and threw it into the water for Tess. She bounded in and swam out to the wood then back with it between her teeth.

The water was glasslike, the reflection of the wispy clouds skimming its smooth sapphire surface. She wanted to submerge herself in it, to feel the coldness against her body. To blow away the cobwebs that were smothering and confusing her mind. So she stripped off her clothes and threw them back onto the stones behind her. In her bra and pants she stepped into the sea. She was mad – it was March, possibly the coldest time of the year. They were only just emerging out of the dark, icy winter, the water yet to be heated by any warmth from the sun. But she needed to feel it. She needed something to clear the clouds from her thoughts and so she strode in. Her feet throbbed with pain. Her legs stung and then went numb. She was up to her waist, and then her chest. She couldn't breathe. She thought of Jake, his words that first time. *Just breathe, short sharp breaths.* She launched herself under the water, circled her arms in breaststroke but still she couldn't breathe. Pains shot through her chest; she kept swimming further and further out. Her arms and legs ached with cold and still the shooting pains darted in her chest, as though her heart had been caught in a vice and was being squeezed and squeezed. She continued to swim. *It will go.* Soon she would get that wonderfully tingly feeling, and the endorphins. Where were the fucking endorphins? She turned round; she could see Tess barking on the shore. She ran into the water to follow her but then turned round and jumped back out. And suddenly the shore felt very far away. There was a figure climbing down onto the beach. She heard shouting – was he shouting at her? He was waving and Tess was barking. She started to swim back to the shore, but she couldn't feel her legs moving any more, they just seemed to drag her down. She felt light-headed and her breaths became even shorter. And then she swallowed some water, icy-cold salty water that clogged her throat. She tried to kick her numb limbs and the pain, it was still there, shooting across her chest, down her arms. How could she be so stupid? She was going to die there, in the sea. She slipped under the water, but something pulled her up. A man, an arm around her neck. And then she was being dragged through the water. She strained to keep her face above the surface, and her mouth kept filling up. She coughed, she spluttered. She could just see the blue sky, the trail of wispy cloud. Then she was on the beach, the hard stones piercing her back, and she was shaking and her teeth were rattling in her mouth. And the man, he was covering her in a coat, and clothes, he was piling them on top of her and he was holding her and rubbing her arms. But she still couldn't stop her teeth from chattering. She tried to tell him she was sorry, to thank him for saving her. She tried to tell him to call Jake. 'Jake!' She kept saying his name over and over, and then there he was. Between the two of them they carried her back across the beach and somehow hoisted her still-rattling body up the rope and into the field, where Jake's quad bike was parked. They drove her home and put her to her bed. Still she shivered. They piled on blankets and an old-fashioned eiderdown of her mother's that smelt of mothballs. Jake disappeared to find her a hot-water bottle and he was gone for a while and she drifted off into a fitful, trembling sleep. She woke to find Jake in bed with her, his arms and legs around her body, the trembling finally beginning to calm.

'Hi,' she said quietly.

'Jesus, Flora,' he said, kissing the top of her head. 'What were you thinking?'

'I'm sorry,' she croaked. Her mouth felt incredibly dry.

'You scared the shit out of me. You weren't trying to...?'

'What?' She turned her head to look up at him.

'You know, do yourself in.'

'No! Is that what you thought?'

'Well, things have been a bit rubbish these last few days, and—'

'Jake, I wasn't trying to top myself, quite the opposite. I was trying to snap myself out of the self-pitying mess I was in.'

'Oh Flora, I'm so sorry.' He kissed her head again and squeezed her between his legs. 'God, when I saw you on the beach, you were totally blue, and your eyes were wide and confused and it was pretty scary. If Joseph hadn't been there...'

'Joseph?'

'He arrived at the house looking for you, and Lisa told him you had gone for a walk so he followed you down to the beach and when he saw you were in trouble he ran into the water. He saved your life.'

'Wow, who is he? What did he want?'

His eyes darted around the room. 'He, er...' He unwrapped his body from Flora's and climbed out of the bed. 'Well, he's downstairs. Let me bring you a cup of tea and when you're feeling stronger, I'll bring him up here to introduce you.' He leant over and kissed her firmly on the head. 'I'm so glad you're OK, but don't ever do that again, you hear me?' She nodded and he left the room.

It was Lisa who came back and brought her a cup of tea and a piece of banana cake, warm from the oven.

'Jake has been called out to some sheep emergency at the farm. Jeez, Flora, I said go for a walk, not a bloody swim. What were you thinking?'

'Don't you start. I just got it in the neck from Jake.' She took the tea and had a sip. The warm liquid soothed her throat as it made its way down. 'Lis, will you please tell me who this Joseph is who saved my life and carried me out of the sea, practically naked? And how come Jake was there on the beach?'

'Well, Joseph had a phone. He didn't have this number but he's staying at Rosehill Cottage and called Dorothy Moore and she called Jake, who drove the bike down to pick you up.'

'Oh god, how embarrassing. It sounds as though I caused a bit of a scene. I just, well, the water looked so calm, and I just wanted to do something a bit radical. I was feeling so bloody useless and confused and I wanted to feel good, and alive, and...'

'There are other ways to feel better, you know. Ones that don't result in hypothermia and near death.'

'True. You still haven't told me who this Joseph is.'

'I think he needs to tell you himself.'

'That sounds cryptic. Where is he?'

'Downstairs.'

'Right, well, I'd better get out of bed then.' She pulled the covers back and then realised she was naked.

'I think you'd better put some clothes on for this next meeting.'

'Very funny. Pass me those jeans and the jumper, will you?' Flora pulled the clothes on but had to get Lisa to do up the button on her jeans as her fingers were still white at the ends and wouldn't work properly. She shivered and Lisa threw a blanket over her shoulders and found some thick socks and slippers which she put onto Flora's still-numb feet. She walked down into the kitchen where an Asian man was sitting at the table building Lego with Toby. His black hair was damp and streaked with grey. He was hunched over and focusing very hard on placing a tiny piece of Lego onto the wing of a fighter jet.

'Hello,' Flora said tentatively. He looked up and smiled, a wide, generous smile that lit up his round face. 'I gather I owe you my life.'

He stood up and crossed the room to Flora in the doorway and took both of her hands in his. 'Flora, I am so glad that you are OK.'

'Well, it's thanks to you.' He was the same height as her and yet she couldn't quite look him in the eye. 'I don't know what would have happened if you hadn't been there... I, it was a very stupid thing to do.'

'Hey, it's OK.' He was still holding onto her hands and he squeezed them and smiled again and the corners of his eyes creased. He was wearing a shirt of Jake's that was far too big for him and a pair of jeans that were tied around his waist with a rope.

'Oh god, of course, your clothes...'

'There wasn't time for me to take them off!' He laughed. 'Come, you must sit down. Do you feel OK?'

'Yeah, a bit stupid and cold, but OK really.'

'Please don't feel stupid, I was just so glad I was there and able to help. Even if I haven't felt water that cold for a very long time, maybe ever!'

They all laughed and Lisa went over to Toby. 'Hey Tobes, Elsie is watching Harry Potter next door, do you want to come and join her?'

'But I'm doing my Lego with Joseph. We're nearly finished.'

'How about we finish it later, Toby?' Joseph said in a quiet voice. 'I'd like to have a chat with your mum.'

'OK,' Toby said grumpily, and Lisa followed him out of the room.

'So, er, have we met before, Joseph? I'm sorry, I've got a dreadful memory.'

'No, no. We haven't. Gosh, this is harder than I thought.' He rubbed his hands together and sat down in the chair across the table from Flora.

'Why do I feel as though you're about to tell me something really bad?'

'No, no. I'm sorry. It's just, well, this hasn't exactly gone according to plan, Flora,' he said, and closed his eyes and took a deep breath which he then seemed to exhale not through either his mouth or his nose but somewhere in between, and it sounded like a wave on the beach.

'Go on...' she said tentatively.

'Well, I've come from the Philippines, just flew in this morning, in fact, and I came straight here to find you.'

'Oh?'

'Yes, and I have something to tell you, and it is going to be a bit of a shock.'

'All right.'

'I've been thinking long and hard, for sixteen hours on a plane, about how to say this, and I don't think there's an easy way, so I guess I just have to come out with it.'

Flora's stomach rumbled in anticipation and she hugged herself tight. 'Please do.'

'You have a sister in the Philippines.'

'I'm sorry?'

'You have a beautiful sister called Romy. She is eighteen months older than you. Your father, well, he left your mother when she was pregnant with you. And he took their daughter Romy with him. With me. We went to the Philippines.' She couldn't process the words as quickly as he said them. A sister. A father. The Philippines? The alien phrases echoed around her head like an announcement over a loudspeaker in a foreign country.

'What?'

'I know it's a lot to take in right now.' He was staring at her but she couldn't look at him. Her gaze was focused on her hands on the table; she clasped them together and squeezed her knuckles with the tips of her fingers still wrinkled from the water.

'No, no – my father died in a car accident when I was a baby,' she said, daring to look up at him.

'I'm afraid not. That was just what Lizzie, your mother told you.'

'You know my mother?'

'Not really, no, I met her once but...'

'So let me get this straight. My father and you and my sister Romy... you left my mother and me and went to the other side of the world and have never been in contact since, until now.'

'Yes.'

She unclasped her hands and rubbed her face, trying to compute what she had just heard. 'So I have a sister and a father in the Philippines?'

'Not exactly, Flora. I'm afraid.' He leant forward to take her hands, his skin surprisingly smooth and warm against her still-cold hands. But she pulled away, suddenly unsure of this man who she didn't know, touching her. 'Sorry, Flora, I didn't mean... Oh god, how do I say this? Your father, well, I'm afraid he died fourteen years ago.'

'Oh.' And the tiny spark of hope that had been struck some-where deep inside of her was extinguished. She felt suddenly empty.'

'He was a wonderful man. He was kind and loving and generous.'

'But he left me, you all left me?'

'He didn't know about you when he left. It was his biggest regret. He wouldn't have left if he'd known your mother was pregnant with you.'

'So how did he find out?'

'He stayed in touch with Jamie, Lizzie's brother, they were close and—'

'Uncle Jamie, he's known about this the whole time?'

'Yes.'

'And my grandparents, did they know too? And Auntie Bella and Uncle Damian?'

'I don't know about them. Jamie was the only one in touch with Ted.'

'Oh my god, I can't believe this... I...' She could feel her hands start to shake. She tried to rub them together but they just shook even more. She put them up to her face and could feel them clattering against her jaw.

'Flora. Flora, are you OK?'

She felt giddy. 'I, er, I don't, I don't know...'

'OK, you're OK.' He took her hands again and this time she didn't pull them away. He squeezed them between his fingers which were delicate but strong. Then he picked up the blanket that had fallen to the floor and wrapped it around her shoulders. He rubbed the tops of her arms underneath it.

'I am sorry, Flora, this is all too much for you, and with everything you've been through today. I am going to make you a hot toddy.' She sat on her hands and jiggled her legs up and down while he pottered around the kitchen. He disappeared next door and she heard him talking to Lisa and he came back with a bottle of brandy. When he gave her the mug she wrapped her still-shaking hands around it and took a sip. The brandy was warming, the lemon and honey soothing on her sore throat. Neither of them spoke again until she had drunk the whole cup.

'Where is Romy?' Flora asked eventually.

He faltered, doubt wrinkling his brow. 'Well, er, she is in hospital, and that's why I have come.'

'To tell me she is ill?'

'To ask for your help.'

'My help?' She felt a sudden burst of anger towards this man who had come into her kitchen, into her already miserable life, and turned it upside down and inside out with his stories. And he wanted her help!

'She needs a kidney transplant, and I hoped...'

'Woah, woah, woah.' Flora went to stand up but her legs still felt shaky so she sat back down again. 'That's why you've come here?'

'Well, I, er...'

'Tell me, Joseph, if you didn't need my kidney, were you ever planning on finding me?' He didn't answer, couldn't even look at her. 'OK.'

'Flora, please. I know this is a shock, and a lot to take in, but if you would just think about it.'

'I think you should go now,' she said without looking at him.

'Yes, of course.' He stood up and hovered by her side for a moment, as if he might be waiting for her to change her mind. But when she didn't, he walked out of the door and Flora buried her head in her hands at the table.

She sat there for a long time unable to move as she tried to process everything she had just learned. She was still there as the setting sun dipped beneath the window and she felt its mellow glow on her face. And that was how Lisa found her.

'Has he gone?'

'Yeah, he's gone. Did he tell you who he was?'

'Yes, while you were asleep upstairs he told Jake and me who he was and why he had come. He was in quite a state.'

Flora ran her fingers through her hair, still damp and crisp from the sea. 'Just when I thought my life couldn't get any more confusing.' She leant into Lisa who wrapped her arms around her.

'You've had quite a week, my friend. But they say things come in threes, so that's got to be your lot.'

Flora went back to bed and slept all evening. She woke in the middle of the night and reached out to the cold, empty sheets next to her. And before overthinking it, she got up and walked down the corridor to the spare room where Jake was sleeping. She climbed into the bed with him and he woke up with a start.

'Are you OK? Flora, what is it?'

'I just didn't want to be on my own,' she said. He draped his big heavy arm over her and pulled her into him. He kissed the back of her neck and she snuggled into the warmth of his body and went back to sleep.

The following morning, she went to find Joseph at Rosehill Cottage. Dorothy was hanging the washing up outside and told her that he had gone for a walk. So Flora set off down the path in pursuit. She found him sitting on a bench overlooking the sea. His eyes were shut and he was totally still. Was he meditating? She watched him for a while. His skin was impossibly smooth for a man in his fifties – she presumed that was how old he was. And his mouth peaked at the corners into a subtle smile. His chest rose and fell with every deep and slow breath. He seemed so peaceful, so calm.

'Joseph.' She approached him tentatively. She didn't want to shock him. But he opened his eyes slowly and turned to face her with a serenity that was far from shock. 'I'm sorry, I didn't mean to disturb you.'

'No, Flora, it's lovely to see you. Come, please join me.' He moved towards the end of the bench to make room for her and she sat down next to him. 'How are you feeling this morning?' he asked.

'Fine, thanks. I slept for an age last night.'

'That's good, you needed it. After something like that, your body needs sleep to recover.'

'Yeah, it took a long time before I stopped feeling cold, though.'

'Me too!'

'Joseph, I'm so sorry, about the way I reacted yesterday. After everything you did for me.'

'Flora, please, I realise it was a dreadful shock for you. There really is no need to apologise.'

'I was wondering whether you would like to come and stay at ours tonight? I don't know how long you're here for.'

'I'm booked on a flight tomorrow – I must get back to Romy. But that would be lovely, Flora, thank you.'

The rain came in that afternoon and so they lit a fire and hunkered down in the sitting room. Joseph built Lego with Toby at the table while Flora did a puzzle with Olive on the floor in front of the fire.

'Look, Mummy, I just did the clownfish, it's like Nemo.'

'Well done, darling. Now how about finding the tail of this stingray?'

'Do you like fish, Olive?' Joseph asked.

'I like Nemo and Dory.'

'You know, where I live there are lots of Nemos.'

'Wow!' said Olive.

'Turtles, too. Maybe you could come and visit someday.'

'Yes please, oh can we, Mum?' She bounced up and down on her knees with her hands clasped together in prayer. 'Please, Mummy, please can we go?'

'Maybe one day,' Flora said, laughing. 'Will you tell us about where you live, Joseph?'

'Well, it's a tiny private beach on an island called Siquijor. There was nothing there when we arrived thirty years ago, and we built our house at one end of the beach and the guest house and dive school at the other.'

'You run a dive school?' Flora asked.

'Yes.'

'I have always wanted to try diving. Jake and I were going to go to Egypt to learn to dive on our honeymoon, but then I discovered I was pregnant and, well...'

'I would love to teach you, Flora. We have our own reef right there on the beach. And while coral reefs all over the world are dying, ours continues to thrive. I don't know how. It's a miracle! I swear it's Ted, smiling down on us, keeping it alive.'

'Who's Ted?' asked Toby.

'Ted was your...' He looked at Flora, unsure whether to say the word *grandfather*, and she shook her head at him, a tiny movement. 'Was my friend,' Joseph continued. 'Edward was his name, but he liked to be called Ted.'

'There's a boy in my class called Ted. He shoots pieces of paper out of his mouth at the back of my head,' Toby said matter-of-factly.

'That doesn't sound very nice. My Ted would never have done that. He was incredibly kind and gentle.'

'Was?' asked Toby. 'Did he die?'

'Yes.'

'That's sad, was he ill?'

'Yes, he was very ill. For a long time, so he is in a better place now.'

'My friend Theadora's grandpa died and was really ill. He lost all his hair. Did your Ted lose all his hair too?'

'No, he never lost his hair.' So not cancer then? Flora's mind raced with further questions but she knew she had to wait until the children had gone to bed before she could get any answers.

Jake returned home from the farm as she was reading the children a story that evening. By the time she came downstairs he and Joseph were drinking whisky in the kitchen and discussing ecosystems and crop rotation like they had known each other for years. Joseph was sitting at the table peeling potatoes while Jake diced lamb at the counter.

'You're cooking,' she said, fetching a wine glass from the cupboard and pouring herself a glass.

'Lancashire hotpot. Thought I'd show Joseph a typically English dish.'

Flora smiled. She wasn't too sure about Jake's Lancashire hotpot and its lumps of chewy meat floating around in a greasy gravy, one of the old-fashioned favourites he had inherited from his father. But she really didn't have the strength to cook and appreciated the effort he was making.

'I think Joseph used to live in England, Jake. Didn't you, Joseph?'

'Yes, I came here when I was nineteen for five years. I haven't been back since I left with Ted thirty years ago. And I definitely never had Lancaster, how do you say it, hotpot?'

'Lancashire, like the county.'

'What did you do when you were here, Joseph?' Flora asked as she sat down at the table next to him and began to chop the potatoes he had peeled.

'I was studying architecture.'

'Oh right, you're an architect?' Jake asked.

'No, I tried to continue my studies when I got back to the

Philippines but it was a long way to the university in Cebu, and then we built the dive school and I transferred my energies to that.'

'And Ted, my father. Was he a dive instructor, too?'

'No, god no, Ted hated diving. He was claustrophobic. He was a writer, well, a poet, actually.'

'Really? Did he get published?'

'Oh yes, he was quite successful. Edward Thatcher, you may have heard of him.'

'Edward Thatcher is my father!' Flora shrieked, and wielded the knife perilously close to Joseph's face. He backed away. 'Sorry, sorry, Joseph.' She put the knife down. 'But I can't believe it. Of course I've heard of him, I studied him at university. His poems, they are so beautiful, but dark too, so much sadness...'

'You're interested in poetry?'

'I love it. I love all forms of literature.'

'Flora was working at a publishing company before I dragged her down here to the dark depths of rural Dorset,' Jake said.

'It was a long time ago. I never got very far.'

'Ted would be so happy to have a literary enthusiast in the family. He tried to interest Romy in writing, but she could never sit still for long enough.'

Flora got up and poured some water into the pan and put the potatoes on the Aga.

'So your mother didn't tell you who your father was?'

'No, she just said he had died in a car accident when I was a baby. She wouldn't even tell me his name. When she married Jeremy, my step-father, we both took his name. She said we were so lucky to have a fresh start, a new family. She would say it over and over again when I was little, as if convincing herself as much as me. It makes sense now, she was always so cagey, so reluctant to talk about him and well, things didn't end well on the few occasions I tried to delve deeper so I learned to let it go.' She was leaning up against the warmth of the Aga, Jake walked over to her and put his arm around her but she didn't dare lean in to him for fear of releasing the tears that were burning the back of her eyes. She pulled away and sat down at the table opposite Joseph. 'Tell me about Romy,' she said with a forced smile.

'Well, she has the same eyes as you. But she is shorter, and really skinny.'

'Like our mother.'

'Yes, I guess she got that from her.'

'But what is she like? What does she do?'

'Well, she's a free spirit. And she has a strong mind. Once she has decided to do something there is no way of stopping her. She would disappear for hours as a child, sometimes a whole day, and I would be fraught with worry. Ted was calmer, always telling me to let her be. He said that she was sensible and brave and would come back to us when she was ready. He was right, she always came back – with a gecko she had captured in a matchbox, or a collection of shells. She would tell us about her adventures, with added embellishments to make the story better! She was her father's daughter in that respect.'

Flora lit the candles on the table. 'Does she know about me?'

'I told her just two days ago, before I came here.'

'So all this time she didn't know either?'

'No.'

'And if she wasn't ill and needing a kidney, would you have told her?'

He looked down in his lap. He didn't need to answer that; it was written all over his face.

'I see.'

'Romy only just came back into my life. Unfortunately, after Ted, your father died, I was very depressed and I wasn't there for her. She was only eighteen and she was very frustrated with me, understandably. And she met a guy. I could tell that he was no good but I had lost her respect and the right to voice my opinions and so she left with him. She left the Philippines for the first time since we arrived. She went with him to Hong Kong. I didn't see her again, not until just over a week ago.'

'She came back because she was ill?'

'She didn't tell me she was ill. I knew something was wrong, of course, instantly. I wanted her to tell me in her own time. But she didn't, and then she collapsed and we had to rush her to hospital, and now... well, the disease has progressed faster than they expected and she... she needs the transplant or she will die.' His plea was so calm, so lacking in any histrionics, and it was all the more devastating for it. He looked down at his hands clasped together on the table and then up into Flora's eyes.

'And there's no one else who could give her a kidney?' She couldn't hide the desperation from her own voice.

'I would give her mine, but unfortunately I can't. I am HIV-positive, you see.'

'Oh, so that is how Ted...?'

'Yes, Ted's virus progressed more quickly than mine. And I was lucky enough to still be here when the antiretroviral therapy came in.'

'I see, so when, I mean how...?'

'Don't worry, Flora, we contracted the disease after we had left the UK. There is no way that you or Romy could have been infected, or your mother.'

'Right, I see. This is all...' She ran her fingers through her hair and felt Jake's hands on her shoulders.

'And your mother could be a match. But I gather, well, Jamie has kept me informed over the years, that she has not lived a very healthy life.'

'Yeah, you could say that.'

'This is all a lot for Flora to take on, Joseph,' Jake said and squeezed her shoulders.

'I know, and I am so sorry. And Flora, you may not even be a match. Just because you're her sister doesn't mean that you have the same markers.'

'Markers?'

'Yes, that is what they call them. I think it's to do with blood types and tissue types.'

'Right, so I just need to have a blood test?'

'Yes.' There was a glimmer of hope in his eyes and Flora imagined how she would feel if Toby or Olive needed a transplant to survive.

'OK, I'll have the test. I'm not saying that I will definitely give up my kidney, but I may as well have the test, right? Just so we know if it's even an option.' Joseph smiled a huge smile that made his eyes sparkle, and she looked up at Jake and saw the fear in his wide eyes, and he forced a smile and squeezed down on her shoulders a little harder.

CHAPTER EIGHTEEN

LIZZIE

Lizzie left Edward outside the pub that night and promised him she wouldn't tell anyone until they'd had time to think. Her mother took one look at her pale face when she walked in the door and knew instantly that there was something wrong. Lizzie pushed past her, said she was tired and needed to go for a lie-down. But her mum blocked her at the bottom of the stairs, held onto her shoulders with both hands and looked into her glassy eyes.

'Where have you been, Lizzie?'

'Just into town. I told you, I had to get some more books.'

'So where are they?'

'What?'

'The books.'

'Oh, I, er, they didn't have the ones I wanted, they've ordered them.' She shrugged her mother's arms off her shoulders and walked up the stairs, feeling her scepticism burning into the back of her head. She had perfected the art of lying in the last eighteen months. There was still a whirlpool of angst churning her up inside, but she somehow managed to restrain the heat from flushing to her cheeks. She spent the evening in her bedroom and when Edward arrived at the house the following morning, her mother made no attempt to hide her surprise.

'Edward, how lovely to see you!'

'Hi, Rosemary.'

'It's been a while, what have you been doing?'

'I've got a job at a bookshop in town.'

'Really? Lizzie didn't say.' She raised her eyebrows at Lizzie, now standing at the top of the stairs. 'Well, it's lovely to see you. I hope you're going to cheer this one up, she's been a right misery guts these last few weeks.'

'Oh, Mum,' she groaned. 'Come on up, Eddie.' And he ran up the stairs two at a time.

'I've found a place, Lizzie,' he said once they were safely ensconced in her bedroom with the door shut.

'What sort of place?'

'An abortion clinic. I called them, they could fit you in tomorrow.'

'Fit me in! You make it sound like a haircut.'

'I'm sorry, you don't have to go, of course. But I wanted to help, to give you the option.'

'What do they do?'

'What do you mean?'

'Well, how do they get it out of me? The baby, I mean?'

'I've no idea, Liz, you're the scientist.'

'Or maybe not.'

He took hold of both her arms; it hurt where his thumbs dug into her skin. 'But if you do this, Lizzie, you could be. I mean, you could still go to university, become the doctor you always wanted to be. This doesn't have to be it for us, Liz.'

'Do you have to pay?'

'Er, yeah, but don't worry about that. I've got the money.'

'How? Not from your dad?'

'No, god no, I'm not going to tell him. From the shop, I've been saving.'

'But you need that for Oxford!' He didn't reply to that, just fixed her with a look that said, well, I won't be going to Oxford if you don't go through with this.

'I- I'll think about it,' she said, and he smiled and let go. He picked up some of the textbooks that were piled on the floor, waiting to be packed for Manchester, and he flicked through the pages absent-mindedly. He couldn't sit down but wandered up and down the room, fiddling with the trinkets on her desk and the tassels on her curtains until she could bear it no more and agreed to go to the appointment.

'It will be OK, Lizzie,' he said, trying to contain the smile that was making its way across his cheeks as he drew her in for a hug. And then he left.

The following morning Lizzie ran out of the house while her mum was on the phone, doubting her capacity to fool her again. She had been told not to eat anything before the appointment and her stomach churned with the emptiness. Edward was waiting for her at the station when she got off the train and they walked together. The clinic was on the outskirts of town and they walked around the ring road in silence. The cars whizzed past them at speed. Edward was just ahead of her and was walking fast. He wanted this, Lizzie thought, he wanted this situation to be over and done with so he could go to Oxford and leave her behind. He was walking fast into his life without her, and she was struggling to keep up. Struggling to stay next to him on the pavement as the cars and lorries raced past and nearly knocked her off her feet. He turned down an alley behind B&Q and startled a fox who was working his way through a bin bag of rubbish. It ran away and they had to step over the cartons of milk and shredded kebab wrappers that had spilled out onto the street. It turned Lizzie's stomach and she had to swallow down the vomit that crept up the back of her throat.

'It's just down here,' Edward said, taking her arm and guiding her left at the end of the alley. The clinic was a Portakabin with bars on the windows in a car park surrounded by a high metal fence. Lizzie faltered at the gate.

'You OK?' Edward asked.

THE SAPPHIRE COVE   235

'It looks pretty grim, Eddie. Did you say we have to pay for this?'

'Come on, it will be fine. It's a proper clinic with proper doctors, not some dodgy place like you see in the movies.' He put his arm through hers and they walked towards the door. Edward did the talking, checked her in with a woman behind a plastic screen whose eyes never left her computer as she thumped the keyboard with her fat fingers and fake nails. He knew her address but had to ask what her date of birth was. The woman looked up for the first time at the date of birth and scowled at Lizzie, then handed her a clipboard with forms to fill in and a leaflet secured under the clip. It had the strapline 'What is a termination?' in blue bubble writing at the top and a list of bullet points beneath it. Lizzie tried to read it but the words blurred and jumped at her without context or meaning. Vacuum, foetus, suction, gestation, aspiration. Her stomach gurgled and she held onto the base of the plastic seat to stop her head from swimming. There were two other girls waiting, one with her mother, the other with a friend. They were both older than her but not by much.

'Lizzie Claybourne?' A woman in scrubs with a black bob and dark-rimmed glasses came into the waiting room. Lizzie looked at Edward, who willed her on with his eyes. 'Good luck,' he whispered. There was no question of him accompanying her, and so she followed the woman down the corridor, her trainers squeaking on the shiny floor.

The doctor was kind despite her severe haircut and spoke to Lizzie with a soft voice. She asked when her last period was and whether she had told her parents. Lizzie considered lying but then figured it was pointless. Then she asked whether she understood what would happen to her today if she decided to go through with the termination. And Lizzie was surprised to hear her answers, articulate and bright, though her heart hammered hard inside her chest and her feet were sweating inside her trainers. The doctor said that she would examine her now, and there would be a chat with their psychologist, just to make sure she knew what she was doing. Then she would go upstairs for the procedure. She used the words from the leaflet, vacuum and suction and aspiration, and suddenly all Lizzie could think of was Isabelle. She'd been vacuumed and pumped and sucked in the hospital that night, when they pumped her stomach of all the pills and vodka, but it was too late.

The woman asked her to take off her pants and lie down on the bed. 'Try to relax,' she said as she inserted a cold, hard probe inside her, and it felt as though she was being ripped apart. She looked up at the ceiling; there was a world map which had pictures of animals on the corresponding countries. Lions in Africa, monkeys in Asia, koalas in Australia. And she thought of the nuns and their geography lessons, of Sister Agatha with the stick that she would point at countries and demand the capital. And then she thought of Isabelle and of all of the world that she wouldn't see. All of the world this baby wouldn't see. The probe delved deeper. She would be vacuumed and suctioned and aspirated. Just like Isabelle. And then came the sirens and the screams, the sounds of her nightmares. And the nuns were there again, herding them into their dormitories where the blue light still flashed through the window and lit up the walls. And Sister Teresa made them get down on their knees and pray for Isabelle, for her soul, for her sins. And they could still hear the screams of Vanessa Simpson who had found Isabelle in the woods while she was walking Sister Beatrice's dog. And sister Beatrice was trying to calm her, to physically restrain her as she writhed and shouted as though she was possessed. Lizzie bit down on her lip, punctured the skin, the taste of blood in her mouth. The probe was removed, and the doctor gave her a tissue to mop up the jelly, the flecks of blood.

'Are you OK, Lizzie?' the doctor asked.

'I can't,' she stammered. 'I can't do this.'

'It's all right, no one is making you do this. You can go away and think about it.' The doctor reached behind for a leaflet from her desk, the same leaflet, the same words.

'Just take this, talk to your parents. You know where we are.'

'I'm sorry, I...' Lizzie ran out of the room, down the corridor and into the waiting room. She didn't look at Edward; she ran past him and out the front door. Out into the car park where she gasped big lungsful of the fetid air.

'Lizzie.' Edward was beside her, his arm around her shoulders.

'I can't... I couldn't do it...' she gasped, and she felt him stiffen.

'It's OK, it's OK,' he said and drew her into his chest. 'It's OK.' He said it again but she knew it wasn't. He walked her back to the station, and this time he didn't rush. He scuffed his feet and dragged behind her. They didn't speak, each lost in their own dark thoughts.

When she walked back into her house an hour or so later, her mother was waiting at the front door. Had she been there all that time? She took one look at Lizzie and she didn't ask where she'd been and Lizzie fell into her arms and told her. There was no open-mouthed shock or hysterical retribution. Just a weary nod of recognition. And Lizzie was carried along on the wave of events much in the same way as when they'd pulled her out of school only eighteen months earlier. The same familiar sensation of travelling underwater. Her senses dulled, her reactions slow and tempered. Her father was told and she heard them rowing from her bedroom that night. But when she emerged the following morning, the table was laid for breakfast as usual. He sat in his chair at the head, reading his newspaper and decapitating his boiled egg as if it were any other day.

'So, Lizzie, your mother has told me your news,' he said without lifting his eyes from the broadsheet next to his breakfast plate. 'Obviously it's a shame that you won't be able to take up your university place, but, well, what's done is done.'

She slumped into the chair next to him. His eyes moved from newspaper to egg and then back to the newspaper again. 'We've got it all sorted, your mother and I. You can go and live in the flat in London with Edward. I have been on the phone to an old mucker at the *Herald* who says he can give him a job. I will stay at the club. You wouldn't want your old dad there while you're starting your family, would you?' He spooned some egg onto a triangle of toast and put it in his mouth, wiping the corners of his lips with the napkin in his lap.

Lizzie couldn't speak; she felt as if her life was on fast-forward with someone else at the controls. Not just her life, but Edward's too. Edward, who couldn't even touch her in the broad light of day; Edward who had lied to her. Edward who had wanted her to have an abortion so that he could pursue his dreams at Oxford. She looked at her dad who was now shovelling the last spoonful of boiled egg into his mouth, pieces of dried yolk stuck to his lips. How dare he tell her what to do with her life? Edward's, too? It was none of his fucking business! But she didn't; she swallowed down the bile rising at the back of her throat and left the table.

And because Edward was an honourable and kind soul, that is what happened. They moved into her parents' flat in Kensington and Edward took the job at the *Herald*, where he wrote up births, deaths and marriages and made cups of tea. They got married, in a registry office on the King's Road, with only her parents there as witnesses. 'More like security,' Edward joked. 'Here to make sure we go through with it!' But nobody laughed. After the deed was done her parents headed straight back home and she and Edward had a cup of tea and a slice of ginger cake back at the flat. It curdled in her stomach and came back to haunt her half an hour later.

Lizzie was horribly sick. Her mother and the midwives all told her that it would stop at twelve weeks which was when they moved into the flat, but it didn't. As her baby grew from a pea, to a plum, to an orange it carried on. Week after week she was plagued with a sickness that only stilled when she lay on her side in a dark room. Even the flicker of the TV made her want to throw up. She tried, for the sake of Edward and her own sanity. They walked up Kensington High Street, bought noodles and browsed in the market. But the smell of incense turned her stomach and she threw the noodles back up so promptly they barely looked any different on the pavement as they had in the takeaway carton. Edward tried to be sympathetic but Lizzie could see the weary look of despair that he carried around with him. His shoulders were hunched and he dragged his feet across the floor just as he had that time she went to his house on Wilton Street.

He would come home after work and find her still in her pyjamas. Dirty plates and mugs were strewn across the flat and she knew he was disappointed in her, and yet she was just too tired to do anything about it.

'What have you done today, Lizzie?' he'd ask, trying to sound cheery.

'Nothing, Eddie, as usual. But I managed to keep my ham sandwich down for lunch, so that has been a highlight.'

He slumped onto the sofa next to her and picked up the plate smeared with butter that was balancing precariously on the arm and put it on the coffee table in front of them.

'This place is a shithole,' he said with a sigh.

'I'm sorry, I promise I'll do a clear-up tomorrow. I tried today but I just felt so rough. How was work?'

'Same old. Had to write an obituary on some anthropologist, so I guess that was better than most days.'

'That's good, I thought they usually got Gregg to write the obituaries.'

'Yeah, well, Gregg was off sick so I got to do it.'

'That's great, Eddie. Once they see how brilliant your writing is they will surely give you more to do.' A glimmer of hope; she so wanted him to be happy, for him not to resent her for the life that he had unwittingly found himself in. 'I'm sorry about the flat, promise I'll sort it out tomorrow.' He smiled at her but there was a blankness behind his eyes, a dark cloud that he was so obviously fighting. 'Maybe we should go out to celebrate?'

'I don't think it really merits a celebration, Lizzie.'

'Oh, come on, I haven't left the flat all day and I haven't puked since this morning, so that's double cause for celebration.'

'I don't know, Lizzie, I'm really tired.'

'Come on, Eddie, we need this. We should be out getting high at student club nights and drinking our body weight in snakebite and black.'

'You don't need to remind me.'

'So come on, then. Let's go to the Wok Inn at the end of the road. You got paid today, didn't you?'

And so Lizzie changed out of her pyjamas for the first time in two days and went out into the cold night air. They pretended not to peer into the windows of the houses as they passed. Families seated around dinner tables and snuggled up on sofas, the reflective flicker of the TV on their faces. Lizzie linked her arm through Edward's.

'We're going to be OK, you know,' she said cheerfully. 'We've totally got this family thing nailed.' And as she spoke, she felt the now familiar movement of the baby inside her.

'Oh, there it goes.'

'Really? You can feel it move?'

'Yeah.'

'You never said.'

'I wasn't sure the first few times, it just felt a bit like an air bubble. But then it kept on happening and I'm pretty sure now.'

She pulled his hand under her coat and rested it on her bulging tummy. He waited expectantly, a sparkle in his eye that faded slowly with no sign of movement. 'Wait, just be patient,' she said. And there it was again, a tiny flutter of hope. Edward drew in a quick breath; his eyes lit up.

'Was that it?'

'Yeah.'

'I felt it!'

'Yeah, that was it.'

'I can't believe it! That was our baby!' He put his arm around her and they continued to walk down the street, smiles on their faces.

The Wok Inn was surprisingly busy for a Tuesday night. There was only one table left by the door. The windows were all fugged up with smoke and steam and the smell of chilli and garlic caught at the backs of their throats. They settled into their table and Eddie ordered two beers and prawn crackers, spring rolls, Peking duck, steamed dumplings and chicken chow mein, all of which he devoured greedily. Lizzie picked at the prawn crackers and took tentative sips of her beer, determined to enjoy the evening.

'So, what do you think we should call this baby?' she asked with forced cheer.

'What about Oliver or Heathcliff for a boy?'

'Oliver maybe, but I'm not sure about Heathcliff. What about Oscar?'

'Yeah, I like Oscar, as in Wilde.'

'It doesn't have to have a literary significance, you know. What about girls' names?'

'Juliet?' he suggested tentatively. 'Or Rosamund or Velvet?'

'There you go again! Velvet? No daughter of mine is going to be named after my mother's favourite ball dress material.'

He laughed. 'What about Scout?'

'Sounds like a dog's name.'

'All right then – you come up with some.'

'Um, I like Daisy, and Lily and Rose...'

'Flowers.'

'What's wrong with that?'

'It's a bit...'

'A bit what?'

'Wishy-washy.'

'Really? OK, well, we're going to have to come up with something in between wishy-washy flowers and Shakespearean heroines then.'

'Shouldn't be too hard!' He picked up the last spring roll from the plate and Lizzie had a sip of her beer and it didn't burn as it made its way down her throat.

'Edward!'

Edward swung round to see a tall man in a navy overcoat and felt trilby tapping him on the shoulder. 'David, hi.'

'Do you live around here?'

'Yes, just down the road. You too?'

'No, just met up with an old friend, Joseph, and he lives round the corner.' He patted Joseph, a man with a generous smile and kind eyes, on the back. 'Joseph Cruz, this is Edward Thatcher, he works on births, deaths and marriages.'

'Don't forget obituaries,' Lizzie piped up.

Edward blushed and blinked a few times. 'Sorry, this is Lizzie, my wife Lizzie.'

'Nice to meet you, Lizzie.'

'You too.' She held out her hand and shook David's in his leather gloves and then Joseph's ungloved, surprisingly soft hand. 'Do you work at the *Herald* too?'

'Yes, I'm the arts and literature editor,' David said.

'Really? Well, you need Edward on your team then, he's wasted on births, deaths and marriages. Have you read any of his poetry?'

'Lizzie, please...' Edward blushed a deeper shade of crimson and wrung his hands together in his lap.

'No, I haven't!'

'You really don't have to,' Edward said, and shot Lizzie a look, but she was on a roll.

'You should, he is extremely talented. Oxford wanted him after reading his poems.'

'Oxford indeed?'

'Yes, well, that's another story...'

'One I'd like to hear, I'm sure!' David laughed and exchanged a glance with Joseph, who smiled.

'Lizzie, please,' Edward said under his breath.

'Why don't you bring some of your pieces into the office, Edward?'

'You really don't have to...'

Joseph laughed. 'How wonderful, David, just think, if we hadn't bumped into Edward and Lizzie here you might never have known that here was the next poet laureate stuck on births, deaths and marriages in the corner of the office.'

Lizzie beamed at Edward, delighted with herself. It was most unlike her to be so brazen but she felt invincible, buoyed by the beer, the baby kicking, the glimmer of hope.

'Well, we must be off, don't want to intrude on your dinner any further. But Edward, please do bring them in, if your Lizzie here thinks they're worth something.'

'I don't know.'

'Oh, go on.' Joseph nudged Edward's shoulder with his elbow. 'What have you got to lose? It was lovely to meet you both.'

'You too,' Lizzie said with a smile.

'Yes... er, see you tomorrow, David,' Edward said, barely able to look up from his plate.

'That was excruciatingly embarrassing,' he said after they had gone.

'Oh, come on, Eddie, you've got to put yourself out there. What else are you going to do with all those poems? Just leave them lying in the bottom drawer of your desk? And what are the chances of bumping into the arts and literature editor on our one night out? It was fate, I tell you, Eddie. I've got a good feeling about tonight. Maybe our life isn't over after all.'

CHAPTER NINETEEN

ROMY

Romy's condition stabilised in the week that Joseph was away, and every day she became a little stronger. She checked her phone obsessively for news from England and her heart missed a beat every time it rang that it might be her sister or even her mother. But it never was. Joseph called every day at four o'clock her time, eight in the morning over there. He told her about his gallant rescue of Flora from the freezing sea. She struggled to imagine it. To her sea was warm, colder in Hong Kong than the Philippines but not the icy cold that Joseph described. He said he too struggled to breathe and worried that he would drown while trying to rescue her. It all felt so alien to Romy, this world that she had never experienced despite her English heritage. Joseph told her about Flora, that she was beautiful and kind and insecure. 'A gentler version of you,' he had said. 'Less confidence, fewer sharp edges.' She was anxious, he said, and the prospect of flying to the other side of the world and undergoing this operation would be a lot for her to take on. But she had hidden depths, and maybe this was the opportunity she needed to realise them. It was going to be a long process before they found out whether Flora was a match. Months, possibly, of tests and interviews and scans. And even then, apparently, there was only a twenty-five per cent chance of a sibling being a full match. Right now, Romy would settle for anything. The doctors said that if they managed to do all the testing quickly and Flora was a match, then there was a possibility they might be able to avoid putting her on dialysis. But there were so many ifs before they could get to that point.

And her mother never called. After those first few days of her heart racing every time her phone beeped, Romy settled into the disheartened knowledge that her mother had no intention of coming to find her. In fact, she scolded herself for harbouring any such hope. She hadn't tried to find her for the past thirty years, so what made her think that she would come rushing to the other side of the world to find her long lost daughter now? And so Romy blocked her mother out of her thoughts as she had learned to do time and time again with each sadness in her life, swallowing the resentment down every time it reared its bitter head, like a bad dose of heartburn.

She spent a lot of time looking out of the window in her hospital bedroom, trying to remember the people she had watched all those years ago in the flats opposite. She wondered whether the young mother with a baby on the fourth floor could in fact be the teenager that she had watched sneaking out of the apartment after her parents had gone to bed. Or if the man who now lifted weights in the middle of the night was the same man she had watched with a wife and two children playing Uno at their kitchen table every evening. She was also delighted to see that the lady with the noodle stand across the road was still there after all this time. One evening she persuaded the nurse on night duty to let her go for a walk. The noodle lady had grown a little wider but had barely aged a day in the fourteen years since Romy had seen her. She greeted Romy like a long-lost friend, hugging her and pinching her cheeks. And Romy bought some of the noodles and took them back to her room in the hospital, and she was so delighted to be able to eat something other than the dried-up hospital food that she wolfed it down hungrily. She was busted by the night nurse, but seeing her appetite returning she pretended not to notice and turned a blind eye when she disappeared for a walk at the same time every evening.

One night she arrived back with her noodles to find Stefan, Joseph's boyfriend, standing at the window.

'Stefan!' she said, putting her noodles down on the table.

'Romy, hi. I hope you don't mind me coming. I brought some treats from Angel.' He pointed to a box on the table by the window. She peered inside. There was freshly baked bread and cookies, and mangoes and a bowl of adobe chicken and rice. 'She didn't like to think of you surviving on the hospital food, but it looks like you already figured that out!'

'Thanks, please tell her I am so grateful. And, er, don't tell about the noodles.'

He laughed. 'Don't worry, your secret is safe with me. Oh, and here, I brought you these.' He handed her a bunch of flowers, orchids, pink kalachuchi and jasmine. They were tied together with a piece of string. She took them from him and buried her face in the sweet perfume. 'Did you pick these?' she asked.

'Yeah, I remember Joseph telling me that the kalachuchi was your favourite.'

'It is. Thanks, they're really lovely.'

'Please. Eat your noodles. They will be getting cold.'

She perched on the edge of the bed and pulled the pot of noodles out of the plastic bag and snapped the chopsticks.

'Do you want some?'

'No, I had some of the adobe chicken earlier.'

'Angel's famous adobe chicken.'

'She sends you lots of love.'

'Thank you, it's really kind of you to come.' He smiled.

'Have a seat,' she said, pointing with her chopsticks at the chair and then shovelling a mouthful of noodles in. It wasn't the easiest thing to eat while chatting, and strands stuck to her chin.

'It's good to see you up and about. You gave us all quite a fright that night.'

She had forgotten that he'd been driving the boat. That he saw her in that state. 'Sorry. Thanks for driving the boat. Apparently, you got us here at record speed.'

'Yeah, I came home early, I was meant to be in Manila until the next day but my meeting was cancelled.' It hadn't even occurred to her that he wasn't meant to be home.

'Thank goodness you were there.'

'I've never driven the boat at night. It was quite a baptism of fire!' She hadn't seen the humility in him before; it had been hiding beneath all that bravado.

'I bet. You didn't crash into any ferries then?'

'No, thank god. I think something or someone must have been guiding me here as I couldn't see a thing.' She looked at him, unsure whether he was alluding to her father or not. 'Look, Romy, I know it must have been a shock to find Joseph with someone else, and he should have told you about me. But I just want you to know that I'm not here to replace Ted. From what I gather that would be a really tall order.' He laughed and she swallowed down another mouthful of noodles so she didn't have to respond. 'But I would really like to get to know you, if that's OK, I mean.'

'Sure,' she said, and laughed as the sauce dribbled down her chin.

'He really missed you, Joseph I mean. He talks about you all the time. And he follows you on Facebook, you know, spends hours every evening looking at your photos and telling me what you've been up to.'

'No way! Joseph, on Facebook?'

'I know, not such a Luddite after all.'

'So he knew all about me, my job, my friends, boyfriends...?'

'Well, as much as you can glean from Facebook, but yeah, he knew.'

'Wow! I guess that explains why he didn't ask many questions when I came back.'

'You know Joseph, a man of few words.'

'He's not big on chat, is he?'

'God knows what he sees in me, I never know when to shut up!'

'It's obvious why you work together.' He looked pleased when she said that and settled back into his chair. And she realised she was enjoying herself; she hadn't spoken to anyone other than the doctors and nurses since Joseph had left, and it felt good to discuss something other than kidney function. 'Stefan, do you play cards?' she asked on a whim.

'I do. Bet I could whip your ass at gin rummy.'

'You're on.'

And so they played rummy, and then whist, and he came back every other day and they chatted and played some more. Every time he brought more treats from Angel, and she didn't get noodles on those nights, so they would eat supper together. He told her about his career as a journalist and war zones he had been to, the atrocities he had seen. She liked him, she enjoyed his company. He was funny and dry and didn't shy away from her questions. And Romy was pleased that Joseph had found someone not that dissimilar to Ted after all.

In the week that Joseph had been away Romy's anger had weakened to a gentle simmer. She was still cross about the lies he had told and the relationships with her mother and sister that they had denied her. But she had really missed him while he was gone and realised that having only just got him back, she wasn't ready to give him up again. When he walked tentatively into the room, she jumped out of bed and threw her arms around his neck.

'Wow, you seem better,' he chuckled as she held onto him.

'I am, they say I can go home.'

'That's great!' he said, pulling away to look at her. 'And which home will you be going to?'

'I was hoping I could come back with you. I have to come back here very week to check my kidney function, so...'

'I would love that.'

Stefan came to pick them up that afternoon and drove them back to Siquijor on the boat. There was a storm approaching and it was a bumpy ride, and for the whole journey Romy could feel Joseph's eyes on her, wincing for her every time the hull crashed down on top of a wave.

'I'm fine, Joseph,' she shouted to him on the other side of the boat. 'You're gonna have to stop worrying about me all the time or we'll go bonkers.'

He didn't answer but nodded unconvincingly and she turned round to Stefan who was smiling at her behind the wheel.

'Wooo-hoooo!' she screamed into the wind, and Stefan laughed while Joseph held onto the side of the boat, his forehead wrinkled with angst.

Romy was surprised at how easily she settled back into life on the island. She would get up late, and nibble at the plate of fruit that Joseph prepared for her. Some days she felt strong enough to swim, or at least sit on the end of the jetty and dip her feet in the water. She would watch the fish that came up to inspect and sometimes nibble at her toes. She read every book in the guest house library and then she started on the more cerebral ones in Ted's study. She hovered outside the door that first time, summoning the courage to enter his sacred space as she had done even when he was alive. But when she dared to enter, she was surprised to find it exactly as he had left it. Except cleaner, no one other than Ted was allowed to touch anything in there when he was around, not even Joseph. And Ted was oblivious to the piles of dust and the smell of mildewed books and festering coffee cups. But that day everything glistened in its haphazard piles, a sure sign that Joseph was a regular visitor. He was quite affronted when he found Romy in there with her feet up on the desk reading one of his books of poems. But once she had sheepishly put her feet back on the floor he smiled and left her to it.

She had never had the time nor the inclination to fully invest in his poems before. But now, in the wake of so much emotional turmoil and on the edge of something so monumental, they gave her an insight into his soul that she had never seen before. It was as if somebody had shone a light on his heart, and where she had only seen shadows there was now clear definition. He had obviously carried the guilt of what he had done to Lizzie and in turn Flora around with him like a lead weight dragging him down. Always there, lurking in the shadows, even on those glorious days of sunshine and flowers, dive trips and tropical beaches. Romy had thought him artistic and morose, but it ran so much deeper than she could possibly have imagined.

In the afternoons, exhausted by the morning's activities she would doze. Sometimes in a hammock on the balcony, other days in her bed under the mosquito net which swayed in the breeze of the fan. In the evenings they would play backgammon. Stefan was sometimes there but more often than not he was away on business. Romy couldn't help wondering whether he was manufacturing these trips to give her and Joseph time together and she was partly grateful, but she missed him when he was gone. He brought a lightness to the villa, and to Joseph, whose mollycoddling was driving Romy slightly mad.

Every week Joseph would take her over to the hospital on the mainland for more tests. Her kidney function was getting worse, and each week they told her that they might not be able to hold off dialysis for much longer. After these visits, Joseph would phone Flora. She had been assigned a kidney coordinator, apparently, a severe-sounding woman called Megan. Flora had passed the initial health and psychological screening and was going to be called in for a day of more comprehensive testing. CT scans and more bloods; she was even going to be injected with some radioactive tracer to see how her kidneys functioned in response. It felt strange to Romy, that this woman who she had never met living on the other side of the world was going through all of this for her. They were still communicating only through Joseph. That had been Romy's call, at the beginning; she didn't want to meet her long-lost sister for the first time on a screen. And she looked so ill and skinny – she didn't want Flora seeing her like that. Joseph had suggested that it might help her cause, but she didn't want Flora to be guilted into this. She needed to know that she had gone into it from an informed and unemotional perspective. So Joseph continued to speak to Flora. Sometimes Romy was in the room and she could hear her voice, echoey and distant, and she wanted to grab the phone, to speak to her sister for herself, but something always held her back. It was ten weeks to the day after she had left hospital that the call they had all been waiting for came through.

Stefan was away and Joseph and Romy were sitting at the supper table on their balcony. It was dark and the citronella candles were burning low. The sea was gently lapping at the shore beneath them and the buzz of the cicadas fizzed all around them. Then Joseph's phone glowed and Flora's name shone on the screen. Romy had learned not to get her hopes up every time she rang. So she picked up the empty plates and took them to the kitchen while he answered.

And it was as she was the scraping the remnants of her vegetable stir-fry into the bin that she heard his scream. '*What?*' he was saying as she rushed back into the room. 'And you're sure? You're really, really sure?' He turned to Romy who was standing in the doorway and he smiled and nodded, slowly at first and then with a manic, crazed look in his eyes. 'Hang on, hang on, Flora, I just have to tell Romy, she's here. What? well, er, OK. You tell her then.'

He walked towards Romy who was venturing slowly into the sitting room and he handed her the phone. She tried to push it away, mouthed '*no*' to Joseph but he forced it into her hand.

'She wants to tell you herself, Romy,' he said.

Romy put the phone to her ear. 'Hi, Flora?' she said, her heart pounding so hard in her chest she thought it might burst out of her ribcage.

'Yeah, Romy, hi.'

'Hi,' she said again and then realised how ridiculous it sounded.

'So it turns out I'm a match!' Flora's voice was deep and smooth, like something out of an English period drama.

'Really?'

'Yeah, really! In fact, I'm a good match, ten out of the twelve markers are the same as yours.'

'Seriously?'

'Seriously. I'm going to book myself a flight.'

'I- I don't know what to say. Are you sure? I mean, are the doctors sure? Like... really sure?'

'Yeah, they're sure. They've done every single bloody test under the sun and they're sure. I'm coming, I'm going to see you really soon!'

'OK, I can't believe it. Fuck!'

'Yeah, fuck!' She could hear Flora smiling on the other side of the world.

'But wait, Flora, are you sure you want to do this? I mean, you don't even know me. We haven't even met. Have you really thought it all through? It's a hell of an ask, I just—'

'Romy.'

'Yeah.'

'I have never been more sure of anything in my whole life. I'll see you soon, OK?'

'OK.'

And then she was gone, and the moment, that moment she had been waiting for on so many different levels was over. But it was OK. She was coming. She was going to meet her sister.

CHAPTER TWENTY

FLORA

The testing process for Flora had been thorough and relentless. Joseph had set up the initial meeting for her at the hospital in Dorchester only two days after she agreed to do the tests. He delayed his flight for a couple of days so that he could accompany her. They met with Megan, the kidney coordinator. She had small eyes, made even smaller by thick glasses, and she wore a layer of foundation on her pointy features that gave the impression that she was made out of plastic. There was nothing warm about Megan. She grilled Flora about her motives. Why was she doing this? Had she really thought it all through? Was she fully aware of the dangers? Did she realise that only fifty per cent of live kidney donors who have this meeting actually end up becoming donors? 'They have second thoughts, they aren't fit enough or discover an underlying health condition they never knew they had. People get pregnant, or there's divorce, family breakdown.' She rattled the reasons off as if she was dictating a shopping list, and every time she said the words 'live kidney donor' Flora winced.

'What's the alternative? Dead ones?' she asked with a laugh.

'Of course,' Megan answered with disdain.

'Look, Flora, I am not here to reassure you.' You're not kidding, thought Flora. 'My job is to make sure you are fully aware of what you're getting yourself into, so that you don't go halfway down this whole process and then become one of the fifty per cent that don't make it. Obviously, you can't help it if that's for biological reasons and out of your control. But I need to know that you are fully prepared psychologically. If you are a match, and we have a long way to go before we get to that point, but if you are, you will walk into that hospital in the Philippines a well person and leave a sick one.'

Flora left that first meeting with Megan and ran into the bathroom thinking she might throw up. She retched over the bowl but nothing came up. She splashed cold water on her face and looked at her pallid complexion and dilated pupils in the bathroom mirror. Megan was right: she had no idea what she was letting herself in for. She had come along today full of altruism, fancying herself as a heroine, saving her long-lost sister. But in doing so she would be putting herself at risk. She had to think about her children. Her own family.

Joseph was waiting for her outside the bathroom, pacing the corridor and looking worried.

'Are you OK?'

'Yeah, she was just... Well, it was all a bit much.'

'Look, Flora, you really don't have to do this...'

'But I do, don't I?'

'Only you can decide that.'

'She is really full on, that Megan,' Flora said and exhaled through puffed cheeks.

'Yes, she is, but I think it's all part of the process.'

'What do you mean?'

'She was out to scare you.'

'And it worked, I'm absolutely terrified.'

'That's part of her job, she said it herself. They don't want people wasting hospital time and resources.'

'I guess.'

'Look, Flora.' He touched her arm. 'You could just go home now. You could still meet Romy. She could go into the scheme, she is young, I'm sure a match would come along.' He was trying so hard to be understanding, to take the pressure off her, but Flora could feel the undercurrent behind his words. How could he not? She thought of her own children and the lengths she would go to, to save them.

'It's OK, Joseph. I'll do the tests. There's no point worrying about all of this until we know whether I'm a match or not, is there?'

'OK.' Relief flooded into his features and Flora felt the noose of his desperation tighten around her neck.

There were so many tests: for blood type, tissue type, kidney function, liver function, chest x-rays. They did them all that first day with Joseph at her side. It seemed strange that only a few days earlier she had never met him and yet there he was, this pillar of strength, right next to her. Every muscle in her body ached with exhaustion by the time they were finally spat out of the hospital and into the dusky drizzle late that afternoon.

'Hopefully see you soon,' Flora said with forced optimism as his taxi pulled up to take him to the airport.

'Flora, I, well we, Romy and I, can't thank you enough for what you're doing right now.'

'Let's just wait and see if I'm a match, hey?' she said and hugged him. As his taxi drove off she considered whether she meant what she had said. Did she hope to see him soon, or not? She couldn't answer that. There was no doubt that it would be a relief to be let off the hook and told she couldn't donate, but then who would? Who would save her sister? The sister she had never even met.

She called Doug from her car that evening in the hospital car park. She kidded herself that she wanted his medical opinion about all of this. But really, she wanted to hear his voice. He was shocked to hear her news, but calm and compassionate in his response. 'Any time you want to talk, or need some medical jargon explained, or just need some reassurance that you're doing the right thing, I will be here. It is an amazing thing you are doing, Flora, an extraordinary and wonderful and generous thing. You should be so proud of yourself. Your family, Romy, they will all be so proud of you.' She knew he had perfected his bedside manner, an essential part of his role as a doctor. But it worked. She felt buoyed by his words, calmed and encouraged as she drove home and confident that she was doing the right thing. An amazing thing. Something she should indeed be proud of.

But that confidence ebbed and flowed with the relentless interviews and tests that followed over the next few months. Jake accompanied Flora once, but he had never liked hospitals. He was quiet and surly and put Flora more on edge than when she'd just had Megan for company. So she told him not to come again and he didn't try to talk her out of it. Flora was surprised to find that Megan did in fact lighten up. Joseph was right; the pit bull she'd encountered on that first day was all part of the test that she hoped she'd passed. As the weeks wore on, Megan's dry but wicked sense of humour shone through her icy exterior. She had a good relationship with all the doctors and nurses they dealt with. They seemed to find her mildly terrifying but it helped Flora to get results fast and no-nonsense answers to all of her questions. And there were so many questions asked of Flora. She was grilled about her family medical history and had to tell the story over and over again about her father and how he had disappeared, about her mother and her depressive episodes and substance abuse. Every time she told the story of her past, a little more acceptance took root in her soul. There were psychological screenings as well. Flora recalled her failed attempt at therapy with Dr Jane and thought she would be proud of how far she had come. It was amazing how confidently she had learned to talk about her feelings when there was so much suddenly at stake.

She was, however, yet to confront her mother. Jeremy had called a few times since that fateful night of the row. Lizzie was doing well on crutches and the cast would come off in a few weeks' time. Flora responded with pleasantries but neither she nor her mother asked to speak to one another. There was an impasse between them that ran so much deeper than Lizzie realised. And it made Flora's blood boil to think of her mother's current grudge now that she knew about the lies she had been fed all her life. The nights were the worst; hours and hours of darkness devoid of distraction. When her mind reeled with memories of her child-hood, altered now with the knowledge of what could have been. Several times she got up and went downstairs to call Lizzie. To demand some answers to the questions that kept her awake. Why had she never looked for her sister? Why had she never told her about Romy so that she might look for her? Then she pictured her on the floor at the bottom of the stairs. Or in the hospital bed. Or on her bedroom floor caked in her own vomit, and she put the phone down and went back to bed.

There was a final intense day of testing at the hospital. A long day, Megan told her, when they would repeat blood and tissue tests but also do heart scans, inject her with radiation to test her kidney function, her liver function. It would finally give them the answers that they needed to ascertain if she was a match, and if she was, then how good a match. Flora felt the familiar prickling of nerves as the day approached. She considered asking Jake to accompany her but then thought of his awkward shuffling of feet in the corri-dors, his nervous cough that permeated the conversations with consultants. On a whim she called Doug two days before the big day, and without even asking he said he would like to come with her. That it would be fascinating for him in terms of his career and that he happened to have the day off anyway. And she had seen through all of that and welcomed his suggestion with relief.

She didn't tell Jake about Doug, and it gave her a bizarrely warming sense of satisfaction to hold onto that secret. They hadn't mentioned Jodie since his confession. Their lives had been thrown onto a different trajectory by Joseph and his revelation. But it still underpinned Flora's every waking thought and contributed to her sleepless nights. She tried not to picture them in the barn, their bodies fitting together like a puzzle that should never have been broken. Now she knew what had happened, there was no going back. Jake's moods swung like a pendulum. One day he was concil-iatory and overly attentive, insisting on cooking supper, putting the children to bed, sending her off to have hot, relaxing baths. And other days he was surly and introspective, hating himself or her, she couldn't quite tell which. He had moved back into her bed when Joseph came to stay and she hadn't asked him to move out again when he left. But they slept at either side, a cold chasm between them. One night she had actually fallen asleep and woke to find him crying. She wrapped her arms around his body which shivered with desperate sobs, and she kissed him and told him it was going to be OK. But the following morning there was no mention of it, and they skirted around each other's emotions once more.

Doug greeted Flora in the hospital car park with a hug, and when he pulled away his cheeks were flushed and his eyes glistening.

'Thank you so much for letting me come today,' he said.

'I'm sure I should be the one who's thanking you!'

'Shall we do this, then?' He put his hand gently on her back and guided her towards the hospital entrance.

'I did some of my training here,' he said as they entered through the double doors. His hand was still on her back and he tried to direct her to the left.

'It's this way,' she said, turning to the right.

'Oh, really? I could have sworn the Renal Unit was that way.'

'Maybe it's moved. Do you still know any doctors that work here?'

And he proceeded to list all the doctors he had trained with that might or might not still work at the hospital. Then he went on to talk about his training and which departments he had worked in for the entire seven years that it had taken for him to qualify as they made their way down the corridors and into the waiting rooms. Flora asked questions initially, pleased to have something to distract her from the nerves that fluttered in her belly. But she soon realised that he would continue with or without her probing.

During the meetings with the consultants and the blood tests with nurses, he asked questions on her behalf and explained processes that she had been told about countless times already. In the corridors and the waiting rooms between each test he talked about his son Harry, about his ex-wife, about the surgery he had done the day before, the meals he had cooked, even the brand of fluoride-free toothpaste he had recently discovered. His soft, mellow words soon lost their significance and echoed around her head like the background noise of a distant radio or fan. And the support and distraction that had boosted her at the beginning of the day turned sour, like the radiation pumping around her body. She prickled at his proximity and winced at the monotonous drone of his voice. Then he had taken her hand outside the MRI scanning room, and she had instinctively snatched it away. What followed was an uncomfortable yet welcome silence for ten minutes that felt like an hour. Her legs stuck to the back of the chair in her hospital gown, and her body flushed with heat despite being so scantily clad. She was actually relieved when they called her into the room and Doug wasn't allowed to accompany her. As she lay there in the tunnel that clanked and screeched like a steam train, as she listened to Mozart trying so valiantly yet hopelessly to drown out the noise of the machine, as she shut her eyes and tried to forget about the metal arch positioned so perilously close to her face, she wondered what on earth she was doing there with Doug. Doug, who had seemed to have all the answers in Oxfordshire. With his fresh face and boyish charm, his successful career, his heart on his sleeve. And yet here in the cold light of the hospital, when her sister's life was at stake, Flora realised that Doug wasn't the answer. Her racing heart slowed and the panic settled to a gentle fizz.

Doug hugged her with less enthusiasm in the car park at the end of the day.

'Thank you for coming with me,' she said meekly.

'It was an honour,' he said with infuriating sincerity. 'It really is an amazing thing that you are doing, Flora.' She thanked him again. But she didn't feel the same welling of pride that she had felt when he said it the first time. She rolled her eyes and walked back to her car, cringing. She called Lisa on her way home and told her about the way Doug spoke with his head on one side and his patronising tone while explaining procedures that had been explained to her so many times now that she felt more qualified than him. About how he had grabbed her hand and she had physically recoiled. About how she had got him so wrong.

Lisa had laughed. 'Well, now you can go back to your rugged, emotionally stunted husband with no shame,' she said.

And she did. Flora collapsed into Jake's arms when she arrived home. She held onto the back of his shirt and breathed in the smell of cut grass and sheep. Until Olive muscled her way in between them and Jake swung her onto his shoulders. Flora felt the freeze begin to thaw and in its a place a flicker of light glowing deep down inside.

It was three months after finding out about Romy that Flora got the call she had been waiting for. She was washing up after the kids' supper and was watching the children playing on the swing outside. It was May now, and the window was open and through it came the sound of birdsong and the sweet smell of the pink rose that was trying to clamber through the window frame. Her phone rang and she had to peel the rubber gloves off to answer it.

It was Megan. She asked Flora if she was sitting down. And then she told her that she was a match! She had been anticipating this moment for months, and until it came she had absolutely no idea how she would respond. She was happy, there was no doubt. She yelped, and Megan laughed.

'Really? Are they really sure?'

'Yes. You are a really good match.'

'What does that mean?'

'It means that ten out of the twelve of your markers are the same as Romy's. It means that there is very little chance of her body rejecting your kidney. It is almost the best possible outcome we could have hoped for.'

'Almost?'

'Well, twelve out of twelve would have been a perfect match, but you are pretty close.'

'I can't believe it!' Flora said. 'That's wonderful!' And she meant it. For that moment and at least a couple of minutes afterwards she had felt blissfully happy, and relieved, and excited. She was going to meet her sister.

Megan explained to Flora that normally, as a coordinator, she would accompany her through every step of the process, including the surgery. But that she couldn't accompany her to the other side of the world. She promised to call Flora in the hospital and told her that she could call her at any time, day or night. And then all the inevitable anxieties and doubts crept in. Like a festering piece of mould, they attached themselves to her happiness and tried to rot it. Flora felt her legs wobble beneath her and sat down at the kitchen table. She felt the sun's warmth on her back, heard the children's laughter in the garden, felt the familiar flutter of anxiety in the pit of her stomach. She could do this, she told herself. She had to do this, for Romy.

CHAPTER TWENTY-ONE

LIZZIE

After the night at the Wok Inn, things did pick up for Lizzie. Her sickness subsided a little and she made a conscious effort to clean the flat and make Edward dinner when he returned from work. She was a pretty dreadful cook, and her efforts were generally charred or tasteless, but he seemed to appreciate them. And the frost with which her parents had been treating her seemed to have, partially at least, thawed. They were starting to get quite excited about the prospect of a baby in the family. Her mum took her shopping for a Moses basket and brought up a box of Babygros, flannel nighties and crocheted blankets that she had kept from when Lizzie was a baby. They folded them together and placed them in tiny little piles in the chest of drawers in the spare room that was to become a nursery. Lizzie draped a Babygro over her protruding belly.

'I can't believe this thing growing inside of me is actually going to wear this.'

'I remember you wearing that one. Brought you home from hospital in it. You were so tiny. You screamed the whole way home in the car.'

'Oh god, did I cry a lot?'

'Yep, all the time. You looked so sweet, but you had a hell of a pair of lungs on you.'

'I hope I don't have a screamer.'

'You are going to be fine, darling,' her mother said without looking at her as she took the Babygro and placed it on top of the pile.

Edward was happier, too. He had taken his poems in to David and one of them had been published in the paper the following week. And then David had sent him out to review a play at the Donmar Warehouse and was delighted with his write-up. From then on, he sent David out at least once a week to an exhibition or concert. He was still having to do the births, deaths and marriages, but he was inspired by the culture he was witnessing and the fact that maybe his life wasn't over after all. He even brought Lizzie flowers home, a bunch of dahlias that got squished in his bicycle basket on the journey.

But one night the following month Edward didn't come home after work. He hadn't told her about a theatre trip or gig and he never called, and Lizzie sat up waiting for him. She had made bangers with buttery mash, just the way he liked it. But it grew cold and congealed, and a crust formed on top of the onion gravy. It was 2 a.m. when he finally stumbled in, and she was asleep on the sofa. He fell over the newly purchased buggy in the hallway and the clatter woke her.

'Where have you been?' she asked, wiping the sleep from her eyes.

'Sorry,' he said in a melodramatic whisper. 'Went for some Christmas drinks after work.'

'But it's 2 a.m.'

'Yeah, we had a lock-in. Shh, go back to sleep.'

But Lizzie couldn't sleep. She was thinking about lock-ins and underground bars filled with smoke and booze and all the illicit things that she was meant to be doing with her life and that Edward was doing without her. He had a dreadful hangover the following morning and left in a mad dash without any breakfast.

And then he did it again the following week. He did at least call her from the office that time. He said he was going to some advertising agency's Christmas party at a club in Soho. Lizzie had never been to a club in Soho; she imagined the flashing lights, the cocktails and synthesisers as she drank Gaviscon from the bottle in an attempt to quell the raging acid in her digestive system.

They spent Christmas Day at her parents' house with all her siblings and their snide remarks about their unlikely coupling. Jamie pretended he knew that Edward and Lizzie had been sleeping together in the summer, but she could tell that he didn't. His teasing reeked of resentment. None of them had known. She was secretly delighted that she had shocked and surprised them all. Safe old Lizzie, hard-working, boring Lizzie up to no good under the cloak of darkness. But Edward couldn't cope with their relentless mocking about the dirty nappies and sleepless nights that were heading their way. He became quiet and morose. The only time she saw him smile was at the pub on Christmas Eve after several shots and multiple pints. They sang Christmas carols all the way home and gorged on leftover fish pie in the kitchen. It turned Lizzie's stomach watching them dip it in pools of ketchup and so she went to bed, leaving them with a bottle of port and her father's cigars. When Edward finally joined her in her childhood bedroom hours later, his breath was fetid with smoke and port. He curled his body around hers like he had on those summer nights not so many months before and pressed himself hard into her back. He kissed her neck and her hair and put his arms around her. They landed on the bulge in her stomach and she felt the baby flutter beneath his hands and he froze. She turned over to face him, kissed him on the lips, wrapped her arms around his neck and pushed her leg up between his. But he didn't move.

'What's the matter?' she whispered.

'I can't, Lizzie, not with the baby.'

'The baby's not here yet, Eddie.' She snuggled into his neck. Kissed the bald patch of skin behind his ear.

'Stop it.' He pushed her away.

'What?'

'I told you, I can't do it, it might hurt the baby.'

'The baby is very protected up there, Eddie. I know about these things, I was going to be a doctor, remember?' She laughed and wrapped her arms around him.

'I said no, Lizzie.' He pushed her away, more definitely this time. She could feel the hard pressure of his hands on her side long after he had let go. He rolled over to the edge of the bed and she lay on her back, looking up at the glow-in-the-dark stickers on the ceiling. It wasn't long before he was snoring next to her and she was still staring at the stars, her hands where his had been on her belly, feeling the now familiar wriggle of their unborn child.

They went to see Edward's father on Boxing Day. It was only the second time Lizzie had met him after their brief encounter on the doorstep that fateful day. They drank sherry as they sat on the squeaky leather sofas in the front room and he gave them a giant teddy with a striped bow tie for the baby. He also wore a bow tie.

'That is so kind of you, Mr Thatcher.'

'Oh, please, call me Roger.'

'Is it one of your bow ties, Dad?'

'No, it came with the teddy.' He refused to rise to Edward's jibe and tweaked at the corners of his own bow tie. He was immaculately dressed in a crisp white shirt with creases down the arms and a sleeveless jumper with a diamond pattern, and the bow tie. Lizzie thought he should be working in an antique shop rather than a telesales office on the industrial estate.

'Will you come and visit us in London when the baby's born, Roger?'

'I don't know, Lizzie, I'm not very well, you see. Can't drive any more, and not sure I'm really up to public transport.'

'We'll bring the baby back to see you then. We're going to buy a car, aren't we, Eddie?'

'Neither of us can drive, Lizzie.'

'Well, we'll learn, can't be that hard.'

'That would be nice. I didn't think I'd have grandchildren.'

'Oh really, why's that?' Eddie shot his father a look and he seemed to falter.

'I guess I didn't think I would live long enough. But you two are ahead of the game!'

'Not intentionally, Dad.'

'Well, I think it's marvellous. I just wish your mother was here to meet the little one.'

'Shall I go and mash the potatoes, Dad?' Edward got up to leave the room.

'OK, son, that would be good. Plenty of butter and milk, you know, the way I taught you.'

'Would you tell me about her, Roger, Edward's mum, I mean?' Lizzie asked after Edward had left the room.

'Hasn't Edward told you about her?'

'No, not at all. He said he was too young to remember her.'

'Well, yes, I guess eleven is pretty young, but I know he remembers bits.'

'He was eleven when she died?'

'Yes, a week before his twelfth birthday, in fact.' Edward had told Lizzie he was four. Why would he lie about something like that?

'Well, she was gentle and kind and great fun. She loved music, and she was a very talented artist. She drew these flowers on the walls here.' He pointed up at some miniature watercolours of roses and lilies. They were partially hidden behind the curtain and Lizzie wondered whether that was why she had never noticed them the first time she came to see Edward. 'But unfortunately she suffered from depression, and she drank, and that was what got her in the end.'

'Oh really?'

'He didn't tell you how she died?'

'No.'

'Oh... well, maybe it should come from him... I don't want to...'

'Roger, please...'

'Well, he found her. She... er... she hung herself, and he came home from school and—'

'Oh god, poor Edward.'

'Yes, he, well, he didn't speak for a year afterwards, selective mutism, they call it. I was very worried about him... and then, well, I got ill two years ago, diagnosed with Parkinson's and he didn't take that very well either. And... but now he's got you and a baby, and... I can see you are just wonderful for him, Lizzie.' He reached over and took her hand, squeezed it tight between his shaking fingers.

'Lunch is ready.' Edward came back into the room and saw them holding hands and his pupils widened in alarm.

'Lovely.' Roger stood up, letting go of Lizzie's hand. 'I've cooked a sausage hotpot, Lizzie, it's Edward's favourite.'

'Delicious,' she said, standing up.

'No, you just stay there, we'll bring it all out,' Roger said, heading into the kitchen. Edward glanced at Lizzie and then chased after him and she could hear their heated whispers but couldn't detect the words.

They re-emerged with false smiles and plates laden with sausages and carrots, gravy and mashed potato. It was delicious: the sausages spicy, the gravy full of wine. But Lizzie pushed the food around on her plate and struggled to swallow. Her mind was swirling with all that she had learned.

'It's delicious, Roger. I'm afraid I just can't eat very big portions at the moment.' She gestured to her belly, which was now a significant bulge.

'Of course. Please don't feel like you have to eat it. I remember when Edward's mother was carrying him, all she wanted to eat was pickled onions and Edam!'

'Really? Eddie does love cheese, maybe that's why!' She smiled at Edward but he kept his head down, focused on the sausages. 'Maybe this one is going to have a thing for lemon cheesecake, it's the only thing I've wanted to eat for months!' Roger laughed and

Edward forced a smile. 'I've been painting the nursery,' she said. 'I don't have an artistic bone in my body, but I found this stencil set where you just fill in the fishes and turtles, and it's surprisingly satisfying.'

'Good for you, Lizzie, what colour have you painted it?'

'It's blue, for the sea, with yellow fish. I know blue is traditionally a boy colour, but I've always liked it so I hope she won't mind, if she's a girl!'

Roger asked Edward about his job and he gave curt answers between mouthfuls, and as soon as he had scraped his plate clean he got up and took it into the kitchen saying that they had to get back to London, that he had to work in the morning and there weren't many trains on the public holiday. Lizzie tried to protest; she had looked up the train times and there was at least one an hour until late into the evening. But he silenced her with a look and she didn't challenge him. She was taken back to the first and only other time she had been in his house and realised that, for whatever reason, he couldn't stand it. Or couldn't stand to have her there, she couldn't tell which.

When she went to say goodbye to Roger, he held onto her hands with both of his. 'It is so lovely to have you in the family, Lizzie,' he said and she thought she saw tears in his eyes and tried to hold on but Edward hurried her out the door, saying they would miss their train.

'Why didn't you tell me about your mother?' She hadn't asked on the walk to the bus stop, or on the bus, or as they waited on the freezing cold platform at the station. She had waited until they were on the train. Until it had chugged into action and they were rocking with the vibration past the terraced houses, the car show-rooms, the industrial estate on the edge of town where Roger worked, and into the frost-covered countryside.

Edward didn't answer. He looked out of the window, squinted at the fields and trees that glistened in the dying sun.

'Edward,' she tried again. 'Why didn't you tell me?'

'It's not something I find easy to talk about, Lizzie.'

'But why did you lie?'

'Because...' He shut his eyes, and his face glowed pink in the setting sun. 'Because...' He stopped as they entered a tunnel and were sucked into a vacuum of white noise, their ears popping. 'Because the lie was better than the truth.' His eyes were still closed. He sighed a weary sigh and opened them slowly. He turned to look at her.

'But Edward, we're having a baby together. We must be honest with each other, otherwise... well, what else do we have?'

'OK.' He nodded over and over as if gathering strength and the courage of his convictions.

'No more lies.' She could feel the folds of flesh gathering in her forehead as she looked at him. She knew she looked pitifully desperate but still he didn't answer. 'Edward, please.'

'OK, Lizzie, no more lies, I get it.'

'It must have been awful, finding her like that.'

'I can't talk about it, Lizzie.'

'But—'

'I said I can't talk about it.' His tone was harsh and she got it. Hadn't she shut everyone out with the same tone after Isabelle? She recalled the night of the play, his pressing her for details on the bench. And what came after. It made more sense now, his questions, his desperation to know what part she had played. It was all wrapped up in his own grief, the part that he had played. They spent the rest of the journey in silence and Lizzie didn't know whether to be comforted by the symmetry of their nightmares, or terrified. He went out when they got home, said he needed to go for a walk to clear his head. He was gone for three hours, and when he came back he slept in the bed in the nursery, still smelling of paint and covered in boxes. But he chose that over sharing a bed with her.

In the new year Edward was promoted to arts and literature deputy editor under David and another of his poems was published in the paper. He was given his own column and sent to the theatre at least three nights a week to review plays, and when he wasn't watching he was writing. Or so he told Lizzie. He was rarely home for supper and some nights not until the early hours. He took to sleeping in the nursery so as not to wake her. And every day her bump grew larger and more uncomfortable. The baby was due at the beginning of April and by mid-February she couldn't imagine how her stomach could stretch any further. The skin hurt it was so taught, and a fine brown line had emerged scaling its way down her bump from her belly button. Her body was changing so quickly and so definitively that she sometimes couldn't remember who she was or what she had ever looked like before. They went to some antenatal classes at the hospital in Paddington and felt conspicuous and patronised about their age. So when Edward couldn't make the third one because of a play, Lizzie neglected to turn up on her own.

Her parents were supportive on an ad hoc basis. Her mother liked to drop into the flat en route to dinner or some shopping spree. She constantly reminded Lizzie about the fact that she no longer had a pied-à-terre in London and how lucky she was to have been given the flat in such a salubrious area. But Lizzie didn't feel lucky; she felt lonely and scared, with way too much time on her hands to think about the life she thought she would be living at nineteen and how far from that she had fallen.

CHAPTER TWENTY-TWO

ROMY

Romy was admitted back into hospital on the day before Flora arrived. The doctors wanted to observe her for a few days before the operation. There were more tests to run, scans to do, tissue samples to take. That evening she and Joseph were playing Scrabble in her room in an attempt to distract themselves and calm their nerves. Neither of them was especially good at it.

'Is *nope* a word?' Romy asked, rearranging her letters.

'No, it's slang.'

'But I let you have *snot*.'

'S*not* is an actual thing, *nope* is just slang for *no*. Couldn't you put *open* instead?' He peered over at her letters and she turned them away from him.

'Hey, don't look! I can't do *open*, it will run into *boiler* which you were so proud of.'

'Ted will be turning in his grave,' Joseph said with a wry smile as he moved his letters around.

'Do you think he's watching us?'

'Of course.'

'Do you think he would approve of what we've done?'

Joseph looked up at her, surprised. 'Contacting Flora?'

'Yeah.'

'Definitely, he would just be sad that he wasn't going to meet her himself.' He went back to his letters.

'Well, if you won't let me have *nope*, I'm going to have to just do *not*, but it's on a double word score, so that's six.'

'We could be here all night at this rate.' Joseph wrote down her score.

'We don't have anywhere else to be.' He looked up and smiled at her, then with smug triumph placed his letters down on the board.

'*Project*, that's eight, nine, ten, eleven, twelve and three for *p*, fifteen, times two, thirty! Not bad!'

'So that's why you wouldn't let me have *nope*! You wanted to use the *p*!' He didn't answer, just smiled and wrote the score. 'What happened when he found out? That Lizzie was pregnant, I mean?'

He flinched, like he might have been given an electric shock, and then regained his composure and calmly considered his response. 'He tried to leave, to take you back.'

'Really?'

'Yes. He packed his bags and everything. I found him at the airport. I begged him to stay.' Romy was quiet. She looked down at her letters and moved them from side to side in the stand with her finger. She contemplated how different her life could have been. 'I'm sorry,' Joseph said eventually.

'Don't be,' she said with a lightness she didn't feel. 'I've had a wonderful life, Joseph, and I wouldn't have wanted it any other way.' He smiled but didn't look convinced. 'I bet Flora inherited the Scrabble gene. Didn't you say she worked in publishing?'

'Yes, I think you might be right!'

Romy had a restless night, and didn't get to sleep until the early hours of the morning. She felt as though she had only been asleep for a matter of minutes when she sensed something, someone. She opened her eyes to see her sister standing there, watching her.

'Hi,' Romy croaked. 'Flora?'

'Yeah, hi.' Her voice was soft, barely louder than a whisper. She smiled nervously and bit her bottom lip. 'Sorry I've arrived so early, but my flight landed before dawn and I wanted to come straight here.'

'It's fine,' Romy said, pulling herself up to sitting and hooking the strap of her vest back up over her shoulder. The gentle light of dawn had barely entered the room and Joseph was still asleep next to her in the chair. Romy ran her hands through her short hair; she could feel it standing on end and tried to press it down. Flora, in contrast, had long hair, to below her shoulders, dark with a curl. She looked quite pale with exhaustion and yet serenely beautiful. Her eyes were big and brown, like Romy's, but her face was fuller, rounder. And her mouth was wide and bore a perfect set of bright white teeth. 'It's so nice to meet you,' Romy whispered. She didn't want Joseph to wake up; she wanted to have this moment to herself.

'You too,' Flora said. She was still holding onto a wheelie suit-case behind her, a rucksack on her back. She pulled it from her shoulders and put it down on the floor and then perched on the side of Romy's bed.

'I can't believe I have a sister!' Romy said and laughed.

Flora laughed too, a quiet laugh, and her eyes flicked to Joseph. Maybe she too wanted to treasure this moment. 'Me neither!'

'How was your flight?'

'Long, the longest flight I've ever been on. Had to stop in Dubai and then Hong Kong. I feel quite delirious.'

'I bet!'

Romy grabbed her hand then; she curled her fingers behind Flora's knuckles and squeezed. 'Thank you for coming, for what you are going to do. I know it's such a huge ask... and...' She could feel her voice cracking.

'It's OK,' Flora said. 'I know you would do the same.'

'Flora!' Joseph woke in the chair and stood up so quickly that he had to hold onto the bed to steady himself. Once he had composed himself he walked around the bed and Flora stood to hug him. It felt strange, watching these two people embracing, knowing that they had already exchanged so much. Once Joseph released Flora, he smiled a huge, beaming smile at Romy. 'So you two have met?'

'Yeah.' Romy felt shy, she couldn't quite look her sister in the eye. And there was Joseph, putting his arm around her.

'You must be exhausted, Flora,' he said and squeezed her shoulder.

'Yeah, I have no idea what time it is right now. I feel as though I've just been in a washing machine for the last two days.'

'Shall I get you a coffee, and some breakfast?'

'That would be great!'

Joseph walked out of the room, leaving them alone once more. Romy was so desperate to have her to herself, and yet once he had gone the silence felt bigger, more impenetrable. There was so much to say – where should they start? Flora clearly felt it too; she swung her legs beneath the bed like a small child and looked around the room.

'Joseph says your kids are adorable.'

'Well, they can be, but they can also be little terrors.'

'It must have been hard leaving them.'

She watched Flora's eyes narrow and she pursed her lips together to keep in what she was afraid to let out. 'Yeah, I was a wreck at the airport. I've never left them for more than two nights, and never been this far away.'

'Your husband, he'll look after them?'

'Jake, yeah. He's a great dad, and I know they'll be fine, but I miss them already.' Romy watched as Flora's eyes filled and she blinked away the tears.

'Maybe they can come here someday, come to the guest house on the beach.'

'They would love that.' Flora looked relieved to be able to focus on a more tangible concept. 'Joseph was telling them all about the fish on the reef and they got very excited. Olive is a big fan of Nemo.'

'She's a girl after my own heart.'

'Do I need to introduce myself to your doctor?' She looked around as if he might appear on call.

'We'll get Joseph to go and find someone – he probably already is.'

'I've never had an operation before. Only ever been in hospital to have the kids before this.'

'And you've just spent the last few months of your life in and out of one all the time.'

'Yes, it was a bit of a shock at first. But I got used to it.'

'Well, this is definitely one of the better ones.'

'Is this where your dad, I mean, our dad...?'

'Yeah, he died in a room just like this but one floor up. Freaked me out a bit when I woke up here. But I've got used to it now. It's actually weirdly comforting. I feel like he's here with me.'

'I'm so sorry you had to go through that, losing a parent. I can't imagine...'

'Yeah, it was tough. But I got through it.'

'Joseph is great.'

'He is.'

'Did he tell you about the sea?'

'The sea?'

'About how he had to drag me out of a freezing cold ocean!'

'Oh, *that* sea! Yes, he's going to dine out on that one for years.'

'I feel so stupid.'

'Hey, Flora, everything happens for a reason. Maybe Joseph had to save you, so that you could save me.' Flora couldn't answer that; she just nodded and looked like she might cry again. 'I think Joseph has booked you into a nice hotel. It has a pool.'

'Really?'

'So, ladies.' Joseph was coming back into the room with two steaming cups of coffee and two paper plates with scrambled egg and rice. He handed a plate and a cup to each of them. 'Traditional

Filipino breakfast I'm afraid, Flora. I asked whether they had toast but apparently not, just rice.'

'It's fine. I don't know whether I can eat anything anyway.' But she took the plate, and after a tentative first bite, she wolfed down the whole lot.

'Maybe you were hungry after all,' Romy said while picking at hers. Her appetite was small at the best of times, but right now her stomach was doing backflips and somersaults all at the same time, and there was no way she could eat.

'See, Romy, that's how it's done. Get those eggs down you, girl, you are going to need all the strength you can get.' He turned to Flora. 'I spoke to Romy's doctor just now on the phone, and he isn't in till later. So why don't you go to the hotel and get yourself sorted? Maybe have a sleep and a swim and come back this afternoon.'

'OK, I think that's probably a good idea,' Flora said, standing up.

'I'll help you with your bags and get you a taxi,' Joseph said.

'See you later,' Flora said at the door.

'Yeah, go get into your bikini, girl.'

She walked out of the room and Romy felt her chest constrict and then swell with something so syrupy and warm that she couldn't quite catch her breath. Flora had been everything Romy had imagined, kind and beautiful and funny and humble. And she had travelled across the world to do this thing. This huge, terrifying act of generosity and selflessness, and Romy was struck with a debilitating flash of fear. What if it went wrong? What if something happened to Flora and it would be all her fault? She closed her eyes and tried to take some of Joseph's deep, stabilising breaths. Romy recalled the look on Flora's face when she had talked about leaving her children. The tears that threatened to fill her eyes. Romy had never felt that before, that intense protective love for another person. Until now. She was pretty sure she was feeling it right now.

It was an unbearably long day waiting for Flora to come back.

Like she had been given a bite-size piece of something so delicious, and then they had taken the plate away. Romy had to endure more tests, more examinations, more scrutinising from nurses and doctors, and all the while her stomach churned with anticipation and excitement. As they prodded her and stuck needles in her arms she recalled her sister's features, the pale skin, wide smile and kind brown eyes. There was a gap between her two front teeth and a smattering of freckles on her nose. Romy looked at her own reflection in the hospital mirror: her pointy features, her short, cropped hair and tattoos on her tanned body. They couldn't be more different.

When Flora finally returned after lunch, her hair was wet and shiny, her cheeks flushed and her eyes looked considerably brighter.

'You've been in the pool?'

'The sea, actually.'

'Oh yeah, a bit different from your sea at home.'

'I am definitely more suited to these warmer climes,' Flora said, 'although I think I've maybe burned my nose in the half an hour that I was in the sun this morning, so maybe not!'

'You'll get used to it. My skin is like leather now, it has seen so much sun.' She slapped her upper arm.

'Hardly leather – you have a suntan to die for.'

'Years of work, my friend!'

'Flora, you're back!' Joseph came into the room with Dr Ramos behind him. 'Flora, this is Dr Ramos, he will be performing the surgery. I think he has some questions and needs to run a few tests.' The glow instantly flushed out of Flora's cheeks and her eyes widened with worry.

'It's OK, Flora, there is nothing for you to worry about. I have done this operation many times.' He proceeded to tell Flora how she would go under first and they would take her kidney out and then Romy would be put to sleep and the kidney transferred to her. It sounded so basic when he explained it, like a child swapping out a piece of Lego from his model. Romy was grateful to him at that moment for not going into the terrifying detail that she had been subjected to over and over again. Flora was whisked off for tests and scans for the rest of the afternoon, and by the time she returned she looked as exhausted as when she had first arrived.

'That's a hell of an afternoon for someone who has just travelled across the world. Most people would be lying on a sunlounger right now.'

'It was pretty intense,' Flora said. 'I would love to sit and chat with you, but I'm not sure I can even string a sentence together. I'm going to go back to the hotel and try to get a good night's sleep. They need me back here first thing in the morning, apparently – they want to do the operation the day after tomorrow!'

'Yeah, they told me. I'm sorry it's so full on. But don't worry, we'll have plenty of time to get to know each other when it's all over.'

'Yeah.' She looked like she might cry again, and Romy wanted to hold onto her and never let go. Flora turned to leave, but she stopped in the doorway and rushed back to the bed where she threw her arms around Romy and squeezed her really tight. She smelt of suntan lotion and antiseptic.

'I'll see you tomorrow,' she said, when she eventually pulled away from her.

'Have a good evening, sis!' Romy said, her voice wobbly with emotion.

CHAPTER TWENTY-THREE

FLORA

When Flora woke up the following morning she was disorientated. The air-conditioning unit was buzzing and the room was so cold that she had buried herself under the crisp white sheet. Her throat was dry and sore when she swallowed and she panicked that she could have picked something up on the aeroplane and would not be allowed to have the operation.

The operation. The events of the day before came back to her like the wave she couldn't quite catch on the beach. She got up and opened the sliding doors on to her balcony and was hit by a wall of heat and the buzzing of insects interspersed with the beeping of horns and whirring of motorbikes. The air was hot and perfumed with sweet-smelling fruit and flowers. She could see the sea through a gap between the buildings, and thought of her swim the day before in the warm water. The way the sea had gently lapped against the golden sand and around her toes. It was so impossibly warm it felt dirty, and yet it was the clearest, bluest water she had ever been in. She had walked out for miles and still it only came up to her thighs. So she had lowered herself into it and wallowed, staring back at the palm trees, the jumble of multicoloured buildings, the alien smells and sounds.

Arriving at Cebu had been a shock. Her senses numbed by the

brandy on the plane were snapped awake by the heat, the frenetic crowds, the shouting and beeping of horns, while the sun was only just peeking into the hazy sky. And then she had gone straight to the hospital on impulse, the adrenalin still firing in her veins. But when she was shown into Romy's room and saw both her and Joseph still sleeping, she regretted her impulse. She stood there, not sure what to do with herself, afraid to make a noise and wake them yet afraid that they would never wake up. She studied her sister's face. Her long dark eyelashes and tanned skin, pinched over high cheekbones. Her cropped hair, ruffled from sleep. Her nose stud, her many earrings, the tattoo at the top of her skinny arm. It was a few minutes before Romy woke up and caught her staring, and heat flushed to her cheeks with shame. She needn't have been embarrassed; within seconds she could tell that Romy wasn't someone who suffered from self-consciousness. Her face had lit up in genuine happiness with a slightly wonky smile and a sparkle in her big brown eyes, just like hers.

Her phone rang and she scrambled across the bed to pick it up, couldn't wait to tell Jake about her meeting with Romy the night before. It had been too late to call when she left the hospital. But it wasn't Jake, it was Megan, her kidney coordinator from the hospital back home.

'Flora, how are you doing?'

'Hi Megan, I'm OK. I went to the hospital yesterday for loads more pre-op tests, and I'm going back this morning. They're going to operate tomorrow.'

'Great, Flora, no point in hanging around. Are you OK? Nervous?'

'Yeah, pretty nervous. It all feels very strange and foreign out here. But the doctors all speak really good English and the hospital is actually quite posh.'

'Well, there you go. You're going to be fine. I've spoken to the surgeon. He is very experienced. You are in good hands.'

'I just, well, I can't help thinking about everything that could go wrong.'

'Flora, listen to me. There's no point in thinking about any of that right now. You have made your decision, and it was the right one. You are saving your sister, and you are strong and brave and you are going to feel like shit for a while. But not for long, and then you will be home with your children again and you will have a sister. And your kids will have an auntie. And an amazing place to go on holiday!'

'Yeah, you wouldn't believe the colour of the sea here!'

'And you'll be swimming in it in no time.'

'Thanks, Megan.'

'Good luck, Flora. I'll see you on the other side.'

Flora hung up the phone and considered calling Jake. She counted on the hours. It would be three o'clock in the afternoon back at home. Jake would be on his way to the school. She would call later. She packed her bags and tried not to think about the hospital. The clinical smell, the strip lights and shiny floors, the machines, the doctors in scrubs, this alien world which was fast becoming her normal. She wondered whether Romy had ever been scared. Her confidence seemed boundless; it oozed from every pore of her steely body. They were so different. And yet again and again it was confirmed with every blood test, every tissue sample, every scan. They had the same genes.

When she arrived back at the hospital there was an extra bed in Romy's room.

'I hope you don't mind, I asked if you could sleep in here with me tonight.'

'Really?' Relief flooded through Flora; she had anticipated being in ward with lots of sick people, all speaking in a language she didn't understand. 'So I can stay in here tonight? Just you and me?' She couldn't quite believe it.

'It's like a sleepover!' Romy said. 'But no midnight feasts, I'm afraid. We are both nil by mouth.'

They spent the afternoon catching up on each other's lives between tests and conversations with doctors. Flora was fascinated to hear about Romy's childhood on the island. But most of all she wanted to hear about her father, Ted, the poet whose work she had studied and analysed. She learned about the man who couldn't sit in the sun without burning his pale skin, and yet had decided to live on a tropical beach where there was no escaping it. About the man who came out in hives if he ate strawberries; the man who liked to dress up in costumes made from anything he could find around the house or the beach and act out stories to his daughter. The man who was larger than life at times, and the same man who would lock himself in his study at the top of their house and not come out for days. The man who would forget to eat or wash or take Romy to school when he was working on a piece. The man who chose to spend much of his life trapped in an alternate world of mystery and ghosts. And Flora tried to suppress the feelings that these stories evoked; the jealousy of the relationship her sister had had with this extraordinary-sounding man, the father she would never meet.

They were told not to eat anything after ten o'clock, and so their supper of chicken and rice took on a 'last supper' significance. They toasted each other with plastic glasses of orange squash and Flora encouraged Romy to eat just a little bit more of her chicken. And then they snuggled down into their beds, side by side.

'I used to dream of having a sister to do this with,' Romy said after they had turned out the lights.

'Me too.'

'But you had your brothers.'

'Believe me, younger brothers are nothing like sisters!'

'I'm sure.'

'On the odd unfortunate occasion that I would have to sleep in a room with them, they would fart in each other's faces and crack crude jokes all night long. They snored and ground their teeth, and then more farting in their sleep!' Romy laughed. 'I would go downstairs and complain and Mum and Jeremy would just laugh and tell me not to be such a prude and send me back to bed.'

'She has a sense of humour then, our mum?'

Flora considered this before answering. 'Yeah, she does. When she is relaxed and happy, she can be quite funny.'

'Was she not relaxed and happy most of the time?'

'Not really, no. It makes sense now. I don't think she ever got over you leaving.'

'What did she say when you told her about me?' Flora had been anticipating this question but was yet to come up with a response that didn't make her sound trite and pathetic. She didn't answer. 'Flora?'

'I... I didn't tell her.'

Romy sat up in bed. 'What?'

'I haven't spoken to her for a few months.'

'But, why?'

'We had a massive fight and I couldn't bring myself to talk to her so I got Jake to call her after I left.'

Romy didn't say anything for a while, and Flora watched as her eyes darted around the room, a thousand thoughts obviously invading her brain. 'What did you fight about?' she asked eventually.

'She slapped Olive, round the face.'

'What?'

'Yeah, and I lost it. To be honest it had been a long week, and that was the final straw. She had broken her leg and I went to stay to look after her. And, well, let's just say she was a pretty trying patient. Then I walked in and found her shaking Olive, and she had this crazed look in her eye and Olive looked so frightened and something snapped in me.'

'Oh god, Flora, I'm so sorry.'

'Yeah, she has always been a bit strange in the way she treats Olive, she is short-tempered with her and overly strict... She adores Toby but has always found fault with Olive. I figured she just liked boys better than girls – it always felt like that to me as a child. But now I'm wondering whether it's because Olive looks so like you. Not just looks, her character, too. Joseph said you were quite determined as a little one.'

'Oh.' Romy suddenly looked like a worried child herself, her confident wings fraying at the edges.

'It's not your fault, Romy.'

'I know, it's just... Well, I imagined you had a showdown with her, demanded to know why she had lied to you all these years. Asked her why she didn't come after me. Didn't you want to know any of that stuff?'

'Of course,' she said immediately, and then a little quieter: 'But...'

'But what?'

'But, well, arguments with my mum don't go well. And I just, I couldn't face it, to be honest. Her lies, there would be more of those, I'm sure, and I knew she would probably try to convince me not to come, and I couldn't risk that. I did wonder whether you would have contacted her, though? After you found out I mean.'

'I, well I was kind of waiting for her to get in touch, I thought you would have told her and...'

'Oh Romy, I'm so sorry. I just didn't think about the fact that you would have been waiting for her to call.'

'Yeah, well I guess I am kind of relieved, I thought she just didn't want to know me.' Romy shrugged with a nonchalance she obviously didn't feel, and Flora's heart pulled with guilt. She hadn't even considered how selfish her obstinate silence had been. She imagined Romy waiting for their mother to get in touch all this time and her eyes filled with tears.

'Flora,' Romy reached for Flora's hand and squeezed it. 'You're having a massive operation tomorrow. We, we're both having huge, life-changing surgery, and you're on the other side of the world. Don't you want to talk to her before it happens?' Flora considered this. She could see how it must look to Romy, that she was being stubborn and trying to prove a point. 'Look, it's half past nine here, which means it's six thirty in the morning there. Not too early to wake her up. You won't want to do it in the morning.' Flora didn't answer. She stared ahead of her; through the gap in the blinds she could see lights in the apartment block opposite. She half closed her eyes in attempt to halt the tears and the lights blurred. 'Flora, please. Will you do this for me?'

Flora sat up reluctantly. She found her phone on the table between their beds. There was a message from Jake saying he loved her. Asking her to call before the operation in the morning. And there was a video of Toby and Olive, in their pyjamas, their faces flushed and shiny after their bath. They both shouted, 'We love you, Mummy, and we miss you.' Flora smiled.

'Can I see?' Romy asked.

'Sure.' Flora handed her the phone and it lit up her face with a blue glow and she smiled, and then laughed.

'They are so cute!'

Romy handed her back the phone. 'I'm sorry, Romy, I know it looks like I'm being pathetic and selfish, and maybe I am. But you don't know our mother like I do. I have a complicated relationship with her, and it's beginning to make more and more sense now that I know about you. But she has ruined so many big moments in my life, and I am not going to let her ruin this one. This is about me and you, and if it was up to her, we wouldn't have known either of us existed, let alone met each other. If, sorry, *when* we come through this and are feeling fit and strong, I will have it out with her, I promise. But not tonight. Besides, she could have called me. She's had two days to call since Jake spoke to her from the airport, and there has been radio silence.'

'OK, I hear what you're saying and I think I get it. I just, well, I just hope you don't regret it.'

'I guess that's just a risk I've got to take.'

'What about Jake?'

'What about him?'

'I thought he would come here with you.'

'He wanted to, he desperately wanted to, but it would be so difficult with the children. And there was no one we could leave them with for all this time, and so we thought it was best that I just come on my own.'

'I guess. Life gets more complicated with kids in the mix.'

'You can say that again.'

'I spent twelve years not going home, not calling Joseph after Ted died, and now, well, I really wish I hadn't wasted all that time because of a stupid row.'

'What did you row about?'

'It wasn't stupid, really, it was pretty huge. I told him it was his fault that Ted had died.'

'Oh.'

'Yeah, I was a bitch, but I was hurting and I was young and confused and it all came out as rage.'

'Was it his fault?'

'I thought so at the time.'

'And now?'

'No, not now. But I know he has spent every day since blaming himself, and he really didn't need me blaming him too.'

'But you've made it up now? You seem... you seem so close.'

'Yeah, we are.'

'Everything you've just told me has made me more convinced that now is not the right time to call. I still feel so angry with her. It's as though everything in my life has suddenly been called into question. Every memory, every relationship, every fucking piece of my existence is not what I thought it was.'

'I know.'

'They robbed us, Romy, they robbed us of a different life.'

'A different life, Flora, but not necessarily better. Who knows what would have happened if our parents had stayed together? I wouldn't have Joseph, and you wouldn't have Jeremy.' Flora snorted. 'And they would probably have been horribly unhappy, and...'

'But we would have had each other,' Flora said quietly.

'True, but we have each other now.' And she held out her hand to Flora, across the gap between their beds.

CHAPTER TWENTY-FOUR

LIZZIE

The baby came two weeks early. Lizzie was out for a walk in Hyde Park. Spring was starting to appear and the trees were dripping with blossom. The air was cool and scented with freshly cut grass and sweet-smelling hyacinths. London was different in the spring; people emerged from their houses, blinking into the light like creatures coming out of hibernation. The parks and pavements were filled with yelping children and intertwined couples, and Lizzie felt her own mood shift. Every day that week she had left the flat first thing in the morning and walked until her feet were sore and her back creaking under the weight of her belly. And then she had sat on a rug in the park and soaked up the sun and the happiness all around her. She was watching a father playing football with his son, trying to imagine Edward kicking a ball, when she felt the first twinge. There had been similar squeezing sensations for days, so she thought nothing of it. But by the time she had walked the several blocks home the twinges were coming more regularly and there was a heaviness that pulled down at her insides with an intensity she hadn't experienced before. She called Edward at work, and by the time he got back to the flat she was holding onto the mantelpiece and wishing she had bothered to attend the rest of the antenatal classes.

'I'm scared,' she told him. 'I don't think I can do this, I don't know what to do.'

'Just listen to your body, Liz, you've got this. You're the strongest person I know.'

She rolled her eyes, but inside she was smiling. It was probably the nicest thing he had ever said to her. 'Do you mean that?' she asked.

'Yeah, you are so hardcore. So brave. You're going to be fine.'

In the hospital twenty-six hours later and still no baby, she didn't feel fine or brave. She felt exhausted and demoralised, and angry. She didn't want to do this; she hadn't asked for this baby. This baby who had been coming and coming but not coming, *not fucking coming*. A whole cycle of the sun had come and gone and the time on the rug in the park with the joy and the football felt like a distant dream.

'Come on, luvvie, you can do this. I know you're tired but you have got to give it everything you've got. You've got to push with all your might.' The midwife held onto her arm with her pudgy fingers, leant into her with her soft shelf of breasts.

'I can't,' Lizzie cried.

'You can!' said the kind, strong lady who Lizzie had never met until two hours ago. She stroked Lizzie's hair out of her face and wrapped a wayward sweaty strand behind her ear before taking her hand in both of hers and squeezing it hard. 'Come on, Lizzie.'

Lizzie looked up at Edward on her other side. He looked as exhausted as she felt, maybe more. His hair was also wet with sweat and stuck to the side of his flushed face. His eyes were bleary behind his fogged-up glasses.

'Come on, Liz, one last push. We're about to meet our baby.'

And so she did. With the next overwhelming wave of squeezing, crippling pain she summoned all the resources she could muster and she pushed. And she pushed, and the burning, tearing, searing pain she felt then was different. It was fruitful, it was real, it was pain like cutting your finger or scraping your knee. She could cope with this pain. She pushed, and then came the slither of limbs between her legs. And then the cry. The crying of her child.

'It's a girl,' the midwife said, and handed her the baby. An alien-like creature, covered in blood and mucus with swollen eyes and slow, Neolithic clawing motions with its wrinkled hands. It whimpered, it tried to open its eyes, it wriggled in her arms. Lizzie, terrified, looked up at Edward, at his sparkling eyes through his steamy glasses. He smiled, a huge, genuine smile, more huge and more full of love than she had ever seen before.

Edward was besotted, that night in the hospital, and when Lizzie was too exhausted to conjure any emotion at all he carried the baby around in his arms. He gazed adoringly into her little round eyes while Lizzie dozed in and out of consciousness. Her parents came, and she could barely speak. They took turns in holding her, cooing at her, saying she looked like Bella as a baby. How typical! She wasn't even to be thanked for her nine months of puking and twenty-seven hours of labour with a child that bore her any resemblance. Bella could enjoy that pleasure like she enjoyed most things, with no effort. Lizzie looked at her baby in her mother's arms and searched for a glimpse of herself, or Edward, but there was none. She felt utterly detached from this creature who had just mercilessly torn her insides apart with her arrival and left her feeling so battered and bruised she wondered if she would be able to walk, or sit or pee ever again.

They went home the following day and Lizzie waited for the moment when her emotions would heat up, for the thaw to happen and the numbness give way to a tingling love. But it didn't come. For days and then weeks Edward would swoon and sing and smother his daughter in love and kisses while Lizzie was slowly dying from the inside out. She tried to pretend that she loved the baby as much as him. And that the jealousy that raged through her soul when he gazed at his daughter with a love that she had never known, wasn't really there. That it wasn't making her think bad thoughts. Bad, bad, crazy thoughts that left her crying in the dark for hours while he was out at work.

There were better days, when the sun was shining and she forced herself out of the flat and took the baby into the park and sat on her rug under the same tree. But as she watched the happiness all around her, the children playing and their parents loving them, it only highlighted her deficiency further. And she would retreat to the flat, frightened and overwhelmed.

She usually rallied in the evening, terrified that if Edward saw her like that, he would love her even less. But one day he came home in the middle of the afternoon and found Lizzie wrapped in the heavy, draped curtain of the bay window. The still unnamed baby was crying in the Moses basket on the other side of the room and Lizzie was rocking back and forth. The curtain creaked on the rail.

'Lizzie, what's going on?' He walked into the room and she flinched with the light that he brought with him. He didn't go to her, of course, he picked up the baby.

'Shh, it's OK, Daddy's here... shhhh, it's OK...' He kissed her and held her against his chest, rocking her back and forth with his soft mutterings. Her cries calmed to a whimper and his rocking slowed to a gentle sway as her eyes drooped and her tiny body relaxed into his. Lizzie watched from the window but her rocking didn't stop and nor did her tears. It felt like a lifetime before Edward gingerly placed the baby back in the basket and turned his attention to her.

'What's going on, Lizzie?' he whispered so as not to wake the baby, but his tone was still harsh. She couldn't answer, just looked up at the weary disdain on his face. He rubbed his temples and sucked in deep breaths, blowing them out through puffed cheeks as he paced the room. 'I just came home to grab a piece I wrote last night and forgot, but I need to get back to work.'

She still didn't answer but sniffed and nodded her head in acknowledgement. He crouched down facing her then, held her shoulders in his hands and looked at her straight in the eye. 'Look, Liz, you've got to pull yourself together, OK? I can't do this, I've got to go to work and earn us some money. You need to look after our baby.' She wiped her eyes and then her nose and nodded at him.

'OK,' she whispered between sobs. 'I'm sorry, it's just so hard.'

'I know, and you're doing great. And it will get easier. OK?' His tone was softer now, encouraging, but behind it there was desperation. 'And we're going to give her a name, tonight. No more procrastinating, she is five weeks old. She needs a name.'

'OK. Tonight.' He unwrapped the heavy damask curtain from around her body and tried to hide his surprise when he saw she was still in the milk-soaked nightie that she had slept in.

'Why don't you have a bath while she's asleep?' He pulled her to her feet. She wanted him to take her in his arms, to cradle her and kiss her on the head like he had the baby. But he left her there swaying unsteadily on her feet in the bay window, the sour smell of milk wafting up from the crusted stain on her filthy nightie.

But she did pull herself together. She had a bath and washed her hair and by the time he came back at eight o'clock, she was wearing fresh clothes and chicken Kievs were cooking in the oven, filling the flat with the smell of garlic butter. The baby was awake, but not crying, on a sheepskin rug on the floor. Edward walked into the flat and couldn't hide the relief that warmed his features. Neither of them mentioned the afternoon. They forced their way through their chicken Kievs and drank red wine while the baby was quiet.

'So, I found this book of names at work today. Apparently they do an article on the most popular names and their origins and then compile it into a book every few years.' He flicked through the pages and stopped at one towards the end of the book. 'How about Rosamund? Gentle horse, beautiful rose.'

'Haven't we been here before? It sounds a bit pretentious,' Lizzie said, wiping her finger around the edge of her plate to get the last smears of garlic butter.

'Pretentious?'

'Yeah, a bit too long and formal.' She licked her finger.

'OK, so what do you suggest then?' He handed her the book and she looked up and down the same page.

'Rose?'

'Back to the flowers.'

'I'm a scientist, you are a culturist.'

'I'm not sure that's a word.'

'Never mind. What about Rosanna?' He shook his head. 'Romily?'

'Maybe.'

'Romina?'

'Too foreign.'

'Romy?'

'Romy, I like that, what does it mean?' he asked.

'Rose, beloved, sea of bitterness,' she read from the book.

'That sounds ominous.'

'Rebelliousness.'

'Nothing wrong with a bit of rebellion.'

'Wished-for child.' She looked up at Edward and his eyes flashed with the irony.

'I like it,' he said with authority and went over to the baby on the floor who was starting to grizzle. 'Are you going to be a rebellious little rose?' he said, and picked her up and kissed her on the nose. She wrinkled her features in surprise and then looked up at him and the corners of her mouth peaked and gave way to her pink little gums beneath. Her eyes narrowed, glistened in fact. 'Did you see that?' Edward turned to Lizzie, who had been watching them. She had seen it.

'Yes!' She laughed.

'She actually smiled. Did you smile, Romy? Is that going to be your name? I think it has to be now.' Lizzie got up and walked over to join them. She peered over Edward's shoulder and smiled at her daughter and her daughter smiled back. And there it was, a flutter of joy, a warm melting of the ice so deep down inside.

'She did it again!'

'Romy it is then!' Lizzie said, and she rested her cheek on

Edward's shoulder and he turned and kissed her on the top of the head.

The next few months passed in a hazy blur of sleepless nights and delirious days. Lizzie's temperament seemed to vacillate wildly. There were days when she didn't leave the flat. She never got dressed and lay on the sofa with Romy at her breast while she watched snooker on the TV. But then there were also the days when Romy had slept for more than four hours the night before and they would head out to the park and Romy would lie on the rug under a tree, kicking her chubby legs and gurgling with delight at the fluttering leaves against the cerulean sky. And every day the ice in Lizzie's heart melted a little bit more, and slowly but surely the good days began to outweigh the bad.

Sometimes her mother came to visit, and they would walk along the river or go out to lunch in a café in South Kensington. On a couple of occasions she even offered to look after Romy so that Lizzie could have a couple of hours on her own. She left the flat without a buggy, or a bag of nappies, and walked for miles, just because she could, her footsteps light and dangerously free. On one of these occasions she walked all the way into the West End and decided on a whim to surprise Edward at work.

'Ah, Lizzie.' It was David from the restaurant who found Lizzie in the lobby of the tatty high-rise that was home to the *Herald*.

'I've come to see Edward. He isn't expecting me, thought I'd surprise him.'

'Afraid you've just missed him, he's gone to review a Van Gogh exhibition at the National, not sure he'll be back in today.'

'Oh, that's a shame.' She swallowed down the disappointment.

'How's that baby of yours then? Keeping you up all night, is it?'

'She's getting better, thanks, slept for a whole six hours on the trot last night.'

'Six hours, and that's a good thing, is it?'

'Well, it's better than two. I'd best get going, it's a long walk home.' She turned to leave and then had a thought. 'The National Gallery, did you say? Is it far from here?'

'Just round the corner, on Trafalgar Square. Van Gogh. It's meant to be wonderful. I'd have gone myself but I have a dreaded management meeting.'

'OK, thanks.'

She looked at her watch; she had already been gone for an hour and a half. She felt the tingle of milk flowing into her boobs. Romy would be wanting a feed. She should head back. But she had walked all this way. Besides, if she nipped into the gallery, she could always get the tube home.

The Van Gogh exhibition was on the first floor. She looked up at the frescoes on the domed ceiling as she walked up the stairs. She had been to the National Gallery once before on a school trip. She and Isabelle had sneaked out to a shop at lunchtime and bought a packet of cigarettes which they smoked one after the other in a side street behind the gallery. Then they had giggled the whole way round the exhibition, thrilled by their audacity. She squeezed her tingling boobs with her arms and thought how very different her life was now.

Then she saw Edward. He was standing in front of a painting of a yellow house on the corner of a street. And she was taken back to that first time that he visited her yellow house, the smell of sausages, the flowers in jam jars, his triumphant lap of the croquet lawn in the wheel barrow and something clenched so tight around her heart that it missed a beat. His head was slightly cocked. He carried a rolled-up leaflet in one hand which he squeezed bigger and smaller in his fist as he focused on the painting, no doubt writing his review in his head. If she could see his lips, she imagined they would be twitching with the words. She walked slowly towards him, anticipating the moment that she would gently tap him on the shoulder. Or maybe she could just take his hand. Would he flinch? Her shoes squeaked on the shiny floor but he didn't move; he was totally entranced by the painting. And then a man cut her up, walked straight in front of her with bold determination and went over to Eddie. He said something to him and Eddie turned and smiled. Lizzie froze, and then darted behind a pillar. She watched as they talked in hushed tones, both staring at the painting. Eddie turned towards the man again. He was Asian and familiar, though she couldn't think why. She could see Eddie's profile, the smile lines at the sides of his eyes behind his glasses. Then he put his hand on the small of this man's back, and he didn't seem remotely surprised by his touch and together they walked away. Smiling. Talking. Totally at ease with one another. Lizzie didn't follow. She watched them until they rounded the corner of the adjacent room, her heart pounding in her chest.

The tube was claustrophobic. The train stopped in a tunnel and she had her face in someone's armpit, and she struggled to draw the hot air down into her lungs. The image of Eddie and that man, the touch of his hand on the small of his back. There was a bitter taste at the back of her throat, and her blood pulsed in her feet and up the back of her neck.

Lizzie could hear Romy's screams from outside on the pavement. She ran up the two flights of stairs and in through the door where her mother's assault began. Where had she been? She promised to be back hours ago. She had tried to give Romy a bottle but she wouldn't take it. She obviously wasn't mature or responsible enough to be a mother if she could just leave her child hungry and crying. Lizzie could see her mother's mouth moving fast, a shower of saliva dancing in the beam of light from the window. She took the screaming baby to the chair in the window and unbuttoned her shirt to expose her now swollen and leaking breasts. The tingling let-down of milk was at once painful and a relief as Romy latched on and continued to sob while she sucked in a desperate fury. Her mother hurtled out of the flat, still shouting as she slammed the door behind her, saying she would probably miss her train now as well. Finally, Romy's sobs slowed to a whimper and she held onto Lizzie's necklace and gazed into her eyes. Romy had read somewhere in a book that a baby could see the exact distance between its mother's breast and face, and as she looked down at her daughter's glassy eyes staring up at hers, she felt something deep inside that was at once wonderful and terrifying. And then Romy's eyes closed and she dozed while continuing to suck in her sleep. Lizzie found herself alone once more with her thoughts. She shut her own eyes, but on the back of her glowing lids all she could see was his hand on the small of his back.

That was the first night she drank gin. She drank until her thoughts no longer crowded her mind. Until they were numbed to a blurry recollection like a childhood holiday or a teenage kiss. Eddie was furious the following morning and threw the curtains open, letting in the harsh reality of day as he presented her with Romy.

'What the hell happened to you last night?' he demanded. 'Romy was in a filthy nappy and you were passed out on the bed in your clothes. Anything could have happened to her.'

'Well, where were you?' Her words were sticky and bitter in her mouth.

'I told you, I had an exhibition and then a dinner.'

'Who with?'

'What?' He stormed around the room, picking up Romy's clothes and throwing them onto the bed.

'Who did you have dinner with?' she asked, shielding her eyes from the sun that now burned into her face.

'With David and some people from the gallery. They were schmoozing us, wanted a good review for the exhibition.' She wanted to challenge him, to tell him that she had seen David, that she knew David hadn't gone to the exhibition. That she knew he was there with someone entirely different. But a wave of nausea crashed over her head and she had to run to the bathroom where she vomited violently. Eddie found her a few minutes later, sitting on the floor between the bath and the loo.

'Jesus, Liz, you must've really gone for it last night. I have never known you to drink alone before. Has something happened? Did you have a fight with your mum, or something?' He passed her a toothbrush loaded with toothpaste.

'Uh, yeah, I did. I came back late and Romy was upset and she shouted. And, well, it got to me. Sorry,' she whispered pathetically.

'Hey, it's OK. We've all done it. But I've got to get to work.' He pulled her up to her feet and helped her back to the bedroom where she collapsed onto the bed. Romy was happily cooing in her cot. She had just discovered her feet and was holding onto them both and rocking from side to side. 'Are you going to be OK?'

Lizzie couldn't speak but nodded in response and he left. Maybe she had imagined it. Maybe she had read too much into the hand on the back. But then a few nights later Eddie didn't come home again and Lizzie found herself dining alone and imagining the worst. She tried wine; it seemed less desperate somehow, drinking wine alone. But while it calmed her nerves it didn't quieten her mind in the same way. So she left Romy in the flat on her own while she visited the corner shop to buy more gin. She was still sleeping soundly when she returned and Romy sat on the floor next to the cot and drank straight from the bottle as she watched her daughter's chest rise and fall through the bars.

Again and again she drank, and Eddie's sympathy waned with every evening he came home to find his wife unconscious. Sometimes she didn't make it to the bed. One time he told her she had been sick in her sleep; it was still matted in her hair the following morning. And every time she would cry, she would beg his forgiveness, promise that she wouldn't do it again. He threw out all the booze in the house. But she just bought more. She would go to the corner shop during the day now, with Romy in the pram, en route to the park. She would hide the bottle under the pile of blankets and muslins at her feet. And then stash it in the bathroom cupboards or under the bed in the flat.

One evening she had started drinking early in anticipation of a long and lonely night. Eddie was going to the theatre. Except he didn't; at seven o'clock he arrived home saying David had decided to take his wife instead. He presented her with a bunch of tulips and a rotisserie chicken and bread still warm from the oven, that he had picked up from a deli in Soho. She could already feel the warming effects of the gin curdling in her stomach but she wasn't past the point of no return. On the contrary, she felt happy and brave and buoyed by his efforts. She drained the contents of her glass while he went to kiss Romy goodnight, and rinsed it out to mask the smell. They ate the chicken with torn-off chunks of warm bread and mayonnaise. Lizzie tried not to think about the absence of wine which only a few months ago would have accompanied this gesture.

'Are you OK, Liz?' Eddie asked her tentatively halfway through the meal.

'Yeah, why do you ask?'

'The drinking, Lizzie. Are you unhappy?'

She dipped a piece of chicken into the pot of mayonnaise and considered her response. She could ask him, straight out, about that day in the gallery. He was offering her an olive branch, making an effort. But as she looked at him across the table, his concerned brow above his glasses, the way his hair flopped in front of one eye, she couldn't face his reply.

'I'm just lonely, Eddie. You're out most evenings. And all day it's just me and Romy, and then when I'm on my own in the evening too, well, it's a bit much.'

Relief flooded into his features. He leant forward and grabbed her hand which was still coated in mayonnaise. She snatched it away and licked the ends of her fingers before putting it back and wrapping her fingers around his. He smiled, and she smiled back.

'And...' She felt bolstered by the gin, by his gentle response. 'Well, we haven't made love in such a long time. And I know I didn't want to after Romy was born, but I feel so much better now, and...' She lowered her chin and looked up at him coyly. He continued to smile, but she could see his throat constrict as he swallowed.

'OK...' he began slowly. 'I'm sorry, Lizzie, I know it must be hard for you. This is not exactly the life that either of us imagined. You're such a brilliant mum, and I am going to try to come home earlier in the evenings at least a couple of nights a week – OK?'

She nodded. But she was painfully aware that he hadn't answered her plea. She stood up and walked around the table. She sat on his lap and kissed him gently on the mouth; she took off his glasses and placed them on the table next to the chicken. She kissed him again, felt his body stiffen as she kissed his neck, his mouth. And then she led him over to the sofa.

'What about Romy?' he asked.

'What about her, Eddie?'

'Well, she might hear, might wake up.'

'She's a six-month-old baby, what's she going to do?' She took off his tie and unbuttoned his shirt. And then she took off her own dress and he just stood there, swaying slightly as if he was on the edge of a cliff and considering whether to throw himself off. Something switched in him then; he grabbed her around the waist and pulled her against him. He kissed her hard, his tongue invading her mouth. There was a sense of urgency, of desperation as he moved her down onto the sofa and pulled off her knickers. It reminded her of that night by the swing seat, the night it had all begun. He pushed into her, so hard, so deep that it hurt. The corner of the sofa banged against the wall and she watched as every thrust sent another crack through the plaster. When he finished, he collapsed on top of her like an exhausted marathon runner crossing the finish line. And then he kissed her cheek, and avoiding her eyes he stood up and fumbled his way back into his trousers, retrieved his glasses from in among the chicken. She lay there, naked and sore, as though both her body and her heart had been torn in two.

CHAPTER TWENTY-FIVE

ROMY

Romy watched as Flora called Jake on the morning of the operation. She strained to hear his voice on the other end of the phone but couldn't; it was muffled and the words were unintelligible.

'I'm going into theatre now, I've only got a minute,' she said. 'Scared... I know... are the kids OK?... I miss them so much.' Her voice cracked when she said this. 'Yeah?... Jake, you don't need to do this now...' Romy watched her sister fight back the tears as she took in whatever it was that her husband was saying to her. What did he not have to do right now? What had he done to her? A protective surge of rage took her off guard. She held onto the bed to steady herself and watched the expression on Flora's face. A smiled tweaked the corners of her mouth as she listened, and then nodded. 'I know you do,' she said, fighting back the tears. 'I love you too.' Her words were barely audible. Then she hung up the phone and Romy went to her. She held her tight and Flora's tears soaked into her hospital gown.

'I'm sorry,' Flora said, pulling away and wiping her nose on her hand.

'Don't be.'

'I was doing really well until I spoke to him.'

'He loves you very much.'

'Yeah, yeah, I think he does.'

'Well, you're very lucky. And you're going to see him, and the kids, really soon. And in the meantime, you've got me. This evening we are going to be through this and out the other side.'

'I'm sorry, I don't know why I'm crying. I mean, what you are doing is even more full on, and—'

'Hey, Flora, look at me.' Romy put her finger on the bottom of her sister's chin. It was wet and sticky. 'We're in this together, OK? I have only just found you, and there's no way anything is going to come between us again. Yeah?'

Flora nodded and curled her lips over the tops of her teeth. 'OK,' she whispered.

'OK, Miss Flora, we are ready for you now.' The nurse came into the room. 'You hop on the bed, missy, and we take you down. Say goodbye to Miss Romy now, you see her later.'

And she was gone. For a long time Romy sat on the bed and stared at the space where she had been. She was still sitting there when a petite lady with a walking stick and a tall man in a Panama hat knocked on the open door.

'Romy?' the lady said in a quiet voice.

'Yeah?' she said, almost absent-mindedly, still lost in her thoughts.

'I, um, I'm...' Romy looked at the lady, so small and frail. She leant on a cane with a dented brass knob on the top and had big brown eyes, almost too big for her face. She smiled nervously revealing a wide mouth, Flora's mouth. 'I'm Lizzie. Your—'

'Mother,' Romy finished the sentence for her.

'Yes.' She took a tentative step into the room. The man strode past her and held out his hand.

'Romy, it's lovely to meet you. I'm—'

'Jeremy.' Romy said it with a smile and took his hand. It was large and slightly clammy.

'Has Flora...?' Lizzie asked nervously, her eyes darting around the room and settling on Flora's bag in the corner.

'She just went into theatre, you missed her.'

'Oh, OK.' Lizzie's face fell with disappointment and her knuckles whitened where she was gripping onto her stick.

'She didn't know you were coming?'

'Well, we didn't know this was happening until Jake called, and then we, well, we...'

'We got on a flight the same evening. Lizzie was quite insistent.' Jeremy finished her sentence for her.

'Right! Sorry, come in.' She got off the bed and cleared Flora's stuff off the chair so that Lizzie could sit down. 'There's only one chair, I'm afraid,' she said to Jeremy. 'But if you go and ask, I'm sure they could find another one.'

'Why don't you do that, Jeremy?' Lizzie said quite quickly and assertively while lowering herself into the seat.

'OK,' he said and strode out of the room, his shiny shoes clacking against the hard floor.

Romy looked at her mother once more. Despite the fragility there was a sense of power to her that she hadn't appreciated when she first walked in. She wore white linen trousers that were creased, presumably from the journey, and a pale pink embroidered shirt. She was painfully thin but elegant. Her fingernails were painted coral and on her fingers were clusters of rings, diamonds, rubies and emeralds. Her hair was dark and in a stylish bob. She wore bright red lipstick, some of which stuck to her teeth.

'I don't really know where to start,' she said with a laugh, turning the rings round and round on her slender fingers.

Romy laughed too. 'Yes, I thought I would be better at meeting my long-lost relatives by now, but it doesn't seem to get any easier!'

Lizzie swallowed and clasped her hands together in her lap. 'How was it? Meeting Flora, I mean?'

'It was... amazing. She is amazing...'

'Yes, yes, she is. How, er, how was she? This morning? She hates hospitals, always refused to go to the doctor as a child.'

'She was OK, a bit nervous. She spoke to Jake just before she went in and I think that made her a bit wobbly.'

'Yes, well, it would.'

'Why do you say that?'

'He is not the easiest of husbands. Not really a communicator.'

'Really? I can't imagine Flora with someone like that, she's so open.'

'Yes, well, I think that may be the problem.'

'Here we are...' Jeremy came back into the room with a chair and Lizzie rolled her eyes at him. He put it down on the other side of the bed and was just lowering himself into it when Lizzie said, 'Jeremy, I'm gasping for a cup of coffee, do you think you could...?' He hovered over the chair and sighed before straightening back up again. 'Yes, yes, of course, good idea. Would you like one, Romy?'

'I can't, nil by mouth. There's a vending machine in the corridor down there but it's pretty disgusting. The coffee is slightly better from the café downstairs.' He winced but tipped his brow as if doffing an invisible cap. 'OK, one weak coffee coming up,' he said and left the room once more.

'How's your leg?' Romy asked, looking at the cane propped up against the chair. 'Flora said you broke it.'

'Yes. It's still a bit stiff, but getting better.'

'Must have been sore on the plane.'

'It was fine, we, er, we had a bed.'

'Oh!' Romy had never met anyone who had flown first class before, never even seen what it looked like. At least Lizzie had the humility to be embarrassed by this admission. She looked around the room and twisted the rings round her fingers again.

'Flora told me you had a row.'

Lizzie's head snapped back towards Romy. 'Oh! Did she tell you what it was about?'

'Er, yeah.'

Lizzie nodded. 'I'm not very proud of the way I behaved that day. Not very proud of a lot of things, actually.'

'Well, it's never too late to put it right...'

'Do you believe that?' Lizzie whispered and her eyes watered. Was it with hope? Or relief? There was something incredibly vulnerable about her, behind the steely composure and the mani-cured nails, the perfect hair.

'Yeah, I'm beginning to think I do.'

Lizzie smiled and a tear escaped her eye and made its way slowly down the side of her cheek. She leant towards Romy, who wondered if she might touch her, but she seemed to bottle it at the last minute. 'Are you scared?' she asked quietly.

'About the operation?' Lizzie nodded. 'Yeah, yeah, I'm scared. Of quite a lot of things. I'm scared it won't work. Or that I'll die, or worse still I'll be left a vegetable or in a coma. But most of all I'm scared that something will happen to Flora. She's so kind and generous and she has those gorgeous kids at home, and...' Romy could hear her voice start to waver.

'She will be fine. Flora is strong. She might not seem it, but she is. And she's fit and young and healthy.' Lizzie had regained her composure while Romy's was unravelling. Romy nodded, afraid to speak in case she totally fell apart. 'And this seems like a very good hospital, much cleaner, smarter than I imagined.' She looked around and nodded her approval and it made Romy smile to think of what she had imagined when she heard her daughter was having surgery in the Philippines. Both her daughters.

'Yeah, it is. I've spent quite a lot of time here, over the years.'

'Have you been ill for a long time?'

'No, not that long. But my dad, Ted. He died here.' Lizzie's body stiffened and she gripped onto her trousers with both hands.

'Oh,' she whispered.

'In a room just like this.'

'Were you with him, when he...?'

'Yeah, me and Joseph were both here. It was quite peaceful. He had barely woken up for days, and then he just slipped away.'

Another tear fell from Lizzie's eyes and she wiped it away with the back of her hand. Romy hadn't dared to imagine that her mother might have actually loved her father and how much his betrayal might have torn her apart. Joseph had painted a picture of an unstable woman, unfit to be a mother, but now she was here Romy could see that there was so much more to the story.

'Did you love him?' she asked.

'Yes, very much,' Lizzie replied.

'Romy?' It was Joseph coming into the room.

'Joseph.'

Joseph's eyes flitted to Lizzie and widened in surprise. She had taken a tissue out of her bag and was wiping the tears from her cheeks, and some mascara had smudged underneath her eye.

'I, er, just went to check on Flora, but she's still in theatre so there's no... news.' He looked at Lizzie while he spoke and his voice trailed off at the end as he recognised her. 'Lizzie?' he asked tentatively.

'Hi, Joseph,' she said, pulling herself up from the chair and grappling for her stick.

'No, please, sit down.' He rushed over to help her back down into the chair. 'I didn't know you were coming.'

'Surprise!' she said with a laugh and threw her shaking hands in the air as her bottom landed on the chair. Joseph looked back at Romy with concern and she forced a smile.

'They got on a plane that night after Jake called and told them. Came straight here.'

'Wow, I... er.'

'I just had to see her, them, both of them,' Lizzie said.

'Of course,' Joseph said and smiled. Then he sidled up to the bed and placed his hand on top of Romy's. 'Are you OK?' he asked.

She nodded. 'Yeah, a bit nervous, and overwhelmed. It's turning out to be quite a big day!' She wanted him to hold her hand but was afraid that his touch would be her undoing and so pulled hers away and ran it through her hair.

A nurse came in. 'Quite a party in here, Miss Romy. Are you ready?' she asked.

'What, now? Are we going now? I thought I would see Flora before...'

'Not yet, don't worry. She is OK. Still in surgery.' She picked up Romy's hand and measured her pulse. She looked at Joseph and then at Lizzie and back to her watch while she counted. 'OK, so you need to stop exciting her. Her pulse is racing. Miss Romy doesn't need excitement today. She need calm. We need to get your pulse down before you go to surgery.' Lizzie and Joseph both nodded and bowed their heads in shame like small children being told off.

'Yes, of course. We can leave her be,' Lizzie said and picked up her bag from the floor.

'No,' Romy said quickly. 'Please, let them stay. I don't want to be on my own right now.'

'OK, they can stay, but no excitement, no upset, just calm, yes?' She looked at all of them and they each nodded in turn. 'I'll be back in half an hour to take you down. You can see Flora in recovery before you go in.'

'OK.' Romy nodded, but her heart didn't grow calm. It thumped in her chest, fast and irregular. She closed her eyes and tried to take a long, deep breath. Joseph took her hand and breathed with her, deep and slow in, deep and slow out. When she opened her eyes again, Lizzie had turned her whole body round and was staring out of the window, as if she felt like she shouldn't be intruding on this private moment between father and daughter.

'Did you come on your own, Lizzie?' Joseph asked, and she turned around. Romy could see that her eyes were still red and watery. The mascara had made its way down her cheek. She looked like a Pierrot doll, silent and sad.

'Jeremy went to go and get coffee,' Romy said. 'He's been gone quite a while – maybe you could go and see if he's all right?'

'Really?' Joseph looked at her, reluctant to leave.

'Yeah,' she said.

'OK, but remember what the nurse said.' He looked at Romy and then at Lizzie, who nodded silently, and he left the room.

'He is kind,' Lizzie said after he had gone.

'Yes.'

'I met him once, in a Chinese restaurant.'

'Really?'

'It was a happy night. You were in my tummy, and it was the first time Eddie felt you kick. We talked about names.'

'Did you come up with Romy then?'

'No, that was later. Eddie wanted to call you Rosamund or Titania or some other Shakespearean heroine.'

'That sounds about right. What did you want?'

'I like simpler names, flowers: Rosie, Daisy, Lily.'

'Flora!'

'He wasn't around to challenge me on that one.'

'Sounds like Romy was the perfect compromise.'

'Yes, yes, I suppose it was.'

'Was it the first time they met, that night in the restaurant?'

'I think so. They didn't seem to know each other before. Eddie didn't even want to go out. It was all my idea!' She laughed. 'Imagine if we'd just stayed in, or got a takeaway!' She bit her lip and looked like she might cry again and then shook her head. 'I'm sorry, your heart rate. We need to keep you calm. Let's talk about something else. Tell me about you. What do you like? What do you do?'

'I'm a tattoo artist.' She watched for Lizzie's response, anticipating shock or surprise, but she didn't even flinch.

'Are those your own designs?' She pointed to her arms.

'Yeah, I designed them but my boss did it.'

'They're beautiful,' Lizzie said and she really seemed to mean it.

'Are you married? Children?'

'No.'

'Do you live here?'

'No, I left here after Ted died. I've lived in Hong Kong for the last fourteen years.'

'Is it fourteen years since...?' Lizzie asked, and then seemed to remember her change of tack. 'Tell me about Hong Kong. Jeremy and I have travelled a lot, but mostly Europe and America, the Caribbean. This is my first trip to Asia.'

'Well, it's mad and frenetic, and the buildings are crazily high and all jammed up against each other on this tiny island. At street level you barely see the sun there are so many skyscrapers. It was a bit of a shock after here. The island where I grew up is pretty quiet. We lived on the beach. My dads, they built a guest house and a dive shop. Sorry, do you know any of this already?'

'No. No, I don't know anything.'

'And yet he knew everything about you, and Flora.' Romy hadn't meant it to sound so vitriolic, but her words packed a punch. Lizzie's eyes widened. And suddenly she found herself on higher ground and it felt good to be in control of the conversation. 'Your brother. Is it Jamie?'

'Jamie.' She nodded slowly, digesting the significance of this.

'Yeah, well, looks like he kept Ted informed. Joseph too, after Ted died.'

Romy could tell she hadn't known this and yet she didn't seem all that surprised. 'They were close, your father and Jamie.' She spoke with weary recognition.

'Weren't you curious?'

'What?'

'About where I was?'

'Of course.'

'But you didn't try to follow, to find me.'

Lizzie didn't answer straight away. She smoothed her trousers down over her legs and looked up at the ceiling for inspiration. 'I wanted to. Believe me, I wanted to so much.'

'So why didn't you?'

'Because, well, because I couldn't.'

'Couldn't or wouldn't?'

'Couldn't. He... Ted left a letter and, well, there was something I had done, something I wasn't very proud of, and he said that if I tried to follow him, to find you, that he would tell, and—'

'Here we are, two rather cold and weak coffees. Joseph found me in the wrong queue at the wrong café, selling rice and chicken apparently.' Jeremy strode into the room, his booming voice bouncing off the walls. He handed the cup to Lizzie who took it between her shaking hands, not daring to look at Romy. Joseph was behind him and immediately picked up on the tension in the room. He looked at Romy and then at Lizzie, and back to Romy again.

'Everything OK?' he asked.

'Yeah, we're just getting to know one another,' Romy answered with an unconvincing smile.

'Great, well, not long now. She'll be back any minute to take you down.'

Romy looked at Lizzie, who was taking tentative sips of her coffee. The plastic cup rattled against the rings on her fingers.

'This isn't so bad, is it?' Jeremy wandered over to the window. He was so big, his presence seemed to fill the whole room. 'And thank god for the air conditioning. How do you live in this infernal heat?'

'You get used to it,' Joseph said. Romy could feel him looking at her but she didn't dare catch his eye. She smiled at Jeremy and then followed his gaze out of the window.

'Any news on Flora?' Jeremy asked. He was obviously not one for silences.

'Not yet, no,' Joseph answered.

'Do we know how long it will take? The op, I mean?'

'Could be a couple of hours. Romy's will be longer.'

Romy felt her stomach rumble. Her chicken and rice the night before was a long time ago. She hugged her stomach tight and willed her heart to slow.

'OK, Miss Romy, time to go down.' The same nurse came back in. She picked up Romy's wrist as before and tutted. 'I said no more excitement.' She looked at Lizzie, who averted her gaze. 'OK. *Don't worry. Be happy...*' she started to sing, and then laughed a high-pitched hyena squeal and Jeremy guffawed loudly. 'OK. Say your goodbyes now.' She pulled up the side of Romy's bed.

Joseph held onto her hand. 'You've got this, Romy,' he said, squeezing it.

'Yeah, I got this. See you on the other side.' She looked at

Lizzie, who was no longer trying to conceal the tears than coursed down her face.

'Bye!' Romy said and waved at her with a smile, but Lizzie couldn't respond. She just nodded and the tears dripped off the bottom of her chin.

The nurse turned her bed around and wheeled it towards the door.

'Wait!' Lizzie had got to her feet and forgetting her cane, was hobbling towards the bed. She grabbed Romy's hand and put it up to her lips. They were warm and smooth as she kissed Romy's palm, leaving a red stain on her skin from the lipstick. She looked like she was about to say something but couldn't.

'Hey,' Romy said, and took her hand in her own. 'Don't worry, I'm going to be back really soon. You look after Flora while I'm gone.'

'I will,' Lizzie whispered, and let go of her hands. And Romy was wheeled out of the room.

CHAPTER TWENTY-SIX

FLORA

Flora peeled open her eyelids. Her head throbbed, her mouth was dry and sticky. There was someone there, a shadowy figure obscuring the light. A man or a woman? She couldn't tell. She opened her mouth to speak but couldn't find the words. Her throat felt tight and raw, and she struggled to swallow. The figure was still there, she felt its animosity. It wasn't helping her, why wasn't it helping her? She couldn't ask, couldn't speak, could barely open her eyes and it didn't seem to care. And then she was sucked back down.

When she woke again the light scorched her eyeballs. She shut them again. There were muted sounds, like she was underwater; chatter from people in the corridors, traffic on the streets below, the beeps and bleeps of the machines.

'Flora?' She heard her mother's voice. She felt her touch on her hand, her tiny fingers squeezing hers. 'Flora.' She tried to open her eyes; the lids fluttered but they felt so heavy.

'Mm,' she mumbled through closed lips.

'Oh Flora, thank god.' Her mother was there, blurred but smiling.

'Mum?' she asked.

'Shh, it's OK,' Lizzie said with a smile. 'Don't speak, you're

OK. Just rest.'

She lost the battle with her eyelids. It could have been seconds or hours before she opened them again; the passing of time had become intangible. She drifted in and out of consciousness. She dreamed of tropical seas, and icy-cold waters, of Jake, of Romy, of a younger version of Lizzie plaiting her long brown hair. Every so often she would open her eyes, like a turtle coming up to the surface for air. And her mother would be there and then she would drift away again.

'Flora?' It was Joseph obscuring the light from the window the next time she surfaced.

'Romy?' she whispered through cracked lips.

'She's still in theatre. She didn't want to go under until she knew you were OK, that the surgery was a success.'

So it was a success? Flora scanned her body mentally. Would she feel a cavity where the kidney had been, pain where they cut her open? She felt nothing but a heaviness that sucked her down onto the bed and with all the will in the world wouldn't let her get up.

'How do you feel?' Joseph asked.

'Numb, and so tired.'

'Just rest. Lizzie's just popped out for a walk. She'll be gutted to have missed you.'

'Lizzie?' Her eyes sprang open with more vivacity then. 'My mother, she's here?'

'Yes, she said you saw her, that you spoke to her.'

'I thought it was a dream.'

He smiled with relief. 'Well, it's not, she's here. Got on a flight the minute Jake told her.'

'Oh.'

He patted Flora's hand. 'I'll go find her. She will want to know you're awake.' And he walked out of the room. Left Flora on her own to digest and process the news that curdled with the drugs in her empty stomach. A wave of nausea swept over her and she shut her eyes and gripped onto the sheets until it passed. When she opened them again a nurse with a round smiling face and a gold tooth was peering down at her.

'Ah, Miss Flora, you awake. How you feeling?'

'Awful.'

The nurse pressed buttons on the machine by Flora's bed and picked up her wrist to feel her pulse. There were cannulas in the backs of both her hands and the needles pulled at her flesh. Tubes of clear liquid leading to bags were suspended on poles above her head.

'Your vitals are good. Do you feel any pain?' she asked.

'Er, no, not yet, I... can't really feel anything. Do you know anything about my sister Romy? Is she out of theatre?'

'Shh now, you just look after yourself and let us deal with your sister now, hey?' Her eyes darted to the side as she spoke and she couldn't hold Romy's gaze. Did she know something?

'Has something happened? Is Romy OK?'

'Shh, Miss Flora, please, you have just had major surgery.'

'But is it going OK? The surgery?' Flora tried to sit up but a pain shot across her abdomen. 'Ow, fuck!' she screamed.

'Miss Flora, please, you need to rest.' The nurse put her hands on Flora's shoulders and laid her back down on the pillow. 'You cannot start moving around just yet. I will go and find out what is happening with your sister, OK?'

'OK,' Flora whispered.

'Now, promise me you won't try to move again.'

'I promise.'

'I'll be right back.'

She walked out of the room, and Flora could feel her heart pounding in her chest in the wake of the pain. It had startled her. She lifted up the sheet and peered down at her body wrapped in bandages. She stroked the fabric tentatively; there were bumps underneath where she assumed the stitches were. They felt tender under her touch. They told her there would be two incisions, but it felt as though her entire stomach had been ripped apart. She certainly couldn't tell where one cut stopped and the other started.

She couldn't imagine ever standing up again. Ever going to the loo. Ever actually getting out of this bed. Her hand was still under the covers padding her stomach carefully when she heard a voice in the room.

'Flora?' She pulled the sheet down and saw her mother coming into the room. She looked like she had aged a decade since Flora had last seen her on that fateful night only a few months ago. Her hair was slightly frizzy and make-up had leaked from her eyes and trickled down her sunken cheeks.

'Mum!' Lizzie walked towards her with the help of a cane which clacked against the hard floor. 'I can't believe you're here!' Lizzie kissed Flora on the forehead. Then she abandoned the cane which clattered to the floor and gathered her into her arms. She smelt of lily of the valley and Flora was transported back to her childhood. 'I can't believe you're here,' Flora said again, holding onto her mother's shirt.

'I had to come, my daughter was having an operation, both my daughters.' Lizzie pulled away from her and perched on the end of the bed, still holding Flora's hands in hers.

'Romy, is she...?'

'There's still no news. Joseph has gone to see if they will tell him anything.'

'Have you seen her?'

'Yes, we arrived just after you had gone into theatre but Romy was still here.'

'How was it? Isn't she amazing?'

Lizzie smiled. 'That's what she said about you!'

'She did? What did you talk about?'

'Well, er, she told me about Hong Kong and her tattoos. They're quite something, aren't they?'

'I knew you'd hate them.'

'I don't, actually, Flora. They're rather beautiful, in fact.'

'Really? I don't believe you!' They had slipped back into their familiar roles of dissension with such ease that Flora could almost pretend the gaping chasm between them wasn't there.

'Yes, well, it has been an interesting few days.' And there she was, the Lizzie that Flora loved to hate, with the familiar bitter tinge to her words. Flora withdrew her hand and Lizzie bristled.

'Mum, why... why didn't you tell me? All this time...'

'I wanted to, so many times I nearly told you. But—'

'But what? What could have possibly been more important than telling me I had a sister? More important than finding your daughter? The daughter that was stolen from you!'

Lizzie considered her response. She rolled her rings around her fingers like she always had. She looked like she was about to say something and then changed tack. 'You're right, Flora. Nothing should have been more important. But with every year that passed it became harder to tell, it became...' She faltered, put her trembling hand up to her mouth.

'Easier to forget?'

'No,' she responded quickly, with fire in her eyes. 'No, I never forgot her. Every day I have thought about her. I have wondered where she was, what she was doing. Did she still have to have Baloo, her teddy, to get to sleep at night? Did she still suck her fingers? Did she have Eddie's nose? My hair? Your eyes? Every single day I would ask whether they were loving her like she should be loved.'

Flora felt a pang of longing for her own children, so far away on the other side of the world. She imagined what it would be like for them to be taken away and another wave of nausea crashed over her head. She shut her eyes and waited for it to pass.

'Flora, are you OK?'

'Yeah.' She swallowed, her throat still raw and burning. 'Just feeling a bit sick, all the drugs...'

'Shut your eyes. I will be here.' Her mother's voice was soft and nurturing. And she was taken back to being sick as a child when Lizzie would sit with her and stroke the hair off her face and tuck it behind her ear. Sometimes she sang to her, '*Mamma's gonna buy you a mocking bird...*' She didn't sing now and she didn't stroke her hair but despite everything, Flora was comforted by the knowledge that she was there. And she drifted back into her dreams.

When she woke again Joseph and Lizzie were whispering by the window.

'What is it?' she called to them. Tried to sit up again, but the pain struck her back down. 'Ow, shit!'

'Flora!' Joseph rushed over to her. 'Don't try to sit up, not yet.' He eased her back onto the bed gently, supporting her head until it hit the pillow.

'Has something happened to Romy?' Joseph's eyes darted to Lizzie and then back to her. He took her hand and forced a smile but Flora could see the worry that pulled at the corners of his eyes.

'There, well, there has been a complication.'

'Oh god.'

'They hit an artery and she lost a lot of blood. They had to shock her back.' His voice wavered and Flora felt the nausea creeping up her body and into the back of her throat.

'But she's OK, right? She's going to be OK?'

He took her hand. 'I... I... hope so, Flora. She is in intensive care.'

Romy was in a coma. She was breathing with the assistance of machines and they didn't know when she would wake up. *If* she would wake up. *If* and *when* she woke up, whether there would be any brain damage.

Flora was sick several times as the anaesthetic wore off, and her wound throbbed and served as a constant reminder of what she had done. She thought of Megan's words at that first meeting, how Flora would arrive at this hospital a well person and leave it a sick one. There was a gaping hole where her kidney should be; a hole that should have been filled with a sister. But her sister was now fighting for her life, and what if she didn't make it?

She wasn't allowed to see Romy, who was in the ICU on the other side of the hospital. Joseph went between them and every time he arrived in Flora's room, she looked up expectantly for good news, but his face remained drawn and grey.

When she hadn't been sick for two hours and managed to eat a ginger biscuit, she called Jake. He answered the phone before it had even uttered a ring.

'Flora?' His voice was urgent, desperate.

'Hi,' she whispered.

'Oh, thank god.'

'I'm OK.'

'You are?' His voice cracked with emotion and she thought she heard him cry.

'Yeah, I've been sick as a dog with all the drugs and it hurts like hell, but I'm OK.'

'Is that Mummy?' She heard Toby's voice in the background.

'Yeah, buddy, she's OK.'

'Can I talk to him?' Flora asked.

'Mummy?'

'Hi, Tobes.'

'Does it hurt?'

'It's not too bad. How are you? Are you looking after Daddy?'

'He is really sad, he has been crying a lot today.'

'Well, you give him a big kiss from me, and tell him he doesn't need to cry any more. I am fine.'

'Will you come home soon, Mummy?'

'Yeah, buddy, I'll be home soon, I promise.'

'Flora.' It was Jake again.

'Yeah.'

'Is Romy OK?'

'She... she... no. Jake, she's in intensive care, and they don't know if she's going to make it.'

'Oh god.'

'I just found her, Jake, I can't lose her now.'

'Shit, Flora, I'm so sorry.' She couldn't respond, the words caught at the back of her throat in among the tears that were now spilling down her face. 'Flora, listen to me. She's going to be OK. You have both survived so much, this is not going to be the end.'

'Yeah.' She looked around for a tissue to wipe her streaming nose but there was none and so she used the corner of the sheet.

'Flora?'

'Yeah, you're right. I've got to be strong, for both of us.'

'You've got this, Flora.' She could hear his footsteps on the kitchen floor, and she imagined him pacing up and down. He always paced when he was on the phone.

'You'll never guess who's here?'

'Your mother.'

'You knew?'

'Yes, she called me when she landed. She was in quite a state, I think this whole thing has really rattled her.'

'Yeah, well, there's quite a lot of demons coming back to bite her right now.'

'Are you OK? Seeing her, I mean?'

'Yeah, actually, I am. I mean, there are still so many unanswered questions. But I don't feel as angry with her as I thought I would. Everything is beginning to make more sense. And what with Romy, lying there in intensive care, it puts everything into perspective.'

Flora was exhausted. When she was awake her body hurtled with anxiety for Romy and then she would fall into a deep, dark sleep. Sometimes in the middle of a sentence, she would be overcome with an exhaustion that was so completely impossible to fight that she had no choice but to succumb to it.

One afternoon she woke to hear voices before she opened her eyes.

'Did it start straight away? After the Wok Inn?' It was her mother.

'Not really. We met at a work do a couple of months later.' There was no mistaking Joseph's dulcet tones. 'I had written some pieces for the paper on some new buildings out in the East End. David, who you met that night, had got me the job and I needed the money. And because of the work I was invited along to the Christmas drinks, and that was where I met Ted again.' Flora could tell that they were standing by the window and it sounded as though they were facing away from her, but she didn't dare open her eyes in case they weren't. She wanted to hear this.

'Did he talk about me, about what he'd done?'

'Of course he did, Lizzie.'

'Did he regret it?'

'It tormented him for the rest of his life. You must have read The Yellow House?'

'What?'

'His most famous poem, and his darkest. It is about you and Flora, his guilt.'

'The Yellow House you say?'

'Yes.'

'I think he was always more in love with my house and family than he ever was with me. Or was it Van Gough's yellow house that you saw together?'

'Maybe a bit of both. It is quite complex – as you can imagine.'

'Complex, yes I can, I never really understood the way his mind worked. And I couldn't face reading his poems.'

'Fair enough. You know we never meant to take Romy.'

'What?'

'It was just going to be us.'

'So why, why did you take her away to the other side of the world?' Lizzie had raised her voice, her words desperate and rasping.

'It was that day after you told him you had seen us. He came back from work to tell you that he was leaving. But he couldn't do it. Not when he found you like that. And he decided he couldn't leave Romy with you, in case you tried again.' Lizzie didn't answer and Flora could hear her laboured breathing. When it was obvious that Lizzie wasn't going to respond, Joseph continued. 'After his mother, and everything. It was history repeating itself, and he didn't want that for Romy. He wanted to give her a better life than the one he'd had.'

'Was it really so bad? He had his father, he was so kind. You know he led me to believe that his dad had beaten him? I bet he didn't tell you that, did he? That all that time he stayed with us that summer he let me believe he was living with a monster. His father was such a gentle soul when I finally met him. He came to visit me you know, after you'd gone. He wanted to come after you. More than my own family did. They were quite happy to forget all about him and the shame he had bought on them. Quite happy to forget even their own granddaughter. But not Roger, he tried to find you, but then he got sick and—'

'His father was part of the problem, Lizzie.'

'What do you mean?'

'He was gay too, and that was why his mother did what she did.'

'Oh.' Was this news to her mother? 'I see now. History repeating itself,' she said. It wasn't hard for Flora to imagine what Edward's mother had done. What her own mother had tried to do. She was taken back to that night in the bathroom, her mother on the floor. She squeezed her eyes tight to stop the stinging of the tears.

'He tried so hard to love you.'

'But there were so many lies, Joseph. If he had just told me the truth, maybe I would have understood, maybe I could have helped him.'

'Would you have understood if he had really told you how he got those bruises?'

'He was beaten up outside the hospital. He did tell me, eventually.'

'It was in the park.'

'What?'

'He was beaten up in the park, not outside the hospital. He used to go there to find men.'

'Oh.'

'And once or twice they got violent.'

'I see. Twice, yes, that makes sense now.' Her mother's voice had dropped to barely more than whisper. 'Oh, Eddie.' There was no venom left in her voice; she was just sad and tired, so incredibly tired. 'I thought you were his first.' Lizzie said it so quietly that Flora had to strain to hear. 'There was Jamie, of course.'

'Nothing ever happened with Jamie.'

'I know that. But Eddie wanted it to, didn't he? That night when we first got together, I knew he had been to see Jamie. Handsome, charming Jamie. And I knew that Eddie had read the signs wrong, that Jamie was so incredibly heterosexual and would have rejected Eddie.'

'You knew?'

'I guess I always knew, just didn't want to believe it.' Flora's heart went out to her mother as all the missing pieces of her life were finally falling into place. She could hear someone pulling on the cord of the blind and it clattered against the window. She wanted to open her eyes so much that it took all her strength and resolve to keep them scrunched shut. 'I had to be tested, you know,' Lizzie whispered.

'Tested?'

'When my parents heard that my husband had run off with another man, they frogmarched me down to the hospital. Demanded that I was tested for AIDS. It was all over the media by then. The "gay disease", my dad called it.'

'I'm sorry.'

'It was so humiliating.'

'I'm sure it was.'

'Did you give it to him?'

Joseph didn't answer for a while, and Flora wondered whether he had nodded or shaken his head and she had missed it. She couldn't bear it any longer, and opened her eyes for a split second and looked over to the window. Lizzie was facing the glass and Joseph's head was hung in shame. It was him fiddling with the bobble on the end of the blind. 'Yes,' he said eventually and Flora shut her eyes again.

'But how, when?'

'It was a few months after we got here. I panicked about what we had done, taking a baby from her mother. She would say it sometimes, "Ma ma ma", she would say, and I freaked out and went AWOL for a few days. Hooked up with an old boyfriend in Manila. Of course, I didn't know...'

'I see.' A trolley came into the room at that moment. Flora could hear its wheels squeaking and rattling against the lino floor.

'Just bringing Miss Flora's tea,' the lady said.

'She's asleep at the moment, could you leave it on the table?' It was Lizzie who answered, and Flora didn't move a muscle while she laid the plate on the table next to the bed and then pushed the squeaking trolley back out into the corridor. Neither of them spoke after she had left, and Flora dared to open her eyes again. They were both looking out of the window, their bodies close but stiff. Joseph reached across and placed his hand in Lizzie's.

'I'm so sorry, Lizzie,' he said softly. She didn't pull her hand away. Flora looked at her mother's chipped coral nails on the ends of her tiny fingers as they curled around Joseph's palm.

'I can't lose her now,' Lizzie whispered, and Joseph squeezed her hand.

'I know,' he said, and they stood there for a while, holding hands as they looked out of the window at the apartment building beyond.

Until Flora could bear it no longer. 'Hi,' she said, and they both turned around and separated sheepishly as if they had been caught in an illicit embrace. 'Any news?'

Lizzie wheeled Flora through the hospital the following day to see Romy in intensive care. Joseph was sitting next to the bed and holding her hand. He looked up and forced a wired smile, but his eyes were fraught and his hair dishevelled. Flora looked down at her sister in the bed. She looked so small, almost childlike. There was a mask on her face, and tubes in her arms that sprang out of the octopus tattoo like extra tentacles. Her tanned skin seemed grey and sallow. Had it really only been twenty-four hours since they were laughing together the previous morning? Flora took her hand;

it was cool and soft. The rings had been taken off her fingers but there were white marks and dents where they should have been.

'Can she hear me?' she asked Joseph.

'I don't know, but I've been talking to her. It's worth a shot, right?' He stood up. 'Here, Lizzie, come and sit here. I'm going to stretch my legs for a minute.'

Her mother walked over to the other side of the bed and picked up Romy's other hand and Joseph left the room. The significance of this moment with her mother and her sister reunited was so huge, and Flora's heart thumped hard and loud in her chest. She opened her mouth to speak but couldn't think of any words.

'Hi, Romy.' Her mother's voice was soft and calm. 'It is your... your mother here. And Flora, your sister. We are both here. And we really, really want you to come back to us.' She paused and Flora wondered whether she should fill the gap. But she needn't have worried; her mother stopped to draw a long and cooling breath and then continued. 'It was so lovely to meet you yesterday, but there's so much still left to say. So please, Romy, please come back to us. Let us get to know you better. Let us be the family I have always dreamed of.' Flora looked at Lizzie, amazed at the reserves that she had to draw on. She couldn't quite believe the calm and collected manner with which she was delivering these profound words. 'I know you're strong, Romy,' Lizzie continued. 'You are a survivor. I realised that pretty quickly in those early days when I was falling apart at the seams. You were fighting for your place on this earth, for your place in my heart. And you won! Wow, did you win me over. With your gummy smiles and gurgling noises, your chubby little legs. The way you held onto your feet with your hands and rolled from side to side, blowing raspberries. I have held onto these memories for the last thirty years, Romy, but now I want some more.' Flora was taken back to the photo in the drawer. That bonny baby with her adoring father smiling down at her. Not her, of course, but Romy. The baby who had stayed a baby forever in her mother's memories. A sob blurted out of her mouth and took her by surprise. She hadn't even felt it coming. It was such a physical reaction she worried that vomit might follow in its wake. But it didn't, though her head swam with nausea and emotions so raw and strong that they seemed to tip her upside down and then back up again like the fairground rides that had made her so sick as a child.

'Flora, are you OK?' her mother asked.

She nodded. 'Yeah. Sorry, but I don't think I can...'

'It's OK. We can just sit. Just be with her.' Lizzie reached across the bed and took Flora's hand. Her mother held onto the hands of both of her daughters, like she might have done in another life when they were young and crossing the road. And like this, they sat. The minutes turned into hours, the hours into days.

Two weeks passed. Still Romy didn't wake up. Her body seemed to be wasting away before their eyes. At her insistence they moved Flora's bed into Romy's room. The hospital staff refused initially, but when Flora wouldn't go back to her own bed, they realised it was hindering her recovery and so complied. And while Romy's body was fading, Flora's was slowly regaining strength. Within a couple of days she could walk down the corridor and after a week she could make it up and down the stairs. Halfway through the second week the doctors suggested, no, *forced* her to leave the hospital. To get outside, to feel the air on her skin, to breathe some fresh oxygen into her lungs. Lizzie accompanied her and linked her arm through Flora's for support.

'Makes a change, doesn't it? Me looking after you,' she said as they walked slowly down the street between the hospital and the apartment block. It was the middle of the morning and the sun was high in the sky and swelteringly hot. Romy had lived in that air-conditioned cell for so long she had forgotten the heat of the trop-ical world that lived on outside her window. And the noises: the whir of traffic and beeping of horns, the singing of the birds, the squawking of the gulls. Everything was deafening, like someone had turned the volume up on the world. And the sun scorched her eyes and pounded down on the top of her head with an intensity that was quite assaulting.

'I should have lived in a hot country,' her mother said, tilting her head towards it.

'I couldn't handle it,' Flora said. She could feel sweat trickling down her back between her shoulder blades, the tops of her thighs sticky and rubbing together.

'No, you get that from your father. I can't imagine how he survived here. He was the only person I have ever known to get sunburn in March! He had these pale, freckly arms which rarely saw the light of day. He used to wear long-sleeved cotton shirts even at the height of summer.'

'It's nice to hear you talk about him,' Flora said and pulled herself closer to her mother. 'I want to know more about him. I asked Joseph if he could get Stefan to bring some of his poems into the hospital. I thought that if I read them to Romy—'

'Flora, you need to prepare yourself for the fact that Romy might not wake up. And even if she does...'

'Don't, don't say it, Mum. She is going to wake up. She has to. Come on.'

'But Flora, there is a possibility...'

'No, no there isn't. She's going to be OK. I've had enough of this, it's too hot. Let's get back to Romy.' She turned and started to walk back towards the hospital.

'Oh, Flora, let's stay out a little longer. It will be doing you good.' Lizzie called after her.

'It's not doing me good, Mum, I'm sweating like a pig. And I want to be with Romy.' Lizzie didn't protest and followed, which in itself was uncharacteristic and disconcerting.

Flora wasn't sure whether to be grateful for her mother's new-found strength and wisdom or resentful, as it only served to high-light her own weakness more. Flora had always been the strong one but there were times in the middle of the night when the hospital was ghostly quiet and Joseph and her mother had retreated back to the hotel to sleep, when Flora thought she might actually be losing her mind. When the synthetic noises echoed around her head and the shadows on the shiny walls seemed to come for her, for Romy.

It was in these lonely times that she would talk to her sister. About her time at boarding school when she was horribly homesick and frightened of the dark. About her family, her brothers, meeting Jake, their house in Dorset and the birth of her children. She would have no trouble pouring out her soul to her silent sister in those dark and quiet hours. But during the day when Joseph and Lizzie were present, she felt self-conscious talking to Romy. She couldn't be honest about her life while they were there to judge and take offence. She read Ted's poems to her instead, and marvelled at the mastery of her father's words. She recalled her tutor at university hypothesising about the state of his mind, and only now, as she travelled down those darkened tributaries, could she really imagine where he had gone to. He wrote about childhood, about his sexuality, about guilt and how it eats you up from the inside out. He wrote joyful odes to the sea, to the jungle, to the tropical world he had found himself living in. And more melancholic poems, to the green fields of his homeland. Flora felt as though she was beginning to understand him a little more. Along with the poetry, Stefan brought photograph albums into the hospital. Flora spent hours poring over the photographs of Romy and Ted, learning about their lives on the other side of the world. She would ask Joseph questions and he would try to answer, but he was becoming increasingly quiet and morose and Flora worried that he was relapsing into the depressive state that Romy had told her about after Ted's death. Lizzie looked at the photos over her shoulder and Flora would watch her with bated breath, waiting for her to freak out or break down. But she didn't. Flora had spent her whole life treating her mother like a fragile bird. And yet here in this hospital, in this strange country where Flora felt totally discombobulated, Lizzie had rallied and was looking after them all. It was as if this was the moment she had been waiting for all her life, the moment in which she would keep her head while everyone around her was losing theirs.

Jeremy couldn't stand the hospital so made himself scarce, disappearing for hours at a time to fetch food. Then one day Stefan took him on a trip to their island and he came back burned to a cinder but hugely animated about his experience of swimming on the reef. After that, he was off on an excursion every day. Flora resented his holiday attitude but was relieved that it took him and his booming voice away from the sanctuary of their room.

It had been three weeks since she had seen Jake and the children, and with every day that passed they slipped a little further away from her. Toby was quiet and brave on the phone, but Olive cried and begged her to return. Jake was calm and understanding and said she must stay as long as she liked. But she couldn't help imagining him seeking comfort in the arms of Jodie.

One evening Flora was reading one of Ted's short stories out loud to Romy. He had written it in the first year he arrived in the Philippines, around the time that she had been born. The story was about a lioness losing her cub to a pack of hyenas, and Flora questioned whether she was the lion cub and Lizzie the hyena. Or was Romy the cub, and he and Joseph the hyenas? There were so many different interpretations, given the screwed-up nature of their family. It was seven o'clock and the darkness had crept in and caught her unawares. This country didn't experience long, dusky evenings in the way she knew them; the night arrived suddenly. And so she was sitting with only the light of the machines to illuminate her father's words when Olive rushed into the room and threw herself into her arms. Flora wondered if she might be dreaming – she had visited this scene so many times in her mind. But she looked up to see Jake standing in the doorway, and then Toby hot on Olive's heels. And then they were all in her arms and they were kissing her and holding her tight.

'I can't believe it,' she said. 'Are you really here? Is this really happening?'

'We went on an aeroplane, Mummy, and there were movies and video games and Daddy let us drink fizzy drinks and...' Olive was talking fast, her freckled face stained with chocolate ice cream.

'Did you? What... I...' She pulled herself up to her feet and swayed a little as the rush of blood went to her head. But Jake was there to catch her. He wrapped his big, strong arms around her and she held onto him so tight.

'You're here,' she said again and again, as if saying it enough times really did make it real.

'Is that Auntie Romy, Mummy?' Flora pulled herself away from Jake and looked at Toby, who had quietly made his way over to the other side of the bed. He was staring at the body covered in tubes that were linked to machines with a mix of fear and intrigue.

'Yes, Tobes, that's your Auntie Romy. She's sleeping right now, but she's going to be so happy to meet you when she wakes up.' Jake's arm was still around Flora's shoulders and he squeezed her tight and she leant into him and rubbed her wet cheeks on his t-shirt.

'When is she going to wake up, Mummy?' Olive asked, hiding behind Flora's legs, not quite wanting to look.

'Soon, Olive.' Flora crouched down to hug her daughter. 'Really soon, I hope, my darling.'

'Granny Lizzie! Toby ran around the bed and threw himself into Lizzie's arms as she came into the room. She hugged him tight and closed her eyes, breathing in his smell. When she opened them, she looked at Olive, who was still holding onto Flora.

'Hi, Olive,' Lizzie said with a gentle smile and Olive looked at Flora, her eyes wide and questioning.

'Go and give Granny Lizzie a hug,' Flora said and Olive walked tentatively towards her grandmother who didn't release Toby but drew them both to her body and kissed them repeatedly on their heads, their faces, their necks, until Olive squealed with delight.

'Stop, Granny, it's tickly,' Olive giggled, that wonderful gurgle of molten laughter that Flora had quite forgotten.

'I can't stop, you are just too kissable,' Lizzie said, and Flora laughed, and Jake laughed. And Joseph was there in the doorway, and even he cracked a smile for the first time in weeks, and let out a gentle chuckle.

CHAPTER TWENTY-SEVEN

LIZZIE

Edward made an effort to come home early at least twice a week after the night on the sofa. But he barely touched Lizzie other than to give her a conciliatory kiss on the forehead as he walked in the door. The other three nights a week he would stay out late, and Lizzie found solace in her old friend gin.

Then came the night when she decided to confront him. She hadn't planned it. But he came home before she had reached the point of being comatose. The more she drank, the more her capacity increased and the longer it took to hit that moment when her mind settled to a comforting quiet. And so she was raging and brave when he returned to the flat just before midnight. The lights were off and he was startled by her voice in the armchair by the window.

'I know where you've been,' she said.

'You're awake?' he answered without trying to mask the bitter sarcasm.

'You've been with him.'

'Who? I've been with David at a private view at the Tate, I told you.' She couldn't see his face but she could imagine him rolling his eyes.

'Not David,' she spat. 'Him! I know you've been with him.'

He seemed to falter but only for a second. 'What are you talking about, Lizzie?'

'That man I saw you with in the gallery.'

'What gallery?'

'The National, Van Gogh.'

He was still merely a shadow on the other side of the room but she could see his body tense. 'What?'

'I was there, came to surprise you. But you were with him, your hand... on his back... at the painting of the yellow house. I- I ran away.'

'What are you implying, Liz?'

'Don't patronise me, Eddie, I know. I know who you are. I have always known...'

He didn't respond. Just lowered himself onto the sofa and buried his head in his hands. 'I'm sorry,' he whispered eventually. Lizzie felt her heart sink down towards her toes. He hadn't denied it. There was no longer the hope that she had been wrong. There it was, the truth of her marriage and her miserable existence laid out in all its blatant glory. He would never love her in the way she wanted him to. And then came the sirens, the screams, the familiar soundtrack to her nightmares. She took the bottle from the table next to the chair, she put it to her lips and glugged down the cold, numbing liquid. And she watched him cry, her eyes bleary with gin. Then she gave in to the heaviness, to the welcome relief of darkness and the silence that it brought.

He was gone when she woke up the following morning. Romy was crying in her cot. She pulled herself up, her body stiff and unforgiving as she dragged her feet across the carpet. She picked Romy up, kissed the top of her head. She smelt of sleep and milk.

That was when she decided what to do. She called her mother. Said she wasn't feeling well and asked if she would take Romy out for a few hours so she could get some sleep. Her mother jumped at the chance. It felt good to be taking action, to be doing something constructive. She tidied the house while awaiting her mother's arrival. She dressed Romy in her smartest outfit: a blue-and-white smocked dress and navy tights. Little white leather booties that Bella had given her when she was born. She even clipped a gingham ribbon hairslide into her soft baby hair.

Her mother was surprised when she arrived and saw the gleaming surfaces and immaculate baby. Lizzie manufactured a dry cough and held onto the furniture as she walked. She breathed in the smell of her daughter's head before she placed her in the pushchair at the bottom of the stairs. She kissed her nose, then her cheeks and the tops of her eyes, which made her blink and giggle. And then they were gone.

She sat down at the table in the kitchen and wrote the letter that she had written over and over again in her mind.

Dear Mr and Mrs Rhodes,

I am so incredibly sorry for the loss of your daughter. Isabelle was a wonderful, kind and honest person. She was my best friend, the best friend I have ever had. And I am responsible for her death. We made a pact, Isabelle and I. Only I wasn't brave enough to carry it out. Isabelle was brave, she had more courage than I could ever hope to have. I should have died that day with her in the woods, and there isn't a day that has passed since that I haven't torn myself apart with the guilt and shame of what I did. I gave her the pills and the vodka and arranged to meet her in the woods. But I bottled it, I didn't even show up. It never occurred to me that Isabelle would go through with it alone. Today, however I am not scared. I hope you can take some shred of comfort from the fact that I will soon be with her, where I should have been all along.

I am so sorry.

Yours, no more

Elizabeth Claybourne

She placed the letter inside the envelope and licked it shut.

She had no difficulty in recalling the address. Isabelle had told her about her house in Hampshire that was ironically called Hertford-shire House. How she had imagined as a child that it had been picked up by a giant and moved from one county to another. After addressing the envelope, she propped it up against the salt and pepper mills on the table and went into the bedroom. She put on her favourite dress with poppies on it. She wrapped it around her body and tied the bow at her waist. Eddie liked it, said she looked like she should be riding through a French market on a bicycle. At the thought of Eddie her legs buckled. She sat down at her dressing table. The sirens came while she brushed her hair. The screams as she painted her lips bright red. But she didn't try to block them out. Today she wasn't afraid; today the noises that had haunted her dreams and days alike gave her the courage to carry on. She went into the bathroom, found the Co-codamol she had been given in the hospital after she had Romy. It was stashed behind the Listerine, the cream for cracked nipples and Romy's gripe water. And there on the side of the bath was her sponge, the bottle of Johnson's baby shampoo, the rubber duck that Edward had so proudly brought home from work one day. Lizzie picked it up, still wet from her bath the night before. Could she do this? Could she really leave her daughter behind? But the sirens blared loudly in her ears and she focused hard on the hand on the small of her husband's back. She laid the pills out on the dressing table next to the bottle of gin. And then looked at the clock; she would have to hurry if she was to post the letter and take the pills before her mother came back from the park. She grabbed the letter from the kitchen and ran down the stairs, two at a time. And it was as she came out into the bright light of the glorious day, the birds singing, the scent of honeysuckle filling the air, that she ran straight into Edward.

'Lizzie, where are you going?' He looked at her dress, the hair, the lipstick, the envelope in her hand.

'I, er, what are you doing here? Why are you not at work?'

'I was worried about you, after last night. Thought we should talk.' The panic mounted in Lizzie's stomach and fizzed around her head.

'Oh right, well...' The pills were on the dressing table, the gin. She put the letter behind her back.

'What's that, Liz?'

'Nothing.'

'Behind your back, what is it?'

'Just a letter I was going to post.'

'Who to?'

'Er, to Bella, haven't written to her for a while, and...' He put his arm around her back and tried to grab the letter but she pulled it away from him.

'Stop it, Eddie! What are you doing?' He grabbed hold of her wrist and pulled it in front of her body. He peeled her fingers off the envelope one by one and read the address.

'This isn't Bella. Who are Mr and Mrs Rhodes?'

'Oh no, silly me, it's not the letter for Bella. They are... they are Isabelle's parents. I felt dreadful that I never wrote to them, never offered my condolences after Isabelle, you know, and—'

'Why would you do that now, Lizzie? Why today after all this time?' His eyes were full of angst, flickering from side to side as he drew conclusions.

'I don't know, Eddie, with everything that's going on between us. I guess it's putting things into perspective.' He handed her back the letter and she thought for a brief moment that that would be it. That she could carry on as planned.

'Why don't we go back inside and chat?'

She looked down at the letter. She could insist on posting it first, but then he might see the pills, and the gin. 'OK.' She pushed past him back into the building and up the stairs; she could hear him climbing them behind her, two at a time, trying to keep up. She unlocked the door to the flat and rushed straight into the bedroom. She threw the pills into a drawer in the dressing table but he was there behind her, his hand in the drawer as she tried to shut it.

'Ow!' he said, and pulled out the box of pills. The gin still sat there unashamedly glistening in the shaft of sun from the window.

'What's going on, Lizzie?'

'Nothing!' she said defensively, but she could feel her eyes filling.

'Are you? You're not.' He looked at her and down at the pills and then back at the bottle. 'Jesus.'

'I... I...' She nearly told him then. About the sirens that blared around her skull, about the screams, about how sometimes she woke up and didn't know how she was going to get through another day. But she didn't; she just couldn't find the words. She looked down at the letter in her hands, the letter that was now scrunched between her fists. Eddie looked at it too. And then he took it and she no longer had the strength to fight back. So, she watched him as he read it. She watched his lips moving, his pupils growing wide with horror and she sank onto the bed. She curled herself into a ball and placed her palms over her ears to shut out the noise. The bed wobbled under his weight and she wondered whether he might hold her, hoped that he might tell her that everything was going to be OK. But he didn't. He sat on the end of the bed, cradling not hers but his own head, his own weary sorrows.

CHAPTER TWENTY-EIGHT

ROMY

She was on the beach at Sapphire Cove, sitting near the water's edge. The sun was dipping into the horizon and all around her the sky and the water had turned pink with coral streaks. She dug her toes under the still-warm sand and buried them deeper to where it became cool, the wet grains scraping between her toes. She looked back at her dads on the beach, their flushed faces smiling at her. Ted kissed Joseph and walked towards her. He picked up her hand and led her into the sea up to her waist. The warm water lapped at her tummy, bubbles fizzing and popping on the surface. She looked back at Joseph on the beach. No longer alone, he was flanked on either side by two women. And then Ted dived under a wave and came up and floated on his back with his arms spread wide. His eyes were closed but he was smiling, his face glistening in the pink sky. She looked back at the figures on the sand. Their features were losing definition in the dimming light but she could tell there were more of them. And she could hear their laughter over the sound of the waves gently kissing the shore. Ted was drifting away. She wanted to follow him but the laughter was warming her soul and pulling her back. Ted drifted too far, his body floating towards the horizon. She walked with heavy limbs out of the sea and Joseph wrapped her in a towel and it was her mother who was rubbing her dry and her sister who was making room for her on the rug. There were children and laughter and Skipper licked her salty toes. And her sister put her arm around her and laid her head on her shoulder and together they watched the shadow in the water slowly disappearing into the darkening sky.

EPILOGUE

TWO YEARS LATER

Romy looked around the restaurant and couldn't quite believe that they were all there. Olive was standing behind her, plaiting her hair. It was down to her shoulders, the longest it had been since she was a child. Joseph was teaching Toby how to play backgammon at the other end of the table, their faces serious and creased with concentration. Jeremy was at the bar regaling his encounter with the whale sharks loudly to Mali and Symphony, who made all the appropriate noises while sipping their mojitos. Stefan was behind the bar, teaching Jed how to make the mojitos. Jed, the hiking-not-boyfriend who had actually stuck around! He came to see Romy in hospital when she eventually woke up. Said he thought she had ditched him until he bumped into Mali one day who told him where she was, and he got on a plane straight away. He had to get past Flora, though; she was like a protective Rottweiler that never left Romy's side in those early days. Jake had to drag her onto the plane three weeks later. Romy had made the journey to England when she was feeling stronger. She had thought she might move there, but while the green fields were lush and the rose gardens pretty, the sea was like an ice cube and she couldn't fathom the relentless rain. Romy looked over at her sister. Jake was rubbing some cream onto Flora's peeling nose, then he kissed it and she whacked him on the arm and laughed.

Romy felt a sharp pull at her scalp. 'Ow! Olive!'

'Sorry, Auntie Romy, I just, well, your hair is not as easy as Mummy's and the plait is falling apart when I try to tie it up.'

'Here, Olive, let me.' Lizzie stood up from her seat next to Romy. After Flora had left, Lizzie had quietly slipped into position at her side. Jeremy had gone back to England and she had asked if she could stay. Four whole months she stayed, and they had spent the time getting to know each other. It took a long time for Romy to regain her strength, and Lizzie had sat with her throughout. She hadn't probed her with questions about her life, nor overwhelmed her with stories of her own. She seemed content just to be with her. And over time, Lizzie's skin darkened in the sun and she put on weight with Angel's constant feeding, and all that nervous energy that fizzed off her quietened to a gentle hum. She had been back three times since then, said she couldn't keep away.

Romy closed her eyes and listened to the buzz of chatter and laughter, to the sound of the waves lapping against the shore and the clinking of ice in the glasses. She felt the warmth of the setting sun on her face and the delicate touch of her mother as her fingers ran through her hair.

'*Happy birthday to you, happy birthday to you...*' She opened her eyes to see Angel coming out of the kitchen with a cake that was more an architectural feat than confectionery. A pyramid of profiteroles and meringues, tropical fruit and petals with candles and sparklers protruding at angles like the spikes on a porcupine. Everyone gathered round, the smiles on their faces blurred by the smoke, their brilliantly tuneless singing bouncing off the water. She blew out the candles with the assistance of Olive and Toby.

'Speech!' Jeremy hollered.

'Oh, Jeremy, do be quiet,' Lizzie reprimanded.

'Actually,' Romy got to her feet. 'I would like to say something. I'd like to say thank you. Thank you, everyone, for coming all this way to celebrate my hugely insignificant birthday. And thank you...' She paused, the words momentarily stuck at the back of her throat amid an overwhelming surge of emotion. 'Thank you for saving me.' She raised a glass to Flora, who nodded and wiped the tear that trickled down her cheek with the back of her hand. 'And last but by no means least, thank you, Ted.' She raised her glass out to sea. 'For my weird and wonderfully dysfunctional family, none of whom would be here if it wasn't for you!' Laughter rippled, glasses clinked.

'Here, here...' someone said.

'To Dad.' Flora raised her glass towards the sea.

'To Eddie,' Lizzie whispered, and hooked her arm through Romy's.

A LETTER FROM SOPHIE

Dear reader,

I want to say thank you for choosing to read *The Sapphire Cove*.

If you did enjoy it and want to keep up to date with all my latest releases, take a moment to sign up at the following link. Your email address will never be shared, and you can unsubscribe at any time.

www.bookouture.com/sophie-anderson

I hope you loved *The Sapphire Cove*, and if you did, I would be very grateful if you could write a review. I'd love to hear what you think, and it makes such a difference helping new readers to discover one of my books for the first time.

I love hearing from my readers – you can get in touch on my Facebook page, through Twitter, Goodreads or my website.

Thanks,

Sophie

facebook.com/sophieandersonfiction
twitter.com/MSophieanderson

ACKNOWLEDGEMENTS

Thank you to all the wonderful people in my life who helped me to write this book in what turned out to be an extraordinary year fraught with lockdown and uncertainty.

To my agent Madeleine Milburn for her unwavering support and wisdom. To her assistant, Rachel Yeoh, who never fails to respond and always with such good cheer. To my editor Lydia Vassar-Smith for her brilliantly perceptive critique and boundless encouragement. To Sarah Hardy and the rest of the publicity team for their tireless tweeting and promoting. And to Alex Holmes and all of her amazing tribe of editors at Bookouture who work their magic behind the scenes. To Claude, for sharing her extraordinary transplant experience with me. To Nicole, for her wisdom and yoga, which saved me through lockdown. To my wonderful girl-friends Neach, Sally, Anna B, Phoebe, Clarence, Lily, Gael, Jo, T, Abi, Anna S, Ellen and Claire – for believing in me, mopping up my tears and making me belly-ache laugh. To my parents, Charlie and Fenella, who I have dedicated this book to because of their relentless capacity to love and support me with everything I do, not to mention homeschooling the kids so I could write! To my children, Jago, Albie, Arlo and Delphi – my inspiration. And to Myles, my rock – you rock!

Printed in Great Britain
by Amazon

10847591R00202